The Coven of the Crow and Shadows

Book 1: Legacy

Birdy Rivers

Copyright © 2022 Birdy Rivers
Cover art courtesy of INCO Designs

All rights reserved. No part of this publication may be reproduced, transmitted, or stored in an information retrieval system in any form or by any means, graphic, electronic, or mechanical, including photocopying, taping, and recording, without prior written permission from the author.

PUBLISHER'S NOTE
This is a work of fiction. Names, characters, places, and incidents either are the product of the author's imagination and experiences or are used fictitiously, and any resemblance to actual persons, living or dead, events, or locales is entirely coincidental.

The Coven of the Crow and Shadows

CHAPTER 1
Ari

Today is one of those days; please give me a reason to set shit on fire. You know the kind of days where you have zero fucks left to give as your world crumbles around you at the betrayal of your family. My parents didn't just betray me, though. They also betrayed our entire pack. I'm locked up in a prison cell for my safety because I'm guilty by association. I had nothing to do with them helping the rogues attack our pack, but the pack doesn't care. My parents might be dead, but my fate has yet to be decided.

I'm in defense mode. My aggression is coursing through my veins; it's what wolfsbane does to werewolves. It suppresses our wolves and brings forth our aggression. Werewolves are naturally aggressive. Well, wolfsbane makes it feel like we are on crack. I'm practically foaming at the mouth, wanting to rip someone apart. It's why they have me in silver shackles. The silver weakens me so that I don't have the energy to act on my aggressive thoughts. My mind and body are at war, but that's nothing new, just a different battle this time.

I've been locked up for several hours now. The attack happened early this morning. My parents, along with a few others from the pack, led the rogue pack to our front doors. They attacked, killing and hurting as many as they could. Alpha Liam was able to swiftly counter the attack with the pack's warriors and the help of his warlock friend, whom I didn't know about. Then again, Alpha Liam just took over for his father. Liam spent years training at academies and training programs on how to run a pack and be a leader. All Alphas must have this training as deemed by the werewolf council. Each faction has a council over which they govern. Each council joins to be a part of the grand council. Humans, witches and warlocks, and werewolves each have factions. There are more factions, but currently, my mind can't think straight.

Humans are well aware of our existence thanks to vampires, who are now just about extinct. Humans helped the rest of us hunt vampires to make them extinct. They just couldn't play nice. They wanted humans as blood bags for their food. The rest of us didn't agree. Humans are still pretty suspicious of supernaturals, but they tend to ignore us and us them unless we have to interact. They have their towns, witches and warlocks have their covens, and werewolves their packs. The other factions are smaller and have fewer territories.

The truth is, I don't know what my fate will be. My best friend, Sage, is Liam's mate. She will surely help me. Sage and I are like sisters. She has to know I had nothing to do with the attack. I was with her when it happened. We were planning for her upcoming Luna ceremony when the attack started. Liam marked her the minute he came home, and now it was just the formal ceremony for the pack's sake. Packs, like most of the supernatural world, are all about formalities.

I overheard the guards saying the traitors were going to be executed. For all I know, I'm waiting for my execution. I can only hope Sage will fight for me to have a trial. I sink to the floor as fear kicks in that my family might have gotten me killed or banished. Neither is a good option. Being a rogue wolf is a dangerous life, especially as a female. I'm an omega, too. My chances of survival aren't good.

I'm well aware that my parent's actions are punishable by death. They betrayed the pack and their alpha. They knew what they were doing when they helped the rogues attack. I wonder if they even thought about what it would mean for me if they failed. They either were so confident in their plan that they would succeed that they didn't need to consider what would happen to me if they failed, or the harsher truth, they didn't care. Maybe they thought I would die willingly for their cause. They are wrong. If I die because of this, I swear I'm coming back as a ghost and will haunt everyone.

The sound of keys on the door jolt my attention. My senses are dull from the silver and wolfsbane, but I can hear keys and voices. Sure enough, the doors open, and Alpha Liam, Sage, the warlock, and the guard who locked me up enter the room. The area surrounding the four cells is open. We are in the basement of the packhouse, which is basically our city hall.

"Here's the prisoner." The guard states proudly as if he's why I didn't escape. I inwardly roll my eyes at his lame attempt to impress the Alpha.

"You chained her! Open the door now!" Sage demands, her eyes searing into the guard's face like she could murder him where he stood.

Sage is tiny for a werewolf, but she is a fierce bitch to reckon with. She is in shape as she was training to be a warrior before Liam snatched her up as his Luna. Sage has short dusty blonde hair that comes to her shoulders. Her bangs frame her face. Her light green eyes are the color of sage which is why her parents named her Sage. She has a nice body, but I know I'm the fuller female body of both of us. Overall, Sage is cute and sexy, and she pulls it off with the utmost confidence.

"Yes, Luna." The guard tries not to stutter.

He's clearly confused as to why his Luna is pissed the hell off at him. Here he thought he was doing a fine job of keeping the traitor locked up till the Alpha could get here. The idiot doesn't know I'm best friends with his precious Luna. No one in this pack barely recognizes me. I'm an omega and a low-ranking one at that. I just got lucky and happened to become best friends with a Beta, not just any Beta, but the daughter of the head warrior. Sage's family is well respected among the pack, so it was no surprise that Liam picked her to be his mate. I think they were secretly hooking up beforehand during training, but Sage won't admit it to me.

The guard barely gets the cell door open before Sage barrels past him to me. I'm now standing leaning on the concrete wall with my hands in silver chains. Sage goes to hug me, but I step back so the silver doesn't burn her.

"Don't touch the chains. They are silver." My voice cracks as I speak.

Sage turns on her heels and stomps towards the guard. "You put her in silver chains! Why would you do that?" The guard goes to open his mouth to explain, but Sage cuts him off with her hand. "Nevermind, I don't care why you did it, just undo it now!" She demands.

"Sorry, Luna. It's standard protocol to help counter the wolfsbane we injected into her." The guard defends himself as he walks past Sage and towards me. Sage turns perfectly on her heels once more and lunges at the guard pinning him to the wall.

"You injected wolfsbane in my best friend, and then you chained her with silver? I will have your fucking job. Next time pay attention to who your prisoner is, or did you not care because she's an Omega? Maybe you thought she deserved it because her parents are traitors, but that doesn't mean she is one. She is like my sister, and you hurt her. You will pay for it with your job. Your lack of due diligence makes you unqualified for this job. Give me the keys and get the fuck out. You are done being a guard." Sage is fierce with her elbow against the guard's throat.

There is no doubt in my mind that she couldn't kill him right here and right now. She lets the guard down, and he gives her the keys. He then runs out of the prison.

Sage unlocks the chains and then hugs me. "I'm sorry, Ari," Sage says as she rubs my back.

"It's okay. Just please tell me I'm not going to die." I try to hide the tears threatening to spill over.

I'm overwhelmed, the wolfsbane is causing me to lose control of my emotions, and soon it will fuck with my head, and I'm scared. I don't think I've ever been so afraid for my life before.

Sage steps back as Liam walks in. Sage backs up, so she stands slightly in front of Liam, who stands slightly to her side. His hand goes to her shoulder in a comforting manner. I swallow the lump in my throat as dread overtakes me. I don't like the way Sage looks at me; she's not even looking at me.

"Ari, I need to know if you were involved with your parents." Alpha Liam questions.

Fuck I want to snap at him, but I don't want to. Damn, the wolfsbane is making me aggressive, and I want to lash out. I'm trying to hold back. I take the biggest breath I can and breathe out.

"No. I didn't know what they were planning. I don't know why they would do something like this." I tell the truth.

I didn't know, and I certainly wasn't involved. If my parents had tried to include me, I would have told them no and told Liam right away. My parents probably knew that; that's why they didn't involve me. They knew I was loyal to the pack and our alpha. Sage sighs in relief. I knew she never questioned if I was involved or not. She knows I wasn't, but Liam doesn't know me like she does. He had to ask, and he's also the Alpha. He has no choice but to ask even if he thought I wasn't.

"She's telling the truth." The warlock says from behind Liam. How the hell did he know I was telling the truth? He must have cast a spell.

"Good. In that case, Ari, you don't have to worry about dying because I'm not going to kill you. You are innocent. However, I can't let you stay in the pack. You might be innocent, but you know as well as I that the pack won't care. They will associate you with your parents, and I can't protect you from them. You have two options. Option one, I banish you, and you become a rogue, or option two. You go with Zane and become his familiar." He points to the warlock. So his name is Zane.

Magic was not something werewolves trusted. Magic wasn't natural to us, so some of us fear it, others avoid it, and some think it's unnatural. I fall into the I try to avoid magic category. I don't trust it because of how dangerous it is and how easily one can wield it as a weapon.

I look over to Zane. The handsome, sexy, brooding, and very dangerous warlock. He has ash brown hair that is styled with a short fade haircut on the sides and back with long side-swept hair on the top, a light beard, and dark gray eyes. He seems physically fit, but I can't fully tell with the black trench coat he is wearing. His fair skin tells me he doesn't see much sunlight.

Zane is attractive. It's as if he is calling to my soul. Strange to feel that connection with someone I just met, and I'm not sure you could even say we've officially met.

"I've heard of warlocks and witches making werewolves and other shifters their familiars. Some consider it a form of slavery. So my options are to become a rogue or a slave to a warlock?" I ask in disbelief. Well, that's not the good news I was hoping for.

Alpha Liam is right. I can't stay in the pack as much as I want to. I know I can't because it won't be safe here. No one will respect me, I'll be bullied, hated, shunned, and some might even try to kill me. I'm guilty by association. It doesn't matter if I'm innocent. I guess my parents either didn't give two shits about me. Or they were overconfident. Either way, they screwed me hard.

"I'm sorry, Ari. I don't have any better options to offer you. We don't have much time either. You know the pack will call for blood if you stay too long. You need to choose soon. If you're smart, you'll go with Zane. Leave right from this cell with him."

"What does being your familiar entail?" I ask as I question if this is the better option.

Zane steps forward. "You'll be bound to me. I will own your soul. I will be able to control your werewolf abilities. In return, you'll be able to tap into my magic to strengthen you. It's a type of partnership. You will fight with me when needed, you will be mine to control, and I will protect you in return. I will take care of you, Ari. You will have a safe place to live with me. You will have food, clothes, anything you want or need, you can have it. You know you won't have those options as a rogue."

He's right. Being a rogue is slow suicide. If another rogue doesn't kill me, then a pack wolf will. Pack wolves kill rogues every chance they get. They see them as threats to pack life. They are eliminated and often without question either. It's not much of a life. I'd probably be better off dead. So that makes Zane the only option to have a life. Well, a facade of a life. I'll be his. I don't know him. I'm trusting him with my life, my soul, and who the hell only knows what else.

"Fine. I'll go with Zane, but I get to stay in contact with Sage." I need at least something that is to my benefit. I can face whatever might come of going with Zane if I have Sage in my corner. If I can turn to her for advice or to vent, I'll have a better chance of surviving. I don't even like the thought of being away from her. We've never been apart. We've been friends since we were six. Sage saved me from being bullied by some Beta kids. I started following her around. I felt like I owed her for saving me. We became best friends. She's the only thing I have left.

"I'm fine with you staying in touch with Sage if Liam is," Zane says, looking at Liam, nodding his head.

"I'm fine with it. It's bad enough they have to be forced apart and that Ari can't be here for Sage's Luna ceremony. The least we can give them is contact with one another. Maybe we can arrange for them to meet up. After all, I don't mind hanging out with an old friend." Liam suggests.

Liam is friends with a warlock? Well, that's news to me. Also, was that a little bit of compassion I saw in Liam, but I doubt it was for my benefit. I'm sure he's only doing this for Sage. At least she means something to him. It helps to leave her if I know she has someone. I know Sage doesn't lack friends, but it's still comforting to know she has Liam.

"Works for me. Once Ari and I have completed the bond and adjusted to each other, we can get together. In the meantime, they can call and text. Ari, take this before we leave." Zane commands as he waves his hands in the air. A clump of black mist swirls around in the palm of his right hand. The mist disappears. In Zane's hand sits a round vile with shimmering pale blue liquid. It almost looks too beautiful to drink.

"What is it?" asking as I take the vile.

"Purifying potion. It will cleanse the wolfsbane from your system. You don't want it in your system when we teleport." He answers.

Nodding my head, I open the vile. Then I swallow the pretty blue liquid. It's minty but too minty, like I drank too many breath mints. An overpowering tingling session travels through my body. It lasts for several minutes before I begin to feel normal. My wrists are slowly healing from the silver. I need some food and rest to recover from the wolfsbane and the silver entirely.

Sage hugs me goodbye, and I can't let the gravity of what is happening hit me yet. No, when I'm alone, that's when I will let the tears out. My life is changing. I'm trusting someone I don't know, and it's scary. Warlocks and witches are not a race I want to be around. I don't know what coven life is like. I only know pack life, and that's probably not going to help me much. I push the fear away because I don't like how much I will have to rely on Zane. I have to give him all my trust and hope that he doesn't make me regret this.

"Just remember, Ari, you always wanted an adventure," Sage says with a wink as she breaks our hug.

"Yeah, well, we were kids and didn't want to stay in the confines of the pack territory. We were in a rebellious stage then. This isn't how I pictured my adventure." I reply harshly.

"I know, but maybe it's the adventure you need," Sage replies with a smile. Curse Sage and her impossibly positive attitude. Easy for her to be positive; her world isn't about to get turned upside down.

I stop myself from rolling my eyes at her very cliche statement. She's not wrong. I did want adventure as a kid, but we were rebellious at that point in time. We were in our pre-teens, and the pack territory didn't seem big enough for our adventurous spirits. We wanted to explore and go on a grand adventure. I think I wanted it more than Sage because I was an omega. I've always felt I didn't have a purpose, so I wanted more. Sage was a beta and the daughter of a highly respected member of the pack. Her life was always going somewhere. She was going somewhere before she became Luna, and I was

The Coven of the Crow and Shadows: Legacy

lucky enough to tag along. In some ways, I've been living in Sage's shadow. Not that I ever minded. Being in her shadow was better than any life I'd live on my own.

When Sage accepted Liam as her mate, it made me want more. I know my chances of finding a good mate are slim and now made even slimmer by my parents. It's like they wanted me to fail in life. I never really got along with my parents. They were always so bitter against the pack. I never understood why. My parents always wanted to be above their station. I guess they finally decided to do something about it. Too bad they failed, and now I'm paying for it. Now, I'm trusting a stranger with my life and my soul. Well, this is not how I saw my day going.

Sage and Liam walk out of the cell as Zane walks entirely into the cell. He offers me his hand. I accept it as I look into his swirling gray eyes. Shit, he's even sexier up close. What is it about him that makes me want to rub up against him and get him to claim me? This is how I'd imagine I'd feel if I met my mate.

Mates are strange for werewolves. Some believe we have soulmates and that when you find them, they are meant to be your mate. Others believe you choose your mate, and no one controls who you decide to make your mate. Sage and I always wanted to believe in the fated mate crap. It was a pretty fairytale for two girls who had wild imaginations. Sage swears up and down that she and Liam had a connection, and that's why he picked her. Maybe she and Liam are soulmates. I hope they are, but I know I'm not that lucky.

CHAPTER 2
Ari

Zane whispers words in a language I don't understand. Suddenly, black smoke with a life of its own wraps around us. Chills run up and down my spine as goosebumps show on my arms. It's cold, and I realize it's not smoke. It's a fucking shadow with glowing amber eyes. What the fuck kind of warlock is Zane? The one thing I didn't ask him was what his coven practiced.

The shadows envelop us, and the cold is now accompanied by an extreme suction feeling as if I'm surrounded by tons of industrial fans. It's intense, and I find nausea creeping up my throat. One minute we are in the cell; the next, we are standing on the grounds of a vast dark gray and black manor. The manor is unusual. It almost seems never-ending. I look to the overcast sky that almost appears to have an oily sheen. The stone pathways are lined with statues of black crows. The crow's eyes glow much like the shadow's eyes did. The grass is dark green, like the darkest green grass I've ever seen. We aren't in Kansas anymore, I jokingly think to myself.

"Where are we, Zane?" I ask as a thick mist coats the land. Even the woods around us look strange and dark.

"We are at my coven. Welcome to the Coven of the Crow and Shadows. This is my home and your home now as well. You are safe here."

"I gathered we are at your coven, but this isn't the human realm."

Zane chuckles. "We are indeed in another realm. My coven practices dark and black magic. It's safer for us to be in another realm. I'll give you a tour, explain my coven to you, give you the rules, and then I have someone I need you to meet with before we do the binding ceremony."

"Okay, but I have some questions."

"We will get to them. Come on, let's walk the grounds. We have training grounds outside with obstacle courses, a track, and other things to help us train. You and I will be training together. As my familiar, I will require your assistance in battle." Zane informs me. Well, this just keeps getting better, I think sarcastically to myself.

"Planning on going to war?" I ask as we start heading down the stone stairs that level out to an extensive training field. It's the size of a football field. Holy shit. There's a track in the middle: various obstacle courses and some things I don't recognize.

"No, but my coven's job is dangerous. Most covens have a job for society. My coven serves one of the Five as we are descendants of Death. Most of our magic and power lies in necromancy and shadow magic. We are tasked with gathering souls for Death. We guide souls to the underworld and drop them off with the fairy man who takes them to Death. He decides what happens to their souls. I also help train some of the newer members." Zane tells me like all of this is entirely normal. Maybe it's normal to him, but I really should have asked more questions before I decided to come with Zane. Decedents of Death and what they practiced were crucial things I would have liked to have known before I agreed.

"So why do you need a werewolf as a familiar? I know some like the powers that shifters offer. What's your reason?" I inquire. I have to know what I'm getting myself into.

"Not all members of my coven have familiars. Only the powerful and high-ranking members are allowed familiars.

I've reached the point where I've been granted the privilege. I wanted a werewolf because they have abilities that come in handy when haunting souls. Their heightened senses alone are worth it. Not to mention the ability to self-heal while on the job is helpful. However, I wanted a werewolf from a special bloodline. Do you know why your parents betrayed the pack because I do?"

"Then tell me why did they do it?" I am curious, and if he has answers, I want them. Strangely, I trust that he's telling me the truth.

"They did it because they know they come from a powerful bloodline, more powerful than an alpha bloodline. You come from the dire wolf bloodline or what it's better known as the original Lycan bloodline. Lycans have dire wolves. Dire wolves were cursed to be the wolf counterpart of the original lycans. You're not a werewolf, Ari. You are a Lycan. Lycans eventually realized they could have children with humans, which created the werewolf bloodline. Most lycans died out. Lycans became a myth. Decades ago, it was discovered that some lycans are still around and live secretly among packs," He pauses as if he isn't sure he should keep going. "Your wolf is different from most, isn't she?"

"Yes, she is. I always hide when I transformed so no one would see me." My wolf's fur is a dark steely gray. It's a unique color that no one has. Gray wolves are never this dark. Being a lycan and having a dire wolf would explain my unique fur color, along with my parents and the others like us.

"To fully answer your question. You're a lycan; that's why I wanted you. You are more powerful than you know. Only ancient shifters like lycans can handle being a familiar in my coven. Only they are strong enough. I tracked the lycan bloodline to Liam's pack. Fate was on my side as he tends to like me. When I arrived to ask him if I could take you from the pack your parents were attacking."

"How do you know I'm a lycan besides my weird wolf color?" That can't be the only way he knew. I guess I'm curious if he did some voodoo or whatever it is he practices to find me.

"My research said the surname of the lycan bloodline was Blackwell. When Sage stormed in asking why her best friend, Ari Blackwell, was arrested, I knew I had found you. Fate wanted you to be mine because your parents delivered you to me with a pretty bow. Here I'd thought I'd have to fight to get you to come with me, but instead, you had no choice, which made my job easier." Zane confesses. I'm not sure whether I'm a fan or not that he's being so honest and upfront with me. It should be a good sign, but Zane is a warlock. I don't trust him.

"So glad my parents fuck up worked out for you," I state sarcastically.

At least someone benefits from this. Zane is right about one thing I wouldn't have gone willingly with him. I would have told him to fuck off. I might be an omega, but I'm feisty. Well, I guess I'm not an omega after all. Thanks, mom and dad, for the heads up. There's nothing like finding out you're unique from a man I'm about to give my soul to. It's a little unnerving having to place so much faith in someone I know nothing about.

"I'm sure their betrayal is hard to process." It's almost as if he pities me or is sympathetic to the pain I feel in my heart.

"I was never really close with my parents. I spent most of my time at Sage's. I'd be more heartbroken if I lost her." I state honestly. He's being honest. It can't hurt to be honest back, right?

"Well, lucky that you haven't. I promise you'll get to see Sage and talk to her. We will do the bonding ceremony tonight." He informs me as we head towards the oddball mansion.

"Don't want to risk me running away, huh?" I say as I nudged his arm.

He chuckles. "Something like that. Come on; I want you to meet my brother, Cade, and his familiar, Blair."

I follow Zane into the massively large mansion. I continue to follow Zane through hallways and staircases. As we walk through the strange mansion, it's genuinely odd. Some stairways lead to nowhere, doors that open to nothing, bizarre paintings, and stained glass windows all over the place even where there doesn't need to be one. Shadows move along the walls like swirls, almost giving the illusion of wallpaper. Unease creeps over me as we pass men in long black robes with hoods. I can't see their faces, and somehow I don't think they are alive.

It's like I ended up in some twisted version of the underworld, except there are no souls that I can see. The whole place gives me the creeps. I can't believe I have to live in this weird-ass place. How the hell am I ever to navigate this insane place? Seriously, who has doors that open to nothing and stairways that lead nowhere? What's with all the random stained glass windows? Some of them don't even see the light of day. This place seems almost alive.

Why did the warlock that I get stuck with have to be into dark shit? Why couldn't I have been stuck with the warlock that takes care of nature or something that doesn't involve death and shadows? I hate this place already, and I haven't even spent the night here. Please don't let my room be creepy. I can't sleep if I know there are fucking shadows lurking and possible spirits roaming around. We pass another black hooded figure, and I try not to stare. Somehow, I know to avoid its touch.

"Careful around reapers. They are souls sentenced to serve the coven by Death. Never interact with them and never touch them. Let them be." Zane warns as I swallow hard.

Great, so not only do I have to live in the creepiest mansion to ever exist in an alternate realm, but now I have to worry about these reaper things. For fucks sake, I better not be in some damn death trap. I move closer to Zane.

"Zane, what is with this mansion, and why is it so big?" I inquire, trying to gain some understanding of the new home I find myself in.

"Once you are my familiar, you will have to call me Master while we are around others. The mansion is currently 500,000 square feet and always expanding. Currently it has three libraries, a seance room, an altar room, three kitchens, 160 rooms, most of which have their own bathrooms with modern plumbing, there are two dining halls, a ballroom, an apartment for the coven leaders to live in, and a small indoor training area. You will stay in my bed chambers. I have one of the larger bed chambers. Not all the members live in the mansion. There are few villages and a few towns on the outskirts of the mansion. The forests surrounding the manor are dangerous. Never go in there without me."

"How the hell am I supposed to find my way around? It's like a maze." I state with unease.

I belong with my pack, not living with some warlock doing dangerous shit. I'm also curious what sharing a bed chamber means. I thought I'd at least have my own room. Does Zane expect me to sleep in bed with him? If so, does that mean I have sexual obligations? No one ever said anything about him having access to my body. I didn't agree to that, but would it be that bad?

Not for nothing, but Zane is sexy as hell. He's mysterious and definitely dangerous. I can sense he's powerful. Zane's aura is more potent than an alpha's aura. He demands respect and loyalty. He's not a man to mess with. His job is to collect the souls of the dead and deliver them to Death. Yeah, he's not an enemy I want to have. In a way, I'm intimidated by him, and he doesn't even own my soul yet. Combined with his handsome good looks and fit body, I bet he knows exactly what to do with a woman.

Unfortunately, I'm still a virgin. Sage insisted we save ourselves for our mates. She was a Beta. It looked better if she was a virgin, especially since the alpha chose her. Liam would want his mate to be a virgin. Alphas get off on claiming their mates. I followed Sage with her purity stint for the most part. I kissed guys and fooled around a little, but I could never give up my v-card. I didn't want to disappoint Sage. I always knew I'd never get a high-ranking mate, so it didn't matter to me. I just did it because Sage did. I'm not getting a mate now, so what's the point in staying a virgin?

"You'll learn your way eventually. You'll need me to guide you for a while. The house is designed to confuse any spirits that try to enter our realm. If they do, the reapers will find them. You will learn as we go." Zane reassures me as we open a black door that leads to a lounge-like room. It's gothic style: dark gray walls, black Victorian furniture with dark red pillows. There's a large fireplace with a very intricate mantle. It's carved in unique swirls. Two people are in the room already.

The man who looks very similar to Zane sits on the couch with his arm around a beautiful woman. She has fiery red hair, amber eyes, and fair skin. She's thin and on the taller side. Her heart-shaped face adds to her beauty. She wears a black corset dress that goes to her knees. The man is dressed similar to Zane and has a long black trench coat.

"I see you found your wolf, brother." The man states, nodding towards me.

The Coven of the Crow and Shadows: Legacy

"Yes, Fate was on my side," Zane turns to me. "Ari, this is my brother, Cade Shadows, and his familiar, Blair Simons. Blair is a phoenix shifter. I'm going to let you talk with her so she can help you understand your role better."

On the black coffee table, I notice a spread of food. There are grapes, nuts, cold-cut meats, sliced apples, raisins, and cheese. There are also two glasses, but they are empty. Zane and Cade leave the room, and I'm alone with Bliar.

"Please sit down and help yourself to something to eat," She rises from her spot and walks over to a cabinet that she opens. "Pick your poison." She says, moving out of the way to reveal different bottles of hard liquor.

"Damn, that bad, is it? Vodka." I replied.

"It's not necessarily bad, but it depends on you." She counters as she grabs the bottle of vodka. She comes back over and fills our glasses. She then sits down. "What exactly did Master Zane tell you?" She inquiries.

"That I give him my soul, and he gets access to my wolf abilities," I reply, popping a grape in my mouth. I hadn't eaten since breakfast, and by my estimates of when I left, it was dinner time.

"You'll give him more than your soul," Blair warns.

"Let me guess. I'll give my body and heart too," I say with a half roll of my eyes.

"Exactly. You can't deny the pull you feel towards Zane. He's going to want to own every part of you. Your soul, your heart, your body, your pleasure, your pain, and your loyalty." Her words send a shiver down my spine.

"Let me guess he won't return the feelings." I deflect, not wanting to admit the pull I feel towards Zane.

Blair giggles. "It's not that tragic. He feels the pull to you as well. He will care about you and protect you fiercely. He will love you in return, but he will be bad at showing it.

Think of him as your mate. Fate put you two together. You were always going to be his."

"You make it sound like we're going to have kids." I half roll my eyes.

Blair seems nice, but she also might be brainwashed. The overwhelming sense of loyalty to her master and the fact that she seems unphased by this weird-ass place also unsettles me. Am I going to be like her? Will I just give in? What am I signing up for? Also, am I to believe Zane and I are fated? That sounds like a load of crap you try to sell someone, so they join your cult. I guess covens are sort of like cults. Oh great, that's exactly what I need.

"You might. It's up to you two. Cade and I haven't decided yet. There's one thing you should know about the Shadow brothers. They are sons of the Lord who leads the coven. Cade and Zane will be leading it one day. They are extremely respected and feared, especially Zane."

I nod my head. Well, this just keeps getting better and better. Great, so not only is Zane a warlock who practices dark magic, but he's going to end up leading this weird place. I'm so stuck here forever. I'm a lycan, yeah, that still feels weird to say, yet it also feels right. I like to run free, and I don't see how that's an option when the forest is dangerous and this place is a maze. Sure there is training, but is that all I get?

I spend the next few hours talking with Blair. She's been with Cade for four years now. She told me she was more willing than I was and accepted that she was Cade's. I asked her about what it's like while they are hunting spirits, and Blair made it sound fun. I'm skeptical because I can tell she is trying to sell me on being a familiar. Trying to convince me Zane and I are mates. Telling me, I won't' be able to resist him. I know Blair was supposed to make me feel better, but honestly, she's not helping.

The Coven of the Crow and Shadows: Legacy

Blair's experience is different from mine. She wanted to be Cades. She wanted out of the secret life she was forced to have as one of the handful of Phoenix shifters left. Phoenixes are considered ancient shifters and are thought to be extinct. Clearly, that's not true, as Blair is right in front of me, and I'm one myself. Lycans are also considered ancient shifters. It makes me question some things that I was taught in the pack. Fantastic, now I'm questioning my upbringing and pack. I haven't been here for twenty-four hours. I already hate this place.

I eat and drink the food that Blair had laid out. Overall, Blair seems nice. She wants to help me adjust to my life here. At least I might have a friend here. I don't count Zane as my friend. I can't believe I have to call him Master, although there is a part of me that is turned on by it. Zane is the alpha here. He's going to own my soul, and according to Blair, he will own my everything. I can't even begin to process that.

After some time with Blair, I'm alerted to the arrival of Zane and Cade. I follow them through more twisted stairways and even more winding halls. I swear I will lose my mind trying to find my way around this fresh hell of a maze. I thought I could rely on my wolf senses to help guide me, but nope. The dark magic and creepy shadows make it impossible to tell which way is which. This place is literally my worst nightmare, and I didn't even know this was my worst nightmare. Yet here it is. My new reality is a new layer of hell that I didn't know existed. Hell, for all I know, I am in a layer of hell. Is hell even the correct term to use? This place is more like the afterlife. Not sure that makes it better.

Blair ushers me into a small changing room. She offers me a folded black cotton robe. "Here, put this on. You'll need to take it off when it comes time to transform."

"Wait, I have to transform?" Blair nods her head. "It's not a full moon." I remind her.

"No, but they have ways of mimicking one to get you to transform. One perk to being Zane's familiar is that you will be able to transform at will." Blair says with a wink as she leaves the room.

Not sure transforming at will is worth being enslaved to someone. This is not how I saw my day going, and it's definitely not how I saw my life going. Fate fucked me over, I think to myself as I strip out my jeans and a plain t-shirt. Lastly, I take off my bra and panties. I lost my shoes when I was being dragged to a jail cell for a crime I had nothing to do with, yet I'm being punished. Resentment against my pack rises within me. Why did they have to be such judgemental pricks?

I have a sobering thought as I slip the robe on and tie it. What if my pack was never my home? I hate them for cursing me to this life. Resentment builds within me against my pack, parents, and even Sage. She should have tried to keep me in the pack. Instead, she let Liam give me to Zane like I was a piece of property to be traded. Everything worked out perfectly for Zane, but what about me? I'm doomed to be in this creepy mansion, forced to become a familiar to a warlock I just met. Yeah, this is not how I pictured today going. Not at all. I thought today would be a dull day helping Sage with her Luna shit, but Fate decided to dump a giant bowl of molten lava on my life, melting away everything I knew and loved. Thanks, Fate, you asshole.

Blair comes to get me, and I find myself walking down another long hallway. We come to black double doors. The doors open. I realize that Blair is in a long black dress with sleeves like you would see on a witch's custom; it also has a hood which she has up. She's barefoot. We walk into a stone marble room. The floor is a dark shade of gray that's almost black. The room is circular. There are archways with pillars in a circle around the room. In the center, there is a stone altar with a few steps leading to it. Oh, hell no. I want to run, but my feet keep moving forward. Around the altar, there are three hooded men with unique silver chains around their necks that hold a large black onyx stone that seems to swirl like it's alive.

The more I look at them, I realize there is a living shadow in the onyx amulet. Creepy. Cade is dressed similarly, but his hood is down. Zane is also in a black robe with his hood down. I notice that Zane and Cade have similar amulets around their necks, but these are a dark blue with a black S with a crown on top of the S. It must be related to their status. Zane stands near the stairs. The three hooded men stand on the other side of Zane. Blair joins Cade, who stands at the head of the altar.

Zane motions for me to come to him, and I cautiously walk over to him. I begin to feel nauseous from the anxiety coursing through my veins. This can't really be happening? This has to be a nightmare, a terrible one. I will myself to wake up, but I know the harsh truth. This is real. This is happening. I'm really about to give my soul, and Fate knows what else to this warlock. Fear slowly creeps in as I stand in front of Zane.

"It's time to make you my familiar," Zane states as if that wasn't obvious.

I nod my head, ignoring the fear, anxiety, and disbelief as the conflicting emotions mix into a strange cocktail that threatens to spill everything I just ate onto the floor. Zane waves his hands, and a silver blade with strange black markings appears in one hand while a black chalice appears in his other. Zane holds the chalice between us. "Put your right hand over the chalice." Zane directs.

I do as I'm told. Zane then leaves the chalice floating between us as a shadow comes to swirl around it, keeping it floating in the air. Zane cuts my hand, and blood falls into the chalice. It's not a lot as my self-healing kicks in. Zane takes the chalice in his free hand as the shadow that was holding the chalice moves to swirl around the blade. Both the blade and shadow disappear. That's not creepy at all; I think to myself as Zane instructs me to transform. Behind us, the three men, along with Cade and Zane, chant something. The roof above us opens. It's a giant skylight. The night sky is pitch black, with some stars attempting to shine through the thick fog. Seconds later, a full moon emerges into the sky above.

My wolf stirs within, pushing forward. My skin burns as the need to transform takes over. I remove my robe, and before it can pool around my feet, fur sprouts from my skin and my fingers and toes turn to claws. My bones snap and reform to that of a wolf. Soon I'm on all fours. I shake out my fur and stretch slightly. My wolf is enjoying the extra freedom, and somehow I feel like this part of me will love the hell out of my new life. My wolf will enjoy transforming at will. She might even like the surge of power Zane's magic will give us. However, my human counterpart is very much against this.

"Get on the Altar and sit on it facing me," Zane instructs once more as he moves to the foot of the altar. I do as he ordered. I jump onto the altar and face him. I sit on my hind legs. His free hand rubs my head. "You're very magnificent, Ari." He says with a slight grin.

I won't lie; his compliment did something to me. His admiration was something I realized I wanted. No one ever has complimented my wolf. Not even Sage has complimented me. She always seemed a bit thrown off by my wolf. My parents were like me, so they didn't feel the need to compliment me. Knowing that I have a dire wolf and that I'm a lycan does give me a new appreciation and love for my wolf. I was sometimes ashamed of her because I couldn't be part of pack runs. I guess I don't have to worry about that now.

The Coven of the Crow and Shadows: Legacy

Zane commands a shadow to move his one free sleeve back while the chalice remains in his other hand. Zane then puts his arm out in front of my mouth. "On Cade's count of three, I will drink from the chalice, and you will bite my arm. It doesn't matter if you hurt me. I'll be able to self-heal with your abilities." I nod my head.

"One, two, three." Cade counts.

On the three, Zane drinks from the chalice as I bite into his arm. He doesn't even wince from my bite, and I know I'm crushing his bones. I won't lie; I'm impressed. I thought he'd at least make a face from the pain, but he doesn't. I let go of his arm and lick the blood away from my lips. A strange sensation suddenly washes over me. My whole body feels like pins and needles as I look at Zane's arm. It's healing itself. The minute his arm is healed, the pins and needles sensation stops.

"The bond is formed. I can siphon your abilities. You can come down and transform back." He instructs.

So the pins and needles sensation was him siphoning my abilities. Is that always going to happen? I'm not sure I can get used to that feeling. It was strange and slightly uncomfortable. I hop off the altar and transform back as the skylight closes above us. I quickly put my robe on and tie it. Nudity is common among werewolves, but since I never really transformed in front of the rest of the pack, I am shy about being naked in front of people I don't know.

I stand in front of Zane like before. "We are going to complete the bond now. Say the words that are in your head, Ari."

Words appear in my mind. What the hell? "I, Ari Blackwell, give my soul to you, Zane Shadows, and offer my loyalty as you are familiar."

"I, Zane Shadows, accept your soul and your loyalty as my familiar." He states after me.

Zane puts his right hand to my chest and pulls a white iridescent sphere from my chest as I suck in a deep breath from the emptiness that consumes my body. Zane then puts my soul to his chest, where he absorbs it. The second it's absorbed, I fall to my knees at his feet, breathing heavily as if I just ran a marathon. I also feel like the wind was knocked out of me. My hands go to my chest as the hollow feeling I previously felt dissipates. I almost feel numb. I did just lose my soul. Is that what it feels like?

This is one of those defining life moments. The one where you know nothing will ever be the same. The type of moment that leaves you wondering how you ended up in this situation. The moment where your life is forever changed for better or worse. I don't know what I just did, and the gravity of my situation hits me like a thousand bricks. What did I just do? Maybe being a rogue wouldn't be so bad. Panic temporarily sets in as the uneasy feeling and nausea overwhelm my senses. I gain control over my breathing or try to as I hear the footsteps of the others leave the room. It's just Zane and me, which terrifies me. I just gave him my soul, and now I feel like a part of me is missing as the hollow feeling returns.

"Take my hand," Zane commands softly as he offers his hand.

I take it, and he helps me stand up. For the first time in my life, I stumble from being unbalanced. My reflexes are impressive; they always have been. Better than Sage, and she's a Beta with skilled training, thanks to her dad and brothers. My reflexes, senses, and strength have always been slightly higher than the average werewolf, especially for an omega. I'm starting to think I'm not an omega and that there is more to the story of why my parents began a rebellion or at least tried to. I know it has something to do with us being lycans. I realize there is a secret in my pack. It turns my stomach thinking that perhaps my pack isn't the safe place I once thought it was.

I stumble forward into Zane, who catches me in his arms. "It's alright; it will all pass. Your body is adjusting to the bond."

My head feels slightly heavy, so I lean my forehead on his shoulder. For the first time, I breathe in his scent. It's intoxicating. It's the fresh smell of rain mixed with mint. How did I miss his scent earlier? I must have been so wrapped up with everything I ignored it. In fairness, things went from my usual everyday shit to insanity. Insanity seems to be the new normal, along with weird and creepy. I'm going to lose my mind in this place. I can just feel it. I already lost my soul, so what's my mind too?

After several moments I start to feel normal, as if nothing happened. That somehow unsettles me more because now I don't even feel like I lost my soul, which scares me. If I can adjust to losing my soul like it was nothing, what does that say about my mind, heart, body, and everything else? I'm so fucked. I lift my head off Zane's shoulder as I stare into his dark swirling gray eyes.

"Better?" He asks. I nod my head. "We can head to my bed chambers so you can have the rest of the night to rest. You'll need it. I know you feel fine right now, but trust me, your body is being flooded with the bond; it will overwhelm your senses for a little bit. You should get some rest."

We head out of the ritual room, or whatever they call it. I'm sure I'll have plenty of time to learn how this coven operates. Every coven is different. I ended up needing to link arms with Zane so he could help me walk as I started to feel weak, which is not a feeling I'm used to. Once more, we walk through crazy hallways. I find even more strange things about the mansion. Everything is incredibly detailed. The door nobs, light fixtures, and even the walls have some type of design on them. This place is weird, but it's strangely fascinating. The shadows swirl along the walls as if they are living entities.

Zane leads me down a long hallway with a handful of doors. The hallway is quieter than the rest of the house as I follow him to a dark gray door. Zane puts his hand on the knobless door. When his hands touch the door, it briefly lights up white and opens. We walked into the huge room, which is a cool gray color with black and other shades of gray as well as white. There is no color. There is a sizeable black king canopy bed with gray curtains. A black comforter with matching pillows graces the bed. To the right, there is a little sitting area with a black Victorian looking couch that sits in front of a beautiful black fireplace. The fireplace mantel has intricate and detailed carvings, but it's nothing I can recognize. A black end table is on one end of the couch with a few books on it. Ahead there is a door that I can see leads to a bathroom, and to the left is a closed door which I assume leads to a closet, or possibly nowhere since that seems to be a theme here. I notice a black dresser near what I believe is a closet. Everything is nicely spaced out with plenty of room. The carpet is black with gray specks. Overall the room is nice, and I like the gothic victorian theme of the room.

"I didn't expect you to come with me today when I left, so I'm not prepared for you. I've already requested a bed for you. It will be here tomorrow. I'll also have clothes and anything else you might need." Zane informs me.

I walk towards the bed and then spin on my heels to face him. I'm still a little off balance, but I'm gaining better control. My wolf is very unhappy about being disoriented. We don't like weakness as weakness gets you killed. That's what my parents taught me, and perhaps it's the one solid piece of advice they have given me.

"Let me get this straight. You want me to sleep in your bed with you, naked?" He's a bold warlock. I'll give him that.

Does he think I'll believe his story that he didn't know I'd come with him? He planned this shit. If he didn't, he's a lucky bastard, and I'm screwed.

Zane comes towards me so that he ends up right in front of me. "I never said you had to be naked, but I wouldn't say no if you're offering." He grins.

"Aren't you my master now? Don't you make all my choices for me, or do I have some free will?"

Zane grabs the belt of my robe and pulls me to him. My hands instinctively go to his chest, which I now realize is muscular, and I want to see exactly what he looks like. I look into his stormy gray eyes that swarm with danger and desire. This warlock wants me. I've never really had a male want me before. I was always in Sage's shadow. She is pretty, fit, and a beta. Males went for her over me. There were a few guys I fooled around with, but I never felt desired by them. Zane is different. I can sense his burning desire for me, which turns me on even more.

"I am your master, Ari. If I were you, I would be a good pet and do what my master tells me, or else your life will be very difficult." His voice is low, and I can tell he isn't playing games.

"Is that a threat?" I challenge him.

Why should I make this easy for him? He didn't even have to fight to get me here. Liam handed me to him on a fucking silver platter like my life was his to trade away. Even if I did decide to become a rogue, I have a feeling Zane would have hunted me down and convinced me to come with him. He knows as well as I that a few months as a rogue and I'd willingly go with him just for the safety factor. At least then, he would have had to fight for me. Instead, I was handed to him wrapped in a pretty bow. Thanks, Liam.

Fresh resentment washes over me at Liam and Sage. I never thought I'd resent my best friend or my alpha. I guess

Liam isn't my alpha anymore. No, he's not, but Zane is. He's not just my alpha, though; he's also my master. He owns my soul. No, I won't make this easy for him. He might have easily gotten me to become his familiar, but that doesn't mean I have to submit to him right away. It doesn't mean I have to be a compliant slave. He's coming for more than just my soul, and he's going to want my everything. He may have gotten my soul easily, but I'll be damned if he gets everything else so easily. I just have to resist this pull to him.

"It's not a threat. It's a promise. You have some free will. However, when I make a decision and give you an order, you obey. It's even better if you obey without questions, hesitation, and attitude. I know that will come with time. I don't expect you to obey me so willingly. I expect you to fight me, but you will give in eventually."

"Very confident in yourself that I'll just bend to your will so easily. You might have my soul, you might command me, and I might be enslaved to you, but that doesn't mean I'll bend to your will so easily."

The one hand that isn't on my belt comes to grab my chin. He's a little rough, and it makes my clit tingle. "You can fight me all you want, but you'll give in eventually. You should know I'll enjoy bending you to my will. You'll be mine, my Pet. I'll have all of you. Fate made you for me, and I will enjoy claiming every part of you." His words intensify the tingling sensation between my legs.

"We shall see about that, Master. So, what's it going to be, naked?" I tempt him.

Why am I tempting him to get me naked? I don't know if that's making it harder or easier for him. I know that whatever is easy for him is hard for me and vice versa. I lost the battle for my soul, but can I win the war for what's left? If I'm truly fated to him, do I even have a chance to resist? I'm doomed; it would seem.

"I don't think you want me to choose for you because you won't just be naked if you do. You'll also be under me with your legs spread open as I claim your body and pleasure as mine. So don't tempt me, Pet." He warns. This man is going to be my undoing.

"Is that what you want?"

"Yes, but it's not what you want, not yet. I won't take your body till you're begging me to claim you, and trust me, Pet, you will beg me. You'll sleep naked tonight." He decides as he pulls the knot of my belt undone.

He slips the robe off me, and a slight shiver of anticipation runs down my spine. His gray eyes darken as he admires my body, his desire becoming more evident. I can't pretend I'm not attracted to him because I am. Everything about him sets my desire on fire. He's not even touching me at the moment, and I find my body craving his touch. I'm going to try to resist him for as long as possible, but sleeping in the same bed with him completely naked will be interesting. I'm going to have to try and keep my desires in check. I will not bend to him so easily. It's not even been twenty-four hours with him. He's not getting all of me that easily. Nope.

"Get into bed." He commands, walking away from me and to the other side of the bed.

As I pull the covers back to climb into the bed, I stop in my task as Zane starts to take off his clothes. His back is to me, so he can't see me staring at his nice ass. The muscles of his back are toned and defined. A rather large tattoo of a crow sitting on top of a skull with swirling smoke around it adorns the middle of his back. It's sexy as hell. When he turns around, I can't seem to stop my mouth from dropping. His six-pack alone is worthy of my drool, but the whole of him is sexy as hell. He's not overly muscular like a bodybuilder, but he definitely has them, and he is toned. I didn't expect him to be so fit. I know werewolves tend to have bodies like this because they are highly active and all about strength. I guess warlocks like to be fit, too, and right now, I'm not complaining until Zane catches me soaking in his body. Oh, did I mention his somewhat slightly larger than the average dick? Yeah, that's something to admire by itself.

"Like what you see, Pet?" He asks with a grin.

I quickly gather myself. Yeah, I'm doing a great job at keeping myself in check. Come on, Ari, get it together. Time to bring forth all the attitude, sass, and fire that burns deep down within. I always had to hide that part of myself. I had to be a good omega. Omega's don't act out; we behave and do our best to serve the pack. I would have gotten smacked if I had told pack members to fuck off or do shit themselves. Even around Sage, I had to keep that part under the surface. I was afraid she would stop being my friend if I showed that side of myself.

Thinking about it, I had to hide a lot of myself in my pack. I couldn't show my personality. I had to hide my wolf because she was different. I had to hide that my senses, speed, and overall strength were better than most of the pack put together. I had to pretend to be this pathetic omega who did what she was told, a weak pack member who wasn't worth the ground I walked on. Liam handing me over to Zane like I was fucking dog that he could just give away at will angers me. Liam had no right to give me to Zane. He had no right to make me a rogue either. Instead of giving in to the pettiness of his pack, Liam should have stood up for me. He should be making changes to make the pack better, not keep it the same.

Resentment in waves comes over me at my pack, Liam and Sage. I hate questioning everything I know. I hate feeling like my whole life has been a lie. I thought I was happy in my pack life. I had Sage as my best friend. I'd spend so much time around her and her family. Part of me hoped one of her brothers would find me attractive and make me their mate. As an omega, it's easy to find yourself wishing that someone higher ranking will make you their mate. It doesn't happen often, but I thought I had shot. I spent a lot of time with Sage and her brothers. Her one brother James was attracted to me. I made out with him a few months ago. I thought maybe he'd make me his mate, but then he stopped flirting and wanting to kiss me. Now I wonder if was just hoping to fuck me. The blinders are coming off, and I realize how unhappy I was in my pack. It hurts. Everything I thought I knew, everything I thought I wanted, was nothing more than an illusion that has now been shattered.

"I didn't think warlocks slept naked, that's all." I counter, climbing into the unbelievable soft bed. Seriously, I've never felt softer sheets or blankets before.

I prop myself up in bed and make sure that I'm covered. I don't want to give Zane any more of a peep show than I already have. I know he's going to see me naked. When I transform, I have to be naked, and who knows how else he will see me naked. I live with him now; he's bound to see me naked at some point.

Zane chuckles. "You think werewolves and other shifters are the only ones who like being naked?" He asks, sliding into the bed.

"Well, I've never met any other supernaturals besides my pack. You could have been doing it for my benefit for all I know." I replied, sinking into the bed. Damn, it's comfortable, or maybe the events of the day are finally sinking in, and sleep gives me an escape from dealing with my problems.

"Cute of you to think I'd get naked just for you. I've been with many women, but can you say you've been with a man? I know you're still a virgin. I know your body craves my touch, and your desire burns for me just like mine burns for you. One day you'll accept that we are fated together as soulmates. For now, I'll enjoy watching you squirm as you try to fight your desires. Rest assured, you will give in eventually, and I can be a very patient man when I need to be. Go to sleep; you'll need it for tomorrow." He commands.

Something rushes over me, forcing me to obey. I get comfortable. How did Zane make me do that? I know Alphas have an aura that they can project onto their pack to make them obey. Alpha's love using it as they get off on the power trip. I am bound and enslaved to Zane. He may have something similar to the alpha aura that he can use on his familiar. Every being has an aura, but only some of us can sense it. Zane is my master, just like an alpha is the master of the pack. I stopped saying that alpha's ruled the pack. Alpha's don't lead packs. They are dictators most of the time. Werewolves are vicious creatures, and I take it that lycans are just the same. We are part animal, after all. The weak are picked on, and the strong rule with iron fists. Alpha's tend to get drunk off power.

Roger, Liam's dad, was an Alpha drunk on power. Roger was a bad alpha by most accounts. He punished omega's over little things like spilling a glass of wine was worthy of getting beat up by the warriors. He used females for pleasure, forcing them to his bed with his alpha aura. He was known to take virgins for sport.

Alpha Roger was a crazy man who thought the world was his. He had made plenty of passes at me. He even tried touching me. My mind wanders to that night. The night I never let myself think about. I can't help that my mind goes right to that night. It's like it was yesterday. I was sixteen at the time. I'm nineteen now, and I still cringe at this moment. I never even told Sage about this. No one knows. It's been my dirty little secret.

It was a pack party. The pack throws parties for everything and anything. Every night before a full moon, there would be a giant party at the packhouse. There would be enough food to feed the entire pack and then some. There would be a giant bonfire during the chilly and colder months. This particular pre full moon party was a warm spring night. The type of warm spring night that teases the summer nights to come.

I was in a simple black sundress with black flip-flops. The warm breeze wrapped around me like silk, and I was happy summer was coming. Sage had left me alone because her dad dragged her into talking with Liam. Even back then, Beta Harrison was attempting to pair his one and only daughter with the pack's future Alpha. It wasn't a surprise when Liam picked Sage. They had been thrown together at every turn and chance their parents got hoping they'd fall for one another. I know they did, and I know they were fooling around before Liam officially announced his claim to Sage.

That night I was on my own. When I wasn't with Sage and was forced to be at pack functions alone, I tended to stick to the shadows. If Sage wasn't around, I risked being bullied. Omegas are badly bullied in their teenage years. If I weren't friends with Sage, I would have been fucked. I couldn't show my true strength. I hated getting my ass beat, knowing I could take all of those fuckers down. It sucked being picked on for being weak when I was better than all of them.

Either way, that night, I chose the shadows. I was getting bored of the party, and it was getting late. My parents never came to these functions, so I knew they'd be at home waiting for me. I was heading out to the back entrance, not wanting to draw attention to myself. I knew leaving the front gate, I risked running into some bullies, and without Sage around, I wasn't in the mood for their shit.

I snuck down the dimly lit path that would lead to the parking lot. There I could get to the main road and walk home. Usually, I would have spent the night at Sage's house, but with her gone the whole night flirting with Liam, I doubted she would leave on my account. So, I decided I'd go home and face my parents. I was walking off to the side to avoid being seen. I didn't realize that Alpha Roger was drunk and in the woods pissing.

Alpha Roger stumbled onto the path, and unfortunately, I was nowhere near the exit. The packhouse was too far now. Damn, I didn't want to be near the alpha alone. I knew how he was, and judging the drunken lust written on his face, I had become his current target. He strutted to me and only stumbled once. I could smell the alcohol on him. From what I could tell, it was a lot, at least a bottle or two worth.

"What are you doing out here all alone, omega." Alpha Roger asked.

"I'm heading home," I answered honestly.

"No, you're not going home tonight. Tonight you entertain me." He states clearly, which confused me. Was he just pretending to be drunk?

"No, thank you, Alpha. I'm saving myself for my mate." I state firmly, attempting to get past him and away from him as fast as possible; unfortunately, he blocks me.

He gives a hearty laugh. "That's adorable, but you're just an omega, and I have a right to your body as your alpha." He grabbed my arm.

"Alpha, no. I don't want to go with you." I shouted, hoping someone would hear me and come to see what was going on. I didn't think anyone would stop the alpha from raping me. Not even another omega would help me, but it might startle him if I could draw attention, and I could try to get away.

Alpha Roger was pulling me towards the tree line. I wasn't about to let him rape me. No way in hell I would let him do that to me when I could probably take him. I didn't know if I could have won a fight with him, but I could at least getaway. Once I was on the main road, I'd be okay because there would be traffic and people around.

He got me to the tree line, and I attempted to pull away. I almost got away, but he was quick for someone who was supposedly drunk. I hoped Alpha Roger was drunk because that would have made getting away easier. Alpha Roger pushed me against a tree. He pinned me to the tree with his body as his hands went right to my breasts, grabbing them.

"I can't wait to put my dick in your tight little cunt. I will enjoy taking your virginity, but I won't just take you in your cunt. I'll fuck you in the ass as well. I fuck every hole you have. If I like what I sample, I might be back for more, so do your best to please your alpha. If you do, you'll get my dick again."

His words turned my stomach. Hell no. I wasn't going down like that. I wouldn't let him fuck me like I was his little toy. It was the moment I drew a very fine line for myself. There would be moments when I would use my abilities fully. I wouldn't hold back, not when I was being threatened like this. It's one thing for the bullies to push and shove me. They've given me a good beat down a few times, but this is where I draw the line. I wasn't about to have my first sexual experience be ruined by a drunk alpha who thought I was his because I was an omega.

I shoved him off me. He stumbled backward, stunned that I had such force within me. " I said no. I don't want to be used by you." I firmly stated. I started walking away, but he grabbed me again.

"You should be honored to be used by me. I know what you really are, and I wouldn't want to risk knocking you up. I wouldn't be able to let that child live, and I don't want to have to clean up that mess. Best to let you get going home, omega." Alpha Roger spat at me as he released my arm.

My mind snaps to the present and the thought that comes to my mind as I replay Alpha Roger's words in my head. At the time, I thought he was drunk, but now thinking about it, his words almost indicate he knew that I was a lycan. Is it possible he knew? If Roger knew, does that mean Liam knows, and if Liam knows, does Sage know?

Curling into a ball, I try to push the maddening thoughts from my mind. I don't want to think about that right now. I want to think about sleep because I am tired. The events of the day are taking their toll on me. My body is craving sleep which overrides my maddened mind, and I fall asleep.

CHAPTER 3
Zane

Blinking my eyes open, I roll over to find the warm body of Ari lying next to me. I don't think she meant to move close to me in her sleep. When we fell asleep last night, she was as far away from me as she could get without falling off the bed. Now she's right next to me. Ari is curled under the comforter. Only her head peeks out. I brush some of the hair out of her face as she's on her side facing me.

Ari is beautiful with her black wavy hair. Her hair has natural gray highlights that blend perfectly into her dark hair. It almost creates a smokey effect, especially with natural light waves. She has an ivory complexion. Her dark blue eyes with a hint of violet around the irises pull her appearance together. Her nice sized boobs, sweet little curves, and cute ass only add to her appeal. I also love that she has the cartilage of her right ear pierced with a black hoop earring. She's perfect for me. I didn't expect to feel this drawn to her, but the warlock familiar bond is unique. It's a fated partnership that tends to turn into more. I didn't expect to feel the pull to her so quickly. I knew she was my familiar the moment I saw her in that cell.

I've always known I'd get a familiar. I'm essentially the prince of this coven. My title isn't prince, but they call me Master. Cade and I will rule the coven one day, well, more like Cade will lead, and I will be his advisor. I will only lead if Cade is unable to. Cade has trained his life to lead the coven. I have as well, but for him, it's different as the older son. I'm more or less the backup. I'm okay with it, though. I get a little bit more freedom than Cade. I'm able to go on missions and work in the field. On the other hand, Cade spends most of his time here at the mansion.

I know the mansion confuses the hell out of Ari. She can't even use her wolf senses to guide her. The mansion is designed to confuse the spirits that might escape or follow us back here. Not all spirits get captured. Some get free. The field soldiers do their best to bring as many souls to the underworld. Unfortunately, there are far too many people living, and there are only so many of us. So we go after the ones we can. The souls that get free and roam as spirits eventually find their way to the underworld. Sometimes my missions involve collecting spirits. I only do that when needed. Since my skills are advanced, I am able to take the soul from the human body. Not every member of our coven can do that.

Ari stirs next to me. Her eyes flutter open. She looks up at me as I'm now sitting up in bed. "Good morning, Pet," I say with a half-smile.

"Morning." She says cautiously as she sits up, careful to keep herself covered.

"How did you sleep?" I ask, trying to ease her. I know she is uneasy here.

"Good. Despite how creepy this place is, this room is comfortable. Will the bed I'm going to get be as comfortable as yours." She asks.

I chuckle at her words. "I don't know, but you're always welcome to crash in my bed."

"You'd like that wouldn't you?" Shey eyes me suspiciously.

"Clearly, sleeping in my bed isn't that bad because you ended up on my side of the bed right next to me." I remind her.

The Coven of the Crow and Shadows: Legacy

"It was cold, which is a feeling I'm not used to. The cold here is different from what I'm used to." She tries to make an excuse.

It might be true as the temperature is different in this realm. It's colder, it's always overcast, it does rain, but that's it. There's never any sun. There are no seasons. It's always the same, and I like it, but this place is weird to someone like Ari, who is used to a very different realm.

"I can always light the fireplace for you. It will help keep you warm till you can adjust unless you rather sleep close to me." I raise an eyebrow at her in a challenge.

I want her so badly. I want to touch her, to feel her skin on mine. I want to kiss her, make her moan in pleasure, and taste her. Cade warned me about this. Warned me of the pull I'd feel and the need to have her everything. I didn't think I'd feel all of this so quickly, but I do. Even now, I want to pull her to me and wrap my arm around her. I want her near me, touching me, and kissing me. I want her hands on my dick as she rubs it while I touch her clit. I want everything from her, and I know she'll give it to me, but not yet. She's not there yet.

Right now, I wish I had it easy like Cade did. Blair didn't fight him; she was willing to come with him. She was willing to be his familiar. Cade didn't have to bribe her. All he did was offer the opportunity to her, and Blair took it. She had been hiding in the human realm, afraid to let it be known what she was. If people knew what she was, they would either try to kill her or capture her. Phoenix tears are valuable, as are their feathers. Everyone would hunt her, a trophy to hang on the wall or keep in a treasure chest.

Blair knew that coming with Cade would be the safety she desperately needed. She also needed to be free to be herself. She would be able to transform. Blair is enslaved to my brother, and yet she is free. It's different with Ari and I. Ari was free to be herself to some extent. I know she hid her wolf. I know she hid her better abilities. I know she took shit when she didn't have to. Liam informed me of everything as He knew Ari was a lycan. He knew why her parents attacked. Liam knows the dark history between his pack and the lycans.

Liam was relieved to get rid of Ari. She was the last lycan left in his pack. Ari's parents were killed along with the others who rebelled. With Ari gone, Liam doesn't have to think about lycans anymore. His pack is free from their dirty secret. Lycans remain in other packs and as rogues, but they are getting less and less as time goes on. Soon there will be none left.

I feel bad that Ari got forced to come with me. I knew she'd never choose to be a rogue, and if she did after a few months, she would have come with me. I didn't think I'd acquire her so quickly. I was prepared to fight for her. I knew she was different from Blair. Liam had given me all the details before I had arrived. He wasn't even surprised when I mentioned lycans or dire wolves. He already knew, which surprised me. I've always seen Liam as a good person, but for him to keep such a dark secret changed my view of him slightly. I always thought he'd be an alpha to fight for a change in the way packs were run. Perhaps I was wrong about him.

I don't like that they knew about Ari and the others. I don't like how he let the pack treat the lycans. He didn't have to make Ari come with me. He could have forced the pack to accept her and explain that she had nothing to do with the attack. Ari was loyal to Liam, and in a way, he betrayed her. He gave her to me like she was nothing. He didn't care how it would affect his mate. Sage and Ari are best friends, so Sage must be upset to lose Ari. Liam didn't seem to care about their friendship. It was easier for him to get rid of Ari than stand up for what was right.

The Coven of the Crow and Shadows: Legacy

I've heard of the harshness of pack life. Vampires are just as vicious, but they are cruel to others which is what got them haunted in the first place. Werewolves are only vicious with each other, so the other races don't bother stopping them. Since they are only hurting one another, no one can intervene. Each supernatural race, along with humans, has its own way of doing things. It's chaotic trying to fit it all together, which is why I prefer staying in this realm. The human realm is a mess. Politics run wild, and there's always something happening, someone doing something they shouldn't. Trouble makers upset the balance on purpose because they can. Most covens prefer to operate in another realm for the safety and peace it provides. Witches and warlocks are the only supernaturals who hate the human realm.

It used to just be the human realm. However, in time others from the other realms surrounding the human one started invading the human realm. Vampires realized the humans were free food. Warlock and witches saw it as a chance to explore something new. Shifters saw it as a playground. It all meshed together. Most of the realms collapsed as more and more members invaded the human world and rejected their original realm. Our coven's realm is one of the very few realms left. Most have turned to ash and dust.

"Sleeping next to you isn't horrible, but I don't want you to get any ideas." Ari's words bring me back to the present.

"Oh, I have many ideas. Many ideas on how I'm going to make you mine, on how I can seduce you, and ideas on how I'm going to fuck you." I watch as her mouth slightly drops. She's not used to men being forward with her, nor is she used to a man wanting her. The males of her pack were fools not to claim her. Their loss is my gain.

"Well, just get those ideas out of your head," She demands, but I can tell my boldness flusters hers. "So, are we going to train today, Master?" She says master with some defiance. She's changed the subject from sex to training.

I inwardly chuckle at her. She's so defensive, and her attitude is something else. I can't blame her. Her world is forever changed, and she doesn't have a say. I know she's feeling a million different things right now, and I doubt desire, sex, and lust are top emotions. Right now, she's scared, uncertain, and anxious. I hate that she isn't comfortable with me. It's not even about the sex at this point. I don't want my presence to be something she can't stand. It bothers me. I regret her forced decision, but I didn't want her to become a rogue. I wouldn't be able to protect her, although I would have tried. She is mine to protect. Mine to take care of, mine to love, and mine to claim. She's my familiar and my soulmate. It's vital that she is comfortable with me. Damn it. I didn't prepare well for this. I did not expect her to be handed to me as a wrapped gift from Liam.

"I'll get the dirty thoughts out of my head when you get them out of yours. Don't pretend you didn't like what you saw last night. Don't pretend that I don't heat you to your core. You aren't fooling me with that rebellious act because you can barely fool yourself. Resist all you want. It just makes the chase that much more fun. It's going to make fucking you so much sweeter." The shock on her face tells me that I'm right. She's stunned that I called her out. I can sense her desire. I might not be able to smell it like she can mine, but I can feel her desire. I see how her body reacts to me. I know she was starting to get damp last night with our encounter. I can always siphon her super sniffer if I want to confirm I'm right.

Climbing out of bed, I head to the bathroom. My bathroom is all black marble. Everything from the shower, the tub, the floor, the walls, the ceiling, the sinks, and even the toilet is black marble. The fixtures are all gunmetal-colored. The glass of the shower is clear. It's crisp and clean. I pee and then wash my hands. As I'm washing my hands Ari walks in, and her mouth drops a little.

"This bathroom is amazing!" She exclaims, looking around wide-eyed.

"Glad you like it. I told you my chambers were nice. I know the rest of the mansion is odd for you. You'll get used to it and will learn your way around over time. Once you learn the patterns, you'll be fine." I assure her.

"If you say so. So, are we training today, and if so, what will I wear?" She inquires, stepping closer to me.

I take a moment to pull her close to me. Her hands land on my chest again. I love her natural reflexes to my actions. She looks up at me, unsure of what to do. I want to kiss her sweet rosy pink lips, but I'm not sure how she'd respond to that yet. I have to be patient with her.

"Your clothes will arrive with breakfast. We can eat here as I'm sure you're not ready to face the entire coven. Blair will bring some wardrobe options this afternoon after we finish training. Today we won't be too hardcore. Today is just testing some things and getting used to our bond." I informed her.

"As you wish, Master." She says with a wink.

"I like it when you call me Master," I say in a low husky voice.

"I like it when you call me, Pet." She softly confesses, and I think she shocked herself with her confession. "I don't know why I said that." She quickly says, looking away from me.

"It's okay. The bond is going to throw you off guard. It will make you vulnerable when you don't even realize it. As much as I want you to adjust overnight, I know you won't because you need time. I'm sorry your world got turned upside down like it did. I didn't want you to come with me because you were forced, but because you wanted to." I rub circles on her back, and she relaxes.

"I did want to come with you. I didn't want to be a rogue. I knew you were the safer option, even if it felt more dangerous. I realized I wasn't truly happy in my pack like I thought I was. I was hiding my true self, and that always felt wrong. I don't have to hide with you." There is a level of sadness in her voice. It must be hard to find out you weren't ever wanted in your pack. Packs, like most covens, are like families. They didn't treat her like family. I can't imagine what it must be like to hide from the people who are supposed to be your community, family, and support.

"You will never have to hide with me. I will always accept you for who you are." I assure her. I meant every word as I don't want her to hide from me. I don't want her to hide any part of herself from me.

She gives me a half-smile. "Thank you," She pauses, and I can see she is trying to hide her pain. The pain of realizing her life wasn't as good as she thought. Maybe she was never wanted and was never going to be accepted. I feel for her as I can't imagine such treatment from my coven. We never treat each other like that as we are all respected in this coven. Even the lowest members are treated with respect. We might play with shadows and mess with necromancy, but we don't bully each other. "I need to pee, so get out." She says, pushing away from me and hiding behind her sass.

"Don't think you'll always get away with giving me demands. You only get a pass because I know you're hurting." I say, walking out of the bathroom.

I head to my dresser and pull out my training clothes. I have black sweatpants, a black tank top, black socks, and black sneakers. I'm fully dressed by the time Ari comes out of the bathroom. She's desperately trying to hide her conflicting emotions, but her tough face settles into place as there's a knock on the door. I toss her the robe from the floor as I head to answer the door. Opening the door, I find an initiate with a cart. The top layer of the cart is filled with our breakfast. The second layer of the cart has Ari's training clothes on it. The servant pushes the cart into the room.

"Thank you, Jeremy. You may go." I dismiss him.

"You're welcome, Master," Jermey says with a bow and leaves my room, shutting the door behind him.

"So what, everyone calls you Master?" Ari questions as I go to the cart and pull her training clothes off it.

"Yes, Master is my title in the coven because I will help lead it one day. You call me Master for a different reason. You call me Master because you are my familiar. Now behave, or I'll make you train naked." I tease, handing her the clothes.

She smirks as she takes the clothes. She quickly dresses. Her outfit is similar to mine. She has black yoga pants on that make her ass look amazing. She has a black sports bra, a black tank top, black socks, and black sneakers. "I'm sensing a theme here with all this black." She comments.

I laugh at her comment. "Yes, black and other dark colors are all you will find here."

She shrugs her shoulders. "At least it's not neon colors. I can work with the doom and gloom of this place."

"Doom and gloom?" I raise an eyebrow as I hand her a plate of food.

"I'm used to rustic colors like greens, browns, tans, and even white and blue. I've never been to a place that barely has any color. I oddly like it. Although I think my wolf prefers the colors of nature." She replies, taking the plate of food.

"Does your wolf have a name? I'm curious; some say their wolf counterparts don't have a name while others say they do."

"Well, my wolf is named Sasha, but I think only lycans have names. Sage's wolf doesn't have a name. My parents told me never to mention that my wolf has a name. I guess somewhere along the lines, wolves lost their names, or maybe only Lycan's wolves have names. I'm honestly a little lost on it myself. The only things I know about dire wolves and lycans is what you've told me and what I've been able to piece together from my parents. They kept me in the dark with just about everything it would seem." Ari tries to hide the fact that it bothers her.

"We can find out more information if you want. My coven has a lot of resources at its fingertips. I can help you if you want?" I offer, trying to give her some peace with the storm brewing inside her.

"Thank you. I'd like that. I hate feeling like I don't know who I really am." I don't think she meant to say that last part out loud as she starts to eat her over-easy eggs, turkey bacon, hashbrowns, toast, and fruit.

We eat breakfast in silence, both of us lost in our thoughts. I'm concerned about Ari. She feels like she doesn't honestly know herself or her wolf. She's broken, and I'm not sure she realizes it, or she's starting to. Her life has been lies and secrets kept in the darkness. I want to protect her, ease her pain, and so much for her. I hope she will see that being with me isn't the curse she fears it is.

After breakfast, we head down to the outdoor training grounds. The field soldiers I help train are waiting for me in a perfect line. Ari follows behind me. She's taking everything in. Those in my class are dressed like me. Ari stands slightly behind me on my right side. I stand in front of my twenty or so students.

"Morning. I'm sure many of you have heard, I've found my familiar. This is Ari, and she is a lycan. Today my focus is going to be on her. I want you all to pair off and run field training drills. If you need me, I'll be off to the side with Ari as we work on getting her trained for the field. I expect all of you to behave."

"Yes, Master." They say in unison.

I lightly grab Ari's upper arm and lead her off to the side. "I figured you'd enjoy training outside than inside."

"Yes, thank you." She says with a smile.

Ari is not a caged dog, that's for sure. No, she is a wolf who needs to be free. I'm happy to oblige her wolf and whatever she needs. Shifters are very different from the rest of the supernaturals because they have two counterparts. They have their human counterpart, and in Ari's case, she has her wolf counterpart. A rare combination of human and animal. Shifters are fascinating, and in some ways, they don't make sense, and in other ways, they make perfect sense. They are enigmas.

"Do you have any training with fighting?" I inquire, wondering what I'm working with here.

"Some, but not much. I wasn't allowed to train for obvious reasons. My parents feared it would be hard for me to hide my true skills. I did train with Sage and her brothers, but that's it. I wouldn't even say it was official training."

"Something is better than nothing, and I have a feeling you'll catch on quickly. I'm sure you observed from the sidelines when you could. You don't strike me as someone who just sat by without trying to study for the future."

"Trying to learn all about me already, Master." She taunts me by taking an opposite stance from me.

"I don't need to try because you are like an open book with me. You just don't realize it." I say with a smirk. "You've fought other werewolves, but Pet, you are in a different game now. Now you must learn to fight spirits, other supernaturals, and most importantly, fight the darkness."

"What darkness?" she asks, and I can tell she is confused.

I move my hands and manipulate the shadows, so they swirl around her. She attempts to swat the shadows away. "The darkness within and the darkness around you," I answer with a grin, enjoying watching her squirm a little.

She has to get used to different things attacking her. Being out in the field is a dangerous game, and one can end up dead if they aren't prepared. Ari has lived a particular life. She's also lived a secret life in the shadows. She needs to learn to fight what she knows and allow herself to evolve to her true self.

The shadows consume her, and at first, I can tell she is panicked. That's natural. The shadows are thick black smoke in appearance, and they make the air around the person ice cold. I can see her trying to break through the shadows, but that's not going to do a damn thing against my magic. Then I hear the tearing of flesh and the snapping of bones. I hear a vicious growl and a howl of anger. That's my girl. Her wolf is strong enough to break through the shadows as Ari emerges from the shadows in her wolf form. She growls viciously at me, snapping her teeth.

"Hello, Sasha. Nice to officially meet you." I smile at her.

Sasha bows her head to me, and her demeanor changes. She acknowledges me as her master if only Ari would be so willing, but her wolf is different. Animals know when to submit, but humans don't know when to submit. I approach her and then pet her head and scratch her behind her right ear. She almost purrs at my touch, rubbing her head in my hand. Her fur is soft.

Sasha is truly a sight to behold. Her dark steel gray fur is gorgeous. I notice she has the same blue eyes as Ari. Soft and yet danger lurks in them. She is a giant wolf, but dire wolves are larger than regular wolves. Her tail is almost bushy, and her claws are solid black, as is her nose. She's a beautiful wolf.

I notice my class has stopped training to look at Sasha. It's not because they haven't seen a werewolf before, but because Sasha is a dire wolf. An ancient creature thought to be extinct. Lycans are considered rare, even if they are just in hiding. I doubt anyone has openly seen one in ages. They admire her for her beauty and strength. She truly is unlike any other wolf I've ever seen. She's magnificent, and she's mine.

"You want to show me what you can do, girl?" I ask her, looking down at the very happy wolf enjoying the attention from her master.

Sasha looks up at me and gives me a toothy wolf smile as she nods her head in my hand. A new idea forms in my head. I wasn't expecting Ari to let Sasha out so quickly. I thought she would stay in human form for the first few sessions. Ari isn't used to being able to shift without a full moon, so I assumed it would take her some time to adjust to the idea. However, it would seem Sasha is taking full advantage of being able to shift when she wants. I can also tell she is happy not to have to hide.

I clap my hands together to gain everyone's attention. "Change of plans. My familiar here is feeling playful, and her wolf wants to play. So, you all will go up against her. She needs to learn to fight magic, and you lot need to practice. Line up, boys, and face my lycan's dire wolf. Her name is Sasha, and I don't think she plans on taking it easy on you, so I expect you boys to give her the best you've got. My familiar has had to hide her true identity for a long time. I don't think she plans on playing nice." I instruct and give fair warning.

The trainees line up, and Sasha prances over to them, ready to finally have some real training. I stand off to the side as an observer, prepared to interfere if need be. I watch as Sasha digs her paws into the earth, ready to stand her ground or pounce. She's ready for a fight, and she will not back down. I watch Gill take an opposite stance to Sasha. He's got a determined look on his face which makes me wonder who will win this showdown. My bets are on Sasha as she's my familiar. I'm definitely being biased.

As I watch Sasha and Gill go at it with no remorse, I wonder about Ari. What's it like when she is in wolf form? Is she aware of what's happening? Can she feel what Sasha does? I'm fascinated with my pet. I'm going to learn everything about her. It's not just about owning her whole being. That's the alpha male in me mixing with my dominant side wanting me to own her. It's more than that, though. Having a familiar is very special. I'm responsible for Ari. It's my job to make sure she is safe and protected. Yes, she is enslaved to me, but that doesn't mean I don't care about her. She's my everything, even if she doesn't realize it. In my coven, when a member is granted a familiar, that familiar is also that warlock's soulmate. It's a complex partnership, but it's one I've been looking forward to.

Sasha is a force to reckon with. She is tearing through my trainees with viscousness. I think her years of hiding and being caged make her more aggressive. She's pissed, and it shows with every snap of her jaw and swipe of her paws. Every jump and pounce is extra forceful. My trainees get a few good hits in, but that only fuels her anger. As the trainees repeatedly rotate with Sasha, she keeps her stamina while my trainees look like they've been through the wringer. They are new and not fully adjusted to using so much magic repeatedly. Using my magic hardly weakens me anymore. I have to use a vast amount before wearing me down. I've built up my stamina over years of training and being in the field. Collecting souls is not for the faint of heart.

After hours of back and forth with Sasha and my trainees, I finally call it. Even Sasha is losing steam at this point. She isn't used to being able to use her full abilities constantly, but I have a feeling she will adjust quickly. Her strength is evident. Sasha prances over to me, proud of her work. She should be; she kicked ass out there. I'm very confident that she will be excellent in the field.

"Good job, girl." I pat her head as I give her well-deserved praise. "Now, let Ari take over. I need to speak with her." Sasha whines, clearly not ready to be caged back up. "I know, girl, you're finally free, and you want more time out. I promise you will get more time tomorrow as we will train longer. I promise you will be able to be out much more often than before." Sasha rubs her head against my hand and then licks it in approval of my words.

Sasha walks off to the side as the trainees make their way back to the mansion to attend to whatever their assigned duties are. I pick up Ari's shredded clothes. I doubt she will be able to wear this. Note to self, have her transform before I provoke her wolf. I tell Sasha to wait. She will have to transform in my room since her clothes are shredded.

I have Sasha follow me. She seems just as thrown off with the insides of the mansion as Ari is. I can tell she doesn't like all the tricks and randomness of the mansion. I know it messes with her senses, it's meant to, but she will adjust to it and learn to be immune to the magic that messes with her senses.

We make it to my room, and once we are inside, I watch as Sasha turns into Ari. I won't lie, the transformation process is pretty intense to watch, but luckily it doesn't phase me. When you know necromancy like I do, you've seen some dark and disturbing shit. Ari is kneeling on the floor. I come up behind her and put her robe on her. Then I walk in front of her and offer my hand to help her stand.

"Thank you." She says softly.

"Of course, Pet. You did well today." I compliment.

My mom drilled it into Cade and my heads that women enjoy compliments and that we should sincerely give them as often as possible to our familiars. I wonder if that comes from dad fucking something up. My parents love one another and have an excellent relationship. However, I know that it took years and many mistakes to achieve what they have now.

"Yeah, Sasha enjoyed herself a lot today. I have to be honest. I don't think she's ever enjoyed herself so much." Ari states putting the robe properly on and tying it.

"Well, she is finally free to be seen, heard, and admired. No more hiding in the shadows."

"I thought you liked shadows. I mean, isn't your whole coven about death and shadows." She raises her eyebrows at me as she puts her hands on her hips in defiance.

I chuckle. "I'm born from and in darkness. The shadows have always been a part of my life, so yes, I like shadows. For you, it's different. You were forced to hide in the shadows, never allowed to show your true self. I control the shadows, but the shadows control you, for now."

"You control the shadows and me, so let me guess, you will help me fight the darkness of the shadows within?" She asks in a cynical tone.

I pull her to me because I love touching her and the feel of her body against mine is divine. Once more, she puts her hands on my chest, ready to push away at any moment. I wrap my arms around her back so she can't escape so easily. "No, I'll make you a weapon so that you can fight what's inside of you with confidence. You might be enslaved to me, but you are freer than you've ever been in your entire life. Admit it. Today was the freest you've ever felt."

"I'm not sure being enslaved means I'm free, but you're right. Today was a freedom I've never experienced before." Her voice is soft as she lets her guard down.

The Coven of the Crow and Shadows: Legacy

"Did you enjoy it?"

"Yes." Her confession is barely above a whisper.

"Just think of what else you might enjoy with me." I lower my head closer to her to test my limits. I know she's feeling a little vulnerable, which makes me want to take advantage of her, yet I also want to protect her. Her breath hitches as I bring my lips closer to hers. I expect her to push me away or say something to stop me, but she doesn't. Being the asshole I can be, I decide to thoroughly test my limits and gently plant my lips on hers. I expect her to push away. Instead, she melts in my arms. I don't even think she expected to enjoy it.

Her lips are soft and warm. I want to devour all of her, but I'm not about to push my luck any further. Her not pushing me away is enough of a conquer for today. I go to pull away, but she pulls me back to her lips as she wraps her arms around my neck, which only deepens our kiss.

I won't lie; I'm shocked. Ari was so resistant that I didn't think she would embrace my kiss so willingly. Perhaps all the resistance, attitude, and sass is just a wall from her fear? Maybe claiming her everything won't be so hard, and I won't lie; part of me is relieved if that's the case. I understand it's hard for Ari to fully accept our partnership and even the romantic relationship that is to come. It's not what she is accustomed to. This is not her world, not yet, at least. Right now, she is a stranger in a new world, and it has to terrify her.

Deciding to be a little bolder with her acceptance, I push my tongue past her lips and let our tongues do a dance of their own while my hands move to cup her ass to pull her even closer to my body. Damn, does she feel good rubbing against me. My mouth devours hers as her arms wrap tightly around my neck as if her life depends on it. My hands grip the silky soft skin of her ass. I find myself wanting to consume all of her. I want to push her down onto the bed and make her moan my name as I claim her.

A knock on the door snaps both of us out of lust-filled mindsets. Ari's head whips to the door. I sigh in frustration. I forgot about Blair coming by with lunch and wardrobe options for Ari. Ari turns her attention to me. She looks up at me like she can't believe what we just did. It's not horror, but shock. I watch as her mask slips in place.

"You're dangerous to be close to." She says, jumping out of my arms like I'm going to burn her.

I sigh again in frustration as I roll my eyes at her. "Don't act like you didn't enjoy it. We both know you did." I say, walking past her to the door.

Her denial annoys me as it seeps under my skin like a disease. I get that she isn't going to just bend to my will the first day. I know she is going to resist. I've been trying to prepare myself for her resistance, and I can handle it for the most part. I can't handle her denying her attraction to me. I can't handle her denying that she didn't enjoy what we just did. For fucks sake, I was the one who tried to pull away out of respect. She pulled me back to her.

Opening the door for Blair, who has a smile happily plastered to her face. Blair is more than a willing familiar. She enjoys being my brother's soulmate. The reminder of my brother's easy time taming his familiar irritates me further. My brother always seems to get things handed to him so easily. I love Cade; I do. He's a good brother, and we have a good relationship. Cade just seems to have everything on the more accessible side, while I feel like I get the harder side of shit. I don't like feeling jealous, especially when I care about someone.

Blair strides in with several initiates behind her. I get out of the way and grab some clothes to change into. I pop in the bathroom while they set up the bedroom. I dump my training clothes in the laundry basket. I freshen up and put on my black jeans and a dark gray v-neck t-shirt. I toss my black trench coat on and then put on my black boots.

Walking out of the bathroom, I find my bed chambers completely taken over. A small tray of food is set up for lunch in the corner by the fireplace. There are mountains of clothes by the closet that spread to my bed and most of the room. Yeah, I'm not staying here for girly shit. I'm out.

"Have fun, girls. Ari, behave yourself. I'll be back for dinner." I walk towards the door and leave.

I didn't mean to come off cold, but my irritation is getting to me. I didn't think it would be so fucking hard. Just when I think Ari's walls are coming down, she puts them back up. She hasn't even been here for forty-eight hours, and I'm already losing my cool with her. I can't even really be that annoyed with her. Her world just got turned upside down. She doesn't know me and doesn't understand our bond yet. Everything is so new to her, and she probably has more questions than she's ever had before about her family, pack, and her wolf. I immediately regret my reaction.

Deciding I need to work out my frustrations and get my head on straight. I hit Liam up for a drink. He owes me answers, and he knows it. I manipulate the shadows as they come around me to teleport me to the human realm. Once there, I head to the town near Liam's pack. I hop into my black Dodge Challenger and head to meet Liam. The coven has cars and safe houses all over the human realm. They come in handy.

Liam and I always meet at Mcguire's, an Irish pub in the nearest human town to his pack. His pack resides on a mountainside. Not surprising as werewolves love dense forests and mountains. I arrive before Liam. This also doesn't surprise me either. Liam is always late. Liam might be many things like strong, tech-savvy, a damn good warrior, but he is not one to ever be on time. I head in and take our normal spot at the end of the bar.

Marty, the owner, waves at me as he's friendly and loves paying customers. He doesn't give a shit if you are human or supernatural. If you put money into his business, he doesn't care what you are. Marty pours me my regular order of two shots of whisky. It's my usual before Liam gets here. Once Liam gets here, I drink beer because that's what Liam loves. There is this myth that supernaturals can hold their liquor better than humans. That's total bullshit. Liam can't hold his liquor, as I learned this at a party once with him. Never again will I do shots with him.

I down my two shots, and Marty clears my glasses and places a beer bottle in front of me. Good man. I always tip him generously. I like Marty, and I don't mind giving him extra. While I wait for Liam to arrive, I nurse my beer as I think about how I met him in the first place. It was about six years ago. At twenty-one, all future leaders of the supernatural community have to attend a conference where we get a lecture on keeping the peace as we take over for our parents. It's dull, but it's a must.

Liam and I were paired together for some dumb breaking the ice game. We clicked and hung out the whole conference, which was the entire weekend. We exchanged numbers, and from there, we just became good friends. Liam traveled some to other packs learning and observing. I dove deeper into my practices. I was determined to master everything I could. I wanted to earn my familiar, knowing that she would be my soulmate. I wanted to find her. I was damn determined to earn that privilege, and it has consumed my life for the last six years. Once I earned it, I felt relief, but that relief was short-lived when I learned about my future familiar. Our familiars are chosen for us by Fate and Death. Ari was selected for me. I was thrilled to learn my familiar's name. I learned everything about lycans as I couldn't learn much about her as a person at the time.

I did find it odd that there was so little about her. Even when I found out she was in Liam's pack, I had inquired about her before I told him who she was to me. Liam didn't have much information for me. How invisible did she have to make herself to survive?

Liam walks in and takes his seat next to me. Marty brings him some pale-looking beer. Liam and I have such wildly different tastes when it comes to drinking. "Glad you made it," I say like I do every time I meet him, and he's late, which is all the time.

"Yeah, yeah, I know I'm late. I have to confess I'm surprised you wanted to meet so soon." He eyes me suspiciously. "I ain't taking her back in my pack. I don't care what type of hell she gives you or if she isn't a good fuck. I don't care, man. She isn't coming back into my pack. You wanted her. You got her." He picks up his beer and takes a good sip.

"Why the hell would you think I'd return, Ari?" Irritation flares inside of me at his disregard for Ari.

"She's a lycan, man. They aren't meant to be house pets or whatever a familiar is. Do you even know anything about lycans? They are not welcome in the werewolf community for a reason. They are violent, vicious, and power seekers."

"First off, I know more about lycans than you do, and I'm aware of how they can act. Second, Ari is my familiar, that is the equivalent of you claiming a mate, but she is fated to me. I didn't choose her. Fate and Death did. You don't know the Five like I do as I'm a descendant of one." I glare at him.

"Shit, okay, man. Sorry. I didn't realize it was like that. Look, you know Ari is better off with you, so why did you call me here to meet?"

"I don't know. I guess I'm trying to understand Ari better. She's a little more resistant than I thought. I knew she'd be a little defiant, but damn she's being difficult." I take a swig of my beer.

"I can't help you, bro. I'm sorry. I don't know Ari like that. That's Sage's area. I don't ever recall Ari being defiant. She was always submissive from what I've encountered with her. I avoided the lycans as I was told to avoid them, so I did." Liam informs me with a casual shrug of his shoulders.

"Thanks," I say sarcastically.

"Look, I can ask Sage, see what she knows, but that's all I got for you." Liam offers.

"Fine, see what Sage says," I replied with a sigh in frustration.

After chatting with Liam some more, I head back to the coven to handle some business with Cade. I also have to prepare for training tomorrow for Ari and those under me. Some people think I teach the new recruits as a punishment. The truth is, I enjoy it. I don't always do it as I prefer being in the field. I like hunting spirits. I love using my magic, and I can use it a lot in the field. I thought training new recruits while training Ari would work well, and so far, it has. I have a knack for these things.

Before I know it, it's time to head back to Ari. At least my irritation has faded, and I'm less cranky than I was before I left. I'm looking forward to seeing Ari, even if she isn't thrilled to see me. Her bed should be there by now. Maybe having her own space will help her feel more comfortable. She is in my bed chambers surrounded by everything that is mine. She will have a wardrobe now and her bed. Maybe some of her own things will help ease her transition.

The Coven of the Crow and Shadows: Legacy

CHAPTER 4
Ari

Zane left in a hurry. I could tell he wasn't happy that I acted like I didn't like what happened. I'm surprised that I did. I feel like I'm spiraling out of control. I don't know if I can just fall for him so blindly, but damn, was the kiss amazing. I thought I'd been kissed before, but I've never been kissed like that. Zane had a point, what else will I like doing with him? Sleeping in his bed was nice. Training today was the most fun Sasha or I have ever had. My heart swells thinking about how he was with Sasha.

For the first time in my life, I had someone look at my wolf with admiration and love. I didn't have to be ashamed that I was different. I wasn't expecting Sasha to want to emerge like she did. She saw the shadows around me as a way to transform privately. Sasha was itching to get out, so I let her. She was so happy to be free, and so was I. It's nice knowing I don't have to hide any part of me. Zane knows, and he embraces it. It's the best feeling to be accepted.

Even with his acceptance, I still don't know how I feel about the whole situation. I want to accept it, but it's hard. My entire life has changed in a matter of days, and I don't know what to make of it. Everything I thought I knew is just gone. The slow realization that my pack life was crap and I was lying to myself that I'd ever belong there hits hard. I know coming with Zane isn't the worst fate, but it's hard when I feel like everything I had is gone.

This new life is hard to adjust to. This mansion drives me insane even if Zane insists I'll learn my way. I'm surrounded by people I don't know, which raises my anxiety. I know that with time that will change. I hate that I can't go into the woods. Sure, they are made of black trees with blood-red leaves, and the fog that moves through them is thick, but I've never had a forest forbidden before. I don't even know why it's forbidden. Maybe Blair will tell me.

"Hey, Blair, why are the woods surrounding the mansion off limits?" It can't hurt to ask. I'd rather ask her than Zane.

Blair looks up from the clothes she is sorting through. The initiates have already left. "Master Zane didn't tell you?"

"No." Seriously, if he told me, why would I be asking. Blair is friendly, but she's something. I can't put my finger on it. It's not ditziness, maybe oblivious?

"Well, he probably didn't want to overwhelm you. The reason it's off-limits to us is because we aren't members of the coven. In the woods are Howlers, basically what you would call hell hounds. They hurt anyone who isn't a part of the coven, and while we might be familiars of members of the coven, we are not technically part of the coven, so if we went in there without our masters, the Howlers would kill us." She states in an odd cheery tone.

"Oh," I reply, as it's all I can manage to say. This place just keeps getting more charming by the second.

Howlers or hellhounds will kill me, doors that open to nothing, stairs that go nowhere, and an endless maze of shit to figure out. Yeah, this place is so charming. I bet that it would be on any tourist must-see list. I mean, who doesn't want to live in a creepy ass mansion surrounded by a forest full of creatures that want to kill you.

"You should eat and then come try on some of these clothes. I don't know your preferred style, so I grabbed a little bit of everything."

"Well, that makes two of us because I don't know what my style is either." We didn't have much money, so I wore what I could.

I used to go shopping with Sage, but I didn't often buy anything. Sometimes she would buy me stuff, especially if it was my birthday or a special holiday like Christmas. I just usually got her hand-me-downs. Sage has a very preppy style, so lots of argyle and plaid mixed with cute skirts, cardigans, collared shirts, vests, and such. It's definitely not my style, but beggars can't be choosers, or so I've been told. I just sucked it up and wore what I could. I often just stuck to solid-color shirts and jeans. It was basic, and it was on the affordable side.

The next several hours we spend going through clothes. I land on a gothic chic style. There are a lot of black, dark colors, torn-up jeans and leggings, fringy and lace details, combat boots, and leather jackets. Once we settled on a style, Blair had the initiates clear the other stuff away. We focus on clothes, accessories, and some makeup. I'm not a huge makeup fan, but I can get behind some mascara, eyeliner, and various shades of red lipstick.

By the time Zane gets back, I have an entire wardrobe complete with bras, panties, tops and bottoms, dresses, shoes, jewelry, and makeup. It's like fucking project make-over in Zane's room. Blair helps me put stuff away in the closet and the new dresser that Zane got me. No bed yet. Blair claims that it got held up. I'm not sure I believe her as Blair seems very adamant that Zane will fall in love. She doesn't understand my resistance, but I don't understand her willingness.

Blair explained that immediately she took Cade up on the offer to be his familiar. She was thrilled to be his and to go with him. Like me, Blair had to hide the fact that she was a phoenix shifter, but Blair didn't have a pack. She was on her own. She was an orphan stuck slumming it through life till Cade came in like fucking knight in shining armor to offer her a better life.

In some ways, I guess Zane is my dark knight in shining armor, but unlike Blair, I didn't mind my life in the pack. Well, that's what I thought, but the more I think about it, I'm not sure I was truly happy in my pack. I was constantly being picked on and not being able to kick the bully's asses because I had to pretend to be weak. Hiding my wolf, making up shit like saying I put the gray highlights in my hair when in fact, I was born with them. Having to deal with being looked down on for being an omega when I'm not sure I am one to begin with. There was too much hiding and a lot of wishing I didn't have to. I never felt worthy in my pack. They made me feel inferior when I was actually superior to them. Not that I'm one to care about status and who's superior or inferior. Still, being forced to hide my true self has been detrimental. I didn't realize it till now.

I may not fully trust Zane, but at least he's not ashamed of me for who I am. He's the first person in my life to accept me for who I am. The first person that makes me feel valued and wanted. It's strange to have someone look at me like that when I've been looked at with such contempt all my life. Even Sage never accepted me the way Zane has. Sage was always apprehensive when it came to my strang wolf. She has only seen Sasha a handful of times, and every time she would make some comment that would make me feel like a freak. I'm not sure she meant for her words to make me feel that way, but they did.

As much as it pains me to admit this, I've always questioned my relationship with Sage. She's my best friend, and I'm hers, but there's always been this slight disconnect between us. I thought it was because Sage was a beta, and I was an omega. I also thought my wolf had something to do with it. I know Sage secretly thought I was a freak like the rest of the pack. She knows my hair isn't dyed, my wolf is different, and my senses are damn good. I never felt entirely accepted by her, and it bothered me, but I pushed it away because at least I had a friend. Besides, Sage, no one else befriended me. Everyone wanted to be Sage's friend, and she had plenty of other friends besides me. Corine was her other best friend, but Corine would never hang out with Sage when I was around. Corine and almost everyone else never understood why Sage was friends with me. Even her father didn't like her being friends with me. Still, she kept me around. I wish I felt more accepted by the person who is supposed to be my best friend.

Hell, Blair is more accepting of me than Sage has ever been. Today facing off with the trainees, they didn't fear me, and they didn't look at me like I was a freak. How am I more accepted in a place that doesn't even know me than my own damn pack who's known me my entire life? Everyone knows pack life can be challenging for those considered weaker, but that doesn't mean it's right. It doesn't mean it's something that should be accepted or practiced.

Zane entering the room gets my attention. "At least it's not a total tornado in here." He comments. He seems in a better mood, but he still seems irritated. He looks around the room. "Where is Ari's bed?" He asks, looking around the room.

"It got delayed; apparently, that is," I reply.

Zane eyes Blair. "Are you and Cade meddling with Ari and me?"

"Of course not, Master Zane," Blair says with the sweetest tone and smile.

Zane eyes her suspiciously. "You two better not. This is hard enough on Ari and me as it is." Is it hard on him? How the hell is this hard on him? His life didn't get shaken like a damn snowglobe.

"We would never dream of such a thing," Blair responds by putting the last of my clothes away.

"Then how is her dresser here, but not her bed? I requested both at the same time." Zane is like a damn detective with his questions. I'm half waiting for the cheesy line of 'Where were you on the night of Ari's arrival between the hours of ten and eleven.'

"It's a mystery. I guess we are short on supplies of beds." Blair responds as she shrugs her shoulders.

Zane and I look at each other. Yeah, neither of us is buying her story, but what can we do about it? "Right, I'm sure that's what is," Zane states in a skeptical tone, and I can't help but giggle. "Blair, Cade is waiting for you to join him in the dining hall. You should get ready. Ari, I'll leave it up to you if you want to eat here or go to the dining hall with everyone else. We have our own table with my father, Cade, and Blair if that helps ease your social anxiety."

"I don't have social anxiety." I snap in my defense. He raises an eyebrow at me. Damn it. Thanks to my unforgiving pack of rude-ass werewolves, I have social anxiety. I don't want to appear weak to the coven or to Zane. I'm not entirely sure why I give a shit what he thinks of me, but I do. "We can go to the dining hall." I regret the words as they leave my mouth.

"Are you sure about that?" Zane questions.

"Yes," I state with my chin held high.

At this moment, I regret all life decisions that have led to this point, but I'm committed now. Besides, training wasn't horrible. How bad could dinner possibly be? Not to mention I'm going to have to go eventually, so might as well get this bullshit over with now. Rip it off like a bandaid. I try to convince myself that I didn't just make a stupid decision out of defiance, but who am I kidding? I totally did.

"Oh, this is exciting! I'll pick out a dress for you to wear, but you two might want to shower from training."

"Is that your nice way of saying we stink?" I ask, and I hear Zane chuckle.

Blair just smiles at me. "I already have the dress in mind. This one should do. What do you think, Master Zane?"

"It's perfect," Zane says, looking at the black dress.

The dress has a high low skirt, the shoulders are cut out, halfway down the sleeves turn to lace bell sleeves, and it has a black leather lace-up belt. It's a lovely dress. I'll pair it with black lace flats.

Blair leaves to get ready. I'm still in my robe, so I head to the bathroom to shower. Zane said I could go first. The shower is the best thing ever. It has your traditional shower head and other nozzles that spray water that hits your back and legs. It's amazing. I enjoy the warm water and wash away the grim of the day. By the time I step out of the bathroom in my towel, I feel refreshed. Plus, that lavender soap Blair got me was heavenly. Okay, so maybe this place has some perks.

Zane steps into the bathroom to shower while I get dressed. I put on the dress, my black lace flats, and some dark red lipstick. I do a little mascara and light black eyeliner. I'm a gothic fucking goddess, and I'm about to slay this dinner. I need to keep my self-esteem up before my social anxiety gets the better of me.

Zane steps out in black jeans, a dark red t-shirt, black boots, and his trench coat. I like his trench coat, and he wears it open. It's a simple steampunk-styled trench coat. It has twelve silver buttons with a design on the buttons, and it goes to his knees. He seems to favor this trench coat since I've seen him wear it on three different occasions now. I notice it has a hood on it, but I haven't seen him wear it with the hood up. He is sexy, I think, as we leave the room to go to the dining hall.

On the way to the dining hall, through the maze of the damn mansion, Zane tells me I look beautiful, and my heart melts at his words. I feel like a high school girl whose crush just noticed her for the first time as the butterflies dance in my stomach. No one has ever had this effect on me, never.

My mouth drops when we enter the dining hall. Long tables with benches are lined up in perfect rows. The back of the room has a large table where Cade, Blair, and another man, who I assume is Zane's dad, are sitting. The stained glass windows are beautiful, depicting the grim reaper, crows, skulls, tombs, and shadows. There is a large chandelier overhead with skulls with candles inside them.

Zane and I walk to the large table. The older gentleman stands. He's wearing a fancy black velvet robe. His short white hair and short trimmed white beard add to his sophisticated look. "Ari, this is my father, Blaine." Zane introduces us.

"Nice to finally meet you, Ari." Blaine extends his hand, and I shake it.

"Nice to meet you too, Sir," Blair clears her throat. Shit. "Master, sorry." I quickly corrected myself.

"It's alright, Ari. You are new and still learning the rules of our coven. I'm sure our coven is very different from pack life." Blaine says with a kind smile. I relax a bit at his words.

Zane and I take our seats as food magically appears on our plates. Cade and Zane sit on either side of their father. I sit on the other side of Zane, and Blair sits on the other side of Cade. The food smells so good. A large piece of steak, garlic mashed potatoes, and steamed broccoli fill my plate. I'm starving. I've always had a rather large appetite, but so do most shifters, especially those with carnivore animal counterparts. Sasha, in particular, loves meat and could probably eat ten of these steaks. Everyone starts eating, so I dig in. Holy crap, the food here is so good. I don't think it should be allowed to be this good. My glass in front of me is filled with red wine. Well, a girl could get used to this.

"Have you heard from mom?" Cade asks Blaine. Wait, Zane's mom is alive? Also, is she Blaine's familiar? I realize I know nothing about Zane's family.

"Your mother is fine. She will be home in a few days to a week. You boys don't have to worry about your mother. She is perfectly capable of taking care of herself. Besides, she's helping another coven out for me. She is safe." Blaine replied.

The rest of the conversation is about magic and their duties. I listen in finding out information like that Blaine meets with Death once a month for reports. Strange. I didn't think the Five ever really mingled with us mortals, but this coven is special. Zane said he was a descendant of Death. I've never met anyone who was that close to one of the Five before.

The Five are gods and look after all the realms. The god of death or as some know him as, the grim reaper, the goddess of life, the god of fate, the god of war, and the goddess of peace. The Five rule over us and guide us. Many covens worship them. This coven is very different as they don't worship Death but work for him. They collect souls for him. It should freak me out that Zane is a descendant of death himself, but it doesn't. He is also a necromancer, which alone would freak most people out, along with his dark magic and manipulation of shadows. I should be terrified of him and his entire coven, but I'm not. Maybe it's because I'm his familiar, and that somehow eases that fear.

One thing is for sure: no one here would hurt me. I can't say that about my pack. I was bullied and made fun of for being a freak and omega. It's funny how I'm a lycan who could kick all their fucking asses. I regret holding back now.

My parents may have kept me in the dark, but they used to tell me stories about lycans and their dire wolf counterparts. Dire wolves don't just have better senses. They are faster, stronger, bigger, and our teeth don't just cut through flesh like it's nothing. We can crush bones. Funny how I'm already saying we and not them. I'm a lycan, and I have a dire wolf. I'm better than everyone in my old pack. I hate that I took their shit when I didn't have to. I don't know why they hated lycans or why we were in that pack. There is a history there, and I'm determined to learn about it.

After dinner, Zane and I head back to his room. Well, I guess it's our room now. Zane undresses and climbs into bed while I go to the bathroom to remove my makeup and wash my face. I might be a lycan, but I still get damn pimples if I don't care for my skin. I guess that's the human part of me.

We still slayed our look tonight. You certainly caught the master's attention. A voice echoes in my head. Well, that's new.

Sasha? I questioned.

Yes, it's me. I'm finally free to talk to you. I couldn't before while we were in the pack. It was too dangerous to show too much of our true selves. Werewolves can't talk to their wolf counterparts like lycans can.

"I see that. Do you know about our pack's history?"

Yes and no. Just know your parents were trying to take back the pack that rightfully belongs to the lycans. We need rest. We have warlock ass to kick tomorrow.

I laugh at her. Yes, we do have warlock ass to kick tomorrow in training. I won't lie; seeing Sasha in full action during training made me love her. I used to be embarrassed by her, but not anymore. It's time to embrace my lycan heritage and stop letting pathetic werewolves get me down.

I'm strong and confident. I will prove those assholes wrong that I'm not a freak. I'm a fucking lycan with a kickass dire wolf. Time to step out of the shadows and show everyone what the hell I'm capable of.

I head out of the bathroom and to the bedroom with my newfound confidence. Zane is in bed. He's sitting up with a red-covered book in his hands. Zane looks up at me. I can tell he's naked. I'm in my robe as I toss my clothes in the hamper.

"Should I sleep naked?" I asked him, heading to the other side of the bed.

"Of course. You know you, if you give me a choice, I will pick naked every time." He responds with a half grin.

"I know," I reply as I take off my robe. I may not be used to being naked around others, but oddly I'm comfortable with Zane. I'm going to chalk that up to the bond. I climb into bed. Fuck, this bed is the most comfortable thing ever.

"Sorry, you have to be in my bed again. I'm fairly certain Cade and Blair have something to do with your delayed bed."

I laugh. "They definitely do. They care about you. I'm sure they think they are helping. Honestly, your bed is damn comfortable, so I don't mind it. Besides, you aren't too bad to sleep next to."

He chuckles. "Well, at least you aren't just sharing my bed because it's comfortable." He jests.

"The bed is definitely my main reason." I joke back. He shakes his head at me. "You're a bonus, though. Thanks for today and all the clothes. I know I'm difficult, but I do appreciate everything. I feel welcomed here, which is more than I could say for my pack."

"You are very welcomed here and accepted in my coven. Most importantly, I accept you. You don't have to hide or hold back here. You're welcome for the clothes and other stuff. I told you I would take care of you. I meant that, Ari."

"I know," I say with a smile as I settle in the bed.

Zane puts his book down on the nightstand and also settles himself. There is still a large gap between us. I'm not ready to admit that sleeping with him is the best sleep I've ever had. Nor am I prepared to admit the feelings I have for Zane. They are slowly developing, and I don't know how to feel about it. Zane is being fantastic, and I'm being a stubborn ass, but I can't help it. I'm so used to resisting and pushing back against those around me. I'm not used to being so accepted and welcomed. It's hard to go from being an outcast to being accepted by people. This coven is so different from pack life. At first, I thought I'd hate it, but I'm starting not to mind it. That scares me a little, and I don't know why.

Pushing the frustrating thoughts from my mind, I focus on sleep. Tomorrow will be a full day of training, and I need rest. I'm not used to using so much energy as I've always conserved it by not being physical. I couldn't be. I couldn't show anything about myself in my pack. Now, I can do everything at total capacity, and my body isn't used to it. Not to mention I think my body is adjusting to the bond. It's as if I can feel Zane's magic, but I can't tap into it. He has to allow me access in order to use it. I can still feel it, though, and it's strange. Everything is changing as I find out the truth about myself and my family history. It's overwhelming, but for now, I need to sleep. Tomorrow I can overthink everything, but right now, sleep is what my body wants, and that's what it gets.

CHAPTER 5
Zane

Waking from my deep sleep, I find Ari snuggled against me again. I don't think she means to, but I'm not complaining. Her close to me is something I enjoy, even if she is being difficult and stubborn. It's been a week since she's been here. She is doing well with training, but she is still resistant to me. Sometimes she succumbs to the bond, and in others, she acts like she doesn't feel it all. It's beyond frustrating. I'm trying to have patience with her, but damn, is it hard sometimes.

Her bed that I ordered still hasn't come. My brother and Blair deny their involvement, but I know they are meddling. I want to yell at Cade that not all of us have familiars that bend to our will right away. I know they think they are helping, but I'm not sure they are. Ari hasn't seemed to mind sleeping in my bed. Every night she starts on the opposite side, but she's snuggled up to me by morning. I keep offering to light the fireplace, but Ari doesn't want it. Part of me thinks she likes snuggling with me. I like snuggling with her that much I do know.

I roll out of bed, careful not to wake Ari. She's burned out from training. Poor girl isn't used to training so vigorously due to her hiding for most of her life. My father wants to meet with me. So I get dressed in training clothes and write a note for Ari telling her I'll be back to get her for breakfast. I made sure there was an alarm set for her. She is not a morning person. Waking her up is like trying to get a damn teenager out of bed, but she seems to come around quickly once she's out of bed, especially if I put coffee in her face.

Heading to my dad's office, which isn't exactly close to my room, I decide to take the shortcut. Ari is constantly bitching about how much she and Sasha hate how confusing the mansion is. At first, it didn't bother me, and I chalked it up to her trying to adjust to her new environment. Now, it's on my nerves. This is her home now, and I can't change where I live. I live in this realm for good reasons. Besides, if she would stop bitching about it and just ask me how to figure out the patterns, I'd help her.

Frustrated, I knock on the black door. My dad tells me to enter. He's always up early, probably before anyone in the mansion is awake. His office is circular with two large stained glass windows. One has a crow on top of a skull, much like the tattoos that grace all of our backs. The other one depicts a cemetery. He has a large black desk filled with papers and books. The walls of the room are nothing but bookshelves filled with various books on history, spells, and anything else that's important to our work for Death.

"Good morning, son." He says with a giant smile on his face.

"Morning, dad. You're chipper this morning." I comment.

"I got word from your mother. She will be home by next week. She has successfully helped our fellow coven out with warding off the evil spirits that have been bothering them. She is staying around to make sure they don't need anything else. Today, I'll be going to collect the spirits they captured and send them to Death."

"It will be nice to have mom back around. This place isn't the same without her here."

"I agree. Now, I called you here to see how Ari is settling in. She seems thrown off when she is in the dining hall with everyone."

I sigh. "Ari has social anxiety that she is being stubborn about. She's being difficult with a lot of stuff. Ari is having a hard time adjusting to life here. It's not even like she misses her pack. I don't know what it is. I'm trying to be patient, but it's hard. Cade had such an easy time with Blair." I state, frustrated as I run my hand through my hair.

"You know your mom had a hard time adjusting too. She wanted to be a free gargoyle guarding her city. You would think a gargoyle would have an easy time fitting into our coven, but it was hard for her. She struggled. Perhaps she can talk to Ari when she gets home." He suggests.

"That's not a bad idea. Ari isn't used to being accepted. Her pack was brutal to her, and there is history with her pack and lycans that I can't figure out."

"I can shed some light on that. Ari's pack, the Blood Moon Pack, is complex. Long ago, in ancient times, dire wolves and the humans of the Hunter's Moon village were fighting over land. The problem was that it wasn't their land to claim or fight over. It was sacred ground as it belonged to the Five. The Five were angered that these two species were fighting over land that wasn't theirs. So they cursed the dire wolves and humans to be one creating the first-ever Lycans. Lycans are the only supernatural race native to the human realm. They didn't come from other realms like the rest of us did. The lycans created the Hunter's Moon Pack. The first pack to ever exist. Over time lycans mated with humans to create werewolves. Originally, dire wolves were nicknamed terrible or dreadful wolves. That name carried on with the lycans. Eventually, werewolves feared lycans for many reasons. They found ways to kill them off. Ari's pack was originally the Hunter's Moon pack, but when werewolves overthrew the lycans of the pack, they changed the name. The Alphas and Betas of that pack have carried that secret for decades. They allowed some lycans to remain as omegas and forced them to hide their true identity." Dad informs me.

"That's why her parents attacked. They were trying to reclaim the pack as theirs because it belonged to them. It makes sense. Liam left out all of those details, some friend he is." I say bitterly. I'm pissed. I asked Liam directly about the connection with lycans and the pack. I suspected he was lying, but now I know he was.

"Liam will protect his own before he helps you with a lycan. Ari is evil to him. He hates her because he was taught that. I'm sure Liam was happy to get rid of her and all the lycans in the pack. There is no doubt in my mind that he would have killed Ari if you hadn't gone for her. He only let her leave with you because it solved his problem of not having to kill an innocent."

"I'm sure you're right. How do I help Ari adjust to a world she doesn't understand? This mansion confuses her. Training helps, but I know she wants to run free in the woods, but the Howlers would go after her. She isn't ready for missions in the human realm, and I've thought about taking her there just to let her run wild in the forests for a bit, but I'm not sure it's enough." I sigh.

"Your mother was the same way. I won't sugarcoat the fact that Cade got lucky with Blair. My time getting your mother to adjust was much like you trying to get Ari to adjust. Eventually, she will adjust just like your mother did. Patience is hard, and you will need it when you have kids."

"I'm not even bringing kids up to her right now," I state firmly.

Our coven is unique in many ways. One unique thing about us is that the members can only have males. Also, our dark magic overrides any other DNA making our children only warlocks to avoid hybrids. Hybrids are very rare and usually very dangerous. Ari and I will only have boys, and they will be warlocks. However, we have to have sex before we can even have kids.

I like my dad's idea of having my mom talk to Ari when she gets home. My mom is a gargoyle, a type of shifter. Gargoyles are protectors and guardians. During the day, they turn to stone, and at night they come alive. They can either be in human or gargoyle form. Like Ari, my mom can transform whenever and she no longer has to turn to stone during the day. It tends to be a perk for the shifters that are our familiars.

Gargoyles, lycans, phoenixes, unicorns, and dragons are all ancient shifters. There are not many left of their races. Anyone who gets a familiar in my coven gets a shifter from one of the ancient factions, as they are the only ones who can handle our dark magic. Regular shifters like werewolves, basic shifters, panthers, bears, and others can't handle our magic. It would kill or corrupt them. The ancient shifters can handle the dark magic and use it to enhance their abilities.

My mom is quite the fighter. When she is in her gargoyle form, her skin is impenetrable, she's super strong, her claws are vicious, much like Ari's, and she can fly thanks to her badass wings. She also can ward off evil spirits and serves as a spiritual guardian. She's an impressive woman. I think my mom and Ari will get along well. Ari already gets along with Blair. The two have started to become good friends, which makes me happy because Ari isn't used to having a real friend.

I know Sage was her friend, but I question how much of a friend she was. Just like now, I'm starting to question Liam and his friendship. Sage claims to be Ari's friend, but something is off with her. I sensed bad intent coming from her. I thought I was just overreacting and being protective of Ari, given the situation I found her in. When I showed up and helped Liam take out the other lycans, I didn't realize they were trying to take back what was rightfully theirs. I also knew I had to be on Liam's side, or he would never let me take Ari. He was her Alpha, and only an Alpha can give a member of the pack permission to leave.

Liam locking Ari up was never part of the plan. I was shocked when Sage said her friend was locked up. Liam claimed it was a mistake, but I don't think it was. My dad is right; Liam would have killed Ari if it wasn't for me coming and taking her off his hands. He wouldn't have let her become a rouge. He knew why the lycans were attacking and chose to act like they were in the wrong. I question everything I know about Liam. I'm starting to wonder if he's my friend. I don't care if he isn't. I have plenty of other friends. Cade and I are close. I'm friends with other members of the coven. I also have friends outside the coven as well. Unfortunately, I can't say the same for Ari. She only has Blair and maybe Sage. I don't have the heart to tell her that her best friend might not be her best friend.

I'm aware I will have to. Ari wants to know about her family and more about lycans. She has so many questions about Sasha, her dire wolf. Ari is entitled to the answers she seeks. I'm not sure she is prepared for what those answers might bring her. The truth is seldom freeing like many hope it is. The truth is often harsh and earth-shattering. Sometimes the truth can destroy a person. Ari is strong, and I don't think the truth will break her, but it will cut her deeply, especially if Sage isn't her real friend. Not to mention Ari is angry at her parents for attacking, but would she still be angry if she knew that pack rightfully belonged to the lycans?

Why is it that meetings with my dad often end in headaches? I love my parents and brother, I do, but damn do they know how to drive me insane. Cade and Blair are interfering with Ari and me, it is a bit annoying, but it's also not causing any real issues. Ari is right; they care about me and want me to be happy. What Ari fails to realize yet is that they care about her too. She is a part of our family now. She is my soulmate, even if she can't fully accept that fact yet.

Heading back to my room, I find Ari coming out of the bathroom dressed for training. "Good morning, Master." She greets with a smile.

"Morning, Pet. Why are you so chipper this morning?" I asked skeptically. My dad, I can get. Mom's coming home, and that makes us all happy. However, Ari is in a good mood that I don't know about.

"I slept well last night. Actually, I've slept better in the last week than I have in my whole life. Maybe I was just grumpy because I didn't know what real sleep was." She says, shrugging her shoulders.

I chuckle at her words. If only sleep were why she was grumpy, then half my issues wouldn't be so bad. "I'll work on getting your bed today," I assure her. I've been saying that since she came home with me. I can't help Blair and Cade are meddling in my relationship. I've asked them to back off, but the pair plays dumb like they don't know what I'm talking about. I call bullshit.

"You don't have to worry about it. I like sleeping with you. As much as it pains me to admit, your presence is what helps me sleep so well. That's if you want to share your bed with me." She looks down at the floor and starts fidgeting with her hands. Does she really think I'd say no?

I go up to her and lift her chin, so she is looking at me. "I always planned on sharing my bed with you, Pet. I was only giving you your own bed because I wanted you to be comfortable here with me. It was never my preference for you to sleep anywhere other than my bed."

Ari wraps her arms around my neck and goes on her tippy toes to kiss me. Her lips land on mine. Fuck I love the way her soft lips feel against my own. She presses her body to me. I'm trying to hold back. I don't want to spook her as she is constantly torn between accepting that she is my soulmate and rejecting the idea entirely.

"I think I can be happy here with you, Zane." She says as she breaks our kiss. Her words wrap around my heart like a warm blanket.

"That's I'll I've ever wanted for you, Ari," I reply, kissing her forehead.

"I'm still adjusting, but I know this is where I'm meant to be. I've never felt more accepted before in my life. I've never felt more admired and loved than when I'm with you. It's all still so new to me. I'll come around fully, I promise. Just bear with me, okay?"

"You can have all the time you need. I'll be here when you are fully ready."

She kisses me on the lips, but this time it's a short kiss leaving me wanting so much more of her. Patience, I remind myself. She's making slow progress, and she is trying. I know she is. That's all I can ask for at this point. At least she is putting in an effort, and she is starting to feel like she belongs here. No one looks at her like she is a freak, and no one cares that she is different. Perhaps she is finally seeing that she doesn't have to hide anymore.

I know shadows, darkness, and death have always been a part of my life. I've never feared any of it. I've used the shadows and darkness to hide in plain sight when I'm on missions. I command the shadows to teleport me where I want. I can manipulate them to bend to my will. I'm a necromancer. I play with death by stopping people from dying, bringing them back to life if necessary, and even taking their life. My ability as a necromancer allows me to remove souls directly from their bodies. It's why I get the complex missions.

The Coven of the Crow and Shadows: Legacy

Most of the coven hunts down the spirits that got away from their bodies before we could get to them and send them to Death. I sometimes do that, but I'm usually one of the ones responsible for sending fresh souls to Death. I need Ari to be in top shape when we finally get out onto the field. I don't think she is aware of the dangers we will face. I'm trying to prepare her the best I can, but she doesn't seem to grasp the gravity of the situation entirely.

I'm relieved to know my father had a hard time with my mom. I was starting to think I was the only one with a difficult familiar. I hope my mom can help ease Ari a bit more into things. Perhaps my mom can explain more of what it's like on the field doing actual missions. I haven't even gotten to simulations of what we might face yet. Ari isn't ready for that, and she won't be for a bit. I'm not sure she will ever be fully prepared to go on a real mission. I might just have to toss her into it and hope for the best.

The truth is, I don't know how to best train Ari. I can do it just fine without much thought for my other trainees. Ari is different. Her background in basic fighting is not as much as I hoped it was. She also is hell-bent on transforming all the time, which is not something she will always be able to do. No matter how many times I try to drill that in her head, it doesn't seem to stick. I can't figure out if it's her or Sasha being the stubborn one with it.

She lets Sasha out as often as possible, but I need her to learn how to fight in human form. She won't always be able to transform, depending on the mission and its location. However, I know Sasha has been kept locked up for so long that she can't resist coming out for training. Sasha enjoys ripping my trainees a new one. She is impressive with her size and speed. I've noticed that Ari and Sasha seem to communicate telepathically, a trait that only lycans seem to have. Lycans are proving to be far more superior than werewolves, and I'm starting to see why werewolves feel so threatened by lycans.

I can tell that Ari observed all she could from watching the rest of her pack train. It's clear that Sasha is a natural-born fighter as well. The two of them are a deadly pair. Well, they will be with some proper training to hone their skills. Ari and I together are going to be a force to reckon with. I'm not sure the spirits will stand a chance with us two hunting them down. I'm itching to get back in the field. I like the action, and I have a feeling Ari and her wolf will as well.

Of course, we will start off small and easy for our first handful of missions. Reaping souls isn't for the weak, and it can certainly get complicated. Not all souls are willing to be reaped, as not everyone is ready to die. Some are vengeful in life and in death. You never know what you will get when it comes to reaping souls. Sometimes it seems clear and cut, but it's not. Other times it's exactly what you expect. It's a roll of the dice, and we have to be prepared for everything that might come our way.

Ari has natural instincts she can finally hone in on. She can use all her abilities at full force without holding herself back in fear of showing too much. I understand why her parents wanted her to keep her full capabilities on the down low, why all the lycans in the pack did. The lycans would have beat the werewolves' asses. Werewolves aren't exactly weak creatures, but neither are the warlocks of my coven and right now, Sasha is kicking their ass like it's nothing. The werewolves surely would have freaked the fuck out, whereas my trainees are trying to improve themselves. It goes to show how different the races think.

Ari seems like she is avoiding training in human form, and I'm not sure why. The only thing I can think of is that she feels more equipped to fight in her wolf form. I know this can sometimes be an issue for shifter familiars. They believe they are only at their best when they aren't in their human form as if their other form is more desired for fighting. That might be true, especially in a pack environment. I know just from talking with Liam that he has that type of thinking, so it wouldn't surprise me if that's something that was drilled into the entire pack. The idea that you are only the strongest in shifted form can be toxic to someone in my line of work. I need to break that mentality quickly.

In many ways, I'm relieved mom is on her way back. For one, this place is never the same when she's not around. Only in the last few years has my dad let mom break away from him and the realm to help other covens. Mom has a unique ability that comes in handy for other covens who deal with unhappy spirits. It was too much for my dad to go with her as he couldn't keep up his responsibilities with our coven. Cade would try to help, but he's not fully trained in running the coven. Not only that, but our coven is one of the main three covens. We are powerful, and many seek our help and our particular magic. Our coven is obligated to help other smaller covens out.

It became easier to let mom go off on her own. I've gone with her sometimes, and my dad will go with her if he can. This time no one was able to go with her. The reason we are so nervous about her being away from us is because familiars are more vulnerable when they aren't with their masters. Many take advantage of familiars when they aren't near their masters. They are easier to kill and hunt that way. I haven't exactly told Ari that part yet, not because I enjoy hiding shit from her, but because I don't want to overwhelm her with information. She's barely holding on as it is.

Hopefully, mom can help Ari adjust. She will be able to offer advice and tips. Blair is good to have around, but she's never really been in the field like my mom has. Dad and mom were a lot like me; they loved working in the field. They enjoyed the action and the thrill of it. Dad didn't start learning to take over the coven until Cade and I were young children, as it became too hard for them to keep up with life on the field and as parents. So my parents settled down. Dad started studying under grandpa, and mom took care of Cade and me. She taught us all about our coven, history, and other things that pertain to our way of life.

Cade is the opposite of the rest of us. He's more like grandpa. Cade loves books, knowledge, and being organized. He's perfect for running the coven, while I just help as his advisor. I like the action of being on the field. I'm known to read books, and knowledge is always valuable when it comes to magic, but my abilities are better on the field. The truth is, I'm stronger, more skilled, and more powerful than Cade. I'm built for the battlefield with the way my mind thinks. I'm quick, and I've gotten myself out of nasty situations where others would have died.

Ari has a fighter spirit, and I can tell Sasha was a warrior once upon a time. Sasha is excellent when she fights. She's fierce, fast, and clever, not to mention her strength and heightened senses. She's a force, and I have no doubt she will thrive on the field when I can let her out; that is, the field is a little tricky at times. Humans might know about us, but that means they like us.

On the other hand, Ari might have a fighter's spirit, but she is in a shell. I think hiding her true identity for so long was detrimental to her. It damaged her confidence. While Sasha is full of confidence and ready to kick ass, Ari is the opposite. I think it's why she's been letting Sasha out during every damn training session.

Every day I tell her today we are working on her fighting skills in her human form, and every fucking time, she finds a reason to transform. I started bringing backup clothes for her because she rips the ones she has on when she doesn't strip before she transforms. She's being difficult, and while I know it's only been a week, I had higher expectations because I didn't consider the fact that Ari needs to learn to embrace her fighter spirit that she's been forced to hide for her entire life.

While I am frustrated with her on many levels, I know it's not entirely her fault. None of it is her fault. She was forced to keep herself hidden. No doubt she was picked on for being different in her pack. Then her parents kept her in the dark about everything. I still haven't decided if that was smart of them or not. Then I swope in and make her life even more complicated by spouting shit about soulmates and familiars. I know many shifters see becoming a familiar to a witch or a warlock as a type of enslavement, and they wouldn't be wrong with it.

I can only hope my mom can help. If anything, I need her advice on handling Ari being so hot and cold. One minute she's on the verge of accepting me, and then the next, she's back to rejecting everything altogether. I'm not trying to take it as a personal rejection because I know it's not, but fuck me, is it hard not to sometimes. Like this morning before training, she is kissing me, and now she completely ignores me and transforms anyway during training. I don't know what to do with her. I don't know if I should punish her for disobeying me or not? Does that make me shitty if I punish her when she's struggling to adapt to a new life?

Patience, I remind myself repeatedly until it's a fucking mantra in my head. I need mom to get home sooner rather than later before I lose my shit on Ari without meaning to. I don't like her not listening to me. That could be a problem in the field on missions. It's bad enough she's giving my fucking blue balls and has me in seven layers of lust hell, but then she has to blatantly disobey me, causing anger to arise within me, which risks me flipping my shit on her. Patience and controlling my anger are two things that are not my strong suits, and yet Fate decided to teach them to me in the very tempting form of Ari. Thanks, Fate, you royal dick.

CHAPTER 6
Ari

"Get up, Ari. You will be late for school." I heard my mom call to me. I groan. Not another damn day at that hell hole, I thought to myself.

Glancing at the clock, it's seven am. Who the fuck gets up this early for school? Who even bothers getting out of bed? If I had it my way, I'd never leave my room. What's the point? I'm a freak. One more year, and I'll be eighteen. Maybe then I can be free. I don't know where I'd go. If I left the pack, I'd be a rouge, but perhaps that's better.

You'd think being a damn werewolf was terrific, that my life would be interesting, but it's not. It's mundane. I'm bullied at every chance. Even with Sage being a friend, it's still not good enough to save me from the bullies. Sage is also wishy-washy. When no one is around, I'm her best friend, the person that she turns to for everything. When other pack members are around, I'm not important. I'm no one. She might tolerate me hanging out with her and her so-called other friends, but I'm not welcomed. Having a shit friend is better than no friends, right?

I rolled myself out of my bed. I dressed in my torn-up jeans and old black t-shirt. Fuck I look like a homeless person. We can't afford much, so I get what I can get. I'm sure the jeans came from Sage, and the shirt was my mom's. I tossed on socks and my beat-up canvas shoes. I walked into the small kitchen to find my parents eating. Mom and Dad, I never understood them. They were always talking in hushed tones.

Plotting it sounded like. I never bothered with their crazy ass plans.

"Ari, it's a full moon tonight. Meet us in the forest by the waterfall-like normal. The other lyc... I mean, others like us will be there."

I groaned. "Ugh, mom, do I have to do it? I'm the only one my age in our freak group of wolves. Come on, let me be with the others just once." I begged.

I wanted to be normal to others even though I knew I was more powerful than them deep down. I never understood why my family and those like us were omegas when we could take down the pack's warriors without much effort. Omegas, we weren't allowed to train or do anything other than basically be slaves to the pack. I hated it.

"One, we are not freak wolves. One day you will know the truth. One day you will embrace who you are. Second, no, you have to be with us."

"Fine, whatever." I rolled my eyes, hating my life.

Embracing the numbness that was forming within me, I let it take over. It's better not to feel when I get to school. It's better to be numb and dissociate. Dissociation is like when your spirit leaves your body. Your body becomes an empty hollow shell. Your body acts accordingly, but your mind doesn't register what goes on around you. You have detached your mind from your body. It's like looking into yourself from an outsider's perspective. It's a strange feeling, but the only way I know how to deal with the bullies, rude remarks, and death glares.

My eyes flutter open quickly from the dream that was more like a memory. I hate when I dream with memories. It's always a dark reminder of my life in my pack. I'm reminded that I never fit in. A reminder my parents are gone. I haven't even let myself grieve their death. At first, I was angry at them. I thought they sent me to this fate, but I realized it wasn't true. This was always going to be my fate. Their deaths hurt because they never told me the truth. I never even knew I had a dire wolf or that I was a lycan and not a werewolf. I know they didn't think they could trust me when I showed such fierce loyalty to Sage and the pack. I thought if I were loyal to the pack, it would mean something, but it never did. My loyalty was constantly thrown back in my face. Resentment against my pack seeps into my bones. Anger at my parents for hiding shit and sadness that they are gone. I have so many questions that I know they could answer. Sasha can only answer so much. Then there is the resentment I feel towards Sage. I was an idiot, and she was a shit friend. She never actually cared. I see that now. I was so desperate for a friend that I accepted her shitty friendship because I thought it was better than nothing.

"You alright, Pet?" Zane asks, breaking my thoughts. He's standing at the edge of the bed in his training clothes.

"Yeah, fine. You know I'm not a morning person." I grumble, deflecting my feelings.

I can't bring myself to open up to Zane. I've tried. I just can't seem to break down the wall I built around myself. The wall that I never realized I put up around myself. I'm so used to defending myself against everyone that it's hard to trust. I'm too afraid to trust. I don't think I've ever really trusted anyone before. I didn't trust my parents because I knew they kept shit from me. I thought I trusted Sage, but I realize I never really did. I always secretly questioned her friendship, but I could never admit that she meant more to me than I did to her. I didn't trust my pack since they were bullies and assholes to me. Trust, I don't even know the meaning of the word, so how the hell do I trust someone who crashed into my life? How do I trust the man I call master? How do I trust anyone when all anyone has ever done is lie, put me down, and bully me?

Sure the coven is nice to me, but that's only because I'm Zane's familiar. Zane ranks high in the coven. He's basically a fucking prince or the alpha's son in my world. No one will disrespect me because they don't want to face Zane's wrath. I've heard about his anger issues through the whispers of the coven. Zane is slightly feared by his coven. I don't think he intends for anyone to be afraid of him, but some are. I'm not sure if I'm scared of him or not. I know he's a little scary when angry, and he is powerful. Scarily powerful. Not only that, but he controls shadows and fucking death. Zane is an alpha male, that's for sure, and he fights to control his desires around me.

It's been weeks since I foolishly told Zane I could be happy with him. I wasn't lying when I said it, but I hate that I told him. I can't let him touch me. It's like the bond does something to me. I can't explain it. It's almost how I imagined a mate bond for werewolves and lycans would be if we had fated mates. His touch, I crave it. I desire him, but I'm not ready to give him everything, and I don't know if I ever will. I'm stubborn. I can say that. I can resist pretty damn well, but Zane makes that hard when he is close to me. I know I agreed to stay sleeping in his bed. I don't regret it. I hate to say it; I sleep better with him next to me. I blame the bond and get my ass out of bed before Zane threatens to take me out himself.

I quickly dress, and we head down to the dining hall to eat breakfast before training. I don't exactly love the dining hall. It's not like being in the pack. I don't worry about people bullying me. I can't get around people staring at me. I know it's not evil or malicious stares. Still, I hate being looked at. Thanks to my years of being hated by my pack, I'm self-conscious. I can't seem to let go of my resentment or anger I feel towards them. I've always kept my anger to myself, but it's boiling inside me lately. Anger, resentment, sadness, depression, and anxiety are all battling for the dominant emotion that wins. I wonder where happiness is at? Can I ever be happy? Doubtful.

After breakfast, we head to the training field. Sasha is already itching to get out. Zane has been trying to get me to train in my human form, but I never listen to him. I'm not comfortable fighting in my human form. I was too bullied and picked on in my human form to feel confident. I've tried, but every time someone comes at me with a spell, a kick, a fist, I feel like I'm thrown back to the past where I was beaten up by a group of pack members or tossed into a locker, the floor, or the wall, I just can't get past it. My mind instantly goes to a bad place. Before, I wouldn't let Sasha out, but now I can. I can let her out whenever I want. Instead of fighting, I let Sasha out to play. Sasha is strong, and she can take whatever is thrown our way. I can't, I never could, and I doubt I ever will. I lost that badass feeling I had on the night of my first training. I lost my confidence. I always have lost it so easily. It's frustrating, and I don't know how to get it back.

Zane gets frustrated with me when I transform when he tells me not. He's threatened to punish me, but he hasn't. I'm not even sure how he would punish me. I can't see him starving me or locking me up. Zane is an alpha male, but I doubt he would ever use physical violence against me. I'm not sure what he would punish me with, but I don't even care if he does or doesn't punish me. I can't help my reactions, and I can't help the fucking trauma. Bullying is the trauma of being told you are worthless, constantly looked down upon, beat up, and hurt physically and mentally. Then you add my little run-in with the previous alpha who had dark intentions with me. Oh, and let's not forget my secretive parents, who neglected me for their grand plans, only for them to end up dead. We never did shit as a family. I think I was a mistake. The other lycans didn't have kids, and if they did, it was never planned. I never understood why. I never understood my entire life. I can't even understand my current situation. Conflicting emotions course through me, and I don't know which one will win.

"Come on, Pet, you aren't training with the others today," Zane says as he grabs my upper arm a little forcefully. He's been frustrated with me lately, but I've been difficult, so I guess it's my fault.

We move away from the others and down a slight dip closer to the woods. There stands a woman who looks badass. She has short dark gray hair, fair skin, and a muscular body. She's not like a bodybuilder, but she has muscles and is toned. Everything about her body looks hard. Is this his mother? I've heard about her. Blair has told me some, and she is loved among the coven. I hear the wives of the members look up to her. She was supposed to be back last week, I think. I honestly don't always listen to the conversations at dinner. I should, but I'm so lost in my thoughts that I think I'm going insane. I know she got held up with whatever she was doing. I wonder if Zane will let me go places without him as his father does with his mother. That's a serious amount of trust and loyalty that I'm not sure either of us has earned from the other.

"Ari, this is my mother, Zara. You will be training with her today. Since you can't seem to listen to me when it comes to training, maybe you can listen to her. You two will be left alone, and no one can see you training. Try to behave." Zane says with a warning in his voice.

I feel him push his aura on me as an alpha would do to a pack member. He's holding back his full strength. I wonder if I only feel his aura because I'm bonded to him, or do others feel it too? I still don't fully understand this familiar warlock bond shit. This shit should come with a fucking user manual because it's complicated as fuck, and I'm struggling to keep up. All I know is Zane owns my soul. He's going to own my everything; apparently, that is. I sigh, looking at Zara. She smiles softly at me. I didn't think anything about her could be soft.

"It's nice to meet you, Ari."

"It's nice to meet you too. I don't know what to call you. I'm still learning how to address everyone." I confess.

She gives a hearty laugh. "You can call me Zara, and I know how that feels to be lost in this coven. It took me years to figure out their damn bro code."

I laugh at bro code. Okay, so Zane's mom is super chill. I can work with that. "Yeah, it's weird for sure. Honestly, this whole place fucking weird. Did you ever get used to living here? Blair seems oblivious to everything that isn't Cade." I don't know why I'm being honest with Zara. I probably shouldn't, but her relaxed vibe makes me comfortable.

"You get used to it, but it takes a while. Blair is a sweet girl. I love her, and she is wonderful for Cade, but that girl worships him. Don't get me wrong, Blaine has my everything, but I made his ass work for it. Blair just caved to Cade like a damn puppy who wanted its tummy rubbed. Blair and Cade aren't meant for fieldwork. They are better behind the scenes. Zane, on the other hand, takes after his dad and me. We loved being in the action. We had a hard time adjusting to running the coven because we wanted nothing more than to be out in the field. Once I had Cade, it made it easier not to be in the field. I had something to keep me home that filled me with purpose. Then Zane came along, and I found myself wanting to be more domesticated. I have a feeling you are going to like the field and settle down when you need to. Zane paired you off with me for a reason. Now, to business. Do you know what I am?"

"A gargoyle." I won't lie; gargoyles are badass. I always wanted to meet one. We had to learn about supernatural history and the factions, even the rare ones. Funny, lycans were never mentioned. What is it with my pack and lycans? Do werewolves and lycans hate each other? I don't get it. There is clearly a part of history I am missing.

"That's right. Zane tells me you are having a hard time fighting in human form. You won't always be able to shift in the field. You have to be able to fight and defend yourself." She repeats the words Zane has said a hundred times to me.

"I know. I just struggle with it. I feel weak in my human form." Did I seriously just confess that? Either Zara is someone everyone talks to and tells their secrets to, or Zane put a truth potion in my coffee this morning. No doubt trying to spy on me. He's constantly trying to figure me out, just like I'm constantly trying to figure him out and his damn motives. Does he just want to fuck me? Fuck, it might be easier just to let him at this point. Nope, not there yet. Zara made Blaine work for it, so why can't I make Zane work for it?

Zara seems like a total badass and someone who can make her master work for what she wants. I'm not sure I'm that much of a badass. I'd like to think I could be, but I don't know. My confidence is gone again as I struggle to process my trauma and life. Everything is fucked up in so many ways. I'm questioning everything I know. I hate that I'm lost and confused. Maybe training with Zara isn't a bad idea. Perhaps I don't like training in my human form with the guys because I'm afraid of what they will do if they beat me in the fight. After all, the males of my pack sure enjoyed beating my ass, and if they thought I didn't see their lustful stares, they were wrong. I saw how the males looked at me. Sage's brother took advantage of me, and I see that now. Fuck did that whole damn pack take advantage of me, and why was I so blind to see it? Fuck me; I'm overthinking again.

Blocking my overwhelming thoughts. I focus on training. Zara shows me basic defense moves and simple attack moves. We are starting simple and easy, so I gain confidence in what I'm doing. Halfway through the day, Zane peers down over us with a satisfied grin on his face that I'm actually training in my human form. I roll my eyes and stick my tongue out at him. Then Zara chases her son away, claiming he is distracting me with my progress, making me stick my tongue at him once more. Zane gives me a warning look, and I know I'm getting myself in trouble, but maybe part of me wants to see precisely how Zane might punish me.

The rest of the day goes smoothly, and I feel better after training with Zara. Maybe I just need to train with someone who understands and can encourage me. I know Zane is frustrated with me, but that could partly be the current lust hell I have him in. It's not on purpose. I'm struggling to process so much right now as the weight of my past pulls me down into a dark pit. I want nothing more than to trust Zane. I want to explore our relationship, but it's hard when I feel like I'm damaged goods.

Familiars in Zane's coven are highly respected. They are a unique part of the coven that only their powerful members need for balance. Ultimately that's what a familiar for this coven is for. The most powerful members like Zane's family need familiars to balance the power. Yes, having a familiar does give the warlock more power, but it's a balance, a shared exchange of magic and abilities. It's a partnership in many ways. In one way, it's a soulmate partnership. At least that's the case for Zane's coven.

While the idea of having my soulmate already predestined for me takes the hassle of dating a whole bunch of assholes out of the equation, it still is hard to accept. The idea of giving my everything to Zane scares me. He's my soulmate, but does that mean I can trust him? He embraces me, and I love him for that, but it also makes me apprehensive as I've never had someone accept me for me. Once again, the scars of my past catch up to me, hurting my future.

Zara walks back with Zane and me. "I hope you behaved, Pet." Zane eyes me as we walk toward the mansion.

"She did well today." Zara chimes in for me.

I do like her having my back. She gets the frustration of dealing with a new master and their intrusive behaviors. Alpha males, man, do I love them, and Zane is an Alpha I'd trust, so why do I have difficulty letting him in? Why am I so afraid to connect with him, to fall in love with him? Surely I can't be this messed up?

"I think I should train with Zara for a little bit. No offense, Master, but I like her better than you when it comes to training." Zara high fives me.

"I agree with what Ari said." Zara agrees with me, and we both smile cheekily at Zane.

"I didn't put you two together to gang up on me," Zane says defensively.

"Well, you should know better because we are trouble together." Zara states as she playfully slaps Zane in the arm.

"Yeah, a lot of trouble." I agree with Zara with a smile on my face.

I love ganging up on Zane. Mr. Alpha male doesn't like it too much. Good, that means he has to work for it. I know in the end, I'm going to end up giving everything over to Zane, but while I'm working through shit, he's going to have to wait. Maybe I'm stupidly waiting for him to prove that he means what he says and wants me for me. Perhaps it's wrong of me to expect some proof, but I can't help it. My past makes me question too much right now. Everything has changed, and I need time.

We reach the manor entrance, and Zara departs, telling me she will see me tomorrow. I follow Zane back to our room. We always shower before joining everyone for dinner. The second we are back in our room, Zane pushes me against the wall with his arms on either side of my head.

"Don't think you aren't in trouble for your eye-rolling and sticking your tongue out at me." His voice is low, and desire is dancing in his eyes.

"Well, how are you going to punish me, Master?" I ask, batting my eyes.

"Oh, you try my patience, Pet. I might not be able to punish you sexually yet, but you just wait till I have you so close to your organism, just not to let you finish, and you won't be able to touch yourself either for relief." His even and sexually threatening tone does something to me.

His words make my core tingle. Oh fuck, that was hot, and I probably shouldn't be pissing him off too hard, or he'll make sure I never have a damn orgasm again. He smirks, knowing full well he's got me. Even he knows it's only a matter of time before I give in to him. It's tough not to give in to him when he's this close. I lick my lips since they suddenly feel dry. I test my luck and kiss him. My lips touch his, and his one hand goes around my throat. He nips my bottom lip.

"Trying to get me to forget isn't going to happen." He growls. In desperation, I grab his cock through his pants. He's already a little hard. "You don't know when to stop, do you, Pet?"

"Guess you'll just have to train me better." I retort, and his hand slightly tightens around my throat, but it's not hurting me. Although any tighter and he might start to hurt me. Oddly, I'm turned on by it, and instead of fear rolling over me, it's anticipation.

"Oh, I'll bend you to my will, Pet. Slowly but surely, you'll give me everything, Ari, and I will be waiting till you're ready. You're mine, Pet, mine and only fucking mine. Now, go be a good Pet and shower before dinner." Zane commands, pulling himself from my body. I let go of his dick. I actually miss the feel of it in my hands.

As I walk past Zane, he slaps me hard on my ass which causes me to yelp. I take my shower and then get dressed while Zane takes his. Then while he gets dressed, I do my makeup. I don't have to wear makeup for dinner, but I like wearing black eyeliner, mascara, and different shades of red lipsticks. Zane and I have fallen into a routine, and it's cute. It makes me feel like we are a real couple. I guess it's hard to wrap my mind around the concept of my Master being my soulmate. Don't get me wrong, I like Zane's Alpha Male personality, I like giving him control, I enjoy submitting to him, it calls to this primal need inside of me to be dominated, and it's a bit addictive. I'm even starting to find calling Zane Master a turn on.

Pushing sexual thoughts and thoughts of how badly I just want to give it up to Zane. I mean, it's not like it makes me a whore to give myself to my soulmate and Master. It's weird thinking that they are the same person. It's getting harder to fight the burning desire between my legs, more challenging to ignore my need for him to claim me, and hard not wanting to touch and snuggle him constantly. I'm turning into a steamy pile of sex goo.

After finishing off my ruby red lipstick, I'm ready to go to dinner. I huff, putting my makeup away as I rub my thighs together, hoping to get some relief from the friction, but nope nothing. Ugh, why did I think that would actually work. I should have fucking touched myself in the shower, but damn it, I don't think it would do much to sedate me at this point.

Zane looks at me lustfully in my dress. He's always drooling over me, and I fucking love it. I love how he makes me feel desired and for the right reasons. I link my arm with his, and we head to dinner. Just as we are about to enter the dining hall, Zane leans in and whispers in my ear.

"Don't think I don't know you are getting sexually frustrated. I can practically smell it on you." He states in a deep tone.

"You can't smell my desire." I challenge. "Silly warlock, you aren't a werewolf," I state, rolling my eyes at his ridiculousness.

"I can't? You forget I can siphon your abilities from you, so yes, I can." He retorts.

Fuck I forgot he could siphon my abilities. I know he does it from time to time to get me used to the exchange and feel of it. I didn't think he would practice using my lycan abilities against me. That clever bastard. "Just for being a smart ass, don't think about touching yourself till I say you can. A little pre-sexy punishment, if you will." I can practically hear the smirk in his voice.

I groan as we enter the dining hall. Remember what I said about loving his alpha male personality? I lied because right now, I'm not loving it. I can't fucking touch myself to relieve some of my sexual frustrations. Damn it. This warlock is going to have me go insane. I regret being curious about his punishments. Zane plays a little dirty with his punishments. I'll admit it's a little sexy. I'd dare to touch myself against his wishes, but somehow he'd fucking know if I did. Magic is only beneficial to those who wield it.

Dinner is full of fun conversations. Zara is clearly the life of the party and the one who keeps all these grumpy men happy. I know Zara keeps Blaine happy. Somehow, I feel like they are still very much sexually active. Zara is blatantly flirting with Blaine. Zane and Cade groan several times throughout dinner for their parents to get a room. I chuckle to myself when they do it. Even Blair seems amused by it. It's pretty funny watching Zara and Blaine torment their sons with their flirting and sexual comments.

By the time dinner is over, Zane and Cade have entirely given up on their parents. Zane makes some cranky comment about at least someone is getting laid tonight. Man, how long has he gone without it? I honestly assumed he fucked someone the night before he came to my pack. Okay, maybe that's an exaggeration, but I assume he had sex within the last year, at least a few months. Zane is good looking. He no doubt has an arsenal of women to fuck. Maybe Zane wants to fuck me, so he claims another part of me. Perhaps he wants to fuck me for greedy reasons.

In the end, it doesn't matter. I'm going to give into him. I'm not going to be able to hold out sexually forever; that's impossible. I know that. I'm well aware I'm going to cave at some point. Admittedly getting my ass sexually punished without much sexual experience probably wasn't the grandest of ideas because now I have a higher chance of caving faster. Werewolves and lycans do have high libidos, although I think most supernaturals do. Hell, I've heard of some humans who can fuck just as much as we can.

I might not be able to hold out forever, but I need to hold out long enough to get myself mentally comfortable. I'm struggling to process so many emotions, events that have changed my life, and processing trauma that I have been blissfully ignoring till now. I'm struggling to see the path ahead. I'm trying so hard to picture my life with Zane and not focus on what-ifs. I catch myself doing the should of, could of, would of dance that only adds to cycling frustration and confusion. I'm overthinking as I attempt to burn my mind up with maddening thoughts. I have to burn out at some point, I hope. I don't know how much longer I can keep going through motions without emotions. I'm failing to keep myself together as I fall apart from the weight of everything.

Don't even get me started on the unknowns about my family, pack, and other hidden shit. I'm missing this crucial piece to the puzzle, you know, the one that makes or breaks if I can stop something terrible in enough time. It's this feeling I can't shake, and yet I'm not ready to face those truths. I'm barely processing everything that has happened up until this point. I'm not prepared for family secrets. To be honest, I'm not sure I could handle it mentally.

After dinner, Zane and I head back to our room. We fall into our nightly routine. I take off my makeup in the bathroom, wash my face, brush my teeth, and strip off my clothes, sticking them into the happier. When I'm done, I get into bed while Zane does what he needs to do in the bathroom. Zane comes out naked and hops in bed. We usually sleep on opposite sides of the bed, even though I always end up snuggled against him by the morning. The asshole gloats about it every morning.

Tonight I'm feeling vulnerable and on the alone side. The emptiness of numbing my crazy emotions has me seeking a little bit of affection. I don't like feeling weak like this, but I want to be close to Zane right now. Zane has settled on his back with his hands behind his head. He's relaxed. I snuggle against him. My back is to him because I'm not sure I want to snuggle fully, but I want to feel his skin against mine.

Zane shifts behind me, and his arm comes around my stomach, pulling me close to him. "What's wrong, Pet?" He asks softly as I feel his lips touch my shoulder.

"Nothing. I wanted to be near you." I respond, snuggling closer to him, inhaling his scent to soothe me.

"You never want to just be near me. What's wrong? You can tell me, Ari. You're safe with me." His grip tightens around me.

"I'm feeling alone right now. I'm struggling to process everything. I'm having a hard time refinding my footing again. I don't want to talk in-depth about it. I'm not there yet, so if it's alright, could you just hold me while I fall asleep?"

"Of course, Pet. I won't force you to talk, but when you are ready, I'm here. I know you have a lot going on, so I'm trying to be patient with you. I'll hold you all night and every night if you want. No matter how badly you piss me off, I promise you will always have me, and I will always have your back." He kisses my head as I melt at his gesture and words.

"Thank you, Zane," I reply softly as I can already feel my body relaxing in his arms. It won't take long for me to fall asleep now.

I don't use Zane's real name much. I stick to master because I know how much he likes it. The coven also requires it, and this coven is huge on formalities. Zane doesn't always correct me when I use his real name in private. I never use his real name in public. If I call him his real name to piss him off, he corrects me, but he doesn't at times like right now. He knows I'm being genuine, so he lets me get away with it.

Moments like right now give me hope that I can trust Zane, that he will be good to me, that I'm more than extra power for him or something he needed to complete his training. Moments like now, I can feel how much he cares about me. I'm important to him. I matter to him, and he accepts me for me. Zane seems too good to be true, or maybe that's the fear of my past talking. I don't get to think much more about it as sleep consumes my body.

CHAPTER 7
Ari

A month has passed, and I'm getting more confident with my training. Zara has been training me for the most part. Zane has slowly started coming and working with us for a bit. Zara has been fantastic with helping me get comfortable fighting in my human form and is now helping me gain comfortability with changing from human to wolf form and back while in combat. I was apprehensive at first, not happy about getting naked to transform and then to transform back, but then I learned Zane could wrap me in shadows. So when it comes time for me to transform, Zane covers me in shadows. I can strip and transform without anyone seeing me naked. Even when I go back to human form, he wraps me in the shadows and uses them to put my clothes back on. It's pretty damn cool, but it takes practice.

We have it almost perfectly, but it was rough getting to that point. I ended up naked and exposed a few times, but it wasn't too bad because Zane covered me quickly, either with the shadow or his body, depending on how close he was to me. Zara was the only one who saw anything anyway, as we have been training in the hidden lower part of the training field. Everyone would have to look over the edge down at us to see me. I get why Zane placed me in this patch. He doesn't want anyone to see me naked I'm not even sure he likes his mom seeing me naked. He knows I'd be highly uncomfortable to be exposed in front of other men like that.

I haven't told him about my old alpha yet, or Sage's brother. I know he won't be happy that they did what they did, even though I was sadly more than willing with Sage's brother. I see now how he was leading me on so he could get some free blow jobs and make-out sessions. I was an easy target. I was always around because I was Sage's friend. I was desperate for a boyfriend as I had never had one before and still haven't. I'm not sure if Zane is my boyfriend or not. Hell, if I know what our relationship actually is.

It's a strange relationship. It's not bad; it's just a lot all at once. It's hard to accept that I'm wanted and desired for who I am and not for my body like I have been desired for in the past. I know if Sage hadn't befriended me, I would have ended up sexually assaulted by the warriors. The Alpha was one thing, and I got away, but it wouldn't be just one of them with the warriors. It would be a group of them. I would have no way of escaping. Even if I took some down in my fight, it wouldn't do much other than piss the remaining standing off.

Zane is different. He's the dream guy in some ways. He talks to me, desires me, treats me like I matter, and helps me. He's been patient with me. We still haven't done much other than make out and touch each other's bodies, but that's it. I know he wants to do more, and honestly, I want to do more. I hate to say it, but I'm slowly losing my will to hold out. I enjoy what Zane and I have done, even if it's not much. I want to trust him, but I need something to prove I can. I don't know, a sign or something. I'm terrified of being hurt by him, even though I doubt he would.

I've gotten to know Zane a little. He's a pretty relaxed guy when he's not being an alpha male in charge. I do like his alpha male side. I mean, I don't like it when he punishes me in a sexy way which I'm still not allowed to touch myself. I get a little bit of relief when Zane has hands on me and plays with my breasts, but he doesn't touch me how I want. I think the asshole is waiting for me to beg for it or just offer it up. Knowing his alpha side, that's what he wants. He isn't pushing me, but he will tease me until I give in.

He's been siphoning my abilities and using them against me. It's not fair. I'm still not used to him siphoning my abilities. It feels so weird, like pins and needles everywhere. I don't like it, but I've gotten used to it. I have to. Zane will do it often in the field, so might as well just get accustomed to the strange feeling. What I'm not sure I'll get used to is him infusing Sasha with his magic to make her even more vicious. We haven't gotten to that part of training yet, but it's coming.

Zane and I are walking out to the training field. We pretty much always train outside, even in the rain. We only train inside if it's a bad storm, and storms are bad here. The lightning is fierce, and the thunder is like it's on surround sound. It's intense. Zane insists the lightning can't hurt anything it touches, but I'm not taking my chances. I feel like if I got hit by one of those things, I'd be freaking dead.

"Go to our area. I'll be there shortly. Don't go anywhere."

"Seriously, where would I even go?" I ask, tossing a hand on my hip. Zane gives me a warning look. I sigh in defeat, not wanting to deal with his alpha male shit right now. "Is your mom joining us today?" I ask as she's missed a few sessions.

I think Zane wants us to train without her, as I'm now comfortable with training with Zane. I know eventually that I will have to go back to training with the others, and soon Zane and I will start running simulations in a simulation training room they have. I'm sort of looking forward to the simulations. It means we are getting closer to going into the field. I can tell Zane is itching for action again. To be honest, I'm just looking forward to leaving this realm for a bit. While I'm sure I'll adjust to this realm, I want to be out of it. I enjoy green woods. I can run in and play in rivers and lakes. Sasha wants more than just training. I can feel her craving to hunt.

"Not today, Pet." He answers, nodding for me to get moving to my destination.

Heading down, I decide to jump down from the ledge, it's high, but I can do it. I do a superhero landing. Proud of my epic little stunt that no one saw. I stand up, and I start to stretch out a bit. It helps if my body is limber when I transform. It's less painful. I'm zoned focused on stretching when I hear the eeriest howl. Whipping my head toward the forest, where I heard the howl. Sasha stirs, getting restless. The howl comes again as three sets of glowing red eyes peer from the dark forest.

"Follow it. You need to follow the howl, Ari." Sasha howls in my head.

Has she lost it? I'm not going into the woods without Zane. I listen for him. He's still handing out instructions to the others. He's preparing them for some test coming up. I don't know; it sounds like coven shit to me. Anxiety creeps over me as I hear the howl again. Sasha is howling at me to follow, but I refuse. Sasha, desperate, pushes forward and makes me walk right towards the fucking woods. What the hell is Sasha doing? She's never been able to control my human form like this. In wolf form, she controls our body, but never in human form. She's like a processed wolf following this howl and what appears to be three Howlers. This bitch is going to get us killed. I hope Zane decides to fucking resurrect us. Actually, I don't know much about his necromancer magic.

Zane tries explaining his magic to me, but I'm not used to the terms, and so I'm honestly confused half the time. Like right now, I'm wondering why my dire wolf is being insane. I didn't think wolf spirits could be controlled like this, but what the hell do I know? Nothing, because mommy and daddy taught me shit about who I really am. Thanks, mom and dad, I think sarcastically as we go deeper into the woods. The three Howlers stop and turn to face us. That's when I realized it's three dog heads on one body. Cerberus? No way he's fucking real, and he works for Zane's coven? Sasha gives me back complete control.

"Hello, Ari, or did Sasha not give you back control?" The one head in the middle talks.

I'm too dumbfounded as I stare at the largest fucking three-headed dog I've ever seen. I mean, it's the only one, but fuck, if I weren't afraid of Cerberus, I'd think he was badass looking. Cerberus has dark greasy gray fair with streaks of black running through it. He's massive, like the size of a dozen Dire wolves. His eyes aren't just red; they are literally fire. His mouth is skeletal-like, and I can see every fucking sharp and long tooth individually. Black goo drips from his jaws. He's menacing, and I don't want to fight him.

"It's Ari. What do you want, Cerberus?" I ask, putting one hand on my hip.

"To meet you. The first lycan to come into this realm ever. Here I thought they were keeping lycans from me."

"Why the hell would they keep lycans from you?"

He laughs an evil laugh like the ones in old horror movies. "Because, Little Lycan, I can mate with lycans."

"Whoa, there is no mating happening," I reply defiantly. Oh hell no, I didn't sign up for this shit. I know I'm part animal, but I will not be having sex in my wolf form. Ew, on so many levels. I know some do it, but no, thank you. Not my kink.

"What makes you think I'll give you a choice?" He growls. I take a few steps back as his growl shakes the ground. Zane, where the fuck are you, I think to myself?

"What do you think my master will have to say about you mating me?"

His three hands snap their jaws. "You're master doesn't have to know."

"Why don't you want him to know? Afraid you'll get in trouble?" Cerberus stays quiet and growls low. "My master is also your master, isn't he? I don't think he'd be too happy about it if you mate his familiar, especially since he hasn't even mated me yet."

"I know, Little Lycan, I can smell that you're a virgin. It's enticing." He advances toward me.

I start moving backward when I hear Zane calling my name at the edge of the woods. "Master, help!" I scream as I start running.

"That's right, run away, Little Lycan, run away. I'll enjoy taking you from him." Cerberus growls thunderously after me.

"Ari!" I hear Zane call.

"Help!" I scream as I run towards his voice.

Cerberus might be a mammoth of a beast, but that asshole moves quickly. Way too fucking quick. The ground quakes under his giant paws. He blows fire at me, and I dodge it. Then he blows fire from all three heads, and I almost become a charred lycan. I'm too busy looking back at Cerberus, fearful that the next set of fireballs will light my ass ablaze. I run right into a wall of muscle. I almost fall on my ass, but two strong arms wrap around me. I look up to find Zane's concerned and yet pissed-off face.

"Master! You found me!" I exclaim, wrapping my arms around his neck. He tightens his arms around me as I sense he realizes we aren't alone.

"Cerberus, why are you chasing my familiar?" Zane questions.

"I thought she was an intruder." He replies.

As I slide to one side of Zane so I can turn and face Cerberus a little, I glare at him. "He's lying. He somehow possessed Sasha to lead me out here. He wants to mate me." I say the last part as I cringe at the thought. I don't even want to know how he plans on mating me. Nope, not all. One hand is on Zane's chest while the other remains draped around his neck.

Zane glares at Cerberus. "Go back to your duties, Cerberus. I'll deal with you later, but don't think you aren't being punished for luring my familiar out into these woods. You will not mate her, ever. Get out of my sight, now!" Zane booms his command.

Cerberus lowers his three heads and bows before he turns to leave. I look at Zane, who looks down at me, his gray eyes swirling with anger. "I'm sorry, Master. I couldn't control Sasha. She was able to take control of my human form. It was weird. It's never happened before. I'm sorry."

"I'm not mad at you, Pet. Although I didn't know Cerberus could communicate with wolf spirits, I have no idea why he thought he could mate you. Come on, time to find my parents. This is serious."

Zane then kisses me gently on the lips. "Thank you for coming to save me. He almost BBQed me," I say, breaking our kiss.

"I'll always come for you, Pet." He kisses me on the forehead before leading me out of the woods.

We head to Blaine's office, which I have never been to before. Zara is there dressed in regular clothes helping Blaine look over what appear to be documents. They look startled to see us. I take in the grandness of the office. Meanwhile, I can see Zane glaring at his parents like they are somehow at fault. Maybe they are, but I doubt it would be on purpose. Zane's family is pretty cool, and I like them.

"What's wrong, son?" Blaine asks, concerned.

"Care to tell me why the fuck Cerberus just tried to mate Ari in the woods." Zane spits at him.

"I told you so," Zara says, shoving Blaine. "Your father didn't think it was real. Howlers can mate with lycans because of their Dire wolves. Howlers are created from tormented dire wolf spirits. It's why the coven doesn't normally allow lycan familiars. Ari was chosen for you by Fate himself. We couldn't argue and say no. I said we should tell you to be on the safe side, but your father insisted it wasn't true." Zara gives Blaine an annoyed look.

"Well, it's true. How do we fix it?" Zane questions.

"I don't know, but I will find out. For now, you and Ari should leave the coven. Go to the human realm and train in one of the safe houses. Get ready for missions the best you can because I have to send you back out there, son. No one is quite like you when it comes to reaping souls. We are falling behind."

"Fine, but we don't go on a mission till I say, and it's an easy one to start off with." Zane agrees.

I get a little excited about leaving this realm. I'm not thrilled about the mission so soon, but getting out of here would be nice. Zane and I head back to his room to pack. We leave tomorrow after breakfast. I'm a little giddy about leaving. I asked Zane where we were going, but he said it was a surprise. We are packing our clothes into these bottomless pit duffle bags. It's cool and practical as there's no limit. It looks like a regular duffle bag, but it's not. It's magical. I might not love magic just yet, but it's useful; I'll give it that.

Zane makes sure we have lunch brought to the room. We have a lot to pack as we don't know how long we will be gone and what climates we will be in. There's a long list of shit that we will need that isn't clothes. It's towels, toilet trees, and I need makeup and jewelry. It seems silly to pack those things, but I need them for specific missions as we might have to blend in wherever we are. Zane said we could have to go to a fancy party, a club, a wedding, birthday parties, countless events, and places that might require me to look a certain way.

We are going back to the human realm. I wonder if Zane will let me talk to Sage. Although, I'm honestly not sure I want to speak with Sage. Why should I hold on to her? I'm sure she has moved on with her other friends. I was one of many, and while she claimed I was her best friend, I'm not so sure I was. I know she was mine, but I didn't have many people fighting to be my friends again.

Zane saved me today. He proved I could trust him. I can trust that Zane will always come for me no matter what danger I'm in. He will find me, and he will protect me. I saw his fear that something had happened to me. I know he masked it well, but I can read his emotions through his pheromones. He was slightly scared, but not at Cerberus. He was scared that he might lose me.

We head to dinner, which is a little sad as we are leaving. We will be back. Blaine and Zara are confident there is a spell or potion that will fix the Cerberus issue. They don't know how long it will take to find whatever they need. Not only that, but Zane is required in the field. Zane is very good at what he does, or so I've been told by just about everyone. Zane's skills are admired, and I've seen a little of him in training, but I have a feeling that's nothing compared to what he does in the field.

Excitement zaps through my veins. I get to see Zane in action, and I want to see him use his skills fully. Truthfully, I admire Zane. He trains like a beast, and he is not someone who typically loses. No one has beaten him other than Blaine; not even Cade can beat him. I can't wait to see him in action. He's confident, skilled in his craft and wicked with war scythe.

Zane uses a war scythe to harvest the souls to bring back to Death. It's where the whole concept of the grim reaper's image comes from in the human world. It's because they took the idea from Zane's coven. Of course, at the time, they didn't know. They thought it was all made-up shit in stories. Zane's war scythe is a badass. The top part of the blade has jimppings as the blade curves toward where it meets the staff; it has black bone-like fragments sticking from it. On the bottom of the staff, there is a badass-looking skull.

As we have dinner and chat with Zane's family, who is slowly becoming more and more my family, I suddenly feel sad about leaving here. It's almost like this mysterious place is starting to feel like home. I've only been here two months, and even though this place is still creepy, it's weirdly still home. Everyone here accepts me. Blair and I have become friends. Zara is a chill mom-like figure to look up to. Blaine is a little reserved, but he cares about his family. Cade is more like an old brother who looks out for me. The rest of the coven is nice to me. I've even started joking around with the other trainees and others I've gotten to know. This place is so much different from how I grew up. Part of me wishes I had grown up in this type of environment as Zane did. Oh well, at least if we have kids, they will grow up in this coven and their welcoming environment over a pack that would hate them for who their mother is. I'm not sure how kids work with Zane's coven as there are no hybrids. We haven't even gotten to the kids part of our relationship, but I think I might want kids now that I don't have to worry about them growing up as I did.

After dinner, we head up to our room. It's strange to call it our room and not Zane's room, but he's drilled it into my head that it's our room. Zane looks a little defeated. I think Cerberus coming after me freaked him out more than it did me, but Zane won't allow his full emotions to come out. I've noticed he's very good at hiding what he feels, although sometimes he lets them slip through the cracks of his mask. There is one thing, though, that keeps playing in my mind.

One fear I had, and that wasn't dying. I didn't want to give myself to anyone but Zane. I think I'm falling for him, and I never realized it. Isn't it too soon? Maybe, but one thing is for sure I'm done holding out. I won't risk anyone else having me.

"You should go take a shower, and then I'll take mine. We have to get up at a decent time for breakfast and then get on the road. We will have to do something traveling to get to the safe house I picked out."

"Can't you just poof us there?" I ask.

"I can, but first, we need to scope out a town for some possible ghost issues. Sometimes the spirits that don't get harvested in time haunt the living. The one town near the safe house is reporting issues. I have to go check it out, and it will be good for you to get an idea of how to scout out spirits and issues. Now, go shower, Pet."

I take his hand in mine. "I will, but only if you come with me."

An amused look crosses his face. He pulls me into his arms. "Did Cerberus freak you out?"

"Yes, but you saved me, and that's all that matters. Thank you." I kiss him softly on the lips. That's when I realized I didn't want to shower. I want him to claim me.

"I'll always save you, you are mine, and I protect what is mine." He says, breaking our kiss.

Zane moves us to the bathroom, where we undress one another and step into the bellowing of steamy water. The beauty of magic is that Zane just has to snap his fingers, and the shower is on with steamy hot water. I guess magic has its perks. Even though we didn't train today, I feel a bit grimy from being chased by the fucking legendary Cerberus. I still can't believe he's real. If he weren't trying to burn me alive, chase me, or claim me for himself, I'd think he was cool. I'm just about done with my hair when I see Zane taking the soapy washcloth to his body. I take it from him and start washing him. He looks at me amused as the desire burns a bit brighter in his swirling gray eyes.

Washing his body, I get to appreciate his sculpted muscular body fully. He's not huge like a werewolf warrior, but he's got muscles and toned everywhere. His ass is better toned than mine. I bring the washcloth over his semi-hard cock. I've always thought Zane had the perfect cock. He was on the bigger side with just the right amount of thickness. Like he can pleasure you with it, but he's not going to spear through your cervix with it. I start to rub the washcloth up and down his cock, causing him to get harder. His nostrils flare a bit, and his hand grasps my wrist.

"Careful, Pet, don't start a game you can't win. You will surely get burned by the fire." Zane warns.

"Maybe I don't want to win, so set me on fire because I like the way it burns." I boldly smash my lips to his.

Zane pushes me against the shower wall, the cool marble against my back. He hasn't broken our kiss. Instead, his tongue pushes into my mouth, dominating my tongue before I even have a chance to battle him. I keep rubbing him till he's completely raging hard. He groans into my mouth with a bit of a growl of satisfaction. He's been waiting for this, patiently waiting for me to feel comfortable enough that I'd come to him. He's an alpha male who deems respect and control even from me. However, there is a softness to his demands when it comes to me. Zane is different from the alpha males I know, and that's he doesn't force himself on me or probably anyone he's ever been with. Werewolf alpha males love to take advantage of their status and power. They take what they want and don't care if it's what you want. My former Alpha is a great example. I guess it's a good thing he knew I was lycan, or else he might have indeed been successful. I never felt safe around the alphas in the werewolf community; not even Liam I felt safe around. However, I feel safe with Zane, which makes me want to be with him. I'm safe, I can trust him, and he cares about me. He doesn't care that I'm a lycan. He embraces making me find the courage to embrace this side of me.

Breaking our kiss Zane moves to kissing my neck as he nips at the skin, undoubtedly leaving slight marks along the way. I like a little pain, though. Pain and pleasure have always interested my sexual desires, but I never felt I had someone I could trust with those desires. Then Zane came along, sweeping me off my feet, made me his familiar while getting my damn soul. Now he's about to get my body and pleasure too because I'm losing the will to resist him. Soon he'll have my heart and mind too. Knowing I can trust him and knowing I'm safe with him it's breaking down all the walls I tried to build up.

My thoughts dissipate when his fingers start rubbing my clit. I let out a little moan of satisfaction. I need to release my sexual frustration that has been intensely building. It's been a month of not having a damn orgasm which is usually self-induced because, well, I don't trust men, it would seem. I've realized that as I've been processing things. Being taken advantage of made me feel vulnerable, and I didn't think I could heal from that fear. However, Zane is changing everything as he slowly heals the broken pieces of me, and in the process, he's going to end up with my everything.

Out of nowhere, shadows wrap around us. One second we are in the shower, and the next, we are dried and on the bed. Zane is on top of me. His gray eyes are fully ablaze with desire, and I'm not going to win the game I started. Good thing I wasn't planning on winning.

"Time for me to finally taste that sweet pussy of yours before I claim your body as mine. First, I'll claim your pleasure."

"It's not fair you are seducing me." I protest. Why am I protesting when I said I didn't want to win? Oh right, I'm a defiant she-wolf, that's why.

"I never said this would be fair. You're mine, Pet, and I will always have you when I desire. I told you not to start a game you can't win. Besides, I thought you didn't want to win." He challenges.

"You're right; I don't. I was always going to lose, wasn't I?"

"Yes, but it's not losing if you are enjoying it, now is it?" He asks, raising an eyebrow.

"I guess not," I admit defeat.

Zane smirks. "Now, my lovely Pet, let your Master give you a little pleasure while I claim it. Unless you would rather talk about how it's not fair."

"Well then, Master, claim my pleasure," I reply with more excitement than I intended. I won't pretend that I'm not excited about Zane giving me pleasure. I am. Even with my little experience with Sage's brother, he never touched me or gave me pleasure. He played with my boobs and nipples, but that's about it. On the other hand, Zane is about to provide me with that experience I've been craving.

Zane grins as he kisses me quickly before he moves his kisses to my nipples which causes me to arch my back. He sucks and licks each nipple causing little moans to leave my mouth. Zane moves down my stomach as he nudges my legs apart. He lowers his head and licks between my folds as his tongue lands right on my clit. Zane sucks and swirls his tongue around my clit like he's a fucking pro. I can't help moving my hips. It's so delicious that I close my eyes and let the moans of pleasure escape. Yeah, he's claiming my pleasure, all right. I can feel my orgasm build as his tongue works magic on my clit, making me stupid wet. I don't know how much more I can take, but I'm going to take all that he will give because this is what I have been missing in my life. No wonder people like sex because it's fucking amazing when you're with the right person. Fuck Sage's brother. I doubt that loser could make me feel this amazing. Letting out a growl of a moan when my orgasm comes crashing over me, making me dazed and high off sex endorphins.

"Feel like you still lost the game, or is the fire of my desire the burn you craved, Pet?" Zane asks, covering my body with his.

"You're exactly what I crave, Zane. I think it's time you finally claim my body, Master." I push my hips up, rubbing my wet pussy against his cock, which twitches at the contact.

"Don't tempt me, Pet. I might not be gentle if you don't behave." He warns as I feel the head of his cock at my entrance pushing in slowly.

"Whoever said I wanted you to be gentle, or did you forget I'm a lycan, and we tend not to like gentle." I tempt him.

I'm not sure what I like, but I know soft and gentle have a time and a place. Right now, it's not what I want and so not what I'm craving. I want to feel everything that Zane has to give me. I don't want him to hold back and be sweet. I want him to fuck me like he owns me. Then he can be sweet with cuddles after. Zane doesn't even respond with words. He shakes his head slowly with a look that he will give me exactly what I want. Without warning, Zane pushes himself all the way into me so that his hips grind against my pussy and his hips rub against my clit. I feel the air leave my lungs. Well, hello pain, but it's not bad pain. It is a pain-filled promise of pleasure.

"Fuck, Pet, your pussy feels like coming home." He says lowly with possession. He possesses me that much is for sure.

"That's because I am your home as you are mine. We are soulmates, and I'm all yours, Zane. I know I'm safe with you, and I trust you." I don't know where the romantic side is coming from. I've never really been romantic, not because I didn't want to be, but because I wasn't sure how. Wrapping my arms around his neck, I pull him down for a deep kiss as I taste myself on him. It's a turn-on to taste myself on him. It's just a little reminder of exactly what he can do to me.

Zane starts moving in and out of me as we deepen our kisses, desperate to feel one another. The need to be his grows with every thrust. Zane's claiming my body, and I love every second as I wonder why I held out for two months. Zane keeps up his quick pace as he slams into me, grinds his hips against my pussy which rubs my clit, and then pulls out to do it all over again. It's a delicious cocktail mixed with pain and pleasure that intoxicates me to the point of oblivion. This is so much more than I ever imagined. I love that Zane knows what he is doing. I'm not even jealous he fucked other women because those bitches were just practice to make him experienced for my enjoyment. I know Zane is very much enjoying my body right now. His tongue swirls with mine, and I'm lost in the movement of bodies as we become one, our souls merging, forming the soulmate bond that I thought was just a hopeful tail for helpless girls. Yet, here I am feeling my soul merge with his as he heals the cracks within my heart. Soon he'll have that, too, and right now, I'm not afraid of when that happens. Trust, loyalty, and desire merge, forming love that allows us to face anything that comes our way.

With a groan of desire, Zane finds his release buried deep within me. He takes a few moments to catch his breath before he gets off of me. He lays to my side as he pulls me into his arms. I lay my head on his chest as the satisfying soreness settles between my legs. The blankets come over us as Zane uses magic to put them over us. I can hear his heart thump in his chest as it settles to a normal rhythm.

Moving a bit to see his face, I need to ask him something. "Zane, am I crazy, or did I feel our souls merge during sex? I know you absorbed my soul, but I can feel my soul again even though I know it's not within me." I don't know why, but it was like I could feel my soul again.

Since Zane absorbed my soul, I can't deny there is an empty feeling, almost like I'm hollow without my soul. At first, I hadn't noticed it, but then it felt like nothing had happened. However, the hollow feeling crept back over me within a few days of the bonding ceremony, but I was able to push it aside to focus on training. Now, I feel whole again.

"You never really lost your soul, Ari. Yes, I absorbed it, but it didn't disappear from existence because I did that. The reason you feel your soul again is because you trust me. Every familiar and warlock has to learn to trust one another. It's important for many reasons. Not all covens have familiars, and the ones that do, don't necessarily use shifters. My coven is one of three covens who use shifters as our familiars. For my coven particularly, they have to be ancient shifters like lycans, gargoyles, and phoenixes. Most familiars don't trust their warlocks right away, so they can't feel their souls because of it. Warlocks, especially in my coven, already trust their familiars because we know that our familiars are our soulmates. Just because I claim your everything, Ari doesn't mean you don't have my everything. Yes, it's more symbolic for you, but you still have my everything, Ari, because you are my everything." His hand cups my cheek, and I melt, becoming a mushy pile of goo. His usually stormy gray eyes are calm, and a soft grin graces his face. Damn, he's handsome.

"I didn't trust you at first because I never realized how uncomfortable I was around men. You have to understand before you that my experiences with men, especially alpha males like yourself, haven't been good. Liam's dad tried to rape me when I was sixteen. He stopped because I started using my lycan strength on him. He stopped and said he could never fuck a creature like me. I didn't know what he meant by it then, but he knew I was lycan. Then Sage's one brother, James, totally took advantage of my loneliness and used me for sexual things like blowjobs. Not to mention all the other asshole guys in the pack always thinking they could make sexual comments to me like I didn't matter to them. Today, you showed me that I can trust you, that you will protect me, and you are slowly healing parts of my heart, Zane. Healing pain that I have repressed for so long. Coming here with you, it all came crashing down on me as years of pain and hurt overwhelmed me because I didn't have to fear those people anymore. I finally let those emotions go because I didn't have to hide them anymore. Thank you for not forcing me."

"Remind me to kill Sage's brother and Liam's dad. I didn't know you went through that. Your pack life was rough. I might be an alpha male, but I would never force someone to have sex. That's not a turn-on for me, although I know it is for many alpha males. I might punish you for disobeying me, be rough during sex, but I'll never actually hurt you, Ari. I'm glad that you trust me now. Maybe us leaving isn't a bad thing; it will give us bonding time together without much interference from others, mainly my family." I laugh at his last words.

"I like your family, but yes, I agree we need some time just for us. We still are getting to know one another and building our relationship to be strong and unstoppable. Your parents are kind of relationship goals."

Zane chuckles. "Yeah, they kind of are. Now, get some sleep, my Pet."

"Goodnight, Master." I kiss him softly on the lips before I lay my head back on his chest as I settle into a comfortable position.

"Goodnight, Pet." He says, kissing me on the head.

I'm relaxed, happy, and content. The soreness between my legs reminds me I finally found someone I can trust. Someone, I am safe with. I have no regrets about giving my pleasure and body to Zane. Tomorrow brings new challenges as we head for our first mission. I'm not sure I'm ready to be in the field. Cerberus kind of sped up the plan we had. Maybe it's not a bad thing, though. Zane and I will get time to ourselves, which we need as we strengthen our bond. I also get to go back to my realm and enjoy the things I have been missing. Tomorrow is filled with promises, but I'm not sure if those promises are good or bad yet. I guess I'll find out soon enough.

CHAPTER 8
Zane

Stretching my back as I rub my eyes awake, I find Ari sound asleep on my chest. We didn't move from where we fell asleep last night. I have to admit she surprised the hell out of me last night. I had noticed she was getting more handsy, bolder with her moves, and always asking for a little more each time we did something together. It was a lot of making out and touching each other's bodies like horny teenagers in their parent's basements. I didn't mind it, though, as I had never experienced it myself as a teenager. It wasn't because I didn't have girls to sleep with. That was never the issue. I didn't want to form attachments, so I did my best not to kiss or make out with other girls. I didn't cuddle after I fucked them. I used them for their bodies as they used me for mine. I always knew none of them was my soulmate. None of them were going to be my familiar. Ari has always been the only woman I've let myself grow attached to, even before I knew who she was.

Holding Ari a bit closer to me while I try to process last night before she wakes up. I need to be ahead of her on this to predict what she might do. We are about to head out onto the field. I needed her, and I focused. I have all intentions of fucking her while we are out on the field, but I don't want her to get sidetracked with it. We aren't fully prepared for this, but Cerberus's little stunt has forced us into the field earlier than I would like. It was going to come before we were ready anyway. We are falling behind on our duties, and the trainees that passed are just going out there. It will take time for us to catch up. Not to mention some weird shit going on with extra bitchy spirits. Ideally, we would have about five to seven months before going out on the field. Oh well, nothing ever truly goes to plan the way you want.

Ari stirs in my arms. Her eyes flutter open. She smiles at me and then kisses me gently on the lips. That's a good response. I was afraid she might regret last night. I know she's been resisting her pull to me, but last night she gave in. I'm not sure how she feels about that. So far, it seems she's happy with her choice, which brings me relief.

"Morning, Pet," I say after she breaks our kiss.

"Morning, Master. So are you going to tell me where we are going yet?"

I chuckle. "That's the first thing you want to ask me the morning after we have sex?" At least she's not making a big deal over it, but I didn't expect her to be so casual either.

"Are you afraid that I was regretting last night?" She asks, cocking her head to the side. I wasn't expecting her to read me so well like that. "I don't regret it, and I have a feeling you are going to make sure I never do." She kisses me again, but she has a little more urgency to her kiss this time.

I break our kiss. "I didn't go through all the hard work of winning you over to slack off. I'll make sure you never regret agreeing to come with me. I wanted you to have a choice, but that all went to shit. I feared Liam would kill you because he knew you were a lycan."

"He did? It makes sense, as his dad knew. It doesn't matter how I came to come with you. I'm glad I did, even if I had my reservations. However, you are slowly getting rid of those reservations one by one."

"Good. I want you to be happy, Pet."

"I am happy. Now stop stalling and tell me where we are going." She playfully smacks my chest with her demand.

"Careful, Pet. You don't want to end up punished already?" She bites her lower lip and shakes her head no. Fuck she's sexy even when she not trying to be. "Good girl. Now, if you must know, we are going somewhere cold, so dress on the warm side." I kiss her forehead.

We roll out of bed. We were going to eat breakfast here, but glancing at the clock, I realized we slept in. No big deal, we will just get something on the way in the human realm. We already said goodbye to everyone last night, so it's not a big deal that we missed breakfast. I get dressed in a black cashmere sweater, black jeans, and black boots as I toss on my black trench coat. I grab my war scythe and shrink it to about the size of my Glock, which is attached to my hips like my war scythe soon will be. My Glock is loaded with salt bullets. It comes in handy to slow spirits down.

Ari comes out in a black knit sweater, skinny gray jeans, and black combat boots. Her hair is down around her shoulders. She's cute while also being practical. She has on some black eyeliner which pulls out the blue and purple of her eyes. Ari has not only unique hair but also eyes. Her eyes are dark blue with hints of violet. Fuck, she's gorgeous, cute, and sexy, wrapped into one.

"Are you going to dress that adorably cute the entire time?" I ask, closing the gap between us.

A light pink blush graces her cheeks. A clever smirk graces her face. "Is that your way of asking me if I packed something sexy for me to wear for you?" She teases as she wraps her arms around my neck as my arms wrap around her hips.

"Doesn't matter if you did or didn't pack something, Pet, because I already packed something in your bag for you to wear," I say in a low voice, and I swear I see her rub her legs together, trying to hide her arousal. Fuck she's something. "Grab your duffel bag, Pet. It's time to get on the road. There is a diner in the town we will get breakfast at since we missed breakfast here."

I break our embrace, and we grab our stuff. Once we are set, Ari takes my hand as shadows swirl around us. I realize how excited I am to go into the field with my familiar finally. I'm sure Ari is thrilled to be going back to the human realm. It took my mom years to feel comfortable in the coven's realm finally, and I have a feeling Ari will be the same way. I'm half expecting Ari to ask to see Sage, but she hasn't brought her up once since she came with me. I had agreed to let her text and call Sage, but Ari hasn't even asked for a phone yet. I wonder if she is questioning her friendship with Sage like I am with Liam. I want to find a way to ask her, to bring it up in conversation. I want to know if she has the same vibe and feelings I do, but at the same time, I'm going to have to talk to her about her pack history.

It's not a topic I want to discuss, especially since I had to help Liam kill off the other lycans in her pack that attacked. I wish I had known they weren't totally in the wrong, but even if I did, I'm not sure that I could even help them. I'm not sure Liam would have listened. He might not have allowed Ari to leave. He might have forced her to be rouge. The outcomes are endless, and most don't end well for Ari. I took the way that would guarantee Ari would be given to me. I don't know how she will feel about it. Ari trusts me, and I don't want to lose that. I don't think she will be angry. Ari is a hothead sometimes but can also be rational. It might just take her flipping out for a minute before she can rationalize. She reacts strongly with her emotions. Most shifters do, but lycans and werewolves are known for it.

We pop up in the mountain valley with the town that's having problems. The coven's safe house is up in one of the surrounding mountains. I find the coven's car parked in a small parking garage. We stick our bags in the car and drive to the diner. Parking in the parking lot, we get out. Ari takes a deep breath inhaling the fresh mountain air. There is snow on the mountains. I think Sasha will enjoy the snow and running around in it. It also makes for some reasonable training grounds. Different terrain is always good to practice on.

Entering the old-timey dinner that looks like it's still in the seventies, we are told to sit wherever we want by the red-headed waitress. Ari and I take a booth in the back. I like to be a little hidden. The headed waitress, who looks like she is in her mid-forties, heads over to us. The over amount of wrinkles on her face tells me she's a heavy smoker, and the scent of cigarette smoke surrounds her. I don't even need Ari's heightened senses to smell it.

"What can I get, you kids?" She asks in a raspy voice that once again confirms the number of cigarettes she smokes.

"Coffee, black, please," I answer.

"I'll have coffee too, but cream and sugar, please," Ari says sweetly.

The waitress nods her head and then puts the menus down in front of us. The waitress walks off as we glance at the menu. I already know what I want, and I'm sure Ari does too. I look up at her. She has her elbows on the table, her hands folded as her chin rests on her folded hands. Her eyes sparkle with admiration towards me, and it warms my heart in a way I didn't even know was possible.

Our coffees arrive as the waitress sets them down, pulling my attention from Ari. The waitress gives a stained tooth smile. "You two ready to order?"

"Yes, I'll have the three egg meal with poached eggs, ham, hash browns, and rye toast," I answer her as she scribbles my order down.

She looks at Ari. "I'll have the super breakfast with over-easy eggs, all three meats, french toast, hash browns, and sourdough toast with a side of OJ." My mouth slightly drops.

The Coven of the Crow and Shadows: Legacy

I know as a lycan, she can eat a lot as she has to keep her strength. She won't be able to shift if she doesn't have the energy and strength to do so. I look at the waitress, who has an amused grin.

"Well, damn, it's good to know some in your generation actually eats as a real woman should. I'm Shelly, by the way. Let me know if you guys need anything else. I'll get your orders right in." She smiles cheerfully like Ari just made her damn day. She saunters off as I just look at Ari with desire. She's being herself and opening up to me more. Maybe I should get the not so fun conversation out of the way. I want to enjoy our time in the cabin. The safe house is a log cabin. It's tiny but practical.

Ari is still leaning her chin in her folded hands. I swear I think she's trying to figure something out about me. I'm not sure what it is, but I feel like Ari is studying me for some reason. Maybe she is curious to see how I act in the field, or perhaps she is trying to figure out more about me. Ari opened up last night to me, showing me that she trusted me with the pain of her past. She said I was healing parts of her broken heart. Hopefully, what I'm about to tell her isn't going to undo our progress.

"Ari, I did some digging about your pack. Do you want to know what I found out?" She perks up. Her eyes shimmer with curiosity and some fear.

"I don't know. Do I want to know? I guess how bad is it?"

"It's bad but not earth-shattering. Your pack is the original lycan pack or was before the werewolves took it over. Hunter's Moon Pack became the Blood Moon pack when the werewolves overthrew the lycans. You come from the first-ever pack of lycans, Ari. I think Sasha is an original dire wolf to one of the first lycans ever created. All the leaders of the pack know the truth. For some reason, lycans were allowed to stay as part of the pack, but they had to be omegas. Your parents were trying to take back the pack that was theirs. I helped Liam take out the lycans that attacked because that was the only way he would let you come with me. He forced my hand. I didn't know why the lycans were attacking at the time, but it didn't matter. I had to help, or Liam wouldn't give you to me. I feared he was going to kill you. That's what I've found out and have been able to piece together." I inform her.

"You're afraid I'll be upset with you, aren't you?" She asks, surprising me that she could read me so well. I'm very good at masking my emotions, and I hardly let them show, yet Ari was sometimes able to read me like a freaking book. Our relationship is changing and heading in a positive direction.

"Well, are you upset with me for my part in your parent's death?"

"No, they got themselves killed when they tried to attack with rogues. They were desperate, and it didn't matter if you helped or not. Liam, I'm sure, has other friends he could have called for backup. Many werewolf packs look to the Blood Moon pack. Along with every other lycan, my parents knew what they were doing. They were never going to be successful."

"How do you know that?" I inquired because she said the last part with such confidence.

"I dreamed about it. I dreamed they'd attack, they would lose, and I would end up in jail. I didn't dream of you, though." She answers.

"Wait, Ari, have you had other dreams come true in the past?"

"Yes, but it's just a coincidence. The only big one I ever dreamed of was my parents' attack. I didn't think it would happen, or maybe I was in such denial that they would do that."

She's acting far too casual about this. Lycans don't have premonitions. No supernatural does unless they are blessed by one of the Five. Why would Ari be blessed by one of the Five?

"Ari, lycans don't have premonitions. Only those blessed by one of the Five have premonitions. How often do you get these dreams?"

She looks shocked and nervous. "I don't know, every few months. It's not consistent. I can't control it. I haven't had one since the attack."

"Okay, let me know if you have another one. It's important, Ari. I'm dead serious about this. If you are blessed by The Five, then there is much more to your story and family history than I thought. I'm going to have to contact my dad and see what he suggests our next move is. We will scout this town and then go to the safe house. We will train while we wait to hear back from my dad. Perhaps, Cerberus was into you for other reasons besides your dire wolf."

"Zane, you are scaring me a little." She starts tapping her hands on the table.

"I'm not trying to scare you," I take her hands into mine. "We will figure it out together. You don't have to do anything alone anymore, Ari. I'm with you, and I promise we will get you answers. Have faith in my ability to help you."

She nods her head. "I trust you, and I have faith in you that will help me find the answers I seek. As much as I don't want to talk to Sage, maybe it's time we have a little double date with our supposed friends." Ari states with fierceness. A minute ago, she was on the verge of freaking out, but now she is determined to figure things out. I almost feel like Sasha is pressing forward a little to help Ari get past her fear of the unknown.

Our food comes out moments later. There is so much food on our table that there isn't even room for our drinks. We eat quickly, though, and slowly pile the plates up, making more room. I tend to eat bigger meals as channeling magic takes energy. We stay quiet while we eat as we both take in the information.

On the one hand, I'm happy Ari isn't upset with me. I feared she might blame me for her parent's death or something along those lines, but she didn't. I did not expect Ari to tell me she had premonitions. I don't even know what to make of it. It's not bad that she has them or that she is blessed. I just don't understand why she would be. I wonder if Fate picked Ari for a reason. He gave me a special familiar, blessed by one of them. Fate doesn't have a goal or a plan at all, I think sarcastically to myself.

If there is one thing I know, when the Five bless someone with premonitions, there is usually some type of prophecy or reason the person is blessed. Ari might just have a destiny quest ahead of her, and I think I will get a front-row seat. Somehow, I have the feeling we are soulmates because we are meant to do something meaningful together. We are meant to do a destiny quest, and those are always a pain in the ass, but the reward is usually significant for doing it, so I guess it's worth it.

Ari seems thrown off that her dreams were important. I'm not sure why she didn't think they were. Then again, werewolves don't concern them with stuff like that. That's more warlock and witches who pay attention to that shit. Ari also doesn't seem to have control of her premonitions, and sometimes it's meant to be that way. Other times, it can be controlled. It depends on how the five blessed you. It seems Ari has more mystery surrounding her than I initially thought. I'm not sure if I'm ready for a side mission, but I think we just found one, whether we like it or not.

We finish eating our food, I pay for us, and then we leave the diner. We drive to the town's cemetery. Cemeteries and unmarked graveyards are common places for spirits to spawn from. They also tend to come here confused, searching for their tombstones to confirm their death. This town's cemetery is a mix of an old cemetery with headstones that have dates carved into them to more modern headstones with fancy designs. We walk around checking over the place to see if there are any signs of lingering spirits.

Ari sniffs the air like she is picking up on a scent. I grab her hand and siphon her heightened smell. Sulfur which means spirits have at least been here. If they are coming back or hiding, I'm not sure. The amount of sulfur I smell indicates there were many spirits here at one point. Almost as if there were serge of them coming from something. Strange indeed. We walk around, but that's all there is other than the smell.

"It's quiet, too quiet." Ari comments. I realize she is correct. I don't even hear the sound of birds or any animals. Nothing for miles surrounding the cemetery as if it's been abandoned by the wildlife. Crows love to frequent cemeteries as they are spies for my coven. They alert us to where the spirits are or where there might be trouble which means there had to be a crow here at some point. Something isn't right.

"Something is not right here, Ari. We should go and call my dad. It seems we have a few things to report to him. Let's go back to the town and talk to some locals." I stop siphoning her abilities as we walk back to the car.

We head back into the town. We head into all types of stores, from small shops to large and everything in between. We even buy some of the local stuff like syrup and honey. Ari had asked for it, and I didn't want to deny her, knowing that I wanted this to also be a little fun for her. So we got some local honey and freshly made syrup from the farm. I think we ended up with three or four different flavors. She even bought ingredients to make pancakes and waffles while we stay at the safe house. I think it's cute that she wants to cook for me, and

I'm not about to tell her no. Ari knows how to eat, so it makes sense for her to know how to cook, even if it's just the basics.

After eating dinner at the diner, we head to the log cabin. There is snow on the mountain, and I can see that Ari is excited. I'm sure Sasha is looking forward to playing in the snow. The log cabin is small; it has four rooms. The kitchen and living room are completely open. The living room has a large fireplace and a loveseat couch in front of it. The kitchen has full-size appliances and a small dining area with a square table with four chairs. The backroom is the bedroom with the attached bathroom. There is a queen-sized bed and a nightstand on either side, and a dresser. There's a small closet in the bedroom. The bathroom has a shower stall only, and it's only big enough for one person. There's a sink and toilet with a mirror cabinet over the sink. The cabin is small and practical. There is a closet in the living room stocked with some weapons.

Ari gets to putting the food we bought away. I knew there wouldn't be anything in the fridge, not that I couldn't magic some food for us, but we ended up food shopping while we were doing research. We didn't find much other than there have been a lot of deaths due to OD's. Strangely, I didn't think a large mountain town would have a drug problem, but I guess people get bored out here as there isn't much to do unless you are into winter activities. There are several coal mines and lumber mills surrounding the town that do go into the cities. That may be one of the ways the drugs are getting into the town.

With the increase in deaths, there have been more spirit sightings by humans and other supernaturals with the rise in deaths. Something is off in this town. Nothing adds up. Drugs in a town like this doesn't make much sense, and then why are the spirits so restless? As Ari puts items away, I start a fire in the fireplace as it's getting colder with the sun going down.

The Coven of the Crow and Shadows: Legacy

It's a magical fire that will burn all night as there are no heat or AC units. I spell the fire to burn throughout the night safely. I write my findings in my magical journal. What I write in my journal will magically appear in my father and brother's journals. The three are linked by blood magic. They will get an alert that I've sent a report. Then they will respond with their thoughts. I guess I'll hear from them either tomorrow or the following day.

For now, I'll focus on Ari. She's still shaken. She plops on the couch in front of the fire, taking off her boots. I join her on the couch as I, too, take my boots off. We might as well relax a little. Protection wards surround the cabin, so we are completely safe here. Only people I trust know I'm here, and that's my family. For my family, blood is thicker than water. We will always stand together and will always have one another's back.

Ari leans her head on my shoulder as I wrap my arm around her. We sit there cuddling, enjoying the roaring fire as we try to process the day. It was a lot of information for one day. We ended up with more questions than answers. I'm not sure how long we sit there cuddling, but Ari shifts. She ends up straddling me.

"What are you up to, Pet?" I question, wrapping my arms around her hips so she can't move from her position.

"We are in a cute cozy cabin surrounded by snow in the mountains. There is a fire going, and there is something I'm a little more interested in than cuddling." She teases, sliding her hand between us, touching my ever growing hard on. The little vixen even has the nerve to grind against me.

"You sure you want to play games, Pet?" I ask, grabbing her ass roughly. She lets out a small yelp, followed by a slight growl.

Ari doesn't hesitate as she smashes her lips against mine. One hand moves to her back while the other threads through hair at the base of her neck. I roughly grab her hair and pull her head back as I trail kisses and little bites down her neck. The little vixen lets out a satisfied moan. That's it; she's asking for it. My hand on her back moves off her to wave around, commanding the shadows to come around us as the coldness they bring causes Ari to shiver in my arms. The shadows remove clothes. The second we are naked, the shadows disappear.

I move my mouth down over her nipples, biting and sucking, taking turns with each one till I feel the wetness dripping from her coating my cock. Damn, I love to hear her moan. I stop playing with her nipples as I help guide her onto my cock. Shit, she's so tight, and I can't help the low growl that escapes my lips. Ari's desire dances in swirls in her eyes as she gasps slightly at the new position. Fuck I love that I get to teach her this shit. Ari places her hands on my shoulders as my hands go to her hips to help give her the tempo I want her at. Once she gets one, my hands slip between us, my fingers finding her clit as my mouth claims hers. She moans in my mouth as I rub her.

"Don't come till I tell you to, Pet. I own your pleasure, remember."

"Yes, Master." She murmurs against my lips. Fuck me; she's something else.

Every time she gets close to coming, I stop rubbing her. She pouts each time, moaning her displeasure. Oh, I'm going to have so much fun teaching her edging. Ari is getting lost in her pleasure, and she is starting to struggle with keeping pace, so I take over for her. I stand us up, and she instinctively wraps her legs around my hips. I lower her to the ground on the rug between the loveseat and the fireplace. Ari is under me with her legs still wrapped around me. I start moving in and out of her as my fingers go back between her legs, her juices giving me all the lubrication I need to slam into her tight warm pussy. Fuck she feels good.

"Master, please." She begs for her orgasm.

I grin at her. "Come on, Pet, cum for your Master."

My words send her over the edge as her walls tighten around me and bring me incredibly close to my own release. I love the little moan growl she does as her orgasm shakes her body. I pound into her harder and faster until I find my release deep inside her. I lean my forehead on hers as we both catch our breath. Fuck I love this woman even if she's not ready for me to say to her yet. I kiss her forehead and pull out of her.

We clean up in the bathroom, and then both crash in the bed. Ari is snuggled in my arms like she was last night. I like that she sleeps naked with me. Her body is warm, perks of her being lycan. I almost don't need the blankets with Ari next to me. I stroke her hair gently.

"Get some rest, Pet. We get to do some training in the snow tomorrow," I informed her.

"Sasha is going to have a blast. Don't even expect me to train in human form. Sasha won't let that happen."

I chuckle at her words. "I kind of figured. Your wolf sure loves to show off for me." I joke.

"That she does. I'll let her have it. I have better ways to show off and please you." She teases.

"Seems like you love having me own your pleasure and body," I state huskily.

"I do." She admits as she closes her eyes.

I smile at her ability to be cute and sexy simultaneously. I hold her a little tighter, knowing it soothes her. Sure enough, she's asleep before I am. I'm glad she is comfortable with me. I relax my mind and push the thoughts of uncertainty out. I'm going to be anxiously awaiting my father and brother's replies. I need to know their views on everything that's going on. I'm starting to think it's a good thing Ari and I were forced to the field early even if we aren't fully ready. I have to believe that Ari and I are strong enough and in sync enough to do this. We don't have a choice. It's here whether we like it or not, and I have to believe we are ready to face whatever is to come our way.

CHAPTER 9
Sage

"It's been two months, Liam!" I scream at him as I slam my fists down on his desk.

Liam jumps, startled. We had my Luna ceremony shortly after Ari left with Zane. Zane has thrown a monkey wrench into my plan, which pissed me off. Ari was supposed to die that day. We had it all set up perfectly. We would say that she was part of the attack, and no one would question it. Then fucking Zane shows up demanding Ari as she is his familiar.

It figures that bitch would escape her death. I hate Lycans with passion, but I really hate Ari's bloodline. Her bloodline and my bloodline are mortal enemies. Our bloodlines have hated one another for centuries that goes back to the original Lycans and werewolves. I've known what Ari was for a while now. I befriended her, hoping maybe she would feed my secrets about the Lycan's plans so I could give the information to my dad. Ari's parents never told her shit. They never even told her she was a fucking lycan. Ari was such an easy target.

I watched from afar as others bullied her. Everyone knew her family were freaks like some of the other omegas. They picked on Ari, making her isolated till I came along and befriended her. The bullying stopped around me, but I know it still happened when I wasn't around. I didn't care that Ari was bullied. I made it seem I cared about her, but she was just a pawn in my game to break the werewolf curse. Ari is the key, and Liam just let her go because he didn't think it was that big of a deal.

The problem is, it's a huge deal. I need to kill Ari, her blood is the key to breaking the curse, or more importantly, her dire wolf is the key. Ari doesn't even realize the power she has with an original dire wolf from the first-ever cursed lycans. Ari doesn't even know who she is a descendant from. I know more about her and her history than she fucking does. Pathetic foolish lycan girl, I'm will get her back. I wonder if Zane is keeping her from me. I don't like her being bonded to him as his familiar. She is better protected with him. I had her in my claws, and she slipped through them practically unscathed. A nasty growl leaves my lips.

"Calm down, Sage. For fucks sake, it's not that big of a deal. She is still friends with you. She is going to call or text you soon to meet up." Liam tries to calm me down.

"We don't know that, Liam. Zane could be keeping her from me. I don't know how long their training is. Do you?" I ask as he shakes his head. "I didn't think so. Maybe you should contact Zane to see if Ari can meet. You can even offer it to be a double date so that he can feel like he's in control. I have a feeling he won't let her go anywhere alone with me, not yet at least."

"Fine, I'll text him right now if you want. Babe, tell me what you need me to do, and I'll do it." Liam soothes me by coming behind me and rubbing my shoulders.

"Text him and let me know what he says. We need to get close to Ari. I won't be able to take her right away. We have to get Zane to let down his guard around us so we can take Ari. The sooner she is dead, the sooner our curse is broken. Ari is easy, and I have her trust. I can get her to force Zane to let her and I have girl time. Maybe not on the first meet-up, but I need to know that I still have her friendship. If I

have that, everything else will fall into place as it's meant to."
I relax at Liam's massage.

Liam is a good lap dog. I know he's the alpha of the pack, but let's be honest, I run this pack as Luna. Liam will do whatever I say or want. I've got him wrapped around my finger with sex. He likes an alpha female, and he found me. Liam is weak compared to me as an alpha. He submits like the good boy he is, which is why I've been manipulating him for years to pick me as his mate and Luna. Ari originally had Liam's interest, but I won him over as she was too shy of guys. I knew my brother was using her for some fun. I told him I didn't give a fuck if he raped her or not. He just couldn't kill her; that was for me. Then Liam's dad tried to have a go at Ari, but she stopped him. Liam's father wouldn't let him pick Ari even if Liam wanted her. She is a lycan, and that was never going to happen. Eventually, Liam learned to hate lycans like the rest of us, and that's when he became repulsed by Ari. It worked out in my favor just like I wanted it to.

Now, just to get Ari back long enough to kill the stupid bitch. I'm going to be the liberator of the werewolves. I will free us from only being able to transform on a full moon. I have to do this. I have to prove to all the alpha males that I am better than them. I'm going to be worshiped and loved. Our pack will be forever respected. I will free us from our curse and become a goddess among werewolves making sure I kill every fucking lycan till they are just myths and nothing more.

Liam texts Zane to see if we can meet for a double date. I had Liam feed Zane some bullshit that I missed Ari and needed to see her. With any luck, Zane will tell Ari, and she will want to meet up. If anything, it might make her feel guilty for ignoring me for two months. I'm sure she is pissed on some level that Liam let her go with Zane. Ari has always tried to hide her defiant side among the pack, afraid it would get her ass beat even worse, and it would have. Now she isn't a part of the pack anymore, she is free, and I fear what that has done to her confidence. If she becomes too confident with Zane, she will be harder to kill. I'm going to have to work hard to get her alone and be able to execute a plan to kill her quickly.

I can do this. My father has been preparing me for this since I was a child. I'm the chosen one to set the werewolves free from our curse. By killing Ari, not only do I break the only able to change on a full moon bullshit, but I can also bring back fated mates for werewolves. Ari isn't even aware of how much her lycan bloodline has done to the werewolf bloodline. She doesn't even know the story. Her parents kept her in the dark, and they did me a favor by doing so. Thanks to her parents, I had all the information I needed to get my claws in Ari, and she was none the wiser. She knows nothing, and I can only hope it stays that way.

CHAPTER 10
Ari

Waking in Zane's arms is pretty nice. He's still asleep. I can tell from his even breathing and lower heart rate. I carefully untangle myself from his arms. I go to my bag and grab black leggings and a solid dark red tunic top. I don't even bother putting panties or a bra on. We will be training in the snow today which means Sasha will be out to play. The fewer clothes I have to shed during transformation, the better. Sasha's thick coat of fur will keep us warm in the snow.

Heading to the kitchen, I start making a pot of coffee and gather ingredients for pancakes. Once the mix is made, I fire up a skillet and start making them. I grab the butter and some of the syrup we bought out and set it on the table. I start frying up some sausage links and bacon. We will need a big breakfast with the energy we are both about to burn training. Zane does get worn out towards the end of the day, but he still would be able to kick ass in a fight. Zane's stamina is impressive. I can tell he drilled that into himself at a young age.

I hear Zane get up. He walks out in just black sweatpants. Fuck he's hot, and he's mine. The fire is still burning keeping the cabin warm and toasty. I remember Zane fucking me in front of the fire last night. It was romantic. Zane comes up and slips his hands around my waist as I flip some more pancakes. He pushes my hair to one side, leaving my right side exposed. He kisses my neck.

"Good morning, Pet."

"Morning, Master. Breakfast is almost done, and coffee is ready. It just needs to be poured."

"It smells delicious. I bet it will taste wonderful, but not quite as good as you taste." He kisses my shoulder, and I giggle at his silly comment.

"I don't think fucking me all day long is going to count as training," I comment as he goes to pour himself a cup of coffee.

"I'm your master. Training is whatever the hell I want it to be." He says, winking at me as I place the pancakes on the table. I shake my head at him.

"Sasha wants out, and you promised her." I remind him as I can already feel Sasha growing pissy. She really wants to play in the snow. Sometimes I think she is nothing more than a giant puppy.

"That's true. We train outside, and tonight we can have an inside training session."

"I like the way you think." I kiss him briefly as he passes me to sit at the table.

I plate the meats and stick them on the table as well as our plates for us to stack what we want on them. I grab a cup of coffee real quick as I got busy making breakfast and totally forget to make myself one. Zane compliments me on my cooking which makes me smile. I know I'm a decent cook. My mom made sure she taught me that. That's about all she taught me.

Zane was afraid I'd be upset about his part in my parent's death, but I'm not. Zane was trying to make sure I didn't end up dead along with my parents. I was his priority, and I honestly can't hold that against him. He put me first, and no one has ever done that before. So, I'm not mad. I knew my parents were up to no good. I had my dream that they would die a few nights before it happened. I didn't know Zane would show up at all. Even when I saw them losing, I wasn't sure why they were losing, but now I know it was because of Zane. I wonder why I didn't dream about him? Why was he omitted from the premonition?

Having my dreams sometimes come true always felt like there had to be more to it than just coincidence, but I wasn't sure. I didn't know much about my wolf at the time. My parents never even told me we were lycans. They just said my wolf was different from the others. My dreams coming true were part of my different wolf for all I knew. I wasn't educated about my lycan abilities, just that I wasn't allowed to use them at full capacity or else I'd get in trouble. I had to force myself to be weak to survive even though I wanted to fight. I was taught to keep my head down and listen to my alpha. I still don't understand why they drilled all that into my head when they planned revolting. Nothing they did made sense, and whatever their crazy plan was, it doesn't matter now because it died with them.

Knowing that my dreams are premonitions and knowing that it's not normal scares me a little. I don't know what it means. I hope it's nothing terrible, but I have no way of knowing unless I happen to have a dream about it. Zane patiently waits for his dad and brother to get back to him. I'm anxious for their reply as well as it will have to do with me. I'm not sure I'll like what they have to say. I have no way of knowing if my unique talent is bad or good. I seem to have ended up with more questions than answers.

Thankfully, Zane is on my side, and I don't have to do this on my own. I'm happy I'm with him. At first, I was so mad about having to go with Zane, but now I wouldn't hesitate for a second. Zane is all that I could have hoped for in a mate. I know I wouldn't have found someone like him in my pack. I was right to want to leave my pack years ago. I don't like that I let myself become complacent. I don't know what I was doing in my pack. I'm not sure why I decided I ever wanted to stay. I was always hell bent on leaving, but Sage would always remind me that life as a lone wolf was dangerous. Rogues were killed and not looked upon with fondness. I wasn't sure the world would have been much safer, so I stayed. The moment I convinced myself to stay was when I let go of everything I had hoped for.

I hadn't realized I'd lost my hope or sense of adventure, knowing I was meant for something bigger than what my limited world was offering me. I let fear get me, let Sage convince me not to leave, and I never even questioned her motives. I thought she was a good friend, but I was a fool. She wanted me to stay, but why let me go with Zane? Unless I was never meant to leave. Maybe Zane wasn't a part of Sage's plan either? That's if Sage is truly plotting something evil. I mean, I can't think of a reason she would want me dead. Sure, she might not have been the greatest friend, but Sage cares about me on some level, right?

"Pet, Liam texted me." Zane's words pull me from my thoughts.

"What? Why?" Fear creeps in that something is wrong.

"Sage misses you. They want us to go on a double date with them?"

"Did you tell Liam we were coming back to the human realm?" Wondering why the hell Sage wants to truly see me. I doubt she misses me, and even if she does, I still don't buy it. Not enough time has passed for her to miss me like I'm sure she is claiming to right now. I know her. She might think she tricked me, but Sage isn't the mastermind she believes she is.

"No, I haven't talked to Liam since shortly after you returned home with me. I'm a little pissed at him. He was withholding information from me. I'm not so sure I can trust him anymore." Zane confesses.

"I know how you feel. I feel the same way about Sage. Something is off here, but I don't know what it is. Fuck! We have to agree to this double date. It's the only way to know if we are being paranoid or not. We both are questioning their friendship, and they are a couple. That's a red fucking flag. Also, I'm a little creeped out you got the text not even forty-eight hours into us coming back to this realm." I raise an eyebrow at him as I plop a piece of bacon in my mouth.

"Fuck, you're right, Pet. Alright, I will tell him we are up for a double date, but I won't mention we are back in the realm. I want to see if they know or not because it's odd they reached out so soon after us arriving. Could it be a coincidence, sure, but doubtful?" Zane adds.

"Text Liam back and see when they are free, then we will pick a time and an activity like going to a club or something. We are going to end up in the city investigating." I comment.

"Did you dream that?" Zane asks.

"No, but sometimes I get strong feelings about events that might happen."

"Ari, love, that's another sign of premonitions. Sometimes they don't always come in the same way. I don't think you can control yours. I think you are shown what you are meant to see, which means your gift is probably meant to guide you with your quest." Zane informs me.

Damn, what would I do without him? I'd be screwed. I need Zane to help me figure out my past, family history, and if my supposed best friend is plotting against me for some unknown fucking reason. I don't know why Sage would conspire against me. I can't ignore the feeling that she knows more about something than me, which has given her an advantage over me. I guess I will have to face her sooner rather than later. I'm not going to let her on to the fact that I'm suspicious of her.

After breakfast, Zane helps me clean up, and then he goes to dress in some warm clothes. Sasha is pressing forward, ready to play in the snow. The greedy wolf wants more time to show off to Zane. Sasha enjoys prancing around for Zane. She follows his orders better than I do. Zane treats her like a fucking lap dog, and Sasha loves it like the giant puppy she secretly is. Zane comes out in black jeans, a black winter jacket, a black beanie, black gloves, and black boots.

"Are you ready for the snow?" I tease as I strip, thinking I'd rather change where it's warm.

"Watch that smart mouth of yours, Pet. I can punish you in sexy ways now. Don't forget that only I can give you what you desire." He winks at me.

I roll my eyes. Zane loves our back and forth just as much as I do. "Just because Sasha likes to listen to you doesn't mean I do." I retort.

I jump in the air when his hand lands hard on my ass. I turn to see him slipping the glove back on. "Ow, that hurt, and did you seriously just smack my ass?" I ask in disbelief.

"I told you to watch that smart mouth of yours. You didn't want to listen." He closes the gap between us and kisses me with force, but like the lovesick girl I am, I melt under him. "Now, behave, Pet." He states, breaking our kisses and putting space between us.

Going against my nature to give him a hard time, I figure it's better to let Sasha take over now so I don't get myself in any more trouble. While part of me wants to know what sexy punishment Zane is plotting, I also don't think I want to find out. Zane controls my pleasure now, he could take it away as he did before, and I don't want to lose it. I'll pick my battles, and this isn't one I want to go down for.

Feeling my bones snap and break as fur ripples over me, replacing my skin as I end up on all fours. Sasha is letting me be in control. She usually is all about having control in wolf form, but I think Cerberus freaked her out with how he was able to enchant her with his howls. Sasha is partially in control. She's in control of our body, but I'm in control of our mind. Shifter shit is sometimes hard to explain, and sometimes I don't even know how to explain it other than it's how things are for us.

Zane opens the cabin door, and Sasha bolts out the door at lightning speed as she jumps into the crazy amount of snow. She rolls around, enjoying the cold icy feeling sticking to her fur. Ridiculous fucking puppy, a scary and mean puppy, but nonetheless a fucking puppy. I shake my head internally at Sasha's embarrassing display of rolling around in the snow. Zane chuckles.

"I knew you'd like the snow, girl." He says through his chuckles, clearly amused at Sasha acting like a foolish puppy.

Sasha prances around in the snow, jumping in the air, rolling around in the snow, and overall running around like a mad wolf on steroids. If I didn't know better, I'd think my wolf was fucking high. Then I remember how I kept her locked up out of fear. I feel guilty about it, but I had to be safe. Sasha knows that.

We talk when we have to. I've tried talking to Sasha casually and asking her thoughts on things, but she seems to be withholding information from me. I wonder if she knows what Sage knows. Sage clearly knows something I don't know. I wonder if Sasha knows too. I wonder if she'll tell me or if she will make me figure it out on my own? Sasha is pure animal, and while she is a part of me, she is also just a spirit that allows me to have a wolf form. Shifters are complex. We don't make sense, and yet we do at the same time. Every shifter is a little different. There is even a difference between werewolves and lycans, and we are related.

After Zane lets Sasha bounce around like a mad wolf who just got a sugar high from eating too much candy, except it wasn't candy, it was pure mountain fresh air. Something Sasha loves more than anything. Crazy ass wolf of mine also seems to love snow. I'm fine to let her play in the cold, wet stuff. I'd rather be in the cabin. Now that Sasha has played, Zane is ready to do some training with her.

    He has Sasha practicing moves in sync with his actions as he fights with his war scythe. Eventually, Sasha takes over, and I can rest in my own thoughts. It's strange feeling my consciousness, but I know I'm not in control. Almost like I'm locked in my own mind. I'm at peace, though, because I trust Sasha and Zane.

    Strange how I trusted his alpha warlock ass so quickly, but he's proven himself. I can't deny that he did everything right by letting me come to him. He waited because I was important enough for him to hold out on his desires, knowing that I would come around when I was ready. Zane treats me like his prized possession. It makes me warm and fuzzy on the inside, knowing he accepts me as I am and loves me, but neither of us is ready for that confession. I know that when I make that confession, it's allowing him to claim my heart.

    Shifting thoughts from Zane and how stupidly perfect he is. I'm not complaining. I just can't help but fear there is a catch, something I'm missing. Zane is doing everything right, and soon I'll stop questioning him. Right now, I want to focus on Sage. My old pack was filled with secrets, and I know it ties to my past. Sage is the Beta's daughter; she, like Liam, is privileged with knowledge the rest of the pack isn't. She knows something I don't that much I'm certain. Her timing for missing me seems off. I thought she would have waited much longer before she reached out. I'm surprised that she did. I'm usually the one who has to initiate contact in our relationship. I don't know what her motive could be, but knowing Sage, it's something to do with duty, destiny, honor, or anything else along those lines. Sage always thought she was so damn noble, so it wouldn't surprise me if she has a secret crusade that I'm sure Liam falls into somewhere.

The Coven of the Crow and Shadows: Legacy

I'm concerned that Zane is questioning his friendship with Liam. Liam withheld information from Zane on purpose, but why? Also, how dumb is Liam to not think that Zane wouldn't get the information another way? I always said Liam was never the sharpest tool in the shed. This is why I doubt he is the mastermind of anything. Liam is the muscle. Liam is good for his strength, status, and wealth, and that's it. No doubt Sage is probably running the pack behind closed doors. She used to have notebooks of ideas on how she would change the pack. Sage has always had ambition, while I never really had any. Guess it's time I get some because I'm going to need it along with my newfound confidence as a badass lycan bitch to try and win against Sage's bullshit games.

Then let's not forget the fact that I have premonitions, a blessing from one of the Five. I always knew my dreams and gut feelings were too accurate to be an accident, but I was hopeful until Zane all but crushed that theory. Zane confirmed my fears that there was more than I was allowing myself to believe scares me. I'm not sure what I'm supposed to do or how I'm qualified for whatever reason I have this ability. I know it's something big. The Five don't give out blessings like Halloween candy. You must earn that shit which is why I'm not sure what the hell I did. I wish Sasha would talk to me more, but she keeps telling me shit like it's not time, or soon you will find out. I just roll my eyes at her responses now because clearly, I'm getting nowhere with her furry ass.

I'm pulled from my thoughts to Zane tossing snowballs at Sasha as she tries to dodge them. Zane is laughing his ass off as he plays snowball fight with Sasha, who is snapping snowballs with her jaw, swiping them with her giant paw, or dodging them. I chuckle at Zane treating Sasha like the puppy she is. Seriously giant viscous fur ball puppy. Ridiculous. I shake my head internally as Sasha continues to act like an oversized puppy. Zane enjoys himself as if he always wanted a dog as a kid but got told no. Zane's laughs reverberate off the mountains, and his smile melts my heart. It's not fair that he's handsome and sexy at the same time.

"You're just jealous he's playing with me and not you." Sasha taunts me.

"Oh hush, you oversized wolf, you clearly like showing off for him." I retort back. "Are you finally going to give me some answers?" I ask, irritated at her.

"Not yet, impatient child. Soon. Zane will help you with the path you need to take." Sasha scolds me like I'm the child while she has a snowball fight with our master.

"I fail to see how I'm the child here when you're the one acting like a fucking puppy."

"I'm older than you can imagine, Ari. I'm one of the original dire wolves that was cursed to the humans. I'm the only reincarnation of this wolf spirit because my original human counterpart was someone important. That should shut you up for a bit until Zane will take you to who you need to see." Sasha states, annoyed at me.

"See, was that so damn hard?" I ask snarkily.

"Yes, but this part will be easy." She taunts with a laugh.

I start to feel my bones snap and break, and my fur recedes, returning to skin. Oh, that fucking wolf is going to pay! A shrill screech leaves my lips as I find myself naked in the snow on a fucking mountain. Zane tosses a snowball at me while he laughs at my unfortunate circumstance.

"What did you do to piss Sasha off?" He asks with a laugh as he comes over to me.

"Why do you assume I'm the difficult one?" I ask with snark as I fold my arms over my chest, trying to keep warm. Fucking wolf. Sasha laughs at me in my head. Oh, you just wait, I think to myself.

The Coven of the Crow and Shadows: Legacy

"It's always you. Sasha is submissive and easy to work with. You are always the difficult one, Pet. You're lucky I love your difficult ass. Now, let's get you inside where it's warm." Zane responds as he picks me up and tosses me over his shoulders with my ass in the air for all to see.

I screech at the sudden movement. Zane laughs and shakes his head. Jerk, sexy and handsome jerk. I correct myself. Oh, cool off, lady parts. Now is not the time to be getting aroused, and you were just in snow. If Zane suspects I'm turned on, he will use my senses against me. I hate that he does that, but the jerk does it anyway. I can't believe he assumed I was at fault. Shadows swarm around us as the cold of the mountain is replaced by the unnatural chill of the shadows, which is then quickly replaced by the cabin's warmth. Zane sets me down as I pick up my clothes and chuck them on.

Pouting, I go to the fridge to pull out steaks for dinner and other ingredients as I'm hungry. Zane comes and wraps his arms around my waist and pulls me back into him. I drop the ingredients in my hand on the counter as I let a small growl escape. I'm annoyed with him for siding with Sasha. I know I'm difficult, but I'm not that bad. Most of the time, I submit to his ass, okay, half the time, but I'm getting better.

"Don't you dare growl at me, Pet. You won't like the punishment." Zane says in a low, warning voice. His words send shivers down my spine. "I can smell your arousal." He comments.

I slap his arms. "That's cheating! I don't even feel you siphoning me anymore." I pout a little. I can't believe I got used to that pins and needles feeling so easily.

Zane chuckles. "I'm just that good, Pet, or maybe I'm just teasing you." I can hear the smirk in his voice. Damn alpha male and his games as if I'm in the mood to deal with his alpha ass.

Turning in his arms, I know my mouth is a little open, which causes him to chuckle even more. I snap my mouth close. "You're mean and bad." I weakly defend as I poke his chest. Oh, fuck, this is embarrassing. Now is not the time for me to be all sappy and submit like Sasha. I'm better at standing my ground with Zane, so I like to think.

Amusement dances over Zane's features. "Oh, Pet, I know you can do better than that." He mocks as he suppresses a laugh which earns him a scowl.

"Sasha was at fault, not me. She is withholding information from me." I blurt in defense. Sasha growls in my head, clearly not happy I snitched on her to our master. I'm sticking my tongue out at Sasha in my head, which earns me another nasty growl.

Zane's features soften. "Pet, I was teasing you out there. I didn't think it would bother you so much, sorry, Pet. Wait, Sasha is withholding information?" Zane inquires. Ha, I win, wolf, I think smugly. I block Sasha temporarily before she can growl at me again. I know she will not be happy, but I'm in control, not her. One thing every shifter learns is never to let your animal side have control. It ends badly, and most shifters go savage if their animal side is in control for too long.

"She knows something about my history, but that's it. All I've gotten is that she was an original lycan dire wolf, and this is her first time reincarnating as a wolf spirit. I'm the first one to have Sasha since her first human." I inform him.

"I'm going to tell my father this. This is important. I'll go inform him while you cook dinner, then after, you and I will have a little bit of sexy fun." Zane pecks me on the lips before he leaves me to cook while thoughts of said sexy, fun time fill my head. I do like having sex with Zane. I'm not going to lie. I'm glad I saved myself for him. I'm happy he's the one who took my vcard. I guess if anything, Sage helped me stay pretty pure for Zane. Damn, her old-school values paid off. Well, I guess that's something positive that came out of our friendship.

I make steaks with loaded baked potatoes and roasted broccoli. Zane compliments me on my cooking which makes me happy. I like cooking for him. Zane takes good care of me, so it's nice to repay in a way that isn't sex. Although, I love the sex part so far. It's funny how well we are made for each other. Maybe soulmates are a thing as it seems that Zane and I are meant to be. Perhaps we will get a happy ending as his parents did. I do like the idea of family.

I never saw myself with a family, but I can see that future since meeting Zane, and I like it. I know I'm not ready for kids just yet. First, I have to figure out my family history, take out some possible enemies, and probably have some destiny shit to take off. If I'm lucky, it will all merge to the same path. I have Zane with me, and that brings me comfort. I'm going to need him with what's to come. He's already helping me so much more than I could have done on my own. My life changed when I was given to him, and at first, I thought it was a curse, the lesser of two evils, and it was at that time. Now, I would choose him every time. I'm falling in love with him, I know that, but I don't care. Zane might be the only good thing that comes into my life.

Zane and I have so much to figure out together, both within our relationship and with the other issues. We still need to focus on the excessive amount of spirits that seem to be causing more trouble than usual. Add my drama into the mix plus our personal shit, and we have a lot on our plates. However, I did always want an adventure. I always wanted to do something grand with my life. You know, the whole hero thing that only seems to exist in epic books and movies. Maybe I will finally have that adventure followed by a new, less-action adventure. The adventure of being a mom, having a family, and growing old with someone I love. A girl can dream of having it all, can't she?

CHAPTER 11
Ari

Zane and I spent a blissful almost two weeks in the log cabin. We even have a routine. We get up and make breakfast together. Then we train out in the snow, and by we, I mean Sasha, while I stay safely warm locked inside my head. Sasha and I are on better terms, but I'm still upset with her for withholding shit. I know she is wise and whatnot. I'm sure she has her reasons, but I'm still not thrilled.

After training, Zane and I head inside. I cook dinner, and then we spend the night having sex if we are up for it or cuddling. I do miss showering with Zane. The shower here is far too small for us both. Honestly, Zane barely fits in the stall himself. I'm average height at five-five, but Zane is at least a head or so taller than me.

Tomorrow our little bliss ends as we go to the city. Somehow supernatural drugs are being given to humans. Supernatural drugs are much stronger and deadly to humans. All over there are just random spikes of drug overdoses. It's to the point that the human authorities are getting involved, and the last thing we need is a war between supernaturals and humans again. It gets threatened every handful of decades. I guess we are due for it.

Zane and I are heading to a club in the city. It's a very popular supernatural club, but it's also a trendy human club. It's one of the few places where supernaturals and humans can mingle in peace. Zane knows the owner. Apparently, Ghost, yes, his name is fucking Ghost, and no, he isn't actually a ghost, stupid. Anyway, Ghost is a dark fae who owns the club. He's a sleazy dude who likes slightly crazy women. I'm slightly crazy, so I will be a little flirty, gag. I don't want to flirt with this loser, and Zane isn't thrilled either, but if Ghost thinks I'm interested in him, then we have a better chance of getting information or keeping him distracted so Zane can work some magic voodoo.

"It's not Voodoo," Zane shouts from the bedroom.

"Hey, no mind reading!" I scream at him from the kitchen.

Recently I learned that one of Zane's perks as my master is that he can read my mind. Apparently, I can read his mind as well, but I haven't figured out if he's serious or fucking with me. I'm too stubborn to text Blair or Zara to find out if it's true. One thing I've learned about my alphahole of a master is that he loves to fuck with me. He loves to give painful yet sexy punishments like grabbing my nipples and twisting them painfully till I comply. I secretly love it.

"It's not a secret, Pet." Zane chuckles from the bedroom.

"Zane, I swear on my parent's grave I will fucking...." I stop talking as shadows come around me. Is he fucking teleporting me to him?

"Yes, I am, Pet. Now, what were you threatening?" He asks as his hands come around my waist, pulling me to him. The shadows go away. Fucking A, how am I supposed to compete with that? "I'd say my next words carefully unless you want me to spank that cute ass of yours."

"You'll just do it anyway because you like it." I tease, rubbing myself against him.

"Oh, you think you can play games, Pet?"

"Well, you like to play games, so why can't I?"

"Because, Pet, you and I both know you won't win." He yanks a fist full of my hair suddenly as he pulls my head back, exposing my neck. Fuck he knows how to shut me up. "I think it's time we introduce you to something new, Pet." Zane's voice is filled with promise and authority. There is one thing I can't seem to figure out about my master. Why the hell is his aura so fucking intense?

Everyone gives off an aura in the supernatural world. Werewolf Alphas are known for abusing their auras. Their ability to push their will on their pack is a drug. They get off on it. It seems that only certain shifters can sense others' auras. Werewolves, lycans, and regular animal shifters, those are the ones that can turn into whatever animal they want. While it sounds cool, it's limiting in ways only shifters can understand. I have always been able to sense Zane's strong aura. His command, authority, and strength are so strong. No one in his coven, not even his father or brother gives off this type of aura. Zane is different somehow.

Thinking of what I know about Zane, he's the most powerful in his coven and is the only one who can use necromancy magic. What am I missing about him? It's like it's right there on the tip of my tongue, but my mind just can't fully pinpoint it. Zane is a warlock, that is for sure, but his magic is strong, powerful, and unlike anything I've seen. No one in the coven has the full abilities he has.

"Now, now, Pet, you don't need to be thinking about that right now. Although, I applaud your detective skills. You're right. I am different, and I will tell you why eventually, but I don't think you are ready for that truth."

"Stop reading my mind!" I exclaim, frustrated. "Seriously, I need to be able to think about shit without worrying you're in my head. It's bad enough I have to deal with Sasha in my head. Wait, can you hear Sasha when she talks to me?"

"Yes, and I can read her thoughts too. She can also talk to me telepathically like she can with you. Now enough serious talk. Don't think you are getting away with your little threat by distracting me. Oh, and I'll stop reading your mind when you figure out how to read mine." He smirks at me as he brings me over to the bed.

Shocked by his words that he can talk with Sasha like me is news to me. I'm not sure I like them talking to each other without me knowing. Suddenly I'm not feeling so turned on. I stand there staring at Zane, trying to figure out his game. I'm not sure why him and Sasha talking bother me so much. It makes sense that she is part of me, and we are technically both his familiar because we are one. Still, I don't like the idea that they could be talking and hiding things from me.

"Pet, Sasha, and I don't talk like that. We only talk when we have to, like during training or if you aren't okay and I need to know how to help you. Sasha knows you better than you think."

"Please stop reading my mind, Zane," I beg.

"I only read your mind to try and understand what's going on with you. You have a bad habit of keeping things to yourself, and I can't help you if I don't know what's going on. If you talked to me more, I wouldn't feel the need to read your mind. I'm not doing it to be malicious, Ari. I'm doing it so I can help you. I know you are still processing everything. It's only going to get more complicated as we figure the pieces of the puzzle out. We are in the field now. I need to know what is going on with you. You can't keep stuff from me. It's dangerous."

"I'm trying." It's all I can say as I cling to him. My head rests on his chest, and his arms hold me close to him.

"I know, Pet, which is why what I'm about to do will teach you not to threaten me but reward you because I know how much you are trying. Plus, I'm impressed that you figured out that I'm different from the rest of my coven. I have to be honest. Only my family knows why I'm different. Everyone else simply thinks I'm powerful. They haven't figured out that I'm different for a reason. You have a unique ability to get yourself in trouble and get yourself rewarded at the same time, Pet." Zane states, impressed that I can manage such a thing.

"I like keeping you on your toes." I joke as I kiss him.

"That you do, Pet." He says, breaking our kiss. Zane lays me down on the bed then he takes off my leggings and panties. What is he up to? He chuckles. He's reading my mind. He takes my hands in his one hand and pins them about my head. His hand goes between my legs as his fingers skillfully find my clit. He starts to rub slow, teasing circles around my clit. "You don't get to cum till I say, and you don't want to know what happens if you do."

Oh, crap, I'm in for it, but I also have a feeling the reward part is going to blow my mind. Damn alpha males and their ability to shut you up with just a look, pleasure, or tone. I'm starting to forget what I was even mad at him about. He's teasing me but is slowly moving faster. Zane's one hand holds my hands above my head. He's watching me, enjoying the bliss he is putting me in. I've started moving my hips. He knows exactly how to touch me, and the problem is I'm getting close. Zane knows I am, but I'm trying not to cum. Thankfully Zane stops rubbing my clit and inserts two of his fingers inside me.

After a few moments, his thumb goes back to rubbing my clit while his fingers move in and out of me. I'm completely at his mercy, and I love it. I trust Zane so much that I don't care what he does to me because I know he will never hurt me. He loves me, and I love him even if I can't admit it to him just yet. My hips move with his fingers and thumb. Shit, I'm getting close again. I bite my lower lip, trying not to let myself cum. Zane stops rubbing my clit for several moments, which allows me to come down a bit from reaching my climax. He never stops moving his fingers.

Zane trails little kisses along my jawline and neck, nipping some as he moves. As if on cue, he starts rubbing my clit again. I don't know what he's doing exactly, but I know that when I do cum it's going to be a fucking intense orgasm. I can feel it building in my core, holding on like a slow-burning ember that is trying to burst into a full fire. I can't help the moans that escape past my lips. I'm not sure how much longer I can have him do this to me without the ember bursting into flame.

"Master, please," I beg. I can see the approval in Zane's eyes. Of course, he wants me to beg for my orgasm. He's reminding me he owns my pleasure. "Please, I promise I'll start opening up to you more so you don't have to read my mind." I bit my lower lip, trying to hold back.

"Cum for your Master, Pet." He whispers huskily in my ear. My walls clench around his fingers as my orgasm sets my body on fire. I tremble a little from how intense it was. Fuck me, that was something. "Good girl, Pet. Get some rest before we head to the club. We are meeting Sage and Liam before we meet Ghost." He says quietly to me as he helps tuck me into bed.

We decided to kill two birds with one stone by meeting Sage and Liam and club Haze before we have to meet with Ghost. I'm not thrilled to see Sage or Liam, but I need to talk to them or talk to them. They know shit. I am a little tired as training has been intense and brutal. Thankfully, Sasha has to deal with most of it, but it still drains me. Zane makes sure I'm bundled in the blankets. He knows I like them snuggled around me. Zane gets up to leave.

"No, stay, please. I sleep better when you are with me." I say with a yawn as I tug at his arm.

"Of course, Pet. Maybe I should rest as well." He responds as he gets back in the bed with me. He spoons me as I lay on my side. He puts his arm and leg over me, giving me a weighted blanket effect, and I quickly fall asleep.

However, I wish I hadn't fallen asleep. My dreams start off fine, but then the pretty forest I was running through on a summer evening quickly morphed into the club. The edges of the dream become blurred, signaling I'm in a premonition. Zane and I are talking with Ghost, who is doing drugs, while we sit with him in the VIP lounge. There's different supernatural drugs mixed with human ones. Ghost is mixing supernatural drugs with human ones. Is that how he is selling them? Is he tricking the humans? Ghost is lighting something up to smoke in some weird crystal bong thing. He's using a torch to light the contraption to melt the metallic pink crystals so he can smoke them.

The club is crowded as the club rages around us when I start to hear whispers of people getting sick. Some humans on the dance floor begin to drop, foaming at the mouth. All around, it starts to happen with the humans. Zane gets concerned while Ghost is laughing his ass off as he coughs. He says something about humans being too weak to handle their drugs, but it's not that they are weak. They think they are doing human drugs, not supernatural ones. It's a mass murder in the club. People are screaming, freaking out as humans drop like bugs. The music stops as some supernaturals try to help the humans while others are too shocked to do anything. Some are laughing like Ghost, but most are not. This is serious and would definitely fuel war.

Zane looks furious. I'm stunned as Ghost laughs his ass off at the humans dying. Someone screams for an ambulance. Some people are dialing 911 in hopes that they might be able to help the humans. Every human in the club is sick and dying. Their symptoms are slightly different, which means they all took something different. Zane is yelling at Ghost to explain himself. It's a disaster. All of it is bad. This is what would spark a war, a war we don't need. It's worse than we could imagine. The human authorities arrive, and all hell breaks loose as they try to take out supernaturals that come near them. It's a mess. No, it's a disaster and a nightmare. Suddenly as the chaos unfolds, I find myself awake, sitting up in bed with Zane, who is startled awake.

My body is drenched in sweat. Zane is looking concerned at me as I gaze at him. I haven't had a premonition in months. This one was intense and more vivid than the last one where my parents died. I hold my chest, trying to catch my breath as I realize I'm panting like a dog. I mean, I am sort of a dog, I guess. I can't seem to organize my thoughts. It felt so real like it was happening, and I wasn't in a dream. I shiver, trying to ground myself, looking at things around the room. Zane's concerned look makes me feel guilty. I just told him I would start opening up to him more, and here I am acting like a crazy person.

I end up blurting everything out to Zane because I honestly have no idea what I'm supposed to do with this. I never bothered stopping premonitions in the past because I thought they were just silly dreams. Even with my parents, I just thought I was being paranoid because they had been gone a lot and acting stranger than usual. I don't know if I didn't want to see that they were different, or maybe I just didn't care because they never seemed to care when I was acting differently. I did so many things to try and get them to focus on me, but nothing was good enough. I didn't seem like I was important to them. It's when I started to feel like they didn't want me that I was an accident.

This time it's different. I know my dreams are more than that now. I think I was given this to stop it, and Zane seems to agree. The Five definitely don't want a war between humans and supernaturals. It's a bloodbath that will never have a real winner. Peace is the only way for us to live together.

Once Zane is confident I'm okay, he goes to inform his father and brother, but he throws me off guard when he says he's going to go talk to Death.

"Uh, I didn't realize you knew Death like that." I respond, shocked.

"I do. I will be back, Pet. You don't want to go to Death's realm. If you think my coven's realm is creepy, Death's realm is a thousand times creeper. I think it's creepy." Zane states, kissing me on the head. "Take a steamy hot shower to relax you while I'm gone. I won't be gone too long."

Nodding my head, I kiss him. I watch Zane disappear as shadows wrap around him. I'm not sure if he really finds Death's realm creepy or if he was just saying that, so I wouldn't want to go. I have to be honest. I don't want to see where Death lives. I don't think I will like it and I'm not for it. I'm happy to stay behind and take a hot shower. Zane can deal with Death. I have a feeling Zane is one of the few who can face Death head-on without fear. Just another reason he is different. I wonder why. I know he said he would tell me, but it's killing me to know.

Clearing my thoughts, I head to the bathroom and turn the shower on. Right now, I need to relax, so no thoughts about Zane. I know he will tell me. I trust that he will. I don't want to think about my dream, meeting with Sage and Liam, or about the mission with Ghost. I don't want to think about anything. Right now, I need to pump myself up and remind myself of the badass she-wolf I am. I'm going to get answers. I'm strong enough to handle whatever comes my way.

CHAPTER 12
Zane

Ari's vision is concerning. I wrote to my father and brother in my journal. They agreed I should talk to Death to make sure I was truly meant to stop Ari's vision from happening. I know I can. I'm skilled at necromancy, I can save all the humans who die, and I think they all will die. It's a mass murder and a huge issue. Time to pay a visit to Death himself. The one person I dread talking to.

Shadows come around me, and within seconds, I'm in his realm in his throne room. The hooded figure sits on his throne made from bones. Death's silver-gray eyes glow under the black hood. He's in a full black robe with jagged sleeves. The room is all black stone, lit by fire on the walls in torches. Shadows swirl around. I've seen his true form before, but I'd rather not stare into the face of Death as he's a scary fucker. Death holds his silver and black scythe in his right hand. A Howler pup sits near his throne as he loves his hellhounds. The coven calls them Howlers. Cerberus is his fucking favorite. I'm still not happy that fucker came after Ari. The asshole is pissed because Death made him go to my realm to protect me. I'm far too important for Death to leave me unguarded. Cerberus has been an asshole to me for it. Fuck I hate coming here, and I'm so glad I didn't grow up here. I've seen all of the underworld. As much as death doesn't phase me, nor how dark and evil this place is, I'm so fucking glad this was never my home. Fuck, Ari would shit herself if I took her here.

The Coven of the Crow and Shadows: Legacy

"Son, to what do I owe the pleasure?" Death's ice-cold voice cracks.

"Don't pretend to be my father. Blaine is the one who raised me, so he gets that title, not you. You just donated your sperm and convinced a witch to let you knock her up. Speaking of my bio mom, have you heard from her?" I'm so glad Death and Mags didn't raise me. Those two wouldn't know how to be parents if you hit them in the head with a fucking parenting book.

That's right. I'm the son of Death. It's why I'm so powerful, why I'm different. Death started my coven centuries ago. He couldn't keep up with all the souls himself. It was too much, so he decided he'd have many kids to do his work for him. The Five are like gods. Their magic is the original magic and the magic that connects all the realms. Death used his magic combined with dark magic of the witches he knocked up to create a special race of warlocks who could do Death's job. The warlocks controlled dark and black magic, the shadows. They could reap souls with their necromancy magic and save people who weren't meant to die just yet. He made sure every warlock born was a male and that they could also only have males. It worked for a time, but the magic would weaken as the warlocks married or got familiars. The ability to use necromancy died out. The coven members weren't able to control death like their elders. The coven could only harvest souls who passed and hadn't been harvested yet. Death realized that the magic and power of the coven had to always have a warlock linked to Death himself. A new Warlock that was born from Death like the original warlocks were. Someone with the ability to have necromancy. My sons and grandsons will be able to do necromancy. It will begin to fade after my great-grandson's, which means Death will need to have another child.

Death and Mags didn't want to raise me, so Death gave me to Blaine and Zara. They took me in as their second child. Cade treated me like a little brother. The three of them made me a part of their family. They love me, and I love them. They are wonderful people who I'm eternally grateful for. My family is fantastic, and I wouldn't trade them for anything. Ari is now a part of my family, and I love her with everything I have.

Blaine and Cade are powerful enough to have familiars, and they are the coven's leaders. The Shadow family is descended from one of Death's original children. I have no idea what number I am for him, and I don't care. He and Mags are just the people who gave me life. That's it. They are biological parents who had me for one purpose and one purpose only. To keep shit going and help Death out for as long as possible.

"I don't talk to Mags. She got what she wanted from our deal, and I got you. You'll see her soon enough. Now, why are you really here?"

"Ari had a premonition about an event that could cause war between humans and supernaturals. Should I stop it?" I ask, knowing that I want to stop it, but I'm unsure I should. I don't want to piss Fate off. No one wants to ever piss one of the Five off or all of them. Nothing good will happen to those people. The Five don't care if you are human, supernatural, or your parents are one of them. They will punish you, and you will not like it.

"I see your familiar finally figured out she is blessed by one of us. About time." Death states in a bored icy tone.

"Care to tell me why she is and if I should stop her premonition?" Now I'm getting annoyed. I hate being here, and he knows this. I want to get back to Ari. She was very shaken by her dream. I hated leaving her, but I had to talk to this asshole.

"Yes, you should stop it. This is something you need to stop, Zane. Fate gave Ari the premonition for a reason. We want you to stop it. As for Ari's gift, you need to talk to your mother about that. She can help Ari." Death responds.

"Seriously? This better not be some lame attempt at her trying to see me. I told her no too many times. She's had her chances, and she's blown every single fucking one. I will stop Ari's premonition. I already know how to do it." I'm in defense mode.

I don't trust my bio mother much. Death I trust because he's one of the Five. He's all business and doesn't bullshit, ever. He might make jabs at others, but he never fucks around. On the other hand, Mags has fucked around with me over the years. She's tried to stay in contact. Zara wasn't thrilled, but she understood as a mother why Mags wanted contact with me.

The problem was that Mags was selfish. She would often blow off our playdates or meet-ups, miss my birthday almost every year, and not contact me for years. One day I heard from her, and the next, she would be gone without a trace. Zara eventually told Mags she needed to stop fucking around with me. She couldn't come around when she felt guilty. Zara stood up to Mags for me. She saw Mags's games were affecting me. Zara being the momma bear she is stood up for her son. She protected me from a woman who only ever hurt me. It's just another reason Zara is my real mother in my eyes.

Mags reached out to me in my early twenties. I'm twenty-seven, and I still want nothing to do with Mags. Death, I can deal with him when I have to and only when it's absolutely needed. Mags, I'm content to ignore her existence altogether. Death at least never fucked with me. He made it perfectly clear he was nothing more than the biological father, and he expects me to do my job. Cut and dry, but at least I know where we stand.

It figures I'd have to see Mags for Ari to figure out why she is blessed. I'm curious about her past and what secrets it hides. I'll have to suck up going to see Mags, but it's for Ari. I'd do anything for Ari, even visit my bio mom. I'm going to have to tell her about who I really am. It's not that I'm afraid of how she will react. It's because I'm worried it will intimidate her more and not in a way I want. It's a lot to take in that I'm the son of Death. Ari has a hard enough time adjusting to my world as it is. I just hope this doesn't put her running in the other direction. I don't want to hurt the progress we've made. I'm going to have to face it soon. I'll tell her after we stop her premonition and take her to see mags.

"I know you can stop Ari's premonition, Zane. You are one of the most talented and skilled sons I've ever had. You've impressed me over the years. Your dedication to learning necromancy and mastering it is admiral. I made sure you were rewarded with a special familiar. One that would make you happy, be your dream woman, and someone who you can have a family with. It might surprise you, Zane, but I like that you have family values while maintaining the command and respect you deserve. I don't have to force you to have a family like I've had to do with some of my other sons. I think you might just be my favorite. I believe that you will be able to fix the shit storm coming. You and Ari are quite the pair. Nothing will stand in your way. I always knew you were meant for great things. Ari is special like you, Zane. It's why I had Fate pair you with her."

"You picked her out just for me?" I'm surprised, and yet I'm not.

Death loves control, so of course, he would have a say in who my familiar is. I know he's not lying when he says I'm his favorite which honestly feels good to hear. I can't deny the pride I feel for Death to acknowledge me in such away. My hard work paid off. I was determined to be the best there was. I spent most of my life practicing my magic, testing my strength, pushing my skill, studying all there was to learn about my coven, the Five, the types of magic I had and how to use them, reading all the grimoires of Death's other sons, and everything I needed to make myself the best.

"Yes. Don't be too surprised. You've always known you were special. Now go stop the premonition and pay your mother a visit Anything else you need?"

"One, how the hell do I stop Cerberus from trying to mate with Ari?" I need to be able to go home if I need to, and I can't be worried about that fucking three-headed asshole.

Death chuckles. "Cerberus hates protecting you. I can't believe he went after your familiar. Eh, he'll get over it. I take it when he approached her you hadn't fucked her yet?"

"No," I answer.

"Once you fuck her, he won't be able to. In the shifters and beasts' worlds, she is claimed once the female is fucked by her male. Animals are primal, and fucking is claiming to them. You take her virginity; therefore, she is yours. It's that simple. So if you haven't already, I'd fuck her. Is that all?" I nod my head. "Good, now go do the job I know you're very good at." That was when I knew the meeting with him was over.

That's fine. I'm weirded out by my heart to heart with Death, nor am I thrilled I have to visit Mags. I hate that Death refers to her as my mom. I catch myself from time to time referring to her as my mom. I try to refer to her as my bio mom or Mags. I'm also not thrilled that Ari has to meet her. I don't want Mags trying to convince Ari to convince me to see her more or some shit. How much guilt Mags is feeling depends on how much she fights with me to see her. She will try to make me feel guilty or make me appear like an ungrateful son. Fuck, I'm not looking forward to it. Mags loves to push my patience and infuriates me to no end.

I teleport back to the cabin as Ari comes out of the bathroom. I fill her in that Death wants us to stop her vision. I assure her that I know how to stop it. I do. I'm a fucking necromancer, I control death, and I've been told by Death to save the humans, which is precisely what I will do right after I have a little chat with Liam while Ari chats with Sage.

Ari decides to rest some more, and I agree that we should. We need to be rested. I will make sure we eat before we go to the club. We have to be on top of our shit. Our first mission is much bigger than I wanted it to be, but I guess it's now or never. I believe in Ari and I. Hell, if Death can believe in us, we can believe in ourselves. Death is correct. We are a deadly combination. Ari is reasonably confident in her skills these days, which is incredible to see. I don't like her doubting herself because she is fucking badass, and she is all fucking mine.

CHAPTER 13
Ari

Taking deep breaths to calm my nerves as we get ready to go to the city, hoping to pull myself together before we leave. Tonight is a big night. Zane threw me off guard because we are supposed to stop my premonition from happening. I didn't think our first real mission would be so important. It was one thing when it was just trying to get information from Ghost, but now it's saving the humans. The saving part is actually on Zane, not me, but still, I have to be prepared for anything. I don't know what might come our way, even though Zane is very confident in himself and us, which helps me feel better about the whole thing.

I'm curious to see Zane in action, real action. I've seen him in training, but Zane plans to use his necromancy magic tonight, and I'm curious to see it. Magic was something I always feared, and I tried my best to avoid it at all costs, but being a warlock familiar has changed that for me. I still fear magic, well, some of it. I see how useful magic can be and that it's only evil if the person who wields it is evil. Zane has changed a lot in my life and how I view things. I love that Zane is giving me the adventure that I wanted. This is why as nervous as I am, I'm also ready to embrace the edge of the world as I experience the adventures I thought only were for stories.

Glancing over myself in the mirror, I'm pretty impressed with my look. I have a low-cut crop top with a crisscross back and lace detailing on the hem. I have on gray torn-up skinny jeans with a few safety pins attempting to hold some of the rips. It's more for looks than anything. My black combat boots finish off the look, along with my black eyeliner, mascara, and blood-red lipstick. My hair is down as I let the slight natural waves I have work their magic with some product that should hold all night.

"Fuck, Pet, I didn't expect you to look so damn sexy. Ghost won't be able to keep his hands off you, and every other asshole will be eye fucking you." He growls. It's the desire to fuck me, and I almost wouldn't put it past Zane to fuck me in the club in front of everyone so they all know who I belong to.

"I like that thought, Pet, but I know you wouldn't, so I wouldn't do that to you. However, I might not be able to fuck you in front of everyone like your dirty mind has imagined, but I have other ways of making sure people know your mine."

Zane closes the distance between us. He comes up behind me and slips on a black velvet choker necklace with a silver crescent moon charm that has tiny diamonds in it. I touch the charm. "It's beautiful," I state, shocked at his thoughtful gift.

"Just like you, Pet. You're mine, don't forget that." He says low in my ear.

"I'll only ever be yours, I promise," I respond, reassuring him that even though I have to flirt with someone else tonight, I will hate it, but I have to for the sake of the mission. Why do I get the feeling Zane is going to fuck me the second we get home to remind me exactly who owns me. I won't complain, though. I love it when he fucks me like he owns me.

Turning to face Zane, he's dressed in black boots, black jeans, a dark gray t-shirt, and a black leather jacket. I'd ask if Zane is worried about being hot, but that warlock is always on the colder side. Not ice cold, but not naturally warm either.

Another weird thing about him, but I don't care. I like his cooler skin. Being a shifter means my natural body temperature is on the warmer side, so I wore a crop top knowing it would be a bit warm in the club with all those people.

I'll admit that going clubbing isn't really my thing. I can't dance, I wish I could, but I can't. Sage, on the other hand, can dance. I tried dancing when I was younger, but I couldn't get into it. I wasn't graceful. I'm much better at fighting, it seems. I also don't like large crowds, and too much loud noise gives me a headache after a while. I'm not really into drugs or drinking, although I can't say I haven't experimented in the past. My paranoia always got the better of me, so I stopped bothering with it. Even Sage agreed, although not because she was concerned for me, but because I was ruining her high.

Tonight I get to experience a club. Eh, what the hell might as well try it for the hell of it. I don't have a choice, but Zane will be with me, and I feel like I can face my fears head-on. Strange how much it feels like he is the other part of me, my other half that I never knew I was missing. Damn, I've fallen madly in love with him. Yet, I wouldn't have it any other way. I wouldn't change anything. Going with Zane was the best thing that happened to me, and I don't care how it happened. I'm just glad that it did.

The shadows come around us as I take Zane's hand. He's sweet and taking me to a nice dinner in the city before meeting Sage and Liam at Haze. We end up at a steakhouse run by supernaturals, so no one gives a fuck what you look like. The place is nice with all the wooden detailing. A large brick fireplace graces the main and rather large dining area. The main display is a deer antler chandelier that graces the center of the dining area. The whole place has a rustic-chic charm that I didn't think could be a theme, but it works.

Dinner is pleasant with Zane. We review our plans for the night and talk about how it's nice to be on a date. Unfortunately, Zane and I haven't had much time or many chances for dates, so when they do happen, it's nice. It's moments like these that make me feel like we are a real couple. I know we are a real couple, but it's nice to do couple things like go on dates. Sex is fantastic, but it's also nice to spend time together doing something nice.

The food is delicious, and I enjoy my huge and semi-cooked steak. We eat a good amount of food, knowing we will need it for energy tonight. Magic takes energy, and while Zane is very good at reserving his, it's good to top off the tank. The same goes for me as a shifter. My body is constantly working overtime with heightened senses, self-healing, housing a wolf spirit, and everything else it has to do to keep my ass alive.

After a wonderful dinner with my soulmate, I'd call Zane, my boyfriend, but we are way past that. Weirdly with our bond, we are already married in the supernatural world. Humans are the ones who mostly stick to the whole marriage thing, but supernaturals have their own versions of it, and not all are the same. It always seems supernaturals are always rushing things in some way. We don't do the whole dating or courting thing, engagements, and whatnot. It's straight-up tied to one another forever. I don't know how we manage to make the relationships work, but we do for the most part.

Club Haze is in the center of the city on the main strip. The club is massive and takes up most of one block. We don't need to wait in line to get in, as Ghost has generously put us on the VIP list. Zane and I enter the club. It's set up like an old warehouse. EDM music blares in the background as the dance floor is overfilled with people wearing neon paint on their faces, arms, legs, and any exposed area. The club is dark, but light flashes around in various areas, and strobe lights are over the dance floor. Fuck! This would give anyone a seizer, I think, as my heightened senses are torturing me right now. There is a loft-like section overhead that is the VIP area. That's where we'll end up tonight. Along the edges of the dance floor are sitting areas with couches and chairs with tables. The entire walls of the club are one giant wrap-around bar with stools. I've never seen a bar so long and large before. It wraps around the walls of the room with mirrors behind the bar area. It's pretty cool.

We find Sage and Liam sitting in one of the couches between the bar and dance floor. Sage is dressed in a tight black dress with red sparkly heels. Liam is in jeans, a black polo shirt, and simple black loafers. Liam stands and shakes hands with Zane. Sage stands up, and we hug, but it's so fucking awkward. Liam suggests that he and Zane go get us drinks while Sage and I catch up. It seems innocent, but nothing Sage or Liam does is innocent. I give Zane a reassuring smile as the guys head off to the long lines of the bar. Sage and I sit back down on the couch.

"You look well, Ari." She states with a fake smile as she crosses her legs.

"Thank you. You look good too, Sage. Luna really does look good on you." I compliment, knowing it will piss Sage off if I play nice.

"It does, doesn't it?" She says confidently. Still vain, check. "You and Zane seem like you are getting along." She observes.

"Yes, Zane is exactly the man I want. I think you might be right, Sage. Soulmates just might be a thing." At my words, Sage's face turns sour. Okay, what did I say to get that reaction out of her? Deciding to switch gears because I think the topic of soulmates pissed her off for some reason. Usually, Sage loves that topic, and I thought she'd want to hear that I thought she was right, but I triggered her hard for some reason. "Anyway, are you and Liam talking about pups yet?"

"No, not yet. We have pack business to handle first." Sage responds with her new mask slipped in place.

"Oh, is it bad or something? I might not be a Luna, but I'm still your friend, and I do know our pack." I offer. I'm partially truthful with my statement. Part of me still wants to believe that I've misjudged Sage, and she is actually my friend, but that hope dies with the words that come from her mouth.

"You're not a part of the pack anymore, Ari, so don't pretend you care about the pack." Sage sneers.

"Bitch wants to play games," Sasha growls.

"We can play games too." I remind her.

"Am I not part of the pack because I went with Zane or because I'm a lycan?" Sage's eyes go wide for a second before they settle into a glare.

"I see he told you what you are."

"You seem disappointed about that, Sage. How long have you known and kept it from me?"

"I just found out when I became Luna. You know how men are in our pack. The women can't be trusted because our minds are so fragile. They think we are weak. At least you know why you're a freak now." She states like she cares.

Years of resentment come bubbling to the surface, years of being treated lesser than making their way, as well as anger. It's overwhelming me like a power I don't know how to control. I'm so tired of being treated like a weak runt. I'm a fucking lycan, and maybe it's time to put this bitch in her place and call her out on all her bullshit. I'm convinced now more than ever she wants me for something.

"Sasha, can I burn my bridge with Sage and not regret it later when I find out the truth?" I ask, hoping Sasha will answer me for once.

"Burn that shit to the ground. You don't need her." Sasha growls back.

A smirk comes across my face. "I call bullshit, Sage. You know you are a shitty friend. I know I wasn't the perfect friend, but I fucking tried. I tried to be the best friend you said I was to you, but I was just a pawn for something. You always kept me a little too close. Whatever it is you want from me, I'll figure it out." I say, standing up, sensing that the guys are back. This visit was short-lived, but I don't care. I got what I needed. Now, I know Sage wants me for something. She was never my friend.

Sage goes to Liam's side looking fake hurt, but I could see her real emotion of anger she was hiding. Zane comes to my side. "So, Liam, are you going to tell me what Sage wants me for? I don't know why I'm asking. Of course, you won't. She owns your ass like she thought she used to own mine."

Sage laughs. "I still own you, bitch." Sage sneers.

"You're coming back with us, Ari," Liam states firmly.

"Oh, that's cute of you two, but the only one who owns me is Zane, and I'm pretty sure my master has something to say about you trying to claim what is rightfully his." I fold my arms under my chest and lean into Zane, who wraps his arm around my waist, pulling me close to him. Zane smirks at my words, and I know I just made his ass happy. I smile smugly, knowing Zane is about to threaten their asses.

Zane's aura grows as he slightly pushes it out from himself, making Sage and Liam gasp in surprise. "If I remember correctly, you gave Ari to me in exchange for helping you kill the other lycans, which you lied to me about. I don't like being lied to, Liam. You've been lying to me ever since I even inquired about Ari. I don't like it, Liam. It is unacceptable from someone who calls himself my friend. Ari is mine. Don't even fucking try to lay claim to her. You aren't her Alpha anymore. I fucking am. I'm her master, and she is my familiar. You don't want to know the literal hell I will raise if you so much as try to take her from me, so whatever you two have planned for her, just know I'm not someone you should fuck with. If you need proof of that, I suggest you stick around for the fucking show that's happening tonight." Zane's tone is laced with threat, and I won't lie. I'd be shitting my pants right now if he was threatening me.

Zane's aura is strong, so strong he has a decently strong alpha-like Liam cowering. Even Sasha is a little freaked at the moment. We know Zane won't hurt us. For fucks sake, the man is threatening to raise hell. Wait, can he do that? His coven is descended from Death, and Zane's pretty powerful. He did say literal hell. Damn, what is Zane exactly? He's more than just the average fucking warlock.

Walking away from Sage and Liam, Zane keeps his arm around my waist. He's pissed, and I am too, but we are pissed for different reasons. Zane's pissy because those idiots tried to lay claim to me and bring me back with them. Zane is very protective of me, and I'm glad he's protecting me and is not my enemy. I would not want to end up on Zane's shit list, and it would seem that is the goal of those we are meant to meet tonight. I know Ghost will piss Zane off when he tries to kill all the humans in his club.

"Hey, how come you don't have drinks?" I ask as we make our way to the VIP area. I realize that Zane and Liam didn't come back with drinks.

"I was listening in by siphoning those amazing hearing skills you have. I realized shit was going down, so I dragged Liam back. The drinks didn't seem important as I didn't know what Sage would try to do. I know you can hold your own against her, but she would have played dirty. Besides, you don't have to fight things on your own anymore. That's what you have me for, Pet." He says with a grin. Fuck he knows how to make me needy for him, and it doesn't always involve sexual acts either.

"Well, our night with Sage and Liam didn't fully go to plan, but at least we know they are up to something. Their pathetic attempt to get me to go with them proves they want me for something. Somehow I don't think I was ever supposed to be given to you."

"It doesn't matter. I would have waged war if I had to. Liam's an idiot thinking he can go against me. No one fucking takes what mine or keeps what is mine from me." Zane growls.

"I know you will protect me, Zane," I say, hoping to get him to relax. I was not expecting him to get so protective even after we walked away from them. I'm critical to Zane, which makes me feel all warm inside. Damn his ability to get me to come undone with his words, actions, and touch. It doesn't seem fair, yet I don't care that it's not.

Pushing thoughts about what the hell Sage wants with me and the fact that there is a level of pain I feel at the confirmation that she was never my real friend. The one friend I thought I had, I never really had. I feel a little defeated, like I'm a loser because I don't have any friends. Yes, I have Blair and Zara, but that's only because of Zane that they are even in my life. I feel a bit pathetic at the moment that the only reason I seem to have a life at all is because of Zane. I can throw myself a pity party later. Right now, I need to focus on flirting with Ghost.

This mission is important, and I will not fuck it up because I let Sage get the better of me. I'm a badass lycan, and I don't need her. Sasha is right. I don't need shitty friends like Sage. I'm stronger and better now because I left the toxicity of my pack. I'm happy with Zane. I have found my strength and confidence, which gives me the advantage I didn't have before. I've grown as a person, even if it was hard because it meant processing everything I had suppressed for far too long. It was worth the pain because the pain awoke something deep within me. Something that changed me made me want to be stronger, confident, and most importantly, it taught me my worth.

CHAPTER 14
Zane

The audacity of Liam to try and use his alpha status on Ari. I saw red from the anger lacing around me. No one fucking threatens what is mine. I was ready to explode, but Ari stepped in, letting her sass and confidence show. I was proud of her for standing up for herself against her peers who wronged her. When she said that she only belonged to me and that her master had something to say about them trying to take her from me. I was hard instantly. Hard from the fact that Ari is amazing, but hearing her tell someone else that she belonged to me did me in.

Ari was sexy, standing her ground against Sage, and I have no doubt she will be able to fully handle the next part that will be epic levels of cringe-worthy material. I'm not happy that Ari has to flirt with a scumbag like Ghost, but that fucker will be so attracted to Ari he will flirt with her no matter what. If she flirts back, she might be able to get him to loosen that tongue of his or at least buy us enough time till the shit storm of the overdoses hits the fan. I know exactly what I'm going to do, and I can't wait to show off.

I'm a bit cocky when it comes to my abilities, but I have every right to be. The truth to mastering necromancy is that one has to die. I stopped my heart with drugs and was dead for a few hours while I fought the darkness of death to figure out how to revive myself. One can't be the master of death if one hasn't defeated death. It was strange coming back to life after being in the literal black abyss of death. I felt like I had been dead for decades, but it was merely hours. I fought the wastelands of my own consciousness on a journey to learn how to revive myself from within my fucking mind without being able to physically touch my body to do the act. It was an unearthly experience that still leaves me slightly unsettled to this day and will for the rest of my life.

One thing about mastering death is that you come back immortal by bringing yourself back from the dead. I can still die, but it takes special weapons to kill an immortal being such as myself. I can always give up my immortality as a god could in the old folklores, which is what most do after a long life; they give up the immorality and die. I'll be stuck at the age of twenty -seven until till I either die or give up my immorality. I have bonded Ari to me, making her immortal with me. I haven't told her, but I'm going to have to soon. Ari will be able to give up her immortality when I do. Blair and my mom don't have this. It's only because I'm a necromancer.

Part of me feels like shit for keeping this from Ari. She was so freaked out to be in my realm. She had just lost everything and was so resistant. I didn't think she would take the news well as she seemed like she could barely process the basic information of being a familiar, let alone a familiar to a unique warlock. Ari has made a lot of progress since she first came with me. I think she is ready now for the rest of the truth about who I am, or more like what I a,m and how it affects her. I'll handle that after I handle Ghost.

Ari and I have made our way over to the VIP area. We both take a few moments to gather ourselves. Our double date got blown to pieces rapidly before it could even get started. We are a little early to meet Ghost. We decide to get drinks, and it takes everything in me not to take Ari to one of the bathroom stalls and fuck her senseless. I can't do that just yet, but after we are done with this mission, I'm taking her back to the safe house and fucking her like I own her. For now, I have to deal with just flirty touching, which Ari is fucking good a,t only making me want to stop her sweet hands from roaming my body.

"Pet, I need you to take something for me," I state as a small shadow appears in my palm and drops the vial of lavender liquid in my hand.

"What is it?" She asks, taking the vile without question. That's my good girl.

At least she is behaving for the mission. I would be lying if I said I wasn't slightly worried about her being difficult. She has a natural rebellious streak that loves to come to play. I know the mission isn't over, but so far, I think Ari will behave like a good girl. The fact that she is trying to do a good job and not fuck around by defying me means she is taking our mission seriously. Perhaps my pet is afraid of failing and disappointing me. The thought makes me internally smirk. Ari never ceases to surprise me.

"It's a potion that will protect you if Ghost tries to drug you. He's not a good person, Pet, and he will like what he sees when it comes to you. Ghost isn't smart, and he will openly flirt with you because he thinks I'm his buddy. He's ballsy enough to drug you in front of me. I won't be able to say anything because if I do, you and I both know he will end up dead, and that can't happen yet. The potion will protect you, so even if he drugs you, it won't matter as you will be fine. If he drugs you, Sasha will know, and you will need to act high, so he thinks whatever he gives you is working. He might have another motive than just wanting to rape you, so you play along with his games until the time of the big event that Ghost has planned."

"Well, it's not going to go his way, now is it?" She asks, popping the cork on the vile and chugging the potion quickly.

I smirk at her, loving her confidence on full display. She isn't holding back tonight. I like this side of Ari. It means she realizes her worth, her strength, and she is learning to step out of the shadows that once hid her. She's letting her true self show, and it's beautiful, just like her. I love seeing my choker around her neck like a collar for my pet. Fuck I love her. I always knew my familiar would be my soulmate, so I was prepared to have strong feelings for Ari. However, the intensity is so much more than I thought it could be. Ari is mine, and I'm enjoying getting to know her. Our relationship is growing stronger, so let's hope that when I drop the rest of the truth on her tomorrow, it doesn't somehow undo our progress.

Ari is showing me tonight she is ready for the truth. She is ready to know who I am and what I really can do. She is about to see some of it tonight when I bring back dozens of humans. There's one thing I'm going to tell her tomorrow and offer something that might give her closure with her parents. As a necromancer and the son of Death, I can talk to the dead even after their souls are reaped and given to Death. I asked them if they knew why Ari would be blessed by the Five, but they never knew about her premonitions. I think I'm the first person Ari has ever told that her dreams come true. She didn't even know that she was having premonitions. I'll offer it to her. She might not want to right away due to her anger and resentment, but I think at some point, she is going to crave that closure.

"That's right, Pet, it won't." I subconsciously pat my right hip where my war scythe is. It's shrunk right now, and my leather jacket covers it just right, not that I need to hide it in a place filled with supernaturals. The humans here know to expect and sometimes even hope for supernatural shit to happen.

After we have a few drinks, which will not affect Ari at all since she took the potion. Alcohol has had no effect on me since I became a necromancer. Not that it has ever affected me.

The Coven of the Crow and Shadows: Legacy

I used to be able to drink a fuck tone and get at least tipsy. Being related to one of the Five has its downsides. Drugs and alcohol have never been able to affect me, thanks to being a demigod. However, I did with what I could do, but now neither affect me. I'm honestly having a drink for show and to blend in. It's the only time I bother to drink or do drugs.

Sometimes I have to play a part in order to reap some of the more challenging souls that won't go without a fight. Other times it's moments like this where I'll be saving people, but I have to blend into the crowd to do so. I'll admit I've never brought this many people back before, but they are humans, and humans are the easiest to bring back to life next to animals. Supernaturals vary as some are much harder to bring back than others. It doesn't matter if I haven't done this before. I know I can do it. There is a first time for everything, and tonight I get to bring back dozens at once. It should be interesting. I even get to put on a little show for everyone in the club. This is one of those moments where I don't have to hide my powers. This is one of those rare show off moments mainly because I have to. The truth is, I won't be able to save them all without putting on a show.

The humans dying will draw attention, and then when they all come back to life, that will draw attention as well. I also will have to use the advantage of the ledge of the VIP loft to have the aerial view I'll need to save everyone. This is one of those times that I'm glad I had to learn to save someone without touching them. I will also have to use the shadows to be extensions of myself and bring back those I can't see or touch. It's going to take concentration which is where Ari comes into play. She gets the job of protecting me if anyone tries to fuck with me. Although, honestly, everyone will be too stunned to attack. Even if they do, I know Ari has got my back. I trust her.

The time to meet with Ghost has come. Ari goes to the restroom to deal with her nervous bladder from drinking. I chuckle at her as she dances in the line, irritated that it's not moving fast enough. I debate about fucking with her and telling her I'll just put the shadows around her so she can pee in a cup. Somehow, I don't think she will go for me fucking with her right now. Besides, I don't want to piss her off right before a mission. I know for a fact that if I were to mess with her like that, her rebellious side would come out. While I like poking that side, right now is not that moment.

After Ari is done with the restroom, we head to the loft. I give the bouncer guarding the stairs my name. He nods his head at us after checking his list. We head up the black stairs to the loft. There is a bar along the back wall. Sharp black leather chairs and couches are spread around with tables. The VIP area is about half full. Ghost sits towards the front of the loft. The loft is open as a thick glass railing that goes to the average person's hips.

Ghost looks like a king overlooking his kingdom as he sits on the three person black leather couch with a black metal table in front of him. I can already see the variety of drugs on the table. I see his strange glass bong like contraption that he heats up with a mini blow torch to smoke the dark crystals. There are humans drugs there as well. Clearly, he's mixing the deathly concoction as he packs the drugs in mini plastic baggies that you would get something small like a ring. Ghost is a dark fae, which means he's greedy, likes death, and likes pretty women with spunk.

His short white hair is spiked. Ghost wears a black sleeveless hoodie and black and white checkered jeans with black boots. His eyebrows, nose, and lips are all pierced with gages in both ears. His pointed ears give him away that he is fae. Ghost has all black eyes, much like one would think a demons would be if they were real. Some things are just stories made up of distorted truths. Demons and angels fall into that category. Ghost's pasty white skin almost glows under the glow of the flashing lights.

We approach Ghost, who casually looks over at us. "You made it, Zane, and you brought me a pretty friend." Ghost smiles wide, eyeing Ari from head to toe, but settles a little longer on her breasts. I have to keep it together. I will admit I did not ever see having a familiar as a challenge in the field. Right now, I'm trying not to stick my weapon into Ghost's chest for eyeing my woman.

"This is Ari. She is my familiar." I state as Ari sits next to Ghost, and I sit on the other side of her, so she is between us. I drape my arm casually over her. Ghost can flirt, but I still need to feel like I'm putting off a don't fuck with what's mine vibe. I also have a feeling if Ghost thinks Ari is untouchable, he might want her more.

"Well, she is something, Zane. What are you exactly?" Ghosts asks Ari, curious about her.

"A lycan." She answers him with a wink.

"Can't say I've ever been with a lycan before. I've heard they are animals in bed." He starts up his mini blow torch as he drops a few crystals on the glass portion of the bong like contraption to be heated up.

Ari goes to reach for one of the baggies he's made, sitting on the other side of the contraption he is lighting. I'm afraid Ari will get burned for a second, not that it matters. She can self heal, but I still don't like her hurt. Ari grabs the baggies mixed with purple crystals and something that looks like cocaine or heroin.

"Careful, sweetheart, I almost burned you." Ghost says as he heats up the crystals getting ready to smoke them.

"Don't tempt me with a good time, babe," Ari replies, laying her free hand on Ghost's thighs as she leans closer to him. Ghosts chokes on the smoke as he inhales, and I'm not sure if that's because he is inhaling shit or Ari, maybe both. I have to adjust myself because I'd be lying if I said her little comment didn't turn me on slightly. I don't like her touching Ghost, but he's already falling for the bait she is putting out for him. "Now, what's this and will get my high as a mother fucking kite?" She asks Ghost, shaking the baggy in her hands.

Well, that's one way to find out exactly what he's mixing, which can lead to why he's mixing it. Fucking hell Ari is proving herself tonight. Not that she has to, but I like that she is. My pet definitely has a vixen that she has been hiding from me. Ari has been slowly letting the sexy vixen in her out as she's grown more comfortable with me. Her trusting me and giving in to her desires have opened both of us up to one another. I'm happy that she can feel her soul again. It was affecting her. It's adorable that she thinks I stole her soul, I did, but she thought it was gone forever because I took it. I'm merely keeping it safe for her. Our souls are essential parts of us, and many seek to destroy a person's soul. Our souls are where our good and bad intentions lie.

"You don't want that sweetheart that's for the humans. If you want to feel like you're up in the air surrounded by purple skies, then you want Sparkle." Ghost looks over his table, and when his eyes land on shimmering pink dust. "You snort it like cocaine. Have you done that before, sweetheart?"

"No, but you can show me." She rubs his thigh again as she leans a little more into him, allowing her breasts to touch him lightly.

I don't know where the fuck this side of Ari has been hiding and why she is bringing it out fully right now, but fuck me, she is asking for it. It's not even her flirting with Ghost. I know she has to and doesn't want to. It's the flirty show she is putting on it. I'm so burying my cock in her when this shit is over. I don't give a fuck how tired we will be. I'm fucking her. Tomorrow will bring its own bullshit, so tonight, I'm going to enjoy her because tomorrow she might now want to after I drop a bomb on her.

Ghost lines the pink powder up and shows Ari how to snort through the rolled up hundred he has. She snorts it. I guess she should do the drugs on her own rather than him sneaking them in a drink. Ari is also using it as a way to get him talking. Ari rubs her nose; I'm sure it itches. Sparkle will make her over sensitive nose itchy and uncomfortable for a minute. I rub her shoulders with the arm I have draped over the back of the couch behind her.

"You alright, sweetheart?" Ghost asks, going back to mixing the drugs with the baggies.

I notice he's mixing different supernatural drugs and human drugs. Almost as if the concoctions are supposed to be different, or perhaps that's the point. He's just mixing random ass drug cocktails hoping it will do the job and kill the humans. Ghost is reckless, so it wouldn't surprise me if this were his first or second time doing this. If this is the first time, he might be using tonight as an experiment to see if it works. Ghost could be doing this just because he fucking can or because he's working with someone, and there is a purpose to his madness.

"Perfectly fine. What are you doing with all these drugs? Surely you can't be doing it all yourself?" Ari probes.

I'm not sure she should just go for it right now, but hell, she seems to have Ghost eating out of the palm of her hand, so it might work. Ari leans into him, rubbing her breasts a little against his arm. Fuck she is too good at this, and I need to keep my jealously controlled because I know at the end of the night she is coming home with me, and I'm going to fuck her. Ghost can dream that he will have her, but she will never let him have her. She knows she's mine and mine alone. Besides, Ari only wants to be mine, that I know.

"I'm selling them to humans mixed with some of their drugs. I've already had Candy distribute the first round of baggies. These are for later in case the first batch didn't work." Ghost answers.

"Why the hell are you giving humans supernatural drugs?" I ask.

Ghost shrugs his shoulders. "Someone paid me a shit ton of money for this. The number was right, so I didn't ask questions. The drugs are being given out on the house. The guy who paid me also paid for the drugs so that I wouldn't be at a loss. I thought the deal was too good to be true, but the man paid up, so now I do what he paid me to do."

"So some mysterious guy you don't know pays you a fuck ton of money and buys drugs for you to hand out to humans like candy on Halloween?" I ask in disbelief.

Ghost is just a lackey. Ghost wouldn't ask questions if the price was right. He would just do what he was paid to do. Ghost lacks morals and is a club owner of a popular club. He's the perfect accomplice for this type of shit, but why? Why kill humans and risk war? Unless war is the goal, then why?

"Basically. Don't sound too judgy, Zane. The club has been suffering lately. People do not want to come out and party like they used with the threat of war on the horizon. I know you hide in your coven's realm, Zane, but most of us don't have realms to go to. We are stuck in the fucking human realm, and they don't want to share anymore." Ghost sounds like a mad man on a mission. Whoever he is working with wants a war with the humans, and I'm guessing by Ghost's tone they want the human realm rid of humans.

I want to go off on Ghost, but I can't. I know I can be arrogant, but if Ghost thinks that I don't know what's going on in the human realm, he's dumber than he looks. Of course, I know what's going on in the human realm. It's part of my job. I know many like Ghost who know of my coven think that we stay oblivious to the world's issues, and all we care about is working for Death. My coven is so much more than that. We help all the realms that are left. There aren't many left as there are five left: my covens realm, the human realm, and three other realms run by covens. Then there are the realms each of the Five reside in, but only they and those they allow entrance into their realm can enter. The ones who serve the Five knew it was better to keep their realm alive than abandon it. Many supernaturals like Ghost are pissy at their ancestors for letting their birth realm fade to nothing.

Yes, things have been tense, but the humans tend to keep to themselves. Honestly, they're afraid of us, and they rather just stick to their areas where they know it's safe. Ghost is over exaggerating that humans are trying to segregate supernaturals. If anything, humans are segregating themselves for safety. They have learned to share their realm,, and while they get a bit pissy about some things, they are always willing to sort shit out. Humans are oddly peaceful, even if their history books would suggest otherwise. Humans are their own type of monsters, and they know that. It's why they rather keep the peace.

I'm not sure what lies Ghost has been fed, but someone is spreading lies to cause panic. I know what he's saying isn't true. The Five know everything that goes on in all the realms. They give my coven and the others that serve them reports, data, and anything else we might need. Someone wants to turn the supernaturals against the humans. No wonder Ghost thinks war is coming because he doesn't know he's helping start the fucking war.

"Have the humans not been playing nice with us?" Ari inquires as she takes a sip of the fruity drink that the waitress brought over not too long ago.

Ghost must have ordered drinks to be sent over. Dark Fea can communicate telepathically with one another, much like how werewolves have a telepathic link with their pack, or they used to at one point in time. Werewolves and Lycans seemed to have lost certain things over time. It's strange to see a supernatural race lose abilities, but then again, werewolves are technically the first type of half breeds. I know they don't want to be called that, but compared to lycans, that's what they are, half breeds. Lycans seemed to hold many abilities that werewolves do not. Lycans can talk to their wolves, and their wolves have names.

Lycans are the original supernaturals of this realm. I wonder if there is something to that. I never paid much attention to that detail before. Lycans are clearly superior to werewolves because they are the original version. Werewolves are like the knock off versions of lycans. I wonder if the werewolves lost the ability to communicate due to their human DNA telepathically? It's a theory and one to focus on tomorrow.

"No, they never play nice, but it's been worse lately. They demand that supernaturals be segregated because we are too dangerous to live among them anymore. Well, I'm happy to teach them exactly how dangerous we can be. How's your drink treating you, sweetheart?"

"Good, it tastes like strawberries and the sunset." She giggles at herself. Well, at least she can act high or act like the drugs and alcohol affect her.

"Good, sweetheart, I'll keep them coming all night. You let me know if you want more Sparkle." Ghost winks at Ari, and she smiles at him. Ghost definitely wants her intoxicated. "Soon, you should be able to enjoy the show." Ghost comments.

Unfortunately, I know what show he is talking about, but I'll stop it. Ari and Ghost flirt back and forth. As the first wave of humans begins to cry out and fall to the floor, I stand up, leaning down over the glass railing. Ghost comes up next to me, laughing his ass off at the pain of the humans beginning to OD.

"You know, Ghost. I ended up becoming a necromancer since you last saw me," I state casually.

"That's cool. I remember you were so pumped even though I'm not sure I still believe in that type of mythical shit. So what, you can kill people better now and send them to death faster?"

Fuck I hate this asshole. Time to prove him wrong. I notice below that Sage and Liam are on the dance floor. They are dancing, ignoring the humans dying. More and more are falling as panic in the crowd sets in. Ari is now standing slightly behind Ghost and me. It's just about time the last of the humans are dying, and the crowd is losing their shit now. Soon the authorities will be called, but I'll stop this shit show before then.

Taking off my war scythe from my hip, I bring it to fall size. I'm going to need it to help channel so much magic. I didn't get this baby till I became a necromancer. Death made it for me. It's my favorite weapon, and it looks badass if I do say so myself. Ghost's eyes go a little wide at the sight of my weapon.

"Let me clear it up for you then. There is a misconception with my power. Many think it's about the killing, about the action of taking a life. It's more than that. It's about controlling death and manipulating it to bend it to my desires," I state as I close my eyes and feel for all the dying human souls. I reach my hands out with my war scythe in my right hand as I let shadows swirl around me and then extend outward to touch every human. It's a web of shadows weaved around the crowd to touch every dying human soul. The shadows all connect together and to me. I open my eyes to see the shadows touching the humans good. The crowd is now all staring at me, including Sage and Liam. "I can absorb death into myself," I say, as I pull the death out of the humans through the shadows using my war scythe to help channel the abundance of magic I'm using and the amount of death I have to absorb. My body shakes slightly from absorbing the darkness. "Then once I absorb it, I can purify it and give it back as a renewed life source," I state as I push a pure white light through shadows and into every human.

The dying humans all start gasping for air. Sage and Liam's mouths are wide open, as are many others. "Holy shit, you really are a necromancer and the son of Death."

I grin as the shadows dissipate, and in one quick motion, my hand wraps around Ghost's throat tightly. "Hell yes, I am. I'm the most powerful to ever exist in my coven. Death himself has called me talented. Don't underestimate my ability to fuck your shit up, Ghost. Stop handing out your drug concoctions to humans. You will not like it if I have to come back here."

"What about my boss?" Ghost asks. He can barely get the words out with how tight I squeeze his neck.

"Tell him he can go fuck himself. I don't care what you tell him or how you deal with him. It's not my problem. What is my problem, is you killing innocent humans. You pissed off the Five with your little stunt, so they sent me to stop you. So before you think about other ways to distribute your deadly drugs just remember you don't want to piss the Five off any more than you already have. Trust me, Ghost, if I have to come back here, it will end with me taking your life and hand delivering your soul to Death himself on a silver fucking platter." I squeeze his neck tighter till he's turning slightly blue. "Do you fucking understand me?" Ghost nods his head the best he can with my hand around his throat. "Good. Glad we could clear up that little misunderstanding. Let's go, Pet. We are done here." I state as I let go of Ghost, pushing him into the table he had set up with his drugs.

The Coven of the Crow and Shadows: Legacy

The drugs go everywhere as I Ghost gasps for breath. Fucking asshole. I'd kill him right now, but that's not part of the mission. Part of me hopes he fucks up again so I can kill him. I know if he fucks up again and tries anything like he did tonight, I will get to keep my promise of hand delivering his soul to Death on a silver platter. Ari comes to my side and links her arm with mine.

Shadows swarm around us and teleport us right to the cabin. Ari looks at me. "What did Ghost mean by you really being the son of Death?" She asks quietly as she tries to step away from me.

I stop her and pull her to me, snaking my arms around her waist. I was so lost in the moment I forgot Ghost accidentally spilled the beans. "Tomorrow, Pet, I will answer all your questions and fill you in on everything you need to know. I promise, but tonight I need you under me screaming my name. Can you do that for me, Pet?"

"I'll do anything for you, Zane," Ari responds by kissing me as she wraps her arms around my neck.

Fuck she's perfect, and damn do I love her. I'm also enjoying her obedient streak even though I know her, and it won't last forever, which is also why I love her. She really is the perfect soulmate for me. Right now, I'm about to show Ari how much I love her and that her pretty ass is mine.

CHAPTER 15
Ari

Zane kisses me deeply as his tongue invades my mouth and entwines with mine. I melt at his touch and kisses. I can't help it. The man knows how to get me a needy mess for him without trying. While my mind wants to fight this moment and get answers now, my heart and body are telling my mind to fuck off because I know Zane is about to fuck me like he owns my ass, and he does. I've been waiting all night for this knowing my alpha male would feel the need to remind me that he owns me. It makes for good sex, and right now, I'll take good sex over my messy emotions. I want to forget the fucking world right now.

"I didn't like you touching Ghost." He growls lowly as he breaks our kiss. He grabs a fist full of my hair to pull my head back, exposing my neck.

"I didn't like touching him. I feel dirty because of it." I admit.

I feel so nasty on the inside and the outside that I had to flirt with Ghost. Touching him made my skin crawl. I hated watching Ghost eye fuck me every ten minutes or so. I think that slimeball would have had his tongue down my throat if he wasn't busy packing drugs. The second I sat down next to Ghost, I realized Zane was right. Ghost would drug me to rape me or worse. Ghost isn't a good person. He's the type of slimeball that drugs women to rape them. I bet he likes virgins too. Seriously what is it with supernaturals being into virgins? I mean, I guess I get it, but at the same time, I don't. Either

The Coven of the Crow and Shadows: Legacy

way, I realized if he thought I was easy, he wouldn't do something too stupid. I also saw it as an icebreaker to start us on the topic we needed Ghost on.

Truthfully, the whole experience with Ghost was a bit more triggering than I cared to admit. I shoved it down for the sake of the mission. Being successful and now back at the safe house, I feel my emotions flooding to the surface. Tonight brought me back to my old alpha and Sage's brother, who I wonder if he was fooling around with me because Sage thought it would keep me around as her friend. So much manipulation, and I fucking hate it. I hate myself for letting myself be manipulated in the first place. I should have been stronger, but I wasn't. I let myself fall for pretty lies. Being misused makes me feel vulnerable like I can't escape constantly being misused for other's cruel intentions. Tonight made me feel like a whore for some reason. Like that's all I'm good for. After all, that's what my old alpha thought. That's what Sage's brother thought, and tonight Ghost thought it too. At least Zane sees me as more than his toy.

"You aren't dirty, Pet. You did it for our mission which we nailed perfectly. You were amazing tonight. You were focused, fierce, brave, and fucking sexy as hell. You know it took everything in me not to fuck you in the damn club when you told Liam and Sage that you belong to me." I knew he'd like that, and it's the truth.

"That's because it's true, you're my Master, and I'm falling in love with you," I confess softly.

I blame the moment and my crazed emotions for my confession. Let's be honest. Zane probably already knows that. He reads my mind. I have a feeling he knows everything, even if he pretends not to. At least he lets me come to him with it, although I'm still not sure that justifies his actions. At least he's not using it against m,e and I trust that he never will.

Zane grins. "Good because I'm already in love with you, Ari. I've been in love with you even before I knew who you were. I knew that no other woman would matter to me as my familiar would. No one I have ever been with was a serious thing because they weren't you. You've always been the only one for me. I know you think of yourself as a consolation prize, but you are more than that, Ari."

His lips crash to mine in a hungry need. I moan into his kiss. Shadows come around us, and we go from clothed to naked in seconds. Zane's erection presses against my belly as he walks us over to the bed and pushes me down before he's on top of me. He pushes my legs apart. I don't even care if we have foreplay. I just want him deep inside of me to sedate the ache in my core.

Zane inserts himself in one swift movement as if he knows exactly what I want. He's all the way in, and I wrap my legs around his waist, but Zane takes my legs and throws each one over his shoulders. Fuck he's really deep. Zane starts slamming into me. Oh, fuck yes, this is what I wanted. Zane's thrusts are hard and rough as he slams into me without mercy. He reaches his hand between my legs as he rubs my clit. I feel him hit my cervix a few times, and while it does hurt, I don't give a damn because everything he does is just right. The pleasure of his fingers rubbing my clit while he slams his cock into me repeatedly is delicious.

Moans escape my lips as I try to keep up with his thrusts with my hips, but I can't. He's just too fast and rough. Then add the pleasure from him rubbing my clit has my orgasm building in my core, threatening to push me off a cliff that I certainly want to go over. There is this need to be dominated to know that I'm really his. I want him to fuck all the doubt from my mind, which is precisely what he's doing. This man, I don't care what he is, he's mine, and I'm his. That's all that fucking matters. My walls clench tightly around him as I cry out my orgasm followed by a small growl of satisfaction. Zane finds his release shortly after me.

We are a sweaty, panting mess tangled on the bed while we come back down to reality after being on cloud nine. Zane pulls out of me, and he plops next to me. I roll into his arms and lay my head on his chest. His heart rate is going back to normal, as is mine.

"I love you, Ari," Zane states quietly as I close my eyes. I can't help the smile that forms on my lips.

"I love you too, Zane," I reply as the blankets come over us.

The satisfying soreness between my legs reminds me of the great ending to our night. I know tomorrow will bring some things that might be hard to process. I'm ready for them, but right now, I want to bask in a great first mission we had. I have to admit Zane did not disappoint, and watching him in action was badass and slightly terrifying. The aura that comes from him is strong, but if there is even a sliver of truth to Ghost's statement, then Zane's aura makes sense. I honestly don't know the full details of Zane's powers and abilities. I just know he's slightly different from everyone else in his coven. All I know is that I'm glad I'm someone Zane loves because I would not want to be his enemy.

When Zane was threatening Ghost, I saw darkness in him. Not an evil darkness, but a darkness that was like nothing I had ever seen on someone. It scared me, and yet it also thrilled me. I couldn't help it as I started to admire his darkness. He had just saved all those humans showing off his strength and power in a display that aroused me. Then he threatened Ghost, and I knew he meant the threat. There was no doubt in my mind that Zane would kill Ghost, and I think he'd enjoy it too. Then again, if he is the son of Death, it makes sense for Zane to like killing on some level.

Zane doesn't strike me as the type of person that would enjoy killing an innocent. No, Zane likes killing bad guys. I'm okay with that. Someone has to deal with the bad guys, and sometimes you have to take them out with death. Sometimes things can't be nice. The hard truth is that someone has to do the work that others don't want to do. Zane's coven has devoted its life to serving others even if they don't get the recognition they deserve.

My body is far too tired from the evening. Zane is already snoring softly. I'm sure he's tired. The amount of strength and power he used was more than I ever thought I'd see in my lifetime. I'm pretty sure that bringing people back from the dead is tiring. I knew that's what he was going to do, but it was something else entirely to see him do it. It was one thing when it was just a theoretical part of the plot. Hearing Zane talk about his powers how he absorbed the death and purified to give it back as a renewed life force as he channeled the most powerful magic I've ever witnessed through his scythe and shadows. It was impressive and something that would be in a classic human sci-fi movie. Seeing Zane train and in the field are two different things.

Zane holds back when he is training. I see that as clear as day now. I know he's holding back when he trains with anyone, not just me, but even the other warlocks from his coven. He has to. There is no doubt in my mind that if he didn't, someone would end up seriously injured or dead. I guess the dead part isn't a problem since Zane could just bring them back to life. Still, Zane holds back. I almost feel sorry for the assholes Zane has to fight, but honestly, they probably deserve it.

Sleep begins to overtake me, reminding me that I need to rest while I may not have transformed. I was still using my heightened senses. Sasha was pressing on the edges of my consciousness, ready to take over at a moment's notice. She was prepared to fight, and I know she wanted to rip Sage's ass a new one. I can't even begin to process everything that happened last night, and somehow I know that I will have even more to process when I talk with Zane tomorrow. I might as well put the mental breakdown on hold till tomorrow, I think to myself as sleep overtakes me.

Waking the following morning, I find the bed empty. I roll out of bed and still enjoy the slight ache between my legs. Damn, I love it when he fucks me rough like that. I like some gentle, sweet, and romantic, but fuck do I like it rough and dirty. Searching the small cabin, I don't see Zane. My guess is he is either off on coven business or getting something. Shrugging my shoulders, I decide to shower. I'm okay with him not being around at the moment. I want some time to process the whirlwind of emotions that are swirling around inside of me.

The warm water washes away the grime from the mission. I clean my face and body before I scrub the hair products out of my hair. I let the warm water soothe me as I try to slowly process last night. My showdown with Sage didn't go great, although telling her off and calling her out on her bullshit did feel pretty damn good. Still, it hurt to know I was being used. Then Ghost and his fucking trigger shit. Still, the night was a success. Plus, Zane showing off his power was a turn on.

Turning off the shower, I dry off, knowing that when Zane comes back, we will talk. I know there is a level of truth to what Ghost said if it's not the whole truth. Zane is more than a regular warlock, something I've known for a bit now. Zane even confirmed that I was correct, and he promised to tell me. I knew Zane was waiting for the mission to be over before talking to me. Whatever it is, he must think I won't take it well, which made him afraid I'd jeopardize the mission. As much as I hate to agree, the mission was important. We saved lives and stopped a war, for now at least.

Then when Ghost made his comment, it all seemed to click together like a puzzle that I didn't even know I was trying to solve. I knew Zane was powerful. I sensed it the moment I laid eyes on him. There was no denying the command of respect he projected. He was stern and cold, as if he wasn't sure if he should close the distance between us. He was close and yet felt out of reach. I was so hopped up on wolfsbane, though, so I'm not sure what I was feeling other than my feelings felt like they were on crack. I had never felt such a loss of control over myself. I couldn't think straight. One minute I was rational. The next, I was ready to burn everything down. It was intense.

I'm not sure how I feel about Zane being the son of Death. If he had told me right away, I would have flipped my shit. I was so freaked out when he first took me to his realm and tried to explain what being his familiar meant. I wouldn't have been able to handle him being the son of Death. That's if it's true, but my intuition says it is. He also didn't deny it last night. He asked me to forget about it till today. He wanted it last night because he needed it, and I did too. There is something about being intimate with him that makes me feel whole.

They say soulmates are your missing half. That they will complete you in ways you could never imagine. Back when fated mates were a thing among werewolves, at least I think it was real. No one knows for sure. The stories would say that finding your fated mate was finding your soulmate. Two pieces that would fit together because they were made for each other. It was a beautiful story to tell little girls. However, werewolves don't have fated mates anymore, if it was ever a thing, to begin with.

The Coven of the Crow and Shadows: Legacy

Sage was always fascinated with the idea of soulmates and fated mates. She would search texts, books, lore, and everything she could on fated mates. Somewhere in Sage's bitchy girl persona is a romantic obsessed with finding her perfect match. I used to just shrug the whole topic off. I didn't want to think about soul mates, perfect matches, love, or anything like that. Why would it matter to me? I was a freak. Even if fated mates were real, or even soul mates, they wouldn't want me. I thought I was defective, and because of that, I was ruined. I thought I was unlovable because of my differences. So I pushed the thoughts of soulmates away. I laughed it off as a cruel joke for lonely girls, and I refused to feel lonely.

Then Zane crashes into my life, proving so much of what I thought wrong. Showing me that I was so much more than I thought I was. Zane showed me my worth because he values me as a person. I matter to him. Then I remember last night we confessed we loved each other. When I had told Zane, I was falling in love with him. I didn't expect him to acknowledge the words, let alone admit he already loves me and has forever. How do I take that in? It's not bad by no means. It's overwhelming to finally feel what I have longed to feel my whole life.

Even with my parents, I didn't feel loved, not really. They tried, they did. I'd give them that. They did try to do their best, even if it was the bare minimum. I felt like I was a mistake to them. A not so happy accident. I wanted to feel valued, supported, and loved. I never got it from my parents, not much anyway. Then I thought I had some level of it with Sage, but that was just pretending. Zane is the first person to love me the way I deserve, the way I need, and the way I want. It's just another way he healed my broken heart and shattered soul.

The truth is, I don't care if Zane is the son of Death or Death himself. I love him. He's my soulmate. I guess soulmates aren't cruel jokes for lonely girls after all. No matter what, I'm in this with Zane. I'm going to help him in any way I can, love him the best I can, and be his everything because he's definitely my everything. Strange to fall in love and have a soulmate when I never dared to let myself have this dream.

Stepping out of the shower, I shut it off and wrap myself up in a fluffy black towel. I dry my hair as I step into the bedroom. Zane is back as I can hear him in the kitchen. I quickly dress in black leggings and one of Zane's dark gray v necks. Walking out into the kitchen, I see that Zane has Chinese food on the table. When I look at the digital clock on the oven, it says three pm. Damn, I slept in late. I couldn't have been up for more than an hour. Oh well, I needed it.

"You were still sleeping when I woke up, so I figured I would go get your favorites knowing you'd be hungry when you woke up. I like you wearing my shirt." He states as he eyes me up and down before he goes back to unpacking the Chinese food.

"What you are about to tell me must be rough if you are prepared with my comfort food," I say as I walk over to the small dining table.

Zane did get all my favorites. Pork fried rice, beef and broccoli, shrimp lo mein, spring rolls, sweet and sour chicken, Chinese doughnuts, and crab rangoon. He also has a bottle of wine and iced green tea.

"Honestly, I'm not sure how you will take it, but you need to eat either way, and it can't hurt to have this." He replies, taking a seat as I take mine.

We make our plates, and I have a little of everything because fuck it, I'm starving. Zane pours us each a glass of wine and a glass of iced green tea. Since I'm starving, I down about half my plate before Zane can even get a handful of bites in. I never claimed to be graceful when I eat. I can't help it. The wolf in me comes out with food. I know I eat like an animal, especially when I'm in private, but I don't care. We sit in silence as we eat. I'm sure he's hungry too, and whatever he's going to tell me will be better on a full stomach. At least that's what I'm telling myself.

"I don't care if you are the son of Death. It makes sense, but I don't understand why others in your coven aren't." I state when we are almost done.

Zane chuckles. "You've been thinking about it ever since Ghost said something, haven't you?" I bite my lower lip and look away, grabbing the glass of wine. Zane chuckles again. "I'll take that as a yes. Well, I know you don't care for the complexion of magic, and honestly, I can't blame you. It's a lot for people who don't understand it, so I will make it basic for you. My coven was started with the original sons of Death purposely birthed to help Death with reaping souls. After some time, they had children, and their children had children. You get the picture the coven grew. After the great-grandkids, the powers got less and less. The magic weakened as the generations went on. Death realized he always needed to have a son in the coven to keep up with the demands, keep the magic strong, and so on. Basically, the magic he used to create us the way he needed and wanted had limitations, as does all magic, even when you don't see it. Magic has a price, so to speak, and I'm that price. So every so many decades, he has a son and waits till it's time to have another one. I'm just one of the many born to sustain the coven."

"You were born just to serve your father?" Damn, that's a lot to put on someone. Nothing like having a kid to be your slave.

"Basically. It sounds worse than it is. You are just one of the many rewards I get for my troubles, but you are the biggest and best reward. Death and the witch he used to have me with didn't want to raise me, so Death let Zara and Blaine adopt me. The Shadow family has been running the coven since the beginning. They have always run the coven. Death thought it would be good for me to be raised in the coven. Sometimes the witches would want to raise the son they had with Death. He would let them under the pretense that the child would go to the coven to learn at a certain age. My birth mom wasn't like that. I know that the Shadows are my adoptive family, but I never felt that I was adopted. Before you ask, yes, I bear a semblance to Blaine and Cade. That's because we are related to Death on some level and genetics. It's a happy coincidence that we all took on the correct features to resemble one another." Zane informs me as he takes a sip of wine.

"What else do I need to know about you?" I ask. It's a little intense having him confirm exactly who he is. I don't care. It's just wow that my soulmate is a demigod. That's not something the average person can say.

The Five are a big deal, and while I've heard the stories and rumors that they sometimes have kids that are like demigods in the old human stories, it never entirely seemed like it could be real. I know it's crazy because supernaturals exist. Well, most of us, some are just made up. Zane is the son of Death, it's a little intimidating, and as much as I hate to admit it, he was right to withhold this information. I would have flipped my shit if he told me when I first came with him.

"When I became a necromancer, I had to die, and when I brought myself back to life, I came back immortal. When you became my familiar, you also became immortal." My eyes go wide. Okay, that's not something I saw coming. "I know it feels overwhelming, and I should have warned you beforehand, but you were already so overwhelmed I didn't want to push you over the edge. I know the idea of forever is intimidating. We can give up our immortality at any time and die of old age. Just remember you can still die, Ari. Immortal doesn't mean indestructible. I have to stay immortal for a bit to make sure our kids and grandkids are set. I have to have heirs to my legacy, Ari. There's no way around it. At some point,k Death expects me, well us, to have heirs. "

"That's okay. I want kids, so that's not a problem. I'd like to wait, though, I mean, we just started going on missions, and you have so much to catch up on. Then add the whole war and Sage things. It's a lot right now, and I don't know if you know this, but shifters can't shift when they are pregnant. I'd be somewhat useless in the field."

"I know, and I agree. One more thing about my powers, then we move on to the other things. I can talk to the dead, so I can make it happen if you ever want closure with your parents. You can say goodbye to them, whatever you need. It doesn't have to be now, whenever you are ready if you're ever ready." Zane offers.

That's a lot to digest. I'm immortal, but that doesn't mean I'm invincible. I'm still not sure how I feel about living forever or for a long time. I guess it can't be too horrible. I'll get to see my kids and grandkids grow up, maybe even my great-grandkids if we want. Then there's Zane being able to let me talk to my dead parents. Yeah, that's not something I'm ready for, but maybe one day it would be nice. I never thought much about closure with them, thinking it would never be a thing with them being dead. I just accepted that sometimes we don't get the proper closure we need.

The heir thing doesn't bother me. I do want kids at some point. I like the idea of being a mom, and Zane would be a good dad. He would be protective, maybe overprotective. Still, the thought of Zane holding our baby, loving me while I'm pregnant, and us raising our family together brings me a type of hope I didn't think I'd ever feel. Hope for a future that isn't out of reach.

"Wait, there's more?" I ask, remembering his words. I'm not sure I can take more. Yeah, I knew it was a good idea to hold off on my breakdown. Alright, well, let's hope it's not too earth-shattering.

"When I visited Death, I asked him how to protect you from Cerberus. It turns out all I had to do was take your virginity and claim your body. Since that's already happened, you are safe. We can go back home whenever we need to. Another thing Death told me was that we need to see my bio mom, Mags. She will help us figure out why you are blessed."

Alright, that's not horrifying. "Couldn't Death just tell you why I'm blessed?"

Zane laughs. "That would be too easy, Pet. I've made arrangements for us to see Mags tomorrow."

"Will you be okay seeing her, and how do you think she can help me?" I ask, finishing the last of my wine.

"I can handle Mags, she's something else, and you will see what I mean tomorrow. She's isn't scary. Honestly, she's mostly harmless. Mags is a shitty mom, and there is a reason she gave me up to Zara. Mags is a psychic witch. She can read people and their auras and tell what someone's intentions are. She can see a person's future or find a lost person, and she can do a lot. It makes sense that she will help you, although I'm unsure how she can. How does Sasha feel about meeting Mags." Zana asks, and for a minute, I totally forgot Sasha has been cryptic about everything.

"Mags needs to show you my memories," Sasha tells me. "In my memories, you will find the answers you seek. I can't explain it to you as some of the memories aren't mine. Sasha was the name of my first human. The first wolf spirits took the names of their first human. When Sasha and I merged, her memories became mine, but they aren't mine, and I'm just a spirit inside of you. My first human's memories are buried, and only Mags can dig them out."

The Coven of the Crow and Shadows: Legacy

"Sasha wants Mags to show me her memories from her first human. Sasha gets her name from her first human, and when they merged, so did their memories. Sasha needs me to see something from Sasha's memories from when she was human." I Inform Zane.

"I see she is finally giving you more information on the matter. Well, I'm sure Mags can do that for her. We will go see her tomorrow. Why don't we relax tonight and curl up on the couch by the fire? We can watch a movie on my tablet. It will help keep your mind off of tomorrow." Zane suggests.

"I'd like that," I reply with a smile. Zane's right. I need to be distracted right now before my brain goes into overdrive.

We clean up our food and stick the dishes into the sink. Zane and I have become a little domesticated already living in this safe house. I like it because it makes what we have feel real and not some dream that I'm terrified to wake up from. I like that it's just us. At the manor, we are surrounded by so many people. Even though we have our private quarters, it's not the same as this. I don't know if we have to live in the coven's manor all the time or if we could have our own place like this. It would need to be bigger since we plan on kids. I'm still not entirely sure how kids work with Zane. He tried to explain it with the dark magic from Death rewrites the child's DNA to make them a warlock and a boy. Magic confuses the hell out of me, and I can't follow it to save my life. I'll worry about that part of things when we decide to have kids.

Zane and I curl up on the couch as he magically starts a fire. This whole place runs on magic. It's pretty handy. We pick some action comedy movies. My feet are on the couch, and my head is only on Zane's shoulders. I like being curled up with him. While he might frustrate me sometimes, Zane is my home. If I have to spend forever with someone, I'm glad it's Zane. My mind goes to earlier and the topic of heirs. I always loved the idea of kids, a family, maybe because I felt I never had one. I wanted to be able to give someone something I wish I could have had. It seemed like a foreign thing for me since I was shunned. I'm nervous about being a parent, and I don't want to be one at nineteen. I guess it doesn't matter. I'm stuck at nineteen forever now. Still, I want to enjoy being out in the field. I love the action, or maybe I'm riding off the high from last night.

Tomorrow I will get answers. Answers that I fear might only make more questions, and even if it doesn't, I'm sure whatever answers I get might not be exactly what I want. I can't shake the feeling that the truth will be shocking. It has to be. I'm blessed by the Five, and I never even knew it till recently. I have no idea why I have premonitions, and it's unnerving to know that the dreams I thought merely coincidental were so much more than that. I suspected it, but to have it confirmed makes it too real.

Although I'll think I'll be just fine with Zane as my soulmate. He won't let me do this alone, just like I won't let him do his duty alone. Taking a moment to glance at Zane, I realize all the burdens he's carried himself. He's the son of Death, born to serve his father. Zane's life was never really his. He bares the intense burden of doing things that no one in his coven can do to keep the coven's magic and resources going to train others to be the best they can be, and that goes for myself and all the other responsibilities that come with his role. I never realized how important and serious Zane's role in the coven is.

I realize Zane, and I aren't so different, at least where our childhoods were concerned. I was so jealous of him for a while because he grew up accepted, respected, and loved. I felt he had all the things I wished for from my parents and pack. Yes, Zane has those things, but his life wasn't quite as perfect as I imagined. Zane's biological parents wanted nothing to do with him. Death only had Zane because he had to in order to keep his work going. His mom, well, I'm not sure why she decided to be the willing surrogate and egg donor. I'm sure she got something for it because I doubt Death would rape someone. The asshole might be a terrifying fucker, but I doubt he'd stoop so low.

Zane may have been adopted into a loving family that gave him that perfect life I thought he had. Still, Zane had to deal with the pain and disappointment of not being wanted by his biological parents. They gave him up without a second thought. I know not everyone is meant to be a parent, and sometimes the adoptive parents are better, which is the case for Zane. However, there is still a level of pain that comes with the feeling of being rejected. The pain of feeling like you aren't enough. I know that pain.

With all the responsibilities and expectations Zane is burdened with, it's a wonder the man is sane. I can't imagine the pressure he must feel sometimes. I know many depend on him in the coven. Zane's phone is always buzzing with texts, emails, and phone calls. Blaine might be the face of the coven and help run it, but even he needs Zane. Then Zane has to have heirs to help carry on his role. It seems like so much for one person to have to bear, and I worry for our children, but then again, Zane handles it so well. I have no doubt he would help our children.

Thinking about Zane with our kids makes me smile. He will be stern and overprotective, but he will love and support them. I have no doubt Zane will be a good father. I think I'll be a good mom. I might not have had a great example, but I seem to have natural instincts. As a shifter, my pregnancy will be about seven months, and while the actual birth might scare me, it's an experience I can't wait to have. I have no idea why I've become so warmed up to the idea so quickly. Perhaps it's a dream I always had that I never let go of. Maybe deep down,

I always knew I'd find the person who I was meant to be with, my soulmate.

I don't even care that I gave Zane my heart last night. I insisted I wasn't ready to say the words to him and admit my feelings, but it slipped out. It was the right moment. I held back telling myself that when the right moment came, I would tell Zane. I was starting to think the moment wouldn't come, but it did. I'm glad I did. I know I've had such resistance when it comes to Zane and our bond. I'm done resisting it. This is what I want. This is where I know I'm meant to be, and I'm happy for the first time in my life. It doesn't matter what I find out tomorrow or the war that threatens the human realm. Right now, I'm happy. Even if my mind is buzzing around and my heart is still healing from the hurt of others, I know Zane won't hurt me. I trust him, and I love him. So, for now, I'm going to enjoy my happiness and the company of the man I never thought existed but that I always hoped for.

CHAPTER 16
Ari

Waking, I find strong arms wrapped around me. My back is to Zane's chest. I wonder if he is cold because he's the son of Death or because he died? He's not ice cold but cool. I like it as I'm generally on the warmer side. I'll want his cold body against mine when I'm pregnant. I can only imagine the hot flashes I will have to endure. Why is pregnancy on my mind so much lately? How did I go from barely thinking about it to it constantly popping in my head?

"Pet, I can feel your mind swarming. It's far too early for that." Zane groans, annoyed that I woke him from his precious sleep.

"Hey, don't whine at me about it being too early. You are the one who kept us up late after the movie with two rounds of sex with lots of foreplay in between." I say, smacking his arms so I can get up, but the alphahole holds me tighter.

"You complaining, Pet? If I recall, you were begging me for it all." I feel my cheeks heat up. Shit, he's got me. How does he always fucking get me like that?

"It's not my fault you know how to make me crumble," I grumble, squirming against him. I make the mistake of brushing against his semi-hard cock. Shit.

"Careful, Pet, you get me worked up. You are taking care of it." He warns, causing me to still. My struggling is just making my ass rub his dick, and that's what he fucking wants.

Bastard, I'm on to your games, I think to myself. I hear Zane chuckle. "Stop reading my mind!" I whine, irritated at him.

"I told you I'll stop when you figure out how to read mine. I'm not fucking with you, Pet. I'm serious. You can read my mind too. You just have to figure it out. Come on. We have to go meet Mags." He groans, letting me go.

"How badly are you dreading seeing her?" I ask as we get out of bed.

"I always dread seeing her. You know I love you because I'm about to visit her for you. I loathe Mags with a passion. I'd rather deal with Death than her. She is a shit bio mom, and I'm thankful Zara is my real mom. The last time I saw Mags, I was ten. I'm twenty-seven. You do the math." He replies, heading to the bathroom.

I think I'm getting my first look at grumpy Zane. He will be fun to deal with today, I think to myself as I dig through my clothes, wondering what one wears to meet their soulmates, bio mom. I have no idea. Do I want to impress her? Does it even matter, considering Zane loathes her? Eh, fuck it, what do I care? I'm going to wear what I want. I pull out a black and white horizontal striped tank dress that comes to my knees, my leather jacket, and my combat boots. I grab a black lace bra and panty set. I still have on Zane's necklace. I refuse to take it off. I only take it off when I shower, and sometimes I forget. I like having it on. I don't know why. Maybe I really love being Zane's pet so much that the choker reminds me of a collar. It's a sexy way for Zane to always state to everyone that I'm his. I could also totally be delusional. I clearly have issues.

When Zane comes out of the bathroom, I head in. I brush my hair, putting it in a messy bun while I brush my teeth and wash my face. Once I'm dressed, I let my hair down. I like wearing my hair down. Even though it is better to have it pulled back for training, I wear it down when I can. I find

Zane in the kitchen fully dressed. Not fair. He uses the shadows to dress him. He's in dark wash jeans, his nicer boots that he wears when he wants to look on the dressed side and not like he's about to fuck someone's day up. He has a black t-shirt on with his leather jacket.

Zane decides to take me to breakfast before we go see his mom. I can't deny that I wouldn't mind procrastinating. Plus, it gives us a date, and I enjoy dates with Zane. Breakfast is casual and relaxed, which is exactly what I need. I am curious to know the truth, but I also rather avoid it all together.

Enjoying the free time with Zane on a date is always nice. Last night was nice too. Our movie was almost over before Zane started playing with me. I didn't mind it, though. I love being with him, and sex with him is always mind blowing. I get why people like sex so much. I'm not sure if everyone has such an amazing experience, but I have Zane, and fuck does he know what to do.

Once breakfast is over, it's time to face the music. Zane uses the shadows to teleport us to his mother's home. She lives in one of the countryside of the human realm. Mag's house is a cute cottage, small, surrounded by beautiful plants, bushes, flowers, and a wooden fence. Zane looks less than thrilled to be here. Guilt starts to trickle over me as I'm the reason he has to see Mags in the first place. I don't know how Mags hurt Zane, but whatever she did, she hardened him against her.

Taking Zane's hand as I weave my hand with his. He looks down at me. I kiss him softly on the lips. "I can do anything as long as I have you with me, Zane," I say, breaking the kiss.

"I feel the same way, Ari. Come on, let's get this over with." He states as we start walking towards the door.

Anxiety takes over the minute Zane knocks on the door. Fuck, I don't know if I'm ready for this. I don't know if I can deal with whatever I find out. I take a few deep breaths and remind myself I'm strong, and I can do this. No matter what I find out, it will be okay. Most importantly, I have Zane with me. It doesn't matter what happens because I can face anything with him by my side.

It feels like forever before the door opens. A woman with short grey hair to her shoulders opens the door. The woman has a cigarette in her mouth as she puffs on it between her two fingers. She wears an oversized and unflattering dark pink dress with white polka dots. She is barefoot and is on the heavier side. Okay, this is not what I pictured. I hate to say, but I think Zane gets his good looks from Death.

"Zane, my boy, you finally come to see me, and it's because you need something." She states, crossing her arms with a huff.

"I see you let yourself go, Mags. Yes, I'm here because I need something. Why the fuck else would I be here?" Zane retorts.

"Don't talk to me that way, boy. I birthed you." Mags spits at him.

"That's all you did, Mags. You birthed me because Death offered you a deal. Don't pretend you give a fuck. Now, are you going to help me, or do I need to go and get Death? He sent me to your door for a reason. You want to deal with him?" Zane threatens, and I watch Mags's face twist with fear and irritation.

"Fine, come in. I'd rather deal with your ornery ass than his." Mags sighs, giving in.

Well, this is going wonderful so far, I think sarcastically to myself as we enter the disorganized and disastrous place Mags calls her home. The outside looks quaint and cozy, but the inside is a hoarder's paradise. Zane looks like he's ready to attack Mags as anger swarms in his gray eyes. I've never fully seen this side of Zane. He's holding back his aura, trying not to crush Mags. Sure, I've witnessed Zane angry, but this is something else entirely.

Mags moves stuff off a round wooden table tossing the things on the table into the clutter of the rest of the house. Zane sighs, annoyed, and I see Zane roll his eyes for the first time ever. Oh, the next time he tells me not to roll my eyes, I will remind him of this moment. Zane glares at me, meaning he read my mind and didn't like my smartass comment. Zane waves his hands, causing the shadows to clean the table off, and sets three matching wooden chairs around the table that I didn't even know were there. In fairness, they probably were there, but the clutter hid them. Zane sits in one of the chairs. Mags raises an eyebrow at him.

"What? If we waited for you, it would be a century before you were done." Zane comments, crossing his arms across his chest as he leans back into the chair. Zane pissy is definitely not fun. I thought I had bad moods, but no, Zane wins this one.

Mags and I take our seats. "Well, what do you need help with?" Mags asks, putting out her cigarette in an ashtray that was on the table. I guess Zane figured she'd need it.

"Ari is my familiar. She is a lycan, and I need you to help her see her wolf spirit's memories." Zane answers.

"I figured she was your familiar. You'd only ever come to see me if she was important to you, and I know the only woman who matters to you besides Zara would be your familiar. I can do what you ask, but I must warn you, it's intense. You aren't seeing the memories. You'll be reliving them. You'll experience everything that the person did in the memories. Remember it's already happened, and you can't actually die or get hurt even if that's what happens in the memory."

My mouth gapes open as my eyes widen. Well, that's not what I expected. I just thought I'd be an observer, not reliving the memories as Sasha. At least I know nothing that happens to me in the memory is actually happening to me. Still, I'm not sure exactly what I will be reliving. I know that I have to do this no matter how unpleasant it might be. I doubt I'm going to be experiencing all the happy events. I'm expecting there to be something tragic, bad, or fuck me worthy.

"Seriously, Sasha, I've been asking you for months. You couldn't have given me a heads up about this?" I hiss angrily at her. "How bad is it? Tell me that at least."

"I never said you'd like how you got the answers, child. I simply said you'd get them. It's not rainbow and butterflies, well, it starts off that way, but it ends in tragedy. Also, don't judge me when I was just a dire wolf and not a spirit bound to someone. I killed Sasha. That's how the spirits were chosen. It was random. Whatever wolf or human killed the other, they were merged. When I killed Sasha, I was animalistic about it. I'm sorry for the pain you will feel from it, I'm sorry you will suffer through this, but you will end up with all the answers to your questions. Although heads up, you might end up with new questions." Sasha warns. Oh sure, now she gives me a heads up.

Well, fuck me, that's not what I wanted to hear. I was hoping for something a bit more encouraging, but at least Sasha gave me a heads up on something for once. Bickering between Zane and Mags breaks me from thoughts and conversations with Sasha. Zane is literally red faced and standing, pointing a finger at his mother. I'm not sure where things went wrong or why, but while I was chatting with Sasha, shit went to hell.

"Zane!" I scream, frustrated at him that he's acting like this.

I know he hates Mags for justified reasons, but I need him right now. I need him to put his shit aside for me. I'm trying to hide my fear because I'm not sure I'm ready for this. I thought I was. I was determined to get answers. I never stopped to consider how I would get them. I was so focused on the destination that I forgot about the journey. Now I'm faced with a journey I'm not sure I can handle.

Sasha said it wasn't pretty. She warned me that Sasha's death was brutal. Sasha's story started off good and ended fucked, so what does that say for me? I have her blessing from the Five, so does that mean I'm fucked too? The hard truth is I'm not so sure it's a blessing. What if it's a curse? If Sasha was so blessed by the Five, then how the fuck did her life turn to hell? All I know is that I'm about to hurt in new ways I didn't even think of yet. Oh, and the cherry on top of the ice cream sundae is that while I'm getting answers, I'm only going to end up with a new fucking set of questions to solve. Fuck my life!

Zane turns his red face to me. He looks enraged. I don't know what Mags did to trigger him, but I don't think that was wise of her. I hate that he's here dealing with her because of me. I feel guilty. However, I need him to get his shit together. Zane's enraged look melts the moment he sees me. I don't know what emotion is playing on my face at the moment. Hurt, anger, anxiety, and fear have taken hold of me. Shit, I'm trying not to cry, and I haven't even gotten to the bad shit yet. Zane comes over to me. Concern is now etched into his face.

"What is it, Ari?" He's using my real name, which means he's being serious.

"Sasha just warned me that human Sasha didn't have a happy ending, if you get my drift." My voice shakes slightly as I try to gain control of the emotions coursing through my body like a dangerous poison that has me paralyzed. I don't think I could move from this chair even if I wanted to. I am mentally glued to this chair right now.

"Shit," Zane turns to Mags. "Is there a way I can see the memories too?" Zane asks. That's when I realize he's going to try and do this with me. Relaxing slightly now that I have Zane focused back on me and at my side, I feel better. Damn, I do need him. I don't know what that says about me, and right now, I don't care.

"Yes, but it's a bit more complex. I'll have to draw symbols on the floor around where you two lay. I'll need thirteen candles. Six black, six white, and one red. Get your shadows to work, boy, because I'm not cleaning the shit up on the floor, nor am I fetching those candles." Mags demands lighting up a new cigarette.

When the fuck did she grab the lighter and cigarettes? Oh, right, I'm surrounded by magical people. See, this is when I don't like magic. It's not fair that they can just magic shit to them. Some of us have to do that shit physically, and it sucks. So yes, I'm jealous as fuck. That's something I never thought I'd be. Not the jealous part. Let's face it. I'm a lycan bitch. I will fuck a bitch up if they touch Zane. I never thought I'd be jealous of someone who could do magic. That's new, and I'm not sure how I feel about it. Right now, it doesn't matter, so I dismiss the thoughts and focus on Mags and Zane, who are back to bickering. I growl, gaining Zane's attention to let him know of my displeasure. Although I'm sure my face is twisted in a scowl, so he knows.

Zane clears his throat and then goes about manipulating his shadows. Mags looks away from him, so he doesn't see her snicker. Mags thinks he's whipped, and that's why she thinks his reaction is funny. Zane is definitely not whipped, and he very much wears the pants of this relationship. I am totally okay with that. It's how I like it. I don't know what it is, but fuck, I love that he's an alpha male. I might be a crazy lycan bitch, but I like to be tamed. Zane reacted that way because he is trying to keep on task for me.

He's trying to support me while not losing his shit on Mags. Of course, in what I can only assume is classic Mags fashion, she is not making it easy for him. This makes me love him even more. He's proving once more that he cares and loves me. I am important to him.

I think about Zane, choosing to think about happy things and not the daunting task ahead of me. How he's being amazing and how fucking glad I am that he is mine. I don't know who chose me to be Zane's familiar, but I'm sure as hell glad they did. Once again, my mind goes to us having a family. Seriously, what's wrong with me? I've never thought so much about having kids and a family in my life. Is this because I suppressed that want for so long that it's coming back tenfold? It seems absurd that it keeps popping into my head, and at the same time, it doesn't. Damn it! Now I'm confused.

Zane finally finishes cleaning the room and ends up cleaning up the whole house. Is that what took so long? The thirteen candles are on the table with black looking chalk. I assume that's what Mags needs to draw whatever she needs around us. Zane offers me his hand, and I take it. He holds my hand tight as we walk to the living room space that is completely cleared out at the moment.

"You're not alone, Ari." Zane kisses me briefly before we lay down on the floor.

Mags starts to draw around us with the black chalk looking thing. "Few things. One, Zane, you are just observing. Only Ari is reliving the memories as Sasha," Lucky bastard, I think to myself. "Two, Ari, you will feel everything as if it is happening to you, but it won't affect your physical body even if it feels like it is. You will have some control over your thoughts while you relive the memories, so try to remind yourself it's not real." Easy for Mags to say. "You two will wake up from the memories when you are done seeing everything you are meant to see. Your wolf spirit will be in control to show you what you're meant to see. She won't be able to interact with either of you. Think of her as a guide you cannot see."

Fuck, magic is complex. I'm so glad I don't have to worry about it. Mags begins setting up the candles. The black and white candles are alternated around us while the red candle is placed between our heads. Mags steps out of the circle as she kneels by our heads. Mags places one hand on my forehead and the other on Zane's forehead. As Mags begins to chant, Zane squeezes my hand one more time to let me know he is with me. Damn, do I love him, but I can't focus on that. I can't concentrate on anything. My thoughts become overwhelming jumbled as I fade into the darkness around me.

CHAPTER 17
Zane

My mind is blank at first. Then I come to a scene of a little blonde girl in a simple cream colored dress. She must be about ten or so. This must be Sasha. It's strange to be in someone else's memories as an observer. It's like watching a movie while watching it be filmed. It's strange, and I'm not sure I can compare it to anything else. It must be even weirder for Ari.

I watch little Sasha go to an altar in her village, where she places offerings to the Five. She prays to them, asking for her village to be protected, for her family to be healthy, and for the happiness of her village. It's pure, sweet, and innocent. The scene shifts to an older Sasha who is in a clearing. To the right is her village. To the left, it's a crazy wild forest with dangerous looking mountains.

Sasha places white candles in a circle in the center of the clearing. She prays to the Five and blesses the space as sacred. She's now a type of human priestess who serves the Five. Sasha devoted her life to serving the Five. I watch her serve her village with grace as she is the leader's daughter. A princess in many ways, as her father is basically a king. Sasha is filled with purity and grace as she serves her village while serving the Five.

The scene shifts once more, and Sasha is now before the Five on the sacred land that she claimed for them. Her goal was to build a temple in the clearing so that her village could pay their tributes to the Five. This is back in a time when the

Five wanted to be worshiped. They wanted sacrifices, gifts, and devoted followers who served them all. The Five stand before Sasha as they collectively bless her with the gift of foresight and premonitions.

Sasha is so humble she has a hard time accepting the gift. In the end, she accepts it. They tell her that her gift will help her protect and serve her village. The humble princess accepts and goes home. Sasha has premonitions every night. She uses them to do precisely what she should do with them. At first, I'm not sure how this turns bad as Sasha is now in her early twenties, happily blessed while serving both her village and the Five.

Then I see the problem. Her village doesn't think she is actually blessed. They dismiss her premonitions no matter how often they come true. She warns them, and most don't listen to her. They only seem to listen or care when it's something positive. As soon as Sasha predicts something negative, they call her crazy. She is slightly shunned from her village for her blessing. It's a little sad to watch how she tries in vain to help the people she cares about, but they don't care for her.

About a year after she is blessed, the dire wolves come from the wild side of the territory, attacking the villagers. Sasha's father becomes enraged and wants to kill all the dire wolves to end the threat. That's what he does: he sends out hunters to kill the dire wolves, and they kill some, which only fuels the fire of rage in the dire wolves. It goes on like this: the two sides picking each other off slowly. It's tedious to watch the terror games that unfold between the two. It's strange. The dire wolves are different. They can think for themselves. They are animals, but very intelligent ones. The two sides wage war against one another as they begin to fight for the land that separates their territories. It's the land that Sasha blessed for the Five. Her temple hasn't been built yet, as her father refuses her.

The Five are enraged with the war being waged between the Hunter's Moon Village and the dire wolves. Sasha has a premonition that both sides will be cursed by the Five if they continue the war and go to the final battle for a land that is not theirs to claim. Once more, Sasha is dismissed as a crazy person. Sasha pleads with her father as he is dressing for the battle not to go. In his anger and determination, he has Sasha locked in her room so that she can't stop him.

Sasha falls to the floor, defeated and devastated at what is about to come her way. After sulking for a bit. She finds the will to break out of her room. She begins to do everything she can to find a way out of her room. The sounds of war echo in the background. Vicious howls are heard in the distance as war screams from the warriors respond to the howls. It's intense to hear, so I can't imagine what the battlefield looks like.

Finally, after many ideas and attempts, Sasha finds a way to pick her door lock. Sasha barrels out of her room and outside only to find the village is partially on fire. The dire wolves have made it to the village. Sasha runs to the battlefield on the sacred land as she doges wolves trying to attack and falling debris from the war that is waged around her. Her determination to make it to the field before it's too late is impressive.

However, it's already happening when Sasha makes it to the field. The humans and dire wolves merge as they kill one another. Sasha watches her father be torn apart. Death and destruction surround her as the curse is being casted on those she loves. The sun begins to rise as Sasha stands in the center of the battle as the screams fade away.

"Too many have fallen is this is ending to what we have begun. Will we remember what we have done wrong?" Sasha asks aloud just as a dire wolf that I would know anywhere approaches Sasha snapping her jaws.

Sasha accepting her fate closes her eyes and breathes in deeply, apologizing to the Five for failing them. The dire wolf that I know as Sasha attacks human Sasha with such viciousness it's hard for me to watch. I'm the son of Death, and even I'm having a hard time watching Sasha's death. I can only imagine the pain Ari is feeling right now, and I wish I could take it from her. The dire wolf shredSasha's stomach with her impossibly sharp claws causing Sasha to scream as she falls to the ground. Blood spills from her wound along with what appears to be intestines. The dire wolf snaps her jaws around Sasha's right arm, causing her arm to break in half as it dangles. The wolf then slashes her back with her claws as Sasha falls forward. When Sasha looks up at the dire wolf drenched in blood and guts, the wolf snaps her neck with her jaws, killing Sasha as the two merge into one body.

Soon everyone is healed, alive, but they are all cursed. Sasha is allowed to keep her gift. However, Sasha is distraught at her failure to pay attention to her dreams now. She doesn't think she is worthy of the gift and begs the Five to take it from her, but they never do. Sasha leaves her village, not fully realizing what she has become. She knew that she would be cursed to be a lycan, but she didn't know anything else about the curse.

The scene shifts to a seemingly happy Sasha who married a human. They have two children together. Sasha accidentally created werewolves when she mated with a human. Sasha and her husband get a surprise when they are in a town. It took her years to find her human husband. However, now there are many more lycans because lycans have fated mates and have reproduced. Lycans were never supposed to mate outside their race, but Sasha didn't know this.

    Sasha's fated mate, an alpha of her old village, which is now a pack, finds Sasha with her husband and children. Furious that Sasha betrayed him by mating with another, he kills her husband. He banishes the children and leaves them as rouges. The children are in their teens when this happens. Sasha's fated mate captures her and forces her to be his mate. He rapes her until she is pregnant and repeats the process after giving birth. He rapes her enough that she has six pups for him. Sasha is depressed. She hates her fated mate and misses her husband, who she was deeply in love with. She misses her two older children, who she worries about constantly, that she can barely take care of the children she was forced to have.

    Fate is pretty pissed at this rate as he whines and complains to Sasha about how she has caused him issues. Fate has to essentially create wolf spirits for the werewolves so that they can transform. It's a cluster fuck, and Fate is annoyed as fuck. He's also irritated that Sasha ignores her premonitions as they come from him. He's angry, and he curses her to age slowly so she can see the destruction she has caused.

    Due to her slow aging, Sasha watches her children grow up while wondering what happened to her older children. Years pass, and her oldest pup from her fated mate is now in charge of the pack. However, the werewolves that have now been created from Sasha's first children are causing issues. They are killing and taking out whole packs. Sasha's child, who is leading the pack, knows they are coming for their pack and Sasha.

    Now Sasha is faced with another war, but this time she caused it when she ignored her gift from the Five. If she hadn't ignored it, she would have seen this happening. She would have known about fated mates. Once again, Sasha finds herself in the middle of the war on the sacred land. Sasha has fully aged at this point. She must be in her eighties at this point. She's weak and frail, but that doesn't stop her. Sasha stands in the middle of the battle, somehow untouched by the war around her. Sasha falls to her knees.

"Oh mighty and great Five, I have failed you once more. I have no right to ask this, but I want to correct what I have done wrong. I ask that you curse werewolves and lycans to change only on a full moon as they clearly can't handle the freedom of transformation. I also ask that you take away fated mates to avoid another war." Sasha pleads.

The Five grant her request. However, the damage had been done. The werewolves won the war and took over the first pack to ever be created. Sasha is forced to watch as the Hunter's Moon pack is turned into the Blood Moon pack. Lycans are demoted to omegas and treated almost like slaves. It's hard to watch, and for the first time, I get a glimpse of what Ari's life might have been like in her pack.

Sasha leaves and goes back to her home she had with her human husband. Now, she has had many children and many descendants on both the werewolf and lycan sides. She is over a hundred now, and her life is coming to an end. Sasha lays in bed resting. She has one final dream before she passes. One day a savior will come, and that savior will have Sasha as their wolf spirit. Sasha's spirit is never recycled like the rest of the spirits. Lycans get dire wolf spirits, and werewolves get the made up wolf spirits. Fate recycles the spirits, wiping their minds before he sends them back. It was the only way that he didn't constantly have to make new spirits. The savior will unite werewolves and lycans as they should have been. The savior will have Sasha's blessing of premonitions to help guide the savior. Sasha's dream ends with a flash of Ari's face. Ari is the savior.

The Coven of the Crow and Shadows: Legacy

Everything goes black again before I feel myself wake from the spell. Fuck, that was crazy to watch. I look over at Ari, who slowly sits up. "Are you okay, Pet?" I know she's not, but I have to ask.

Ari shakes her head. "That was hard. Her death was so painful. She was blessed and then cursed. What a mess," She sighs deeply. She looks into my eyes. "I'm the savior. How the hell am I supposed to unite lycans and werewolves? Does that mean there are more lycans than everyone thinks? How does Sage fit into this mess?"

"It will be alright. We will start looking into Sasha's descendants. Maybe Sage and you fit into the puzzle that way? Fate likes to do shit like that, so it wouldn't surprise me. Even if that's not it, we will figure it out. My guess is there are more lycans. I just don't know where they are. Once again, I will help you. I have many resources. We can head back to the coven's realm as they have a large library there with records of families from all over. One way we keep track of souls is through lineage. We will start there." I assure her.

Ari is minutes away from breaking down. I can't imagine how painful it was to experience that type of death, not to mention the abuse and rape. That couldn't have been easy for Ari, given her history with her old pack Alpha, who I still want to murder for thinking he could touch Ari like that. I stand first and help a shaky Ari up. The second she is standing, she embraces me. Her arms wrap around my waist, and she puts her head on my chest. Wrapping my arms around her, I start to rub her back.

The conflicting emotions she is feeling are evident. I'm not sure how long we stand there. Mags surprisingly keeps her mouth shut. She walked off the minute we woke up. Now she is in the kitchen making herself tea. I know Sasha warned Ari it was bad, but I didn't think it would be that intense. I won't lie. Some of it was hard to watch, which means it must have been even harder to relive. Poor Ari, I wish she didn't have to go through this. The only thing I can do for her is comfort and support her.

Part of me fears she will go back to reclusing from me like she did when she first came with me. We've made significant progress with our relationship. I don't want to go backward, not after we have come so far and the challenges we had to face to get to this point. Ari only ended up with more questions and a fucking quest. Damn, do I hate destiny quests. Somehow, I have a feeling this ties into the war that a group of anti-human supernaturals is threatening. I'm not sure how it all ties together, but we will figure it out. If anything, I'll have to pay Death a visit. If he won't help, then I'll go to Fate. I will do what I have to get the answers we need. I won't let Ari fail at her quest. Failure isn't an option.

After some time, Ari calms down enough for us to leave. We thank Mags as shadows come around us. I take us back to the cabin to let Ari have some time to process before we head back to my realm. Ari takes a hot shower while I figure out something for us to eat. I know she says she doesn't have an appetite, but she has to eat. She needs to keep up her strength. I am worried about Ari. I know I can help her with her quest, but I can't help her process the information. It was a lot and varying degrees of bad and good.

Of all the people, Ari is meant to unite the werewolves and lycans. I'm not sure why she was chosen for something like this, but she was. Fate never does anything without reason, and it's usually a damn good one. All I know is that Ari is going to need me during this. Things definitely just got more stressful. Now we have two things to focus on, and both are equally complex. Too many questions with not enough answers. I can only hope Fate was kind enough to make our two missions become one because that would be fantastic. As far as I know, both Ari and I are on his good side, so I have to trust he won't fuck us over.

Ari settles at the table while I lay out the food. While she was in the shower, I ran and got her BBQ pulled pork sandwiches, mac and cheese, coleslaw, and pecan pie, complete with iced tea. She smiles when she sees what I got her. I'm not a good cook. Ari surprised me with the fact that she knew how to cook, but then she told me she had to learn because her mother never had time. I never realized how much her parents neglected her. Ari didn't have an easy time given what she's told me and what I know about pack life. Once again, I'm grateful to Blaine and Zara for the family life they have given me. Seeing Mags today reminds me that my life could have been hell. Death did me a favor when he gave me to the Shadow family. Death might be a bastard, but even he cares when it comes down to it. Unfortunately, he doesn't show it often.

Making our plates with food, we stay quiet as both of us try to process things. Ari still looks torn between a mental breakdown involving a lot of crying or she looks like she is about to burn the world to ash and dust. I'm not sure which one is the lesser of the two evils. I want to be there for her, but I'm not entirely sure how. I may have fucked my fair share of women, but I was never in relationships with them. The relationship part is new to me like it is for Ari. Neither of us knows what the fuck we are doing. We both are just winging it and hoping for the fucking best. At least we are trying. We will find a grove that works for us. It's just going to take some trial and error to get there.

Thankfully, Blaine and Zara are always available for relationship advice. They know how to make things work and find that balance between being a couple and knowing who you are individual. They have had their fair share of trials and errors. Cade and Blair have gone to them for advice in the past. Blair and Cade have only been together for a few years now. They are still finding their footing. Ari and I have plenty of people who will help us. Ari is a part of my family, even if she hasn't fully realized it yet. Acceptance is hard for her since she has been either neglected or used by others. I believe she will see it at some point. I also know we will do whatever we can to make her feel like she belongs with us.

"Thank you for being there for me today, Zane. It meant a lot to me. I knew whatever I faced in the memories. I'd be okay because you were there with me. I'm sorry I'm adding to your already heavy load." Ari says with her head lowered, picking at her food with her fork. She ate about half her food. I know she can eat more than that.

"Ari, you aren't adding to my plate. I'm more than happy to put everything else aside and help you. You come first. You are all that matters. I'll always be there for you, just like I know you will be there for me. Luck is on our side. We have favor with the Five. You have a blessing. I'm the son of Death. We can handle it. If Fate is kind, our separate things will become one thing." I state, which gets her looking at me like I'm her entire world. It fucking does something to me that I can't fully explain it.

"I love you, Zane, a lot. I wasn't living before I met you. I think you are my real blessing from the Five and that Sasha's blessing is just coincidence because I'm the savior." She beams a loving smile at me. Her words wrap around me, filling me with a love I don't fully understand but will spend forever trying to figure it out.

"I love you too, Ari. You are my greatest reward out of everything I will ever gain in this life. It looks like Death did me a solid when he picked you for me. I always thought it was Fate, but nope, father dear had a say. I'm glad he picked you."

"I'm glad he picked me too. So are you ready to go home?" She asks with a smile.

"Yes, but I have enjoyed this alone time together. We might have to get our own apartment in the mansion. Blaine and Zara have one. Blair and Cade haven't asked for theirs yet. There are apartments within the mansion. We'd have our own kitchen, bedrooms for us and our kids, a living room, a spare room that we can use for whatever. All in one place. I think we need to be able to have something like this at home." I suggest which has Ari nodding her head up and down.

"Yes, please, Zane. I'd really like that."

"Alright, I'll make it happen when we get back. We'll spend one more night here, and then tomorrow, we head back home. As much as I want to play house with you and shut everything out, we have work to do." I state with a pained face. Ari nods her head in agreement.

I would love to play house with her. Have her cook dinners for us and our little family. Have family nights and do fun things. There's a lot I want to do with Ari. As much as I love what I do, I also want to have simple things like a family. I want to enjoy my family and raise my kids in a good home while helping with the coven. I know kids mean less fieldwork for Ari and most likely me too. I'm sure Zara will love to watch the kids while Ari and I do small missions. I know Ari loves the field as much as I do, and giving it up full-time just isn't an option either of us like at the moment.

We have a group of terrorist supernaturals to take down and figure out how to finish Ari's destiny quest. It will be rough, but I have no doubt we can handle it. Ari and I are stronger than ever right now. Ari proved just now that we are strengthening our bond and relationship. We love each other even if we are still new at this. Soulmates are soulmates, and there's no denying the pull to each other. Now I know why Zara and Blaine always feel like they can conquer the world together. I understand it now, and it's simple. They love each other, and they use it to unite them in everything, even if it's difficult. Whatever is to come, Ari and I will face it together because that's what soulmates do.

CHAPTER 18
Ari

We've been back in the coven's realm for about a week now. It was easier to get back into the swing of things here than I thought it would be. I had come to miss the creepy realm. It still weirds me out, but it's home. I'm safe here. Best of all, I'm accepted here. Zane has already started making arrangements for us to get an apartment. I'm not sure if it's something that is built and added to the mansion or if it's already built. I don't know, but I don't care because we get our own place either way.

While coming back was easier, I'm struggling to process stuff. I'm overly moody and irritable. My anxiety is sky high so much, so my appetite has been all wonky. Certain foods make me want to barf my guts up. It's weird, but the smell or sight of eggs suddenly makes me want to hurl. I've been a little nauseous but not throwing up, thankfully. I've also been more tired lately like I can't get enough sleep. My mind doesn't ever seem like it wants to rest. I toss and turn. It's gotten to a point where Zane has offered to make me a sleeping potion. I've denied it for now because I'm stubborn and apparently like to punish myself for unknown reasons.

Today is our first day back to training, but it's not trainees this time. It's with the family. I'm slowly starting to feel like family to the Shadows. It's nice to have a family, even if I'm having a hard time fully accepting the fact that I have one now. Zane and I have spent the last week in the library researching shit and going over reports in the field, looking for hints that something is going on. So far, things have been quiet. We've had a hard time fully tracking Sasha's descendants. It's doable. It just might take time which sucks. I hate having so many missing pieces of the puzzle, and the frustrating part is I can feel how close we are. Like any day now, the puzzle will complete itself, and we will finally see the whole picture.

Zane decided we should take a break and do some training. After all, we do need to keep in shape. We don't know when we might have to go back out to the field. Since the trainees graduated and there isn't a new class yet. The rest of our family decided to join us. It will be fun to see everyone in action. I've only seen Zane and Zara, so I'm curious to see about the others.

The six of us make our way to the outdoor training field. We are dressed in our standard training clothes. I'm looking forward to training. I need to stretch my muscles and burn off some of the anxious energy. Maybe then I'll sleep tonight and not drive Zane crazy. I know he's a few nights away from telling me I'm taking a sleeping potion, whether I like it or not. Maybe this will help. I have to hope it does because I need sleep. I'm far too tired. Even right now, as much as I'm looking forward to training, I'm slightly dreading it because of how tired I am. I keep getting these hot flashes as well, which help nothing. I need to get my shit together because I have important shit to do. I don't have time for fucking anxiety and mental breakdowns.

I'm fairly certain that destiny quests don't involve me losing my shit at every turn and cracking at the seams. I'm not sure why the hell I got chosen for such a quest. I get it. Human Sasha fucked up pretty hard when she accidentally created werewolves. It's hard to believe that she changed everyone's future when she had us double cursed by making us only able to transform on a full moon and took away fated mates. It makes sense that they once existed. Supernaturals aren't meant to mate with humans or other supernaturals, for that matter. Not saying hybrids don't exist because they do, but they are rare. Werewolves are technically a hybrid as they are part lycan and part human. As far as I know, werewolves are the only hybrid race to exist.

Sasha was so upset that no one was listening to her that they were chalking her gift up to craziness. They ignored her premonitions, and it hurt Sasha that they did this. However, she ignored her gift just like her village did because she didn't think she deserved it. I think part of her was also upset that she failed at stopping the war that caused her to lose her way in life.

Focusing on training, I push the overwhelming thoughts away. To warm-up, we run laps before doing some hand-on-hand exercises. Then the couples pair off, running their individual drills for a bit. Zara transforms first. I always forget how impressive she is in her gargoyle form. Zara's skin turns to gray stone like a thick layer of impenetrable armor. Her wings are enormous and have pointed ends at the top and bottom. Her feet and hands are claw-like and incredibly sharp. Her ears are pointed, and I've always been slightly afraid to ask if they are sharp. Zara's gargoyle form is fierce and highly intimidating. I would not want to have to fight her in a battle. I've fought her in training, and she can kick ass easily.

Zara and Blair practice in their alternate forms while I try to get Sasha to transform, but she refuses. Damn difficult wolf can't give me a freaking break. Sasha always has to be difficult with something. Usually, she is withholding information or something along those lines, but right now, she is being a pain in the ass with transformation, which makes no sense because she loves to train with Zane. I don't know what the fuck her problem is, but enough time has passed now that Zara and Blair are already back in human form.

"Come on. Pet let Sasha out. I need to run some drills with her." Zane commands. I don't like his tone. I feel like he's implying I'm the one who isn't shifting which irritates me. He always seems to assume I'm the one who's always being difficult.

"Okay," I reply, trying to hide my irritation.

"Alright, Sasha, come on, girl, I need you to perk your ass up. You like performing for our master. You're making me look bad and upsetting Zane by not transforming."

"No, I'm not letting you transform. You can't." Sasha replies to my thoughts.

"Why the fuck not?" I ask as my irritation rises.

"You'll figure it out soon enough."

I want to curse Sasha out for her bullshit, but Zane yelling at me to run towards him and shift mid-way has me focused on him. I tell Sasha to stop her shit and transform. I'm not in the mood for games with anyone right now. I just want to do things right and make Zane happy. After being out in the field, he's fucking right training is important, and we have to be able to do things correctly in the field.

Running towards Zane, the shadows come around me. Sasha doesn't shift. She refuses. I try to force it, but she holds strong against me. What the fucking hell? I don't understand why she is acting like this. She's been a bitch in the past, but this pushes it to a whole new level of bitch that I don't like. Confused by my lack of shifting, the shadows disappear from around me. I stumble to the ground, distracted by Sasha's bullshit and trying to force the shift.

"What the hell, Ari? Why are you not shifting? This isn't the time for fucking games because you're in a bad mood." Zane scolds.

I growl at him as he comes over to me. I'm well aware that I'm about to make a scene that will probably get me in trouble, but to hell with it. He wants to accuse me of shit. Then I have no problem being the difficult bitch he thinks I'm being. Zane forgets that two can play that game. I know he's used to winning, but that doesn't mean I won't put up a fight on his path to victory.

"Stop always fucking assuming it's me being difficult because it's not. Sasha is refusing to let me shift!" I scream, which gains everyone's attention.

Blair and Zara come over with smirks on their faces as if my words entertain them. It's almost as if I gave something away that I didn't realize I gave away. Something I said clearly gained their attention immediately. Meanwhile, Blaine and Cade act like I totally didn't just snap at Zane.

"Why the fuck not?" Zane asks as he stomps right in front of me and offers me his hand.

"I don't know. She won't tell me. She's being fucking cryptic again." I reply, taking his hand as he helps me stand.

"I don't think they've figured it out," Blair comments to Zara.

"No, they haven't. Let me try to help them. So, exactly how much fun did you two have in the field?" Zara questions with a smirk. The four of them snicker like they know something we don't.

"What?" Both Zane and I reply simultaneously with the same puzzled look on our faces.

"Okay, let me try. Ari, what's the number one rule for all female shifters?" Blair prompts

"Never shift when you are...fuck!" I scream as it clicks in my brain what they are trying to get us to realize.

"Are you saying Ari is pregnant?" Zane asks in disbelief.

"Why else would Sasha not let her shift? Not only that, but Ari is clearly different. She's more tired. I see you avoid certain foods and the face you make when you smell certain foods, Ari. I know those looks. I had them when I was pregnant with Cade. Food aversions and fatigue are all very common symptoms of pregnancy. I know morning sickness is the big one everyone always thinks about, but there are plenty of other symptoms. Time to make an appointment with the coven's doctor." Zara states with a bit of glee in her voice. I'm sure she wants grandkids.

Zane and I look at each other, both of us in shock. We never used protection. How did we not use protection? We've been talking about kids and having a family, but we agreed after solving everything. Definitely not now. What were we thinking? I guess we weren't thinking. A child isn't a bad thing, just not something I thought would happen so quickly. Judging by Zane's expression, he is also thrilled but concerned.

"Ari, we should go see the doctor. We need to confirm this. If you are pregnant, you can not leave this realm. You have enemies in the human realm. Sage wants you for some unknown reason, and she isn't going to stop, you know that. Our child has to be our top priority over everything." Zane voices his concern.

"I know," I reply quietly, realizing what I thought was my body responding to my anxiety was really pregnancy.

I'm a shifter. I'm probably going to start showing soon. Shifters give birth between five and seven months. I can tell that lycans give birth around five months from Sasha's memories. That's why Sasha said I'd figure it out. Damn it! This is not what we need right now, but I can't deny that a part of me is happy. I guess my mind and body were trying to let me know that I was pregnant. I want to ask how this happened, but I know exactly how it happened. I'm thinking now: why did we never think of using protection?

Zane and I head to see the coven doctor. I didn't realize there was a medical wing in the mansion, but it is fucking huge. It's five stories high and must be the size of a block in a major city. I feel like the damn thing just gets bigger every time I see it. It probably does because fucking magic. It makes sense there would be a medical wing. I still have so much to see and learn about this mansion, but also this realm. As strange as this realm is, it has grown on me. I didn't think I'd ever get used to living here, but I have. I still prefer the human realm, but I know I'm not necessarily safe there. At least here, I know I'm safe. Plus, our family is here.

Making our way through the maze that is the coven manor, we end up in the healing wing. It looks like a mini hospital floor. There are hospital beds divided by curtains, a few rooms with sliding doors, and a huge desk in the center of the room filled with nurses. Apparently, some of the coven's wives are nurses, teachers, and other things the coven needs help with. A blonde hair short female nurse sees us and immediately rushes over to us.

"Master Zane, how can I help you today? I'm Sally" The nurse's tone is polite and sweet.

"My familiar needs to confirm pregnancy." Zane answers.

"Oh, well, that's exciting. Come with me. I'll get you set up in a room. Dr. Grant will see you today. He's very knowledgeable when it comes to shifter pregnancies." Sally informs us as we follow her to one of the rooms with sliding doors.

Sally lays out a gown for me to change into, which I do as she grabs supplies. Once I'm changed, I climb onto the hospital bed and get myself situated. Sally draws blood and asks me some questions like how I've been feeling and if I can remember my last period. The problem is shifter's periods are wonky, and most of us have a type of heat that would be equal to ovulation, but like on crack. I don't recall having a heat, but then again, I wasn't really focused on that. My mind was occupied with other shit to even know if I was in heat. I did have a week of extreme horniness, so that could have been it. I'm trying to recall if there were other symptoms of heat, but I can't. Damn it.

Zane holds my hand in his while Sally pokes and prods me to get what she needs. Sally announces that Dr. Grant will be in shortly to review my test results. Sally dismisses herself and leaves us. The reality that I'm pregnant hits me. I know I am. Looking over at Zane, his expression is filled with concern. I feel bad that I'm adding more to his ever growing plate of shit to deal with. Granted, it does take two to make a baby, but it's an added complication. Now isn't the time for a baby when I'm on a freaking destiny quest, and Zane is tasked with stopping a dangerous group of supernaturals.

Then Zane's words come back to me. I won't be able to leave this realm till I give birth. As much as I don't want to be on lockdown like that, I know it's needed. This realm can only be entered or left by someone of the coven. The coven members can't betray the coven. Zane explained it once. There is some type of loyal blood bond that makes it impossible to betray the coven or Death. If you try, you die before you can even get away with it. With a target painted on my back, I have to stay here.

We still have no idea why Sage wants me. I assume it has something to do with restoring fated mates since she never shut the fuck up about it. I also assume she wants to be able to transform whenever again. I can't blame her on that one. It is nice to transform when you want. Still, I'm not sure how I fit into her plan. I imagine Sage has to have some idea of who I am. Does she want me because I'm the savior? If that's the case, is it a good thing or a bad thing? Oh, who am I kidding? It's a bad thing. I haven't figured out why.

Not only that, but we can't risk anyone finding out about my pregnancy. Our enemies might target our child, and that's even worse. Staying in this realm is the only thing I can do. Oh well, at least it will give me some time to figure shit out with my destiny quest and Sage. Sage is a daughter of the beta, so that means she knows the pack's true history. It would make sense for her to know about a savior. This is stressful, and I doubt it's good for the baby, but I can't help myself. My brain is in overdrive as I can't seem to stop it. Endless thoughts swarm in my head.

Dr. Grant walks in with a clipboard. He's about the same age as Blaine, with groomed short gray hair and completely clean shaven. He bows his head to Zane and then looks between us with a smile. "You are indeed expecting. I'd say you're approaching the month marker even if you most likely conceived a few weeks ago. I expect to see your pregnancy picking up, and you'll start showing soon. The first month is usually slow. Then by the end of the second month, things start to excel rapidly. It will be wise for you to have weekly visits considering the father is…." He trails off, trying to find words. I can tell he doesn't want to insult Zane.

"Because I'm a demigod of death. I understand your concern. As far as I know, Ari's pregnancy should follow a normal shifter pregnancy." Zane fills in the blanks for the doctor.

"Good to know. Still, Ari should be seen every other week at a minimum with how quickly shifter pregnancy progresses. I'll give you a list of vitamins to take. You need to rest, eat proper meals, and no hardcore training. Light training is fine, although I suspect that you won't want to do much training by the end of the third month. All the tests look good, so for now, I will send you off with vitamins. Come back in a few weeks or beforehand if you need to."

"Thank you. Dr. Grant." Zane states as the doctor leaves. "You okay, Pet?" He asks as I get out of the bed to change.

"Zane, we are having a baby. How could we have not thought about using protection? Don't get me wrong, I'm thrilled, but even you have to admit this is poor timing." I feel like I'm about to burst into tears. Oh great, now I get to deal with crazy pregnancy hormones.

"I know. I was always so in the moment that I never thought about protection. Part of me wonders if it would have mattered. If you were meant to get pregnant, it wouldn't have mattered if we used protection or not. I'm not sure why you got pregnant so quickly. I guess it's a good thing I put in for our apartment already."

I laugh at his comment. "Well, since I'm off hardcore training, maybe I should focus on our research. Sage was obsessed with soulmates and if she knows the pack's history, she knows Sasha is the one who took that away. I don't know, maybe there is something there, I don't know, but it's a theory." I suggest as I get dressed.

Zane agrees that I should stick to researching. My gut tells me I'm on the right path, so it's only a matter of time before I figure it out. I also make Zane aware that I agree with him that I can't leave our realm. Our baby is too important. I need to be safe in order to keep our baby safe. Hopefully, whatever we have to do can wait till then. There is still a good amount to figure out for both issues.

While pregnancy was something I didn't think would happen for a while, I can't deny the part of me that is happy it's happening now. Zane is being supportive, but even he is thrown off by the pregnancy. Neither of us is upset about it. We are happy to have a baby. It's the timing that I think has us both on edge. Now doesn't seem like a great time, especially with a giant target on my back. Zane is right, Sage won't stop coming for me. Whatever she needs me for is important to her, and she won't stop till she has me in clutches.

Deciding I want a long nap, Zane takes me back to our room. He tells me to rest while he goes to handle some business. I know his job never stops. I feel bad that I can't help to the full extent like I wanted to be able to do. Pregnancy will limit me, and I can also tell Zane is going to baby me. I wanted to help him with his burdens, not add to them. At least I can handle most of the research while Zane does the things I can't. We are a team, and we will find a way to balance this all. I have to believe that we can handle this, even if it feels a little impossible.

In his confident fashion, Zane seems to think our separate missions will become one giant one. At least Zane believes Fate will throw us a bone and help us out with this cluster fuck of situations. The only happy thing is that we are going to have a baby. Knowing I need to get some sleep, I let my mind wander to happy thoughts about our family. What it will be like to have this experience now that it's here. Happy that I have Zane with me every step of the way. Life might have just become more complex, but hey, I always wanted an adventure. It looks like Fate gave me one, after all. At least I don't have to do it alone because I have a fantastic soulmate and his wonderful family in my corner. It's nice to feel like I'm not alone for once. It gives me the support and confidence I need to know that I can do this because I can do this. It helps to have people around you willing to walk through the shadows of the journey with you. It helps that most of them control the shadows.

CHAPTER 19
Sage

Liam and I are meeting with the boss today. I hope she isn't a total bitch today. Our boss is a bitch, but she is the one who is going to make the realm belong to only the supernaturals. The humans are weak and take up too much space. They fear us and would have every supernatural killed if they could. They are worthless beings that serve no purpose. Not even the vampires have use for them anymore, well, the ones that are left, that is. Humans convinced supernaturals to help them hunt vampires, saying they were a danger to their race. Once I kill Ari and break the curses on my people, we will be strong enough to help the boss achieve her goal of a humanless world.

As Liam parks the car outside the cute cottage, I notice Ghost pull up on his crotch rocket. That idiot, I can't believe Zane pulled a fast one on him. Ari and Zane fucked up the plan badly. Those humans were supposed to die. It was supposed to be the spark that lit the war, but instead, Zane and Ari sabotaged us.

When Ari asked to meet at the club, I was surprised. She was never one for such things. I had tried countless times to get her to come to parties, clubs, and other big social events, but it was a struggle. Most of the time, she would decline with some lame excuse. It was hard being her friend. She was clingy and needy. Ari made it hard to be friends with others because she always seemed to have some crises going on. She's a hot mess and has been most of her life. Mommy and daddy neglecting her did a pretty little number on her. It's what makes her so clingy and needy. I guess Zane likes that.

Zane is a complication I wish I could erase. He's more powerful than I imagined. I knew he was powerful because he was friends with Liam. Liam warned me Zane was powerful, but I thought Liam was exaggerating. He wasn't. Even Liam didn't know Zane was that powerful, nor did we know he was a necromancer. I know necromancers are real and that they only come from Zane's coven. Our boss knows a lot about him. I didn't realize the extent of his power. Watching him save all those people while he simultaneously put Ghost in his place was sobering.

I've known Ghost for a few years now, and he isn't one to bow to someone else, but he did for Zane. Ghost is deathly afraid of Zane now and has been trying to back out of our cause since then. I'm not sure how the boss will handle his sudden interest to leave. It depends on her mood. Liam and I get out of the car and head up the stone path to her door. The cottage is adorable, but the inside is a hot mess.

Ghost toes behind us. There is nothing but awkward silence as this will be a shitty meeting. We failed our mission. The boss is going to be pissed. Hell, I'm pissed at us. Ghost failed at killing the humans, and I failed at getting Ari. I was going to play nice, invite her out privately for a girl's day, then I would abduct her, but the bitch just had to find her claws. I have to admit I was surprised when Ari told me off. I never thought she'd have that in her. For years I manipulated her and made her my little puppet. I had her under my thumb, an obedient bitch.

Being with Zane has brought out her confidence. I always knew if Ari realized her full potential as a lycan, she wouldn't need me anymore. I kept her weak, but Zane is undoing all of that. I knew letting my brother take advantage of her would increase her confidence, so I made sure he only used her. The idiot had real feelings for her. He wanted Ari to be his mate. So I sabotaged it. I got my stupid brother to use her by seeing she was dirty and he shouldn't be with her. Once I told him she was a lycan, he was disgusted by her. I needed Ari compliant, so it would be easy when it came time to kill her.

Then fucking Zane comes in, offering to help fight the lycans in exchange for Ari. Liam let Ari go like a fucking idiot. I was so close to being ready to kill her. I planned on doing it the night of my Luna ceremony. It was going to be a little gift to myself to kill Ari and finally end the curse on werewolves. Somehow that bitch escaped. Zane showed up at the right time. At least Ari wanted to keep in contact. I knew I'd have to get her back by meeting up with her. She took longer to reach out than I thought she would. I was getting worried.

As it turns out, I did have a reason to be worried. Ari moved on from our friendship like it was nothing. I couldn't believe how quickly she was over our friendship. The shock still hasn't worn off. I thought she would be so lonely and would contact me within a few weeks of leaving. That bitch ghosted me. Zane clearly upped her confidence. No doubt he turned her against me. I'm a little jealous that he gets to have Ari basically enslaved to him. She has to spend the rest of her life serving his every whim. Ari will never be free. Unfortunately, I have to kill her, which will free her from her shitty life as a familiar. I would rather watch her be forced to serve a demigod of death who no doubt treats her like shit.

Zane may pretend he cares about her. I bet she thinks he loves her. Zane doesn't love her. He's her master. He will use her for everything she is worth. She's a little pet. I saw the choker necklace she was wearing. Ari was proud to be a good bitch and wore a collar for her master. Pathetic. She might have gotten claws to use against me, but Ari is still pathetic. Even more so now that she is hopelessly in love with her master. She can't see how Zane is using her. Ari believes they are soulmates and that they love one another, but she is only under the illusion that Zane has created for her.

Approaching the door, I take a deep breath as I knock. This is going to suck balls. The door opens, and our boss stands in her oversized floral print dress. A cigarette hangs out of her mouth. "About time you idiots showed up." She states, walking away from the door.

I'm surprised when we walk in. It's clean. Holy shit, did Mags actually clean up her cottage? Ghost and Liam look equally surprised. Ghost shuts the door as we walk in further to the clean cottage. It's actually a nice cottage now that it's all cleaned up. I don't see Mags doing this herself. If she did, then things are worse than I thought. Mags is a known hoarder, and it's got to be bad for her to clean things up. Suddenly I'm a bit more anxious about this meeting. I knew it would be bad, but now I fear I've underestimated the situation again.

Mags sits at a chair around the table in the dining area. Ghost leans against the wall near us while Liam and I take seats at the table. "Looks like you finally cleaned up around here." Ghost comments.

"I didn't do shit. It was Zane."

"Wait, Zane was here? Why the hell would Zane be here?" I question.

"Zane is my son, if you fools must know. He needed my help with something for Ari. I couldn't turn him down, or else he would get suspicious. I'm the only one who is interrogating today. So you three fucked up pretty hard, it seems. How did that happen?" Mags inquires, taking a drag off her cigarette.

"It was Zane who stopped me. It was like he knew what we were planning. I don't know how he knew, but someone tipped him off. He saved all those humans. Zane is on to me, so I can't do any more shit like that till Zane isn't a problem anymore, which it's safe to assume he isn't going anywhere anytime soon." Ghost tells Mags folding his arms across his chest.

"Damn it! I don't know how Zane would have gotten tipped off. Maybe Death or Fate has something to do with it. The boy is favored by his father and Fate. The other Five adore him too. The Five will try to stop us, so it makes sense for them to send my son. He's a good little lap dog for them, especially his father. I was always nothing to Zane. Zara was the better mother, and Death, even though he was a shitty father, still got more attention and respect from Zane than I ever did. We will have to plan a bit more carefully if Zane is going to be on our asses. Damn that boy!" Mags slams her fist on the table.

"What about Ari? I can't get her alone to take her. Zane is guarding her, and she follows him like a loyal lap dog. Thanks to your son, I don't have Ari under my thumb anymore. So how the hell am I supposed to kill her if she keeps evading me?" I'm trying not to snap at Mags, but it's hard.

"I can get Zane to bring her back here. The problem is getting him to leave long enough so that you can take Ari. Zane is protective over her, so getting him to leave her with me will be tricky. We might have to knock Zane out if he won't leave. I need the girl dead so you werewolves can fight at full capacity when the war comes. Figures the lycan we need to break the curse is the one fated to my son as a familiar. The Five just can't help themselves from meddling." Mags bites out. She hates the Five. I can't blame her. I hate them too. They took everything from werewolves. They look at us as abominations.

"What can we do in the meantime? The spark to start the war got stopped, so now what?" Ghost questions.

"We will come up with another spark to start the war. Setting the humans off on a killing spree doesn't take much. For now, lay low. We can't draw attention to ourselves. We can't risk Zane figuring out we all are working together. We will wait for things to calm down. Then I will invite Zane and Ari over. We will deal with Zane and then Sage. You will kill Ari right then and there. We can not risk Zane interfering. If he does, we will never get a chance to kill her again." Mags hates her son, and unfortunately, she is scared of him. She knows the power he wields, plus him being friendly with the Five doesn't help either.

"Zane will go insane when he finds out his familiar is dead. He will get revenge, and it won't be pretty, so what is your plan to deal with that?" Ghost directs his question to Mags. It's a good question. Zane will kill us in painful and drawn-out ways. He will hunt us till we are all dead.

"We will most likely need to kill Zane. He's a danger to our plan in more ways than one. Killing him won't be easy. Maybe we set a trap and kill both of them at once. Kill two birds with one stone. It would have to be quick. We can't allow them anytime to react. While we lay low for a bit, let's think of ways to kill Zane and Ari simultaneously. I can get them both here, but honestly, it might be better if we kill them simultaneously at separate locations. Zane and Ari are stronger together. We just need to figure out how to kill them both simultaneously. For now, go back to your homes, run things like normal, and wait. In a month or so, Zane will give up his suspicions and will have some new lead to chase. It won't be hard to throw him off our scent. Then when his guard is down, we will execute our plan." Mags gives the final decision.

It's not a bad plan. We do have to lay low with Zane sniffing around. Ari was clearly suspicious of me at the club, and now, with her cutting me out of her life, I have no way to get to her. Mags is the only one who can get both Zane and Ari in the same place simultaneously, but that seems to present its own complications. Zane is bad news all around for our plans, so I'm okay with taking him out along with Ari. Zane is clearly a problem, and Ari is her own problem. They are enemies that could very well take us out and stop us altogether. Zane is deadly, and Ari is clearly benefiting from their weird relationship.

I'm surprised Ari has adjusted to being with a warlock so well. Zane isn't an ordinary warlock either. He's powerful and a demigod. I thought for sure Ari would be so scared of him that she'd never be able to love him. Guess the bitch is more fucked up than I thought because she seems to have no problem being with Zane. Zane should be her worst guy option, yet she's madly in love with him. How does that bitch get a soulmate and a love story? Even if it's a darker love story, it's still a love story. I don't have anything. Liam and I aren't in love. We are only together because of the mutual benefits being together gives us. Liam isn't my soulmate, and he's not someone I want to spend the rest of my life with.

Ari triggered me when she brought up having pups. That bitch has some nerve to bring up having pups with me. I don't want pups. It's too much work, and I'm far too selfish to love a child. Having a pup would be my worst nightmare. Liam isn't sure if he wants kids. I fear he does and that if I don't give him one, he will leave me or just knock someone else up. I don't know which option is worse.

Meanwhile, Ari is living some dark love story, completely happy with Zane. I bet they are going to have kids. From what I understand, Zane has to have heirs. It's part of his arrangement with Death or something. I don't know if Mags tried to explain it once, but I didn't really follow. Magic is so fucking complex, and I don't have time to bother with it. I can't do it, so why the fuck do I care about it.

The Coven of the Crow and Shadows: Legacy

Leaving Mags's cottage, I'm more determined than ever to break the curse of my people. It's sweet of Fate to make Ari the person I have to kill to break the curse. I hate that bitch, and I hate that she's happy. I had hoped Zane would make her life shitty, but now he had to turn out to be some dark knight. Such bullshit that Ari is always having things work out for her like it's no big deal. I want my happy ending, and it starts with killing Ari. I'll do whatever it takes to get the happy ending I know I deserve.

CHAPTER 20
Zane

Ari is a few months along in her pregnancy now. I still can't believe we are going to have a baby. As much as Ari and I talked about having a family, I didn't think it would happen so soon, nor did I think it would happen in the middle of two major missions. So far, things have been quiet. Ghost hasn't caused any issues. Liam and Sage seem to be happily ruling their pack. Mags has tried to reach out to me, saying she needed to see Ari and me for something important. Something about the whole thing feels off. Luckily I'm an expert at avoiding Mags.

Right now, I don't have time for Mags and her games. I knew going to see her would open up a line of communication I didn't want. Mags thinks because she helped me that, I owe her by allowing her back in my life. That is never going to happen. I have bigger fish to fry than to worry about Mags right now. I still have no idea who the big boss that Ghost was referring to is. I don't like people hiding in the shadows. I'll find them, though. I always find what I'm looking for. After all, I control the shadows so no one can hide forever from me.

Ari had very little luck researching human Sasha's history. We haven't found anything new. I know Ari is frustrated trying to find a way to unite the werewolves and lycans. She is a nobody in their community, and now she needs them to listen to her. Right now, Ari is relating to human Sasha's troubles of not having people listen to her. Ari has tried reaching out to pack alphas to see if any of them would meet with her to discuss changes, but none are willing. Ari isn't sure how to get them to her side. Then there is the matter of the lycans that are hiding away, trying to survive. Ari needs to find them and speak with them as well. She has to do everything from the limitation of our realm.

Of course, Ari wants to leave the realm to conduct her meetings. She thinks approaching the alphas in person will make them more willing to talk to her. She might be correct, but we can't risk that right now. Sage has a target painted on Ari's back. I don't trust that Ari is safe in the human realm. No matter how nice Sage is playing right now, I don't trust her. Right now, Ari is carrying precious cargo. Our child is more important than any mission we have. Ari is far too vulnerable while she is pregnant. I don't like that she can't transform, which is a major way for her to protect herself against her enemies. Ari is just going to have to sit tight till our baby is born.

Ari is stir crazy as I watch her pace back and forth in the coven library, going over lycan and werewolf history, trying to see if there is a way to unite them through laws. As much as Ari doesn't want to force them to unite, she might have a choice. There is a lot of bad blood between werewolves and lycans. The law might not have to be used as a weapon against them but as something that could help encourage them to unite. Ari has been in this library researching for the last few months. I think it's getting to her. I also think not being able to train like she needs to get out her anxious energy isn't helping her either.

Stepping in her pacing path, I catch her attention. "Zane, you're back from the human realm." She states enthusiastically.

Since she can't go there or really do much of anything other than research, Ari is like a drug addict looking for their next score. Except its not drugs. She's looking for its stories of the human realm. Stories of action in the field get her all worked up. Every time I get back from going to the human realm, she is all over me, asking tons of meaningless questions. She's living vicariously through me at the moment, and it's a bit much. Not that I can blame Ari for her eagerness. She's cooped up and unable to do what normally gives her relief. In a way, I feel for her. Shifters are natural animal like beings and not being able to shift, run, or train must be driving Ari insane and, in the process, driving me insane as well.

"Yes, I'm back, Pet. I told you I'd be back for our doctor's appointment. I can't wait to see our little one." I reply, closing the gap between us, doing my best to keep the topic off the human realm. Anything to have her focus on something else. Distracting Ari with our baby normally does the trick.

"I'm glad you'll be with me. I like having appointments when you're there. It eases my anxiety." Ari states, looking down and away from me. She's hiding something.

"Pet, what's wrong? Tell me before I read your mind." I hate threatening that, but she mustn't hesitate to tell me things.

I thought we had worked past this, but as per the usual, it's one step forward, two steps backward with Ari. I know she has a lot of shit to work through, and her past has definitely given her trust issues, but I'm not just anyone. I'm her master, her soulmate, and the father of her child. I'm the one person she trusts, yet she still struggles with opening up to me.

Ari was doing good with opening up to me, but she still has these moments like now where she clams up on me. I haven't been reading her mind as much since she made a real effort to talk things through with me. Ari still hasn't figured out how to read my mind, but I know that will take her a while. It took Zara years before she figured out how to read Blaine's mind. Blair barely has a hold on it with Cade. It's easier for us since we are used to using magic, and mind reading is much like magic. Sensing the vibrations of one's mind is much like sensing the vibrations of magic.

Ari sighs. "I can't seem to shake the feeling that something is wrong. No, wrong is not the right word. More like I feel as if something is off with the pregnancy. Something that shouldn't be happening. I can't explain it." She sighs again, frustrated.

She still has no idea how to control Sasha's premonitions. It's not just premonitions. It's also these strong gut feelings that seem to be correct. Almost as if her intuition is exactly on point.

"It could just be your anxiety, Pet. If it's not, then we will deal with it together. We are in all of this together." I say, taking her hands into mine. I kiss her lightly on the lips. I haven't been as rough with her since we found out she is pregnant. It's hard to hold back sometimes, but I know she needs me to be gentle right now. Ari is much more vulnerable than she cares to admit right now. She is determined to put on a strong facade for everyone. She doesn't want anyone to see her cracking under the pressure of our situation. I'll admit it's a rough position to be in.

I'm still convinced that our two big missions are one giant mission. Still, it's a lot to handle either way. Then you add in a surprise pregnancy. I can't believe I never thought to use protection. We were always so in the moment we didn't think about protection. The first time we had sex was so unexpected I hadn't expected Ari to give herself to me that night. Also, with us both wanting a family at some point, we never thought to talk about protection till we were ready. It seems so sudden to be adding a child to the mix. Ari and I have just gotten to a good place. It took us months to get to this point, and now we are rocking the boat by adding a baby to the mix. If something is wrong with the baby, it's just the last thing we need. Besides, I don't want something to be wrong with our baby.

"I love you, Zane. I don't know what I'd do without you." Ari says quietly as she breaks our kiss.

"I love you too, Ari. You are my world, and I don't know what I do without you either. Now, let's go get our little one checked up on." I state, rubbing her small baby bump.

Ari nods her head with a smile. Her anxiety is written all over her face. I take her hand in mine and squeeze it gently to let her know I'm with her. We make our way to the medical wing and are immediately put in a room. Ari is usually happy at her appointments. She loves seeing the baby just as much as I do on the sonogram. However, today she is on edge. She fiddles with her hands on her lap as her one leg bounces up and down. I don't know how to ease her through this. I don't know how to help her learn about Sasha's abilities. If her intuition is strong, how can I tell her it's wrong when we both know it's not. I'm not a liar, and I am not someone to sugarcoat things. Ari is the same way, so she appreciates my honesty as I do hers.

Dr. Grant knocks on the door before entering. Ari's eyes dart to him immediately as if he holds all the answers. I guess in some ways, he does. He's one of the only people who can help ease her anxiety by giving her the information she seeks. Ari lays back as she rolls her shirt up and adjusts her pants so the doctor can put the gel on her belly. I hold Ari's hand to reassure her. I can't help but agree that something will be off with our baby. The truth is, I've been able to sense that something is off with our baby, but I kept telling myself it was my anxiety about being a first time dad. If Ari is having intuition as to what my senses are telling me, then something is indeed off with our baby. The question now remains what?

The appointment starts off normal. We hear the baby's heartbeat, which is strong. Dr. Grant turns the screen to us, pointing out various body parts like legs, arms, head, and our baby's belly. Everything seems normal, but then Dr. Grant pauses and hones in on one section like he is trying to figure out why something isn't there. His face scrunches in confusion.

"What's wrong?" I ask, holding Ari's hand tighter.

"Uh, well, nothing wrong, per se. We can clearly see the baby's gender, and I don't know how to tell you this, but it's a girl." Dr. Grant answers.

"Well, that's not the worst thing." Ari answers.

"Ari, Pet, you remember me telling you that members of my coven only have males," I inform her gently as I hold her hand. I know I've told her this in the past. However, I was tossing a lot of information at the time at Ari about magic. No doubt she tuned out most of what I was saying or missed it altogether.

Ari's eyes go wide as she looks at Dr. Grant, who is eyeing her rather suspiciously. "I didn't cheat on you if that's what everyone is thinking!" Ari frantically defends herself.

"Relax, Pet. I know you didn't cheat. One, the master familiar bond only allows you to get pregnant by me. Two, if either one of us cheats, the other will feel it. It would be excruciatingly painful. I never doubted your loyalty to me, Ari. No, this is something I have to see Death about. This has his handy work written all over it." I state, trying to hide how badly I'm fuming right now.

"Well, other than the gender, which seems not to be that big of an issue, everything else looks good. The baby is growing just right. Mom is healthy. I will see you two in two weeks unless you need me before then. Master Zane, if you find out anything from Death that I need to know in regards to the pregnancy, please let me know."

"I will, Dr. Grant. Thank you." I reply as I try to soothe a frantic Ari.

Ari and I leave the medical wing. I take Ari back to our room so she can rest. She looks a little worn out. No doubt she's been up half the night worrying about today's appointment. Ari's intuition was right again. Now, if only she could get some intuition and premonitions on what exactly we are dealing with would be great. I need to go see Death. Damn it! I hate going to his realm. I know I'm a demigod of death, but that doesn't make going to Death's realm any better. It's creepy even for me, and that is saying something.

"Master, don't leave." Master. Ari doesn't usually call me that unless we are in public or we are having sexy, fun times. Ari is feeling more vulnerable than I thought.

"Pet, I will be back. I have to go see Death about our baby. I'm going to get us some answers. When I come back, I will snuggle with you all night and all damn day tomorrow if you want. I have to go do this now. It can't wait. I'm sorry, Pet."

Ari pouts as she climbs into bed. "Promise you will come back to me." What the hell? Why does she think I wouldn't come back to her?

I sit on the edge of the bed next to her. "I'll always come back to you, Ari," I say, brushing her unique mixed black and gray hair out of her face as she settles into a comfortable position.

"You know I didn't cheat, right, Master? I saw how Dr. Grant looked at me like I betrayed you and the entire coven. I can't be hated by everyone again, not when I finally feel like this is my home." Her voice cracks with the tears that threaten to spill.

However, I can't help but smile at her words. She feels like this is her home, which warms my cold dead heart. I also know she is calling me Master because she is afraid I'm upset with her. She thinks she did something wrong.

"I know you didn't cheat. I explained to you why I know for a fact you didn't, and even if those safety features weren't built into the master familiar bond, I still would know you didn't cheat. I know how much you love me, Ari, and you know how much I love you. We are very loyal to one another. Dr. Grant was only suspicious because no one has ever had a girl baby in our coven. Never, not once in the long history of my coven, has there ever been a female born. Dr. Grant also doesn't know fully how the master familiar bonds work. Not many do in the coven. Most don't bother even learning about it as most will never have a familiar." I inform her as I stroke her cheek gently, doing my best to help her relax.

"Why are you smiling like a damn kid at Christmas then?" She asks in a snarky tone.

"Because you said this realm feels like your home. I've always told you were accepted here, and you finally believe me." I respond by kissing her gently on the forehead.

"My home is wherever you are, Zane. Plus, this realm isn't horrible. Your family is amazing, and your coven is pretty great too." At least she's back to calling me by my name.

Don't get me wrong, I fucking love it when Ari calls me Master, but I never want her to call me that because she is afraid of me. That is one thing I never want. I don't ever want Ari to be scared of me. My family and Ari are the only people I never want to fear me. Everyone else can fear me as much as they want. In fact, I prefer they did fear me. It honestly makes my job a lot easier.

"You are my home too, Ari. I love you, Pet. I will be back later. Get some rest. You need it." I say, kissing her once more, but it's on the lips this time.

"I love you too, Zane," Ari mumbles with her eyes closed.

Chuckling at her, I wait till she is fully asleep. She always falls asleep faster when I'm next to her. I'm not happy that Dr. Grant made Ari feel like she did something wrong. It angers me, but I can't go off the rails like I want to because Dr. Grant isn't who I'm really pissed off at. No, I'm pissed off at Death. I don't know what game he is playing or why he decided to let my child be a daughter. I have no problem with having a daughter. I just didn't think it was an option as it's literally never been an option for anyone in our coven before. So why now? Why me? Why my baby? I don't like surprises, and I'm even less thrilled that this is happening in the middle of a shit fucking storm that we already have to deal with. This is literally the last thing Ari, and I need right now. We don't' need another fucking complication. Time to visit Death once again, and I'm not leaving till I have fucking answers.

CHAPTER 21
Zane

Fuming, I head to Death's realm. I need answers because right now, I have more questions than answers and more problems than I know how to fucking solve. I hate being at a standstill waiting for that one piece of information that brings the puzzle together. It's infuriating, and it's taking far too long to get answers.

It doesn't help that I'm frustrated at finding nothing. Ghost is acting like the perfect citizen, as if he didn't try to kill a bunch of humans in his club to start a war. Then Sage and Liam acting all hunky-dory running their pack like everything is right in the world. They are up to something. No way they almost spark a war. Wait, that's an option I never considered before. What if Ghost, Liam, and Sage are all working together for the same boss? Shit, it's possible. They are the scum of the supernatural community, thinking they are superior to humans and other supernaturals. The question remains, who is their boss? Also, if they work for the same boss, does that mean their boss wants Ari? We always assumed Sage wanted Ari to reverse the curse Sasha put on the werewolves. At least that was a working theory wolf Sasha came up with. At least she's helping now and not withholding information from us. Still, what if there is more to Sage wanting Ari dead than to just break a curse?

I push the thoughts aside as I'm in Death's throne room, and I need answers. Besides, my new theory that they are all working for the same boss is something to discuss with

Ari. Death sits on his throne, conducting business as if he doesn't even know I'm here. However, I know that asshole knows I'm here. He knows when someone enters and leaves his realm.

My anger flares the longer he ignores me while finishing up whatever business he is conducting. After some moments, Death glances at me. His dark silver-gray eyes stare at me from under his black hooded robe. His war scythe is next to his throne.

"Son." He greets.

I lose it as his casualness towards me as if he didn't just throw a bomb on my lap. "How fucking dare you use my child as some kind of sick experiment!" I spit at him. Death using my child as an experiment is the only explanation I've come up with for why he would do this.

"Ah, I see you found out the good news." He claps his hands together, and for the first time ever, Death seems giddy. "I was wondering when you would find out."

"How the fuck are you so happy about this? My baby is a daughter, which is something that has never been done in our coven's history. Why the fuck now, and why the hell me? You have half my coven thinking Ari cheated on me because we are having a daughter. She is just starting to feel like she belongs, and you do this bullshit? What happened to me being your favorite, huh?" I rage at him.

"Calm down, Zane. It's not what you think. Let me explain before you come at me like a loose fucking cannon." Death's voice is eerily calm, even with him throwing profanities at me, which is something he doesn't normally do.

"Fine, explain. Now." I demand.

"Zane, you are my favorite and the most powerful child I've ever had. You are the only one whose power even comes close to matching mine. None of my other sons would have been able to pull off what you did in that club.

The Coven of the Crow and Shadows: Legacy

Admittedly, I wasn't sure how you would stop the tragic event, but I knew you could," Death pauses as if he's trying to gather his next works. Almost like what he's about to say is hard for him. "Yes, in some way, your daughter is an experiment. She will be unlike anything ever born. A hybrid born from a mother blessed by the Five and the son of one of the Five. Your daughter will not follow the normal genetics that I outlined centuries ago for the coven. When I started the coven, I didn't know I would have to keep having children to keep the realm and magic alive for the coven I created to help assist me. It took me centuries before I perfected the specific genetics needed to create demigods that could do my job. You have to understand, Zane. Managing millions of souls over multiple realms was too much."

"You were overwhelmed," I state. Admittedly, Death does have the most challenging job out of the Five. I guess even gods get overwhelmed.

"Yes. I worked tirelessly to create the coven. To create a bloodline that would be able to do what I could. I never took into account that the demigod's abilities would fade out over the generations. I was so focused on creating the bloodline I didn't think about the after effects. The truth is, Zane, I'm tired of having kids every so many decades. It's exhausting finding the right witches to mate with, the specific genetics needed, the deals I have to make to get them to agree, and then raising a child that ends up resenting me over and over again. It's too much. I want you to be the last child I have ever have. You are more exceptional in ways I never imagined. Your powers are so close to mine and strong that I could walk away from my throne to let you run the underworld."

His words shock me. I never realized the toll it took on him to create the coven and keep it running. Death is correct. All of his children have resented him at some point. I'm even guilty of it. I don't resent him now. That was more pissy teenager Zane, but adult me respects him. I never realized how powerful I was. I knew I was the most powerful of Death's sons, but I didn't think I could run the underworld.

"How would the coven stay running then? Even now, you only have a few in the coven that can help you with reaping fresh souls. We both know the Coven has grown weaker. Our realm hangs on by a thread when I'm not around. Most of the coven members can only do basic dark and black magic. They only reap souls that have not passed on from not previously being reaped. They have just enough power to fight the tough spirits. Even then, sometimes I'm back up."

"It's true. The bloodline is far too diluted now. It's not enough to have a child who can do what I can and them having children who can also do it. Your daughter is the key to fixing everything. Zane, you are so powerful that I was able to alter the DNA of your hybrid daughter. I've never had a child like you, one that I could create a new bloodline with. Your daughter will be born a necromancer with the full abilities a necromancer has. She will also be lycan and will be able to transform. I've had Fate design her a special wolf spirit. Your daughter will change everything."

"I assume she will have regular dark and black magic like I do?" Death nods his head. "Will she be born immortal?"

"Yes, she will age to about eighteen and then stop. Don't worry. She can give her immortality up when she is ready. She must have children. That is key. I've found a way to tie the coven's thriveability to your bloodline. As long as your bloodline continues, the coven will always be strong and will always be able to thrive. The magic will never die, the realm will be unbreakable, and I will never have to have another child again. You, Zane Shadows, are my legacy and the last son I will ever have." Death states proudly.

"I'm your legacy?" I ask in disbelief.

The Coven of the Crow and Shadows: Legacy

The rage I felt earlier fades away into pride and also disbelief. I always thought the coven was Death's legacy, his ultimate achievement. None of the others have managed to create their own coven. Sure they have other covens and other supernaturals who pay their homage. Some worship them, leave gifts at their temples, devote their life to them much like Sasha did, and some will sacrifice whatever is required of them. Still, Death is the only one to create his own coven and the only one to have children for a long time. There are other demigods like me, but they keep to themselves. Honestly, demigods don't like interfering with the human realm's issues. They don't care for humans as they are just servants to them. As for supernaturals, well, demigods think they are above them. Honestly, we are. There is a pecking order to our world that no one truly likes to acknowledge. The highest members are the Five. The next rank would be demigods, then supernaturals that vary depending on their abilities. Ancient shifters would be on the top end of the supernatural rank. In contrast, basic witches, werewolves, other basic shifters, and dark fae would be at the bottom of the supernaturals rank. Humans, of course, would be the lowest rank.

"Yes, you are, Zane. Your bloodline will be entirely different from what the coven has seen in the past. You should know your daughter is not the only child you will have, but worry about the first one for now. She will be something else, something wonderful mixed with deadly beauty. Ari is also key to making your bloodline my legacy. Ari is a lycan and blessed by the five. The two of you have created a bloodline unlike any other."

"You said, other children. Will they be hybrids too?" I inquire, wanting to know as much as possible. I don't like surprises. The more information I have, the more prepared I can be.

"Yes, at first, I had trouble with the male DNA as it is already bonded to the previous genetic code of the coven, which will continue for everyone that is not from your bloodline. Only your bloodline will be able to have females and hybrids. Because of my complications, I had to make the child a girl. I didn't intend for it to cause a scandal with Ari. I'm sorry. I only recently figured out the coding for the males of your bloodline. I had some help from Life to solve it. As you can imagine, it took some convincing to get her to help me."

"Yeah, she doesn't like you." I joke.

"I'm her opposite, we are natural enemies, and yet we are friends at the same time." His tone remains neutral. Sometimes it's eerie how neutral his tone is sometimes. Almost as if he barely feels emotion.

"I believe the humans call that frenemies," I state.

Death chuckles. "Leave it to the humans to develop a term like that. Their realm was always special. Sasha was special. She was the first priestess the Five had. She started the trend of people worshiping us as they do now. I always hated how her fate turned out. She was so broken after being cursed. She felt like such a failure she ignored her gift and caused a huge hybrid issue that, in turn, caused another war. Ironic because the war was what she was trying to prevent in the first place, and then she accidentally causes a war." I see him shake his head as the hood moves in motion with him.

"Ari doesn't know how to unite the werewolves and lycans without forcing them." I offer the information hoping he might help.

"She can't force it. It won't do her any good. There is only one way to end the curse. Sacrifice. Ari has been targeted as the sacrifice, but she isn't the one meant to be the sacrifice. Do you know why Ari has Sasha's wolf spirit and gift?" I shake my head no. "Because she is the descendant of Sasha and her fated mate. Meanwhile, Sage is descended from Sasha and her human husband. Sage must die to break the curse and with her death will bring the unity of lycans and werewolves."

"Her death will automatically bring unity and end the curse?" He's got to be kidding. Ari will never kill Sage, no matter how pissed she is at her. Ari isn't a killer, but I am.

"Yes. Werewolves were never meant to be, but now that they exist, we can't kill them for it. Sasha was the one to cause the rift. Only her werewolf bloodline can end it."

"Why the werewolf bloodline. Technically the lycans started it when their Alpha killed Sasha's husband."

"True, but the fault still lies with Sasha. She ignored her gift and started a hybrid race. She did something unspeakable by ignoring her gift, which would have told her about lycans having fated mates. Yes, the alpha killed the human husband, but he spared the children even if he made them rogues. He spared them. They didn't have to react the way they did. They started the war out of revenge, and now that bloodline will end it. Before you think about killing Sage for Ari, you can't. It has to be the lycan bloodline from Sasha that sacrifices the werewolf bloodline from Sasha. I'm sorry, Ari has to kill Sage. There is no loophole." Death informs me.

"So, Sage knows this too, but she thinks it's reversed that Ari is the sacrifice, not her?"

"Yes, which is why you must not let Ari go to the human realm till after she has given birth. Ari has a bigger target on her back than you think. I can give you the last bit of information to help you before I piss Fate off for helping too much is that you can't trust Mags."

"What the fuck does Mags have to do with anything?" Now I'm just confused.

"You'll figure it out. You're smart. You should go back to your familiar. She needs you, and so does your daughter. I wish I could tell you more, but I don't want to piss Fate off. That wouldn't do any of us good. He's moodier than a teenage female on her monthly with her face covered in acne."

I chuckle at his words. He's not wrong. I've met all of the Five, and Fate is a moody fucker. "Thank you for telling me what you did. I don't want you to piss Fate off. Somehow that will come back to bite me in the ass." Death now chuckles, and for once, we are bonding like a father and son should be. Strange, but not bad.

Leaving Death's realm, I head back to Ari. I have no idea how the hell I'm going to break the news to her. I don't know how to tell her she has to kill her childhood best friend. Even if they aren't friends anymore, and even if Ari resents Sage, Ari isn't a killer. Yet, she has to become one to fulfill her destiny quest. It's bullshit, but I can't fix it for her like I hoped I could. So, I'm just going to have to be her support.

CHAPTER 22
Zane

Arriving back at home, Ari is sound asleep. Deciding it's best not to wake her and let her rest, I head to see Blaine. I know he's in his office. Zara is busy ensuring our apartment is done before the baby gets here. Cade and Blair are trying to help out in the field for a bit since Ari, and I aren't able to do any missions at the moment. I think Zara is secretly hoping Blair comes back pregnant like Ari did.

I still can't believe we forgot about protection. I can't even blame Ari even if I wanted to. She was a virgin lost in the experience of discovering her sexual desires. However, I am the one who should have thought ahead more. I let my desires cloud my thoughts. While having a child feels so sudden and almost misplaced in time, I'm thrilled to have a child. It's hard to picture someone like me as a person who loves the idea of being a father.

I've always known I'd have to have heirs, so I accepted it. Embraced that future, knowing it was the only option. Some of Death's sons have given him a hard time about having heirs. Most didn't want the family scenario. They fell into the stereotype of demigods, vanity. They didn't want to spend their time raising children with their familiars when they could be off doing whatever their hearts desired. I think I'm one of the few who took his job seriously. I'm not just talking about where heirs are concerned. In general, I'm talking about the job we are tasked with as Death's sons.

Knocking on Blaine's door, I hear him tell me to enter. Entering his office, I find Blaine looking over an old book where the pages are yellowed. He peers up at me, and the moment he sees me, his face spreads into a warm smile. Death may not have been the best father, but I think he tried in his own way. Blaine, on the other hand, has always been the best father. I think he's the reason I want to have a family. His family man personality seems to have rubbed off on me, which isn't totally a bad thing. Blaine and Zara made sure to keep me as humble as possible, knowing my alpha personality might let me get too big for britches.

"Son." Blaine greets. "You look like you need to have a chat. Come sit." He gestures for me to sit in the dark red leather chair in front of his desk. "Is this a scotch or tea type of talk?" He asks, standing up and heading to his little cabinet in the corner where he keeps his stash of scotch and tea leaves.

"Scotch," I reply, remembering exactly why I love Blaine. He's the father who will guide you, be an ear to listen to your issues, support you, and love you. Blaine is the father I hope to be to my children. I know I'm colder than Blaine, more alpha than anyone I know, but still, I want to be a good father like Blaine.

"Ah, well, why don't you start while I pour us some scotch," Blaine suggests as he pulls out the decanter from the cabinet.

"I'm sure you've heard that Ari is having a daughter," I state.

There might be many men in our coven mixed with some women and kids, but the gossip around here spreads like wildfire. The coven isn't overly gossipy, but when something huge like my familiar having a daughter instead of a son happens, people talk. Most keep family life and coven life separate, but it makes its way around when the gossip is too good.

The Coven of the Crow and Shadows: Legacy

Blaine clears his throat like he already knows the rumors aren't good. Damn it! "I have. Now I know Ari didn't cheat, and even if she did, I know that she can only get pregnant by you. I know how the master familiar bond works, whereas the rest of the coven, not so much. I know, Ari. She's far too loyal for her own good like a good familiar is. So, why are you two having a daughter? What game is Death playing at?" Blaine inquires, pouring the amber liquid into crystal skull glasses.

"For once, he's not playing a game. He's using my bloodline to not ever have to have another child, as he wants me to be the last one he ever has. Death found a way to use my bloodline and tie it to the magic and realm of the coven. I'm his legacy." That still feels weird to say. Deep down, I think I knew it, but it's different having it confirmed. Even more so when the thought is spoken out loud.

"That's a huge honor and a big deal, Zane," Blaine replies, setting a glass in front of me as he sits back in his chair, holding his own glass.

"He said I was so powerful I could do his job of running the underworld. I don't know how to take the compliment. I went to see him fuming, thinking he was playing games. Instead, I leave honored and with a better relationship with Death. It was strange to bond with him in a father-son way, but it wasn't bad. He was genuine with his words." I take a sip of the scotch letting the smooth liquid burn slightly as it slides down my throat and ignites a fire in the pit of my stomach. "My children will be hybrids. Born full necromancers and also lycans. They will be immortal and will age till about eighteen. My bloodline will be the only ones able to have girls and hybrids in the coven."

"That's huge. A game changer. We should make an announcement so that the coven doesn't look at Ari badly." Blaine suggests.

"That's not a bad idea. I can announce that as Death's legacy, I'm able to have daughters and hybrids. Play it off like a blessing from Death which I guess in some ways it is."

"I'll set it up for tomorrow. The sooner we clean this mess up, the better. Keep Ari in your room till the announcement. I know how over sensitive pregnant women can be. Your mother was a nightmare when she was pregnant with Cade. She cried over actual spilled milk. It was ridiculous."

I chuckle, trying to picture tough ass Zara crying over spilled milk. "Ari is vulnerable, that's for sure. She's like a wounded animal right now. I don't know how I'm going to break the news to her that Death told me how to complete her destiny mission." I take another sip, but it's bigger.

I might not be able to get drunk, but the psychology of it works as I feel myself relax slightly. I hadn't realized how tense I was. That often happens. I'm always tense, ready to strike, constantly feeling like something will come after me. Paranoid? Definitely, but I'm not exactly sane. I'm damn demigod of death and necromancer. I literally can talk to dead people. I'm not going to be the perfect picture of sanity.

"How bad is it?" Blaine asks, taking a sip of his scotch.

"She has to kill Sage. Sage is a sacrifice to the Five to break the curse that lycan Sasha put on lycans and werewolves. Once Sage is dead, the werewolves and lycans magically unite." I reply bitterly as I take another sip of the scotch, letting the smooth burn ease the frustration building in me. I hate that I can't help Ari with this in the way that I want.

"Well, often, that's how curses work once broken. Like a pretty magical spell casts over them, fixing the problems of the curse. The werewolves and lycans will reunite and have peace with the death of a bad person. It's not the worst thing. At least it's not an innocent person."

"True, but Ari will have a hard time killing someone she looked at as a best friend for most of her life. Ari doesn't like Sage, she burned the bridges of their friendship, and she's been upset with how Sage used and manipulated her. However, I'm not sure that's enough for Ari to want to kill Sage. Even if she doesn't always see it, Ari is a tough badass, but she is also good-hearted. Her intentions are always good, even if she has a rough time showing it properly. Ari isn't a killer, and she has to become one."

"She does have to kill someone to break a curse, but that person isn't a good person. Sage used Ari. Ari isn't the only person Sage has used or manipulated. Sage is also hunting Ari to kill her. It will come down to survival with any luck, and that instinct will kick in. Perhaps Sasha can be in control when the killing happens. Ari isn't a killer, but Sasha definitely is. Use that to your advantage." Blaine suggests. Damn, that's a great suggestion.

"That's not a bad idea. It might help ease Ari into the thought of it. Maybe mom can be around. She seems to relate to Ari well. Plus, it would give them some time to talk about baby stuff. Ari could use the distraction. Besides, now that we know what she must do, she can stop driving herself insane in the library researching. Maybe now she can just focus on prepping for the baby."

"I agree it's not a bad idea. Your mother is skilled at relating to others. Sometimes I think she has secret empathic abilities, even if it's not a common ability of gargoyles. Now, you know Ari will not fully give up helping you take down the big boss you are hunting down. She cannot train or be in the field, so maybe throw her a bone and let her help you with your mission. The worst thing you can do is block her out. Ari is much like Zara. She wants to be and feel useful. If she isn't useful to her master, she starts to feel insecure. It's just how some familiars are. They love us so much they want to make us happy, just like we yearn to make them happy. As masters, we do hold all the power in the bond and relationship, but we need them just as much as they need us. We are two halves of a whole, master and familiars. The bond is sacred, special, and unique. You two love each other deeply. Trust me, son, let Ari help you with your mission. It will make your life easier." Blaine grins as he takes a sip of his scotch as if he has all the secrets to master familiar bonds and how to make them a success. Blaine probably does have all the secrets. I bet he's even written a secret book about it that will one day appear in the library after he passes on.

After chatting a bit more with Blaine, I feel better. Blaine is a great person to talk to get things off your chest. His solutions to most of my issues were helpful. I know breaking the news to Ari won't be easy, but I believe she can do this. I know she can. She's strong, and Blaine's right. With any luck, it will come down to self-defense. It will ease Ari's guilt if it's self-defense. I don't know how she will feel about the situation, but she has time to come to terms with it. She can't leave this realm till our daughter is born. She has about three months, maybe more, because I know she isn't going to want to leave our baby right away.

Despite what Ari may think about herself, she has excellent maternal instincts and instincts in general. She will be a loving and caring mother. Zara, I'm sure, will give her pointers and advice just like I'm sure Blaine will do the same with me. Ari and I will be great parents, even if it's happening sooner than expected. The closer it gets to our baby being born, the more excited I find myself becoming. Ari might be a ball of anxiety half the time, but she is getting excited about our baby. I'm sure helping Zara design the nursery, thinking of a name, and setting our apartment up when it's ready will only increase the excitement.

The Coven of the Crow and Shadows: Legacy

I will let Ari help me where she can with figuring out the big boss and how to stop them. She will also need to come up with a plan to take Sage out. It will have to be on sacred land of the Five for it to matter. It will take some planning that I will help Ari with, and she can help me with my mission. We have to work as a team if we plan on being successful. We are a deadly team when we are working together and not against each other. Even with a big bad looming over us, there is still so much hope for the future. If anything, our daughter will have the hope the coven needs. As the season of change is upon us, it brings a newfound hope, one we all desperately need.

CHAPTER 23
Ari

Finding out I have to kill Sage has been a hard pill to swallow. I have a few months left of my pregnancy before I have to lore Sage onto sacred ground and kill her to unite lycans and werewolves. Out of all the scenarios I imagined how I would finish this destiny quest, killing Sage wasn't one of them. While Sage and I are no longer friends, and I hold deep resentment towards her for how she used me, I still don't want to kill her. Zane suggested I have Sasha take control for the actual killing part. It's not a bad idea and one that I'm going to go with because it's the only way I can even attempt to stomach what I have to do.

Zara has been distracting me with setting up the nursery for our daughter. Our apartment is ready, so we are just moving in and setting up our home. It's been nice for Zane and me to set up our home together. It's allowed us bonding time with something that isn't sex or a mission. Zane and I have been helping each other with our missions. We are still connecting the dots and putting pieces of the puzzle together. I think we are close to figuring things out. I can feel it deep within my bones.

It's been strange embracing my gift from the Five. The more I embrace it, the stronger and easier it becomes to use the gift to my will. At first, I wasn't sure I'd ever learn to control the gift, but I'm learning to overtime. I might not ever have complete control over the premonitions as those seem to come from Fate when he wishes me to stop or do something.

However, mastering my intuition and honing in on it has been relatively easy. Sasha has been guiding me with it.

Sasha and I are on better terms these days. We are working more in sync and as one than we ever have before. The pregnancy seems to be bonding us, and also the fact that I'm relying on her to help me kill Sage. At least we aren't at odds. It's nice not having an internal battle with her. We have to work together more so than ever if we are going to fulfill our destiny quest. It's her quest just as much as it is mine.

Zara has me picking out colors for the nursery as we stand in the room pulling together an idea of how we should set it up. Zara has been extremely helpful with helping me with baby stuff. It's often how I pictured my mom and me doing things. Unfortunately, my mom isn't here, and even if she was, I'm not sure she would want to help me with this. Thankfully, Zara lives for this stuff. She is going to be that grandma that spoils her grandkids. Zane informed me we will have a few kids.

Zane made an announcement to the coven explaining why we are having a daughter. Zane explained it in simple terms to the coven. Our daughter is a blessing from Death, and our children will be different so that the coven could thrive through our bloodline. It ended all the rumors, and many are excited for the first female of the coven to be born. It's strange to be making history in different ways. Our daughter will change the history of the coven, but our children, in general, will change the coven's history because they will be hybrids. Then I will change history when I unite the lycans and werewolves. Zane will make history again when he stops the big bad. I never thought I'd affect the world in such a way.

My life is far from how I pictured it back as a girl growing up in a suffocating pack. I never imagined I would really get an adventure or go on a destiny quest. I never imagined I'd be more than just an average lycan. I certainly never pictured my soulmate being a warlock who is my master. Becoming a familiar was never something I would have wanted for myself growing up. Now, I see it in a different light. I see it with love and admiration, which mirror my feelings for Zane, who I love so much. I never thought I could love someone so much or so hard. I feel so blessed to have Zane, be his, and have a family with him. Even if we are starting our family a little sooner than planned, it doesn't matter because we have time. Literally, we are immortal. We can raise our kids and then go off to do all the crazy things we didn't get to do. While I know we can still die, it's hard to do. Besides, Zane is a freaking necromancer. Pretty sure he could just bring us back from the dead if he really wanted to.

Funny how life turns out differently than you originally pictured. People, places, and events change, altering the future in different ways as it shapes the life you end up living. Crazy how far you can go from the picture you painted in your head. Some of it might still be there, but it's altered. The person I saw falling in love with is very different from the man I did end up falling in love with. I pictured living my life in the pack forever, yet here I am, living in a completely different realm run by a coven who works for Death. Yes, some of the pictures remain the same, yet it's altered in ways I never thought of. My story unfolded in the worst and yet best possible ways. What I thought would be my path of ruin ended up being my saving grace. It's funny how we get exactly what we need right when we need it, even if we weren't fully aware we needed it.

Rubbing my belly, I decide on a nice plumb purple color with gray, black, and white as accent colors. I hand the color I pick off to Zara, who will get it to the painters. Zane and I haven't fully moved into the apartment yet. We sleep in our old room for now till we fully have everything set up.

The Coven of the Crow and Shadows: Legacy

Right now, we are setting up the nursery, the living room, dining area, and kitchen. Our room will be last as all we have to do is move everything in our current room to our room in the apartment. I made sure to replicate the master bath that we have in our current room. I love that master bath, it's what the perfect bathroom dreams are made of, and I wasn't about to part with it. So I had them replicate. Zane laughed so hard at me when I told him I wanted the master bathroom replicated. He had the nerve to call me a pampered wolf.

Smiling at the memory makes me glad that I have such happy, playful, and fun moments to reflect on. Zane and I are steady in our relationship, doing our best to grow it in the midst of the chaos around us. We make time for each other every day. We made a rule that we have to have at least one meal together a day. We make sure to spend time talking and, of course, having sex. I can't have sex at this stage as it risks putting me in premature labor. I still have a few months left, but it's best not to stir the pot too hard with the baby being the start of a different bloodline. My pregnancy hormones make it hard not to have sex, but we do a lot of oral and touching to hold us over till we can finally be intimate again.

After several hours of picking paint colors for the various rooms of our apartment, it's dinner time. Zane and I primarily eat in the dining hall with everyone else. It's our way of staying connected with the members of the coven. So many of them turn to Zane, Cade, and Blaine for advice, guidance, and help with various things. Zara is popular among the coven member's wives and partners. Zara has recently been including Blair and me in as many things as she can. We will have to help her run the coven side of things that deal with the wives and partners of the members.

I never realized Zara's role in the coven as Blaine's wife and familiar. Zara is very involved with the wives and partners of the members. She has a gathering once a month of all the wives and partners. It's this massive brunch-like event with delicious food, drinks, and company. It's been nice getting to know some of the other women. With me being pregnant many of them have reached out to me to offer help, advice, suggestions, books, and other things. It's sweet, and it makes me feel like I belong here. The coven has been overwhelmingly welcoming of me, which is why I was terrified my reputation had been ruined by Death. Thankfully, Blaine is good at damage control. Before any real rumors could spread, Zane had made his announcement. Now everyone is excited for the first baby girl ever to be born in the coven. I struggle to see why it's such a big deal, but it's clearly huge to the coven.

Dinner is filled with lots of chatter about the baby. Apparently, the little one controls everything as everything appears to be centered around her. She's also an active little one, always kicking and flipping around. The child loves to use my bladder as her personal pillow and punching bag. I'm not sure my bladder will survive this pregnancy with the way this baby girl abuses it. Zane enjoys watching me struggle with my bladder. He thinks it's hilarious. I guess I make funny expressions and comments that are funny.

Overall, Zane has been amazing throughout the pregnancy. He's gone out of his way to make me comfortable and happy. I know he feels guilty about keeping me locked up in the coven's realm till I deliver, but as much as it pains me to admit, he's right. I shouldn't leave the realm. I'm safe here, and our baby girl is the most important thing. Zane's done what he can to keep me involved with missions and gives me plenty of little jobs to do around the coven for him since he's gone a lot.

That is the one downside to being strapped to the coven's realm is that Zane has to do everything in the human realm on his own. Sure he's done it before. He didn't always have me by his side, but I'm supposed to be making his job and life easier. So far, I'm not convinced I've done a good job at it. I seem to complicate Zane's life, but he doesn't seem to mind. Zane has shown me how much he loves me and how much he cares about me. I never thought I could love someone like this. To love someone with an underlying passion to know your life will never be the same without them. It's intense and slightly overwhelming at times but in a good way.

After dinner, Zane and I head back to our room to unwind from the day. Zane did some recon today in the human realm while I was off decorating our apartment. We make ourselves comfortable on the couch in front of the fireplace. Zane lights the fireplaces, and I stick my legs on his lap while I lean back and rest my head on the arm of the couch. I rub my belly as Zane puts his hand over mine, and we begin to rub my belly together. Our little girl kicks, amused at our rubs.

Zane chuckles. "She's an active little thing."

"Yeah, she is. You know we should probably come up with a name before she is born." I joke. With all the madness around us, it's easy to forget the little things that come with having a baby, like picking a name.

"Do you have anything in mind?" Zane prompts.

"I always loved my grandmother's name, Everly. I was thinking of Sasha as her middle name. I don't know why, but I feel the need to pay respects to both human Sasha and my wolf spirit Sasha."

"Everly Sasha Shadows. I like it." Everly kicks in agreement. Zane and I chuckle at our Little Nightmare because she will be a handful if she is anything like Zane and me.

"Well, that was surprisingly easy. I honestly half expected us to fight over names." I state with a shrug of my shoulders. "So, how was the human realm today?"

Zane sighs as he stiffens as if he will tell me something I don't like. Dread creeps into my stomach as Everly fips around, making me nauseous from the combination. "As you know, I sent shadows to spy on Ghost, Sage, and Liam. For months it's been nothing but cheery bullshit. A show, no doubt, to give the illusion that everything is normal. I figured they would lay low after the club disaster. There's no doubt that us stopping that night set them back. Well, today, my shadow trackers finally paid off. Ghost went to see none other than Mags."

"Wait, Mags, as in your bio mom?" Okay, I didn't see that one coming. I knew Mags was bad news, but I didn't think she was that level of bad.

"Yes, that would be correct. Not too long after, Liam and Sage showed up at her cottage. I'm starting to think Mags might be the big bad boss we've been looking for. She is powerful enough to be in control of such an organization. Not only that, but Mags, like many other supernaturals, are very vocal about how much they hate humans. Many supernaturals think humans are a waste of space, and since there aren't as many realms for us to spread out over anymore, I think people feel cramped. Humans are the easiest target."

"So you think Mags and her minions want to eliminate humans to make more room in the realm? Why not just create a new realm or two?" I question. If room is the issue, then isn't the simpler solution to create new realms instead of killing off an entire race?

"It's not that simple, Ari. The Five are the only ones who are powerful enough to create new realms, but why should they? How long before the new realms wither away like the previous realms. The Five don't believe those that live in the human realm would be grateful for new realms. Separating the humans and supernaturals has always been important. It's why there were realms in the first place. Each realm was meant to operate unaware of the other realms. That's how it was for many centuries until one day; a smart warlock figured out how to travel to the other realms. He broke the fabric of the universe that the Five created. Multiple realms colliding, invading, and merging into pure and utter chaos. If you want to be technical, we are living in the aftermath of an apocalypse. We technically live in a dystopian world. It's the price for breaking the design the Five had created." Zane explains.

"Wait, lycans and werewolves also originate from the human realm, so why does it matter if supernaturals and humans are now mingling, so to speak?"

"The lyans were created as a curse. Werewolves were hybrids as a result of Sasha mating with a human. It's different because humans were cursed to be supernatural, cursed by the Five. Look, whether you realize this or not, we live in the world that the Five created. They are our gods, and they will always rule supreme.

"Well, that's a blunt way to put it. Okay, so Mags is the big bad boss, so now what? Also, you were right. Our missions just became one."

Zane grins. "I know. I don't know what to do about Mags. I can take her out. I can kill her. I just need to time it right. She's been reaching out to me for months now, trying to get me to come back and visit her. Now I know for certain her claims to have more information on your blessing is bullshit. She's been trying every damn angle to get me to bring you to her cottage. I'm not sure why Mags would care about helping Sage break the full moon and mate curse on the werewolves and lycans." Zane ponders.

"Maybe it's the deal they made. Sage helps Mags eradicate the humans. Mags helps Sage get me so she can kill me. It could be that simple. You know I haven't figured out if killing Sage will bring back fated mates for lycans and werewolves? I wonder about the full moon part too." I'm the one trying to solve shit. I might know the endgame of my destiny quest, but I still don't know what completing it fully entails. All I know is that killing Sage unites the werewolves and lycans; everything else is unclear.

"I'm sure fated mates will come back because the way I see it, having fated mates is a way to keep them united. As for the full moon, doubtful. That might remain as a permanent punishment to serve as a reminder not to piss the Five off. That's my educated guess, at least. I know the Five well, which would be a classic move for them."

"Seems like we have the full picture for the first time in a while, or at least enough to strike when needed. I'm sure I'll be having a premonition when the time is right. Every night I go to sleep expecting to have one, but every morning I wake up, and my dreams have nothing to do with our missions."

"Have you been having premonition dreams more often?" Zane inquires. We don't often talk about my special abilities. I'm not sure why. It just doesn't seem to come up as often as I thought it would. It's also very possible the topic is getting overshadowed by our baby girl.

"I have one about every night. Ever since I started embracing my gift, it's only gotten stronger. Most nights, I just dream of silly things like what will be served for lunch or something I'm going to be doing within a few days. My intuition has been the thing to flourish the most. Every day it gets more precise, stronger, and natural."

"That's good to hear. Well, Pet, we should get some rest. You especially need to rest."

"I know," I grumble.

Zane helps me up. I get into a nightgown as sleeping naked isn't as comfortable when pregnant for some reason. Zane, of course, still sleeps naked, which I greatly appreciate. Settling on my left side, I get comfortable. Zane settles against me, his back touching mine. We haven't been able to snuggle properly since my belly is in the way. Still, just having Zane lying next to me is enough comfort. I love knowing he is near me. I feel safe with him. Relaxing knowing that we made huge progress tonight. In that short amount of time on the couch, we solved more than we had in months.

Months of recon finally paid off. Now we have a lot more answers and a better idea of how to do things. I'm sure I will get a premonition when the time is right for us to strike and end all of this once and for all. While I'm still not totally happy about having to kill Sage, I'm fully prepared to let Sasha have complete control. I rather Sasha be in control and do it than me. I'd much rather be tucked in the subconscious of wolf form where Sasha can have all the damn control. It somehow eases the apprehension I have.

Letting my mind relax and switch my thoughts from my destiny quest to thoughts of Everly. I'm happy we gave her a name. It somehow makes all of this real, as if I've been living in some ignorant bliss these last few months. It's still hard to wrap my mind around the fact that we are having a baby. It's a good shock, and I'm enjoying every moment of my pregnancy, even if my daughter thinks my bladder is her personal toy. Zane is wonderful, and he's so good to me. I'm so happy I'm his familiar. I don't care how our relationship may look to outsiders. Yes, he's controlling alphahole a lot of the time, but he's also caring, and he loves me for exactly who I am. That's all I need. Besides, I like my alpha being in control. I trust him, and I know he has my best interests at heart. Zane is my perfect match, my soulmate, and I'm his. Together we will do great things, have a wonderful family, and do some good for the world.

CHAPTER 24
Ari

Hard to believe I'm days away from popping. My stomach is stretched far too much, my back aches, the fake contractions have me freaking out, and my feet are like balloons. I'm ready for the Little Nightmare to come out. The nickname Little Nightmare seems to be sticking. It's slightly fitting as her father is a demigod of death and her mothers is a lycan. These are definitely two things that would give normal people nightmares, and Everly is a combination of those things. We decided to call her Ever as a cute nickname and Little Nightmare as her nickname for when she is driving us crazy.

Our apartment is finally ready and just in time too. Zane and I are hosting a little get together with our family tonight to celebrate our new addition to the family. Shortly after Everly is born, we will have to finish our missions. Everything has been on pause with my pregnancy. Even Fate seems to have kept things from imploding until I give birth. Almost as if the entire universe stopped so that I could have my baby safely. I'm sure that is true in some cosmic way on some level.

I'm still not sure I'm fully prepared for what I'm about to have to do. I fear labor is going to be easier than having to kill Sage. Sage did me wrong, and I hold strong resentment towards her and my pack. However, I don't want her dead. A new fear has been creeping into my mind as the time to complete my destiny quest looms over my head. What will happen to my old pack once Liam and Sage are killed? I assume Liam will be with Sage and will die with her. Even if he doesn't, he still can't be trusted to lead. I'm not going to be fit to lead. I could maybe temporarily lead till I found a lycan alpha that I trust to take over. The pack will go back to being the Hunter's Moon Pack and will be run by lycans as it was always meant to be.

While I haven't fully brought up my new concerns to Zane, I probably should. Zane has a lot of faith in the Five and their ability to have things work out just as they should. I don't doubt the Five or their power, but everything is so cryptic with them. It's worse than dealing with Sasha when she's holding back information. Maybe Zane understands them better because he is part god. He knows how they think and operates scarily well, but then I forget who his bio dad is. Zane has privileges that most do not. Zane can travel to any of the Five's personal realms that no one other than gods and demigods can enter unless permitted by one of the Five.

Ultimately, I have to believe it will work out just right. The Five wouldn't lead me on this destiny quest if they didn't have every part of it planned out, which means they have a plan and maybe even an idea for someone to run my old pack. Pushing the thoughts aside, I decided to focus on tonight. Tonight is going to be something we all need. The calm before the storm. The distraction we need so we can relax enough to enjoy the happy moment.

Zane is dressed in black jeans and a black sweater with his black dress boots. I'm in a black short sleeve dress that accommodates my huge belly well. I'm wearing black fluffy slippers because it's about all I can tolerate on my swollen feet.

Tonight is casual. We are having a fondue cheese pot with all kinds of goodies to dip in it. We will do a chocolate fondue for dessert with its own set of goodies. For the first time since I arrived here, we will have dinner together in a private setting. We all normally eat in the dining hall or as individual couples. I'm looking forward to some private, quality family time. It was something I never really got with my parents, so I'm thrilled to have it with Zane's family.

The six of us gather around the dining table. Zara set everything up for me since I struggle to move from the couch to the bed these days. Zane helps me into my seat across from him. Zane sits at the head of the table. Zara and Blaine sit on one side while Cade and Blair sit on the other side. We each have our own mini fondue pot. In the middle are soft pretzels, hard pretzels, roasted potatoes, french fries, steamed broccoli, cubes of bread, cold cuts, and roasted brussel sprouts. They all have wine while I drink sparkling apple cider. We load up our plates, passing various things around the table until we are satisfied.

"Thank you for joining Ari and me tonight as we have our first official meal in our new home. The coming days are filled with excitement surrounding the arrival of Everly. I'm grateful for you all, our family, and the love that I know will surround Everly when she arrives." Zane raises his glass, and we clink our glasses together before drinking.

"Do you think you two will have to leave shortly after Everly is born?" Blaine asks, dipping a cube of bread into his cheese.

"I don't know. Hopefully, we will get a few days before we have to leave. I'm assuming Ari will have a premonition about what to do after Everly is born." Zane responds, popping a coated piece of soft pretzel in his mouth.

"Either way, we will take care of Everly when the time comes, and we will be back up if you need us," Zara responds with a kind smile. She is so excited to have a grandchild.

Part of me feels bad because I feel like my pregnancy is putting pressure on Blair. Blair and Cade haven't fully decided if they want children. They are leaning towards yes, but I think they are waiting to see what it's like with Everly before deciding officially. Either way, I feel guilty for the pressure they might feel. I'm sure everyone thought there would be some space before Zane and I had kids. Everyone knew that Zane and I would have children at some part as it's required of us by Death.

"I know Everly is safe with you guys. Hopefully, we don't need backup. I plan on taking Mags out on my own." Zane replies.

"You sure that's a good idea? You might want to take Cade or me with you as your backup. I wouldn't put it past Mags to have a special trap set up for you." Blaine states, worried for Zane.

"He's right, Zane. Neither of us should be alone when we face off with Mags or Sage. We can't be together. They will make sure it's that way. They will set it up so that we are separated, knowing that we are stronger together. They will expect us to come alone." I add.

"How do you know they will separate us?" Zane asks suspiciously, like I've been holding information from him.

"Intuition." I shrug my shoulders as I smother my french fries in cheese. A sharp pain comes across my belly. Damn, contractions. I don't think they are real. At least I hope not, but leave it to my daughter to come right in the middle of family dinner. I shrug it off and focus on the food in front of me. I feel like all I do is eat these days. This child can't seem to get enough food. This is one of those moments where being a shifter will come in handy. Shifters, especially lycans and werewolves, can heal from giving birth quickly, and that includes losing their extra belly quickly too. I will need that as I'm too afraid to know how much I've gained.

I'm sorely out of shape, which sucks because I'm sure I'm going to have to fight with Sage. Sasha hasn't been out in months since I haven't been able to transform while pregnant. So she might be rusty. I hope we get some time for me to get some training in so we aren't so rusty. Sage will definitely not be rusty, and I've seen that bitch fight. She is vicious. Luckily, I seem to have a natural talent for fighting, thanks to Sasha. Hopefully, Fate is on my side with this one, and it won't matter how rusty I am.

I manage to make it to dessert before the contractions become too much, and I'm forced to say something. "I think I need to go to the medical wing. I think I'm in labor." I announce.

In a flurry of motion, Zane teleports him and me to the medical wing just in time for my water to break all over the floor. Everything is happening so quickly as the pain becomes more intense. I'm put in a wheelchair and taken to a room. A nurse helps me get into a medical gown. Zane is right there, letting me squeeze the shit out of his hand with each passing contracting. Everything feels intense as my body pumps adrenaline into my system, egging me on to push as the doctor commands me to. I don't even know when Dr. Grant came in or how I got into the hospital bed. The pain is awfully distracting.

I growl out at the painful contractions as I'm told to push. I don't know how many times I push, but the next moment I hear a baby's cry. I lean back in the bed as Zane beams a smile at me. He kisses me gently on my forehead, which is now covered in a thick layer of sweat. Zane cuts the umbilical cord, and the nurse takes our little one to be examined.

"You did beautiful, Pet," Zane says, kissing me on the head.

The nurses help clean me up and settle me in a fresh bed while Zane announces that Everly has been born to everyone. Once I'm all cleaned up from the blood and gore of labor, I'm settled into a fresh hospital bed as Zane walks in, holding a little black bundle of joy. Zane sets Everly in my arms and beams down at the little sweet thing.

"She's perfect," Zane says.

She has my black hair with the silver mixed in just like mine. She has Zane's dark gray eyes. "Yes, she is."

Blair, Cade, Zara, and Blaine come into the room. They congratulate us, and of course, Everly is passed around while I rest up and eat some food. I'm starving even though I just ate, but my body is healing and requires a lot of food and rest to heal this much damage done. Let's be honest, labor damages a woman's body one way or another. I enjoy my chicken tenders and onion rings with a strawberry milkshake while our family is loving on Everly.

After some time, the doctor clears me to go back to our room with Everly. I settle Everly in her bassinet by my side of the bed. She passed out from me, feeding her right before leaving the medical wing. Zane helps me settle into bed. He then settles next to me as I snuggle up into his arms. My body needs rest and sleep. I'm very willing to comply.

"I love you, Zane," I say quietly.

"I love you too, Ari." He replies, kissing my head.

I'm exhausted. I know I will wake up feeling much better after some good rest, having Zane with me and our bundle of joy sleeping next to us in her black bassinette. Life is good right now. We enjoyed a wonderful evening with our family and welcomed our baby girl into the world. I know what comes next isn't going to be easy, so for now, I'll focus on the joy of the present while I get some much needed sleep.

BIRDY RIVERS

CHAPTER 25
Zane

The sound of a fussy baby wakes me from my deep slumber. The overwhelming groggy feeling of being woken too soon overtakes me as I rub my eyes. I sit up in bed to find Ari standing, rocking Ever back and forth. Ari is so lost in soothing our daughter I don't think she has even noticed I'm awake. Ari is a natural at being a mother, which doesn't surprise me, but seems to surprise her. Sometimes Ari is entirely too hard on herself and doesn't give herself credit for how amazing she is.

Everly is a few weeks old and has been keeping us busy. Ari and I do our best to balance getting up so we both can get some sleep, training in, and eat. I never knew a newborn baby could be so demanding at odd hours of the night. Ever is that baby who is up all damn night and sleeps all damn day. Ari has been desperately trying to fix Ever's sleep schedule. Ari's patience is wearing thin with lack of sleep and the anxiety of worrying when we will finally be called to action. The fear of leaving our daughter behind while we go off on a dangerous mission has been eating at Ari since our daughter was born. Neither of us realized how hard it would be to leave.

Personally, I think we both tried to convince ourselves that it wouldn't be so bad. Ever will be with her grandparents safe and sound, completely protected from whatever upcoming battles her parents will have to fight. Still, there is a fear that something might go wrong. Oddly, I never questioned any plan I made for a mission till my daughter. She has changed everything in more ways than one. She has changed our coven, my family, Ari, and me. She's even managed to change Death and give him the peace I think he has been searching for for a long time.

"Sorry, she woke you. I was hoping I got to her in time." Ari says, coming over to the bed.

"It's okay. What's our Little Nightmare up to?" I ask, putting my hands out for Ari to hand me Ever, which she does.

"Oh, you know the normal being upset that she pooped in her sleep." I can feel my face twist at the sound of a poopy diaper. Ari laughs at my great dislike for poopy diapers as she settles next to me, leaning against the headboard along with me. I'd rather deal with dead people than change a poopy diaper. "Don't worry. She has a fresh bum. However, our Little Nightmare of cuteness isn't what woke me up," Suddenly, I don't like her tone as I realize there is only one other thing that would wake Ari up beside our daughter, a premonition. Fuck! "I had a premonition." She states disappointedly as if she hoped she would never have this premonition. I suppose there is truth to that as it's how I find myself feeling at the moment as I hold my cooing daughter as she settles herself in my arms.

"I guess we shouldn't be surprised. After all, it was inevitable. What was it?" I inquire, trying to hide my apprehension; however, Ari is good at reading me now. She's almost figured out how to read my mind. When she would get bored of researching, she started talking to Zara about how to do it. Of course, my mother had no problem showing Ari, all the while tossing my ass under the bus. Although, I am happy Zara and Ari get along, even if it sometimes bites me in the ass.

Ari sighs as she leans her head on my shoulder as. I'm sure she is feeling exhausted. I think we both will need a week to sleep after this mission and from having a newborn. I've never been one to need a lot of sleep, but the stress of this mission, combined with a newborn, has me drinking more caffeine than I've had in my entire life. For the first time in my life, I actually feel exhausted. Not even after a challenging mission have I ever been this tired. Newborn babies are no damn joke, but it's all worth it looking at our Little Nightmare. I always knew I would have kids. It's part of my requirement for being Death's son. I knew I'd have a familiar who would be my soulmate. It seemed like I had the perfect family all set up before I even had it, which made the whole thing feel slightly out of reach for a long time. Then Ari came into my life, and that future started to feel tangible. Now, I have an amazing little family that I'm terrified will be torn apart before it has a chance to flourish.

"As suspected, they are going to separate us. They have been squirrely with us dodging them for five months. The idiots think they have found a way to lure us out of our safe realm. Mags will text you demanding you come to her as she has vital information on an attack that is going to happen by the rogue supernaturals trying to wage war on the humans. She knows you are tracking them so that she will lure you to her with that."

I scoff. "Of course, Mags thinks she is being clever. She is dumber than I thought. If she hasn't figured out that, I know she's the fucking boss. Of course, she would offer some fake information on an important mission, knowing I wouldn't be able to resist a lead. What else?" I ask as I internally roll my eye at how dumb my bio mom is. Mags has never been the brightest witch. Powerful, yes, wise, not so much. I do not doubt that Mags thinks she is being clever with her plan.

"While you are meeting with her. Sage will text me demanding I meet her at the old cemetery that we played in so that she can give me something that she found about my lycan heritage. She will claim she is making peace with me. She thinks I'm gullible and will come alone. She will demand I come at the same time that Mags demands you."

"One, I don't peg you as someone who played in a cemetery, so I'm going to need more context on that. Two, do they think we are so stupid that we won't see it's a trap? At least demand somewhat different times. They are far too desperate to get rid of us so that they can carry out their plan. They know if we are around that, they will never be able to do what they want. They want to stop us before it's too late." I didn't realize they were that desperate to eliminate us. That's concerning because that could mean there is a bigger picture that we aren't seeing. "We do need to be careful with one thing. Mags knows I'm immortal, and while she doesn't know exactly how the master familiar bond works, she knows I would find a way to make you immortal like me. So they will be prepared to kill immortal beings, which is very dangerous for us."

"I agree, but we will have back up that they won't see coming that much I did see. I also saw you being done with Mags first and joining me. Mags will be alone, but Sage will not be. She will have Liam and Ghost to help her. Sage is under the impression it's going to be three against one. Even with Blair making it two against three, Ghost is a Dark Fae. He is a master illusionist and can manipulate matter. I can take on Sage or Liam by themselves, but I'm not sure I'm in enough fighting shape to take two opponents on. Even before Everly, I barely had enough training for something like that. I've been training hard to get back to where I was, but a few weeks isn't enough time. I've healed incredibly well from having Everly, which got me back to training sooner, but still. Blair will have to take on Ghost. I will only be able to take on Sage and Liam temporarily. You showing up with Cade is what will allow us to win the fight and give me the chance to kill Sage." Ari's worry is evident in her tone.

"I will show up and help you, Pet. Hold them off, and I will come to you in time. When do we get these texts?"

"In three days. We can start preparing with Blair and Cade tomorrow, circling back to the cemetery. The pack cemetery is where Sasha planned to build the temple to the Five. The open space just naturally became a cemetery over the years. It's rumored to be haunted by ravaged wolf spirits. I used to hang out there and read or doodle in my sketchpad. It was the one place I knew no one would bother me, where I was safe from the bullies. Of course, as we got older, the cemetery became a party place, especially around Hallows Eve. Sage and I would hang out at the cemetery when we wanted to escape our shitty lives. Of course, that's back when I thought Sage was my friend and that she had it hard too. So, I have always secretly liked cemeteries because it was the one place I felt somewhat safe from my cruel pack. Ironically, you ended up being my soulmate. When we talk about ourselves before we met, it's become apparent we were destined to be together." Ari states.

"You're right. We have more in common than I realized. Well, our Little Nightmare is asleep. Should we attempt some sleep?" I ask.

"Yes, we should." Ari agrees, taking Ever from me. I like that she has a cute nickname and a sweet one. Also, one nickname is one that only Ari and I will call her. I like that we have our own thing with our baby girl.

Ari places Ever in her black bassinet that is beside Ari's side of the bed. Once Ari is satisfied that Ever is good, she climbs back into bed with me. We snuggle up together as we both seek out sleep. We never know how much time we will have. Ever is an unpredictable baby who doesn't seem to ever want to have consistency. She is a chaotic little thing, but hopefully, the newborn phase won't kill us. Zara insists it won't be like this forever, but we will never have enough sleep now.

Sure enough, in three days, we both get our texts bright in the morning as our Little Nightmare is waking from sleeping a solid four hours. I'm not sure why she slept for so long, but I'm not questioning it. We desperately need sleep. I read over the text from Mags.

Hey, son. I'm sure your father and the rest of the Five have put you in charge of figuring out who is causing issues with the humans. I have some information that you will be interested in. Come to my cottage around seven tonight.

I scrub my hand down my face. As much as I'm looking forward to one final fuck you to Mags and ending her miserable ass existence. I'm not looking forward to having to separate from Ari. I know she can handle her side of things till I get there, but I can't help it. I love her so damn much I can't stand the thought of something happening to her. I know Ari can handle herself, but I'm still her protector. Then there is the matter of leaving Everly behind even though I know she will be taken care of and safe. It doesn't make it easier to leave like I hoped it would be.

Ari sets her phone down on the nightstand as she goes back to pleasing our fussy Little Nightmare. I roll my ass out of bed after replying to Mags that I'll be there. I head to the bathroom to shower and get ready for war. The warm water helps relax me. My eyes are closed as I let the water run over my head, pondering how this is the first mission that I'm torn about. I've never questioned my missions or what was expected of me. It's never been hard to leave for a mission before. This is a new feeling of apprehension I'm not used to.

Soft hands come around my waist from behind. Ari kisses my shoulder. "Your mom took Ever for a bit so we could prepare. I thought we could add something to our preparations." She huskily says as her fingers trail up my arm. I spin to face her as I pin her against the shower wall.

"You like to play games, Pet. It's going to get you in trouble." I respond, pinning her wrists above her head.

Our mouths collide together as our tongues play a game of their own. Enjoying the soft, desperate moans that escape her as my hands trail along her body, making my cock hard. I could easily spend hours with Ari enjoying everything her sweet body can give me. I've never experienced enjoying sex till Ari. I thought I had plenty of great sex before, but I was wrong. Nothing can compare to being with Ari, my familiar soulmate.

Letting her wrists go, I use both hands to cup her ass as I lift her. Ari instinctively wraps her legs around my waist as I enter her. She entangles her fingers in my hair as we go back to kissing while I move in and out of her. Fuck she's everything I've ever needed. I'm content to spend forever with her. I hate that we're both about to fight huge battles to stop a major war while completing Ari's destiny quest. It has to be done. We have responsibilities whether we want them or not, so for now, I'm going to enjoy the hell out of my pet.

"I love you, Zane. I'm so glad I'm yours," Ari states breaking our kiss as I slam deep within her.

"I love you too, Ari. I'm happy you're mine. You're my everything, Pet." I slam into her one more as I spill my seed deep inside her.

After we gather ourselves, we finish off our shower by actually showering. Drying off, we both get dressed. Unfortunately, we can't go in workout gear. We have to appear normal. I'm dressed in my black jeans and a black v-neck t-shirt paired with my black trench coat and black boots.

The Coven of the Crow and Shadows: Legacy

My war scythe and gun are on my hip. I've loaded the gun with Iron bullets. Cade will have his pistol filled with silver bullets.

Ari is wearing torn-up gray skinny jeans and a black tank top. Over the tank, she has a loose mesh punk sweater that hangs off her shoulders slightly and her black combat boots. Ari has on her choker. I love that she seldom takes it off and wears it everywhere. My Pet loves to show off that she belongs to me.

Zara comes back with Ever, and we spend some time with her. Cade and Blair join us as it gets closer for us to leave. Blaine has also joined us. Cade is dressed like me, but his coat is shorter than mine. He doesn't have to conceal two weapons. He only carries his pistol with him. He's a skilled fighter and is a strong warlock. He can hold his own out in the field. Blair is a bit of a different story. Like most familiars, Blair is incredibly dependent on her master when it comes to fighting. She struggles to fight on her own and do well with it. However, when she is with Cade, it's like she is suddenly a fierce fighter. Ari thankfully can hold her own without me. Granted, she is stronger with me as I am with her, but Ari handles herself better in the field and on her own than Blair does.

We gather in the living room as Ever sleeps peacefully in Ari's arms. It's time to finalize our plans. "Alright, Cade and I will go to Mags's cottage. I'm going in alone. Cade will be on stand-by. I trust you will know if I'm in trouble. I suspect Mags to entrap me with some charm or enchantment specific for demigods. She will come at me with guns blazing. I've prepared for this, and Death has given me anti charm and enchants potion. He's eager to help in any way possible. He wants Mags dead like yesterday. Once I get her where I want her, I will kill her. Then we will come to you guys."

"Right. Blair and I will head to meet Sage. Sage will have Ghost and Liam hiding while I'll have Blair hiding. They don't even know who she is, so they will have no idea to look for you. If they find you well, give them hell. Sage will come at me with a cocky attitude which I will use against her. Basically, we hold them off till Zane and Cade come to us. Then we kick ass." Ari adds.

Blair and Cade agree. It sounds simple in theory. I'm hoping everything goes according to our plan and not our enemies. However, we have Fate on our side along with the rest of the Five. Mags and the rest of them have blind ambition guiding them. Still, we can't always plan for everything. Ari's premonition never shows if we win, just how the battles goes down. We have to go with our defenses high, ready for the unexpected.

After all the goodbyes and love yous are said, the four of us head out. I kiss Ari one last time before I wrap shadows around her and Blair to take them to their destination. Cade and I head to Mags. Arriving separately, so we aren't seen together, Cade takes his position outside the cottage where Mags has a blind spot. I think I know more about her cottage than she does. I head up the stone path to the front door.

Knocking, I take a deep breath. I'm so ready for this moment. I've been waiting for this final showdown with her for years now. I knew when I told her to fuck off all those years ago. She would find a way to snake her way back into my life. Mags is predictable. I honestly wasn't surprised when I realized she was the big bad boss the goons were working for. Mags has always had false ideologies and loose morals. She doesn't even bother to hide her greed and never has. She's a walking cliche of a lousy villain. It actually pains me that she is my bio mother. Thank Fate I took after Death. Damn, that's not something I thought I'd ever think.

The Coven of the Crow and Shadows: Legacy

I'm dumbfounded that I've somehow managed to build a better relationship with Death while I'm about to go kill Mags. They sure ended up on opposites of each other in my life. I'm grateful I ended up with Zara and Blaine. At least with them, I had a shot at being a decent person.

Mags opens the door, her usual cigarette puffing its pungent smell into my face. "My boy, you made it." She says in her deep scraggly voice. Fate was not kind to her when it came to aging. She pissed him off badly. Generally, you've done and gone pissed off Fate if you age poorly. It's not always the case, but it is a lot of the time. Sometimes he's a petty asshole, which is why I'll stay on his good side.

"Yeah, you said you had information. I'm here for the information, not you, Mags." I spit at her as I shove past her.

As suspected, Mags has attempted to use a charm amplified by a spell. I can see the engravings of spell markings on the floor. I hear Mags shut the door. Seconds later, she is in front of me. "You were always an ungrateful child."

"Why have entrapped me?" I ask in a threatening manner. I need to play dumb. She hasn't played her cards yet. I need her to think she has me, so I have to play along with her pathetic attempt to take me out.

Mags chuckles. "Here, I thought you were a smart boy, my mistake." Mags thinks she has entrapped me and that I'm immobilized. She also thinks she has suppressed my powers with her pathetic charm. I will hand it to Mags. She did give this a good college try. She has all the right items to take out a demigod. Except she's right. I'm not smart. I'm cunning. I'm always a step or two ahead. Thanks to Ari, I can be three to five steps ahead of the game.

"What is the meaning of this, Mags!" I demand. "I don't have time for your games. Ari needs me."

"Oh, and pray tell why does your precious familiar need you?" She asks, puffing her cigarette as if she has all the time in the world. I also note the jealousy towards Ari that she has my attention when Mags has never had an ounce of real attention from me. I tried to have a relationship with Mags. I tried to let her be a part of my life, but she is toxic. Toxic souls are the hardest to reap. They are resistant and difficult. Mags will not die easily.

"If you must know. I have a newborn daughter at home."

"I'm a grandmother, and you didn't tell me!" She screams. I knew it would piss her off. "How dare you keep something like that from me? You don't even have the decency to tell your own mother that you've had a child, let alone not even bring my grandbaby to see me!" She is outraged. As if I'd bring my child to see her. I roll my eyes at her pathetic attempt to claim rights as my mother.

"Why would I tell you something important like that? You think you have some right to be in my life, to know what's going on in it. You don't, Mags. You have never been a good mother to me. You gave me up before I was even born. You only had me to get something from Death. I was never important to you. Your payday was more important than the life you brought into the world. Stop acting like you are some award-winning parent. You're not. Death is a better parent than you." I growl at her.

Years of pent up anger, hate, and pain bubble to the surface. I will speak my peace to her before I take her soul right to Death. I've bit my tongue for years. I've tried to spare her feelings thinking she was just some misguided soul. I tried so damn hard to justify her actions towards me, the words she said, and all the times she disappointed me. I didn't want to accept that the woman who brought me into the world didn't care if I lived or died. I was her son when it was convenient for her. Any other time I was just a transaction. A payment for whatever she got from Death for having me. Till this day, neither of them has told me what the deal was. I don't want to know as some things are better left unknown. I also don't give a shit.

"You will always resent me, thanks to that bitch Zara acting like the perfect mother. She turned you against me. I should have picked the person you went to, not Death."

"Wow, that's your response? Really? You could have at least lied and said you wish you kept me. It would have been better if you had just given me up and disappeared. I would have been just fine without knowing you."

"You little shit!" She screams as she throws her cigarette at me. "I will enjoy killing you. It's only fitting I brought you into this world, and now I'll remove you from it." She says as the psycho takes out an all black dagger with a red marking on it. That's a sacrificial blade. What the fuck exactly is Mags's planning on doing? It doesn't matter. It's time to end these games.

"Bold of you to assume you can take me out. I'll give it to you, Mags. You planned this out just right, but you forgot one thing. I'm a cunning bastard. I play to win, and win I do." I state smugly.

"You were always an arrogant bastard just like Death. You are like him in so many ways." Mags states, coming closer. She puts the blade to my neck. "Too bad you won't see your daughter grow up."

"That's where you're wrong, Mags. I'll see her grow up right after I go help Ari kill Sage." Mags's face drops. "Yeah, I know she works for you just like Liam and Ghost do as well. I've figured out your whole damn underground rebellion. Death is waiting for you. I don't think you will enjoy the afterlife." I counter as I pull my war scythe out as shadows grab Mags causing her to drop the dagger. "I hope Death makes your time in the afterlife as hellish as possible," I say as I drive my war scythe into her chest.

My war scythe glows a pale green as Mags's soul is absorbed and will be sent right to Death. Finding a towel in the kitchen, I use it to clean off my scythe. As I leave, I pass by Mags's body. Her body is surrounded by blood. I don't feel guilty or remorse towards her death. It's a bond I'm glad to have severed. A chapter I'm more than happy to see close forever. Part of me has always wished Mags just left me the hell alone. I wish she never tried to be a part of my life.

Stepping out of the cottage, Cade helps me set it on fire. The fire won't spread as we've spelled it, only to burn the house down. It will go out on its own when it's turned everything to ash. Watching the flames lap at the cottage as smoke rises to the sky, I feel an odd sense of peace, knowing that Mags is gone and that her evil plans will never come to light. She set her path, made her bed, and now she will pay the consequences.

"You okay, brother?" Cade asks as he puts his hand on my shoulder.

"Yeah, I'm good. Let's go help our familiars." I state as I command the shadows to take us to where they are. One mission complete. Now, it's time to complete the second half of our mission. Ari needs to finish her destiny quest so we can go home to our baby girl.

The Coven of the Crow and Shadows: Legacy

CHAPTER 26
Ari

Blair and I head to my old pack territory. It's strange to be heading back there. I honestly thought when I left with Zane. I'd never be back. At first, that saddened me, but as I realized how shitty my life was with my pack, I was glad at the thought of never coming back. It figures Sage would lure me here. The old cemetery is considered haunted by the pack. Over the years, the stories grew crazier and wilder. I could never figure out why people thought it was haunted or cursed. Knowing the truth, the tales make sense. The cemetery's ground is indeed soaked in the blood of lycans and werewolves, the beginning of a curse that created not only one supernatural race but also a hybrid race. No doubt it's haunted to some degree.

    Facing Sage for a final time and knowing I have to kill her is emotional. Despite Sage not being my friend, she was still my friend. I shouldn't care about killing her after she used and manipulated me. Sage plans on killing me. That alone should be enough to motivate me to want to kill her, and in some ways, it does. I'm not a killer, though. Strange to say that as lycan. You would think killing would be almost natural to me, but it's not. I have too much compassion, which is something Sage loved to remind me of. I'm sure she is counting on that compassion for something.

    Her text was unbelievably unconvincing. She texted me she was sorry and wanted to make peace with me. She promised me secrets about my family, which she knew I would be curious about. She doesn't realize that Zane and I have already figured it out. Even if she suspects we have, which I'm sure she will to some extent, she is only luring me here to kill me. I have to keep reminding myself that she wants to kill me even if I don't want to kill her. I know I have to, and I will. Well, Sasha will do it. I'm alright with letting her take the lead on this.

While I like to think of myself as a badass these days, I'm still not a killer, so this is hard for me. However, Sasha is a killer, and she knows what to do. Sasha will do the killing while I sit locked away in my subconscious. I'm okay with that. I'm even okay with Sasha blocking me out entirely from it, but I'm not so sure I should. Deep down, I know I have to be somewhat consciously aware during the act. At least I don't have to do it physically. Sasha is giddy with sending Sage to the afterlife, knowing Death will make her regret every decision she has made.

I've already had my showdown with Sage, so I'm not looking forward to a second one. Although, I wouldn't mind putting her in place one last time to prove that I'm not someone she can control. The only one who controls me is Zane, and even then, he still gives me control over myself. I have to admit part of me feared what kind of master Zane would be. I didn't know him, and I wasn't sure if I was putting my life in the hands of someone I could trust. I had no choice. I had to go with him, and I was terrified of what my life would be like. I've heard of warlocks abusing their familiars, cruel masters with no heart. I'm not sure if those rumors are true. Thankfully, for me, they are not true. Zane is an extraordinary master and soulmate. He's perfect for me and me for him. We seem to be two halves of a whole who never knew how much we need each other.

Zane might have known to some degree as he's always known he would have a familiar even if he didn't know exactly who she was. Still, I don't think Zane expected us to be so great together. Sure, as a team fighting in the field is one thing, and there was never a doubt we would kick ass at it. Neither of us could be sure how our relationship as a couple would be. I was so resistant at first that it was hard to see us working out like we have. We even started a family. I'm eager to get home to my baby girl and nervous about the battle.

I have no doubt Zane is kicking Mags's ass right now, but I have to keep my fight going till he can get to me. Blair hides in the woods in the trees in a smaller phoenix form. Blair can shrink herself to be any size she needs. Right now, she is about the size of an average bird like a cardinal. Leaning on the headstone is the one mausoleum where I know Sage will come as this is our meeting spot. I look at the cloudy sky. It's going to rain as I can smell it. The cemetery is enormous, so Sage and I made a meeting spot so we could always find each other.

Ironically, the headstone we meet at is none other than human Sasha's stone. It's ancient, and yet it's in perfect condition. The whole cemetery is preserved. No matter how old the headstones or mausoleums are, it stands in excellent condition as if time itself can't touch this place. Somehow, I have a feeling this cemetery is enchanted so that it will never age no matter what. The pack doesn't even bury people here anymore. Not unless it's a family with a plot or mausoleums with room. It's rare considering this cemetery is centuries old, and many generations have come and gone since its creation. Combine that with the haunted factor, and people avoid this place.

Oddly, I loved this old cemetery. It was the place where no one would bother me. Where I could hide away from the world and fade away in a good book or new album from a favorite artist, I would journal or doodle, totally lost in my own world. I spent many afternoons exploring, finding the best places to hide, read, and rock out, shutting out the world. This place became my personal playground. My escape from the restricted and unhappy life I was living.

It's strange being back here. Once upon a time, I would have done anything to stay in my pack because I thought it was my home. The harsh reality is this place, this pack, was never my home. My home is with Zane and our daughter. I have a beautiful family, and I'm surrounded by people who care about me. I was unhappy with my life before Zane whisked me away, but I was in pure and utter denial. I did whatever I could to convince myself that I was happy. I tried so hard to convince myself that life outside of my pack would be horrible. I told myself so many lies to survive. I wasn't living, surviving, and that isn't a happy or peaceful life.

The problem with survival mode is that it becomes the security blanket you wrap yourself in, so you don't have to deal with the reality of your shitty life. Survival mode became comfortable and safe. I felt like I was sleepwalking through my life. My motions were stuck in the mundane life of a girl trying to survive her cruel world. My home wasn't safe either because my parents never made me feel wanted or truly loved. My pack and my parents neglected me; the very people meant to help me. My world was lonely, and I desperately pretended it wasn't.

Zane was a force that unexpectedly came into my life, turning it upside down. Zane taking me away was the radical force that woke me up. He saw into my core, into my soul, and woke me from the numb, cold sleep I had put myself in to survive. I didn't even know that I was without certain things till he came into my life. Zane is the only person to love me in this world. I don't believe my own parents loved me, making me wonder if I was worthy of love. Then Zane came along and showed me my worth.

The Coven of the Crow and Shadows: Legacy

Today I'm going to prove my worth by completing my destiny quest given to me by the Five. Then I'm going to go home with my soulmate and cuddle our adorable baby girl while surrounded by our family. First time to take a bitch down once and for all. Guess I should tap into my unresolved pain and turn it into a weapon.

"You came," Sage states plainly as she approaches me.

"I came because you said you had information about my lycan heritage. That's the only reason I'm here, Sage." I retort flatly, folding my arms under my chest.

"I think it's cute you've finally found your claws, but you can't compete with me in the bitch department. The truth is, you're a filthy lycan and always have been. The only thing lycans are good at is dying, which I plan on doing to you." Sage starts taking off her clothes. She is going to transform. Well, she is wasting no time.

"I think it's cute that you think I haven't figured out your little plan. I know you work for Mags. I know you want to kill me because you think you will break the curse of the full moon and bring back fated mates. You think I don't know that we are both descendants of Sasha. I'm the lycan side, and you're the werewolf side of her lineage."

Sage stops as she is about to shred the last of her clothes. She mockingly claps her hands. "Congratulations, you figured it out. Good for you. I'm not impressed. You knew I wanted to kill you, and you still came to meet me? You're dumber than I thought."

"Not dumber, just more gifted than you. Did you know human Sasha was blessed by the Five?"

"Dumb bitch had premonitions. They obviously did her no good. She couldn't stop the war between humans and dire wolves. She failed just like you will. I know you think you are the chosen one to unite lycans and werewolves, but that will never happen. The only way to fix this centuries-old mess is to end your pathetic life." Sage spits at me as she begins to transform.

"Oh, I know I'm the chosen one because I have Sasha's gift. I've already seen this battle, and I know how it ends." I brag. I don't know how it ends, but Sage doesn't need to know that.

Sage doesn't stop transforming as she is done talking. I was hoping to stall her a bit longer. She is more eager to kill me than I am her. As Sage lunges at me, I'm stunned, lost in the moment as my thoughts race at a mile a minute. Suddenly I don't feel so confident. A moment of self-doubt, and I hesitate. I do the one thing Zane told me never to do, hesitate. My mind goes to that moment.

We were training in the rain just like right now as soft droplets of rain began to fall. The words echo in my head. "Never hesitate, Pet. Always follow through with what you intend to do. Hesitation is all your enemy will need to gain the upper hand." His words swirl around my mind as I feel the harsh, sharp bite of teeth ripping the flesh of my left leg.

Crying out from the pain, I realize Sage will kill me if I don't kill her. It doesn't matter the history we have. Our friendship was nothing more than a master manipulation where Sage was the puppet master and I the stupid puppet. The pain radiates through my leg sending shock waves to my system. The pain awakens something deep within me. I punch Sage's wolf in the face causing her to let go of my leg. I stumble backward, falling on my ass.

The next thing I know, I'm tearing my clothes off at inhuman speed. My bones crack as my muscles rearrange. I don't even feel the pain and discomfort from transformation as adrenaline pumps through my system, driving me forward. I'm completely transformed as my clothes lay in tattered ruins around me. Sasha is pissed and ready to fight.

The Coven of the Crow and Shadows: Legacy

I wasn't sure Id' be ready to fight, but I'm more than ready. My leg is quickly healing. Lycans heal faster. Sage circles me as another wolf comes from the cemetery's tree line. Liam. He snarls as he snaps his jaw. Liam joins Sage in circling me as Blair flies out from her hiding place in the trees. She lands next to me and is almost the same size as me in her full size, which she is now. Blair is a beautiful large bird with feathers in various shades of red and orange with hints of yellow. It looks like she is on fire, but she isn't. The color of her feathers are so vibrant and mimics the flames of fire.

Ghost comes out from his hiding spot as I saw in my dream. Liam and Sage go to either side of Ghost. Liam and Sage growl viciously while Ghost cracks his knuckles. Suddenly, I find myself hoping Zane and Cade get here soon. Blair will take on Ghost while I take on Liam and Sage. This will not be an easy fight, but we have to hold off as long as possible.

Blair takes flight and flies over them, getting Ghost's attention just like she hoped she would. While Blair is busy taking blasts from Ghosts and breathing fire at him like a fucking dragon, I face off with Liam and Sage. Liam is a large brown wolf with some hints of black in his fur. Meanwhile, Sage is a small to medium red wolf with hints of brown in her fur. Sasha is bigger than both, but size doesn't always matter with our kind.

Yes, size is helpful, but I've seen small wolves rip bigger wolves to pieces. Liam and Sage have fantastic stamina and have been trained in fighting much longer than I have. My size will only help me so much, along with my better senses and faster healing abilities. Still, I have to try my damndest to take them on. Sasha is strong, and she is a beast while fighting. She's ruthless where I am not. I trust her.

Sasha and I have our differences. Sometimes I feel like I have a Dr. Jekyll and Mr. Hyde personality. Still, I trust Sasha.

I used to be embarrassed by her, but now I'm proud of her. I'm honored she is my wolf spirit. Our relationship is rocky, but we will always have each other's back. Sasha is fierce. She can handle this. Not to mention she is ancient, which only adds to her strength. The older the wolf spirit, the stronger and wiser they are. Sasha is an original wolf spirit of a lycan; it doesn't get any stronger than that.

Sage and Liam split up and started to approach me on both sides. Sage will strike first, and Liam will strike at me while I'm distracted, fending her off. I have to counter Sage fast enough so I can quickly counter Liam so he can't do any damage. Fuck, this is going to be complicated. Sage lunges at me as I dodge her by rolling towards Liam, who is getting ready to swipe his paw in my backside while Sage had me distracted. I roll into him, knocking him over. Quickly I get on top of him, pinning him under me. Sasha and I are working together as one. We both have equal control, which is a first for us, but damn, we are a lethal team.

Snapping my jaw into his right shoulder, Liam howls in pain. Sage knocks me off, Liam tackling me to the ground. Quickly I kick her off of me and roll to all fours. I get in a defensive position as Liam stumbles up onto all fours. I got him good, but he's already healing. Granted, he is healing slower than I did. I'm still not sure it's enough. If I could injure him several more times, I'd have the advantage. However, Sage isn't wounded, and she is now in front of Liam, protecting him so he can heal uninterrupted.

Sage snaps her jaws and growls lowly at me as she gets into an attack position. Shit. She's pissed. I don't think she expected me to be able to fight. Sage figured she could kill me quickly. She wasn't expecting me to have backup, nor was she expecting me to be able to hold my own against her. However, we both know I won't last forever.

The Coven of the Crow and Shadows: Legacy

Glancing at Blair and Ghost, I see Blair countering Ghost move for move, but she is wearing down. We need our masters in order to be at maximum strength. It's how the bond works. They are weak without us, but we are more vulnerable without them. It's not an equal exchange, but it's pretty damn close. Sage charging at me pulls my attention back to my own fight. I barely dodge Sage. However, I'm able to get past her and take another shot at Liam. I tackle a growling Liam one more time as I hear Sage pivoting on her hind legs, attempting to get to me faster. My paw swipes Liam's wolf's face, and then I quickly jump off him as Sage barrels to me. I dodge away from her jumping up onto a large stone bench. Sage growls angrily that I've avoided her.

Jumping down off the bench, I lunge at Sage, knocking her to the ground. However, she uses her smaller size against my large size as she easily wiggles her way from my claws. I roll away from her. Sage gets a minor bite in before I roll away, quickly getting back on all fours. I'm losing stamina. I'm not in top shape as I didn't train for five months. I'm better than where I was right after giving birth, but I'm nowhere near what I was before I was pregnant. Even then, I'm not sure it would make much of a difference. Where the hell is Zane and Cade? Fear starts to creep in that they ran into complications or worse. No, I can't think worse.

Blair is losing stamina as well. She's not used to being out in the field. It's not her and Cade's thing. They spend more time running the coven than anything else. It takes a lot to run the coven, and Cade is trying to take over for Blaine so that he can retire with Zara in a few years. While Blair knows how to fight, she isn't a warrior. Ghost is wearing her down, and soon he will start doing damage to her. Blair isn't like me; she can't self heal.

Just as Sage is getting ready to come at me again, shadows move around me. I whip my head behind me to see

Zane and Cade have arrived. Cade is already assisting Blair. Zane comes to my side as his shadows have Sage backing away toward Liam. Liam is now mostly healed, which would typically concern me, but Zane is here. Now the real games can begin.

"Sorry, I'm late, Pet. I see you held your own just fine." Zane states, taking out his war scythe.

Zane has the shadows go around Sage and Liam, confusing them. I know how confusing the shadows can be. They overwhelm your senses, and for a werewolf, that's torture. Zane controls the shadows, so he usually makes them friendly towards me unless it's training. Right now, the shadows are definitely not being friendly towards Sage and Liam.

I know the play Zane wants to make. It's one we have practiced many times but haven't used on the field yet. Zane and I enter the shadow tornado that is surrounding Sage and Liam. Zane is going to Liam while I go for Sage. We find Sage and Liam with their wolf butts touching each other as they swipe at the shadows with their paws. They are disoriented and distracted. Zane heads for Liam, and I make my way toward Sage. This is where I let Sasha have complete control. I know I will hesitate again, and I can't afford to make that mistake. I got lucky once. I don't want to test Fate a second time.

I am getting myself lined up with Sage to go right for her jugular. I'm not playing games. I get one shot at taking her out quickly and without having to fight her. Once I'm content with my angles, I charge Sage as a fierce growl tears out of my throat as my jaw opens wide, striking my target perfectly. The warm metallic taste of blood seeps into my mouth. I can taste the iron in her blood. Dropping Sage from my jaw, she falls to the ground. She is so weak she transforms back to her human form.

The Coven of the Crow and Shadows: Legacy

Sage tries to put pressure on her wound, but she is bleeding out too quickly. Before Sage can attempt to heal herself, I forcefully smash her skull with my enormous and deadly paw. Sage is dead. Her blood soaks the ground around her. Suddenly there is a pulse from the ground as a flash of golden light makes waves along with the land around us. The rain stops, and the sky clears. The curse is broken. Werewolves and lycans will be at peace with each other. A premonition flashes before my eyes; it's the first time I've ever had while awake.

I see the lycans coming out of hiding. The lycan who will take over the pack is a distant relative of mine on the Blackwell side of my family. The pack is taken over, and the name is changed. Some werewolves leave and go to other packs while others stay. The two races now work together, fixing the pack systems and striving to live in unity. It's a beautiful premonition. I've completed my destiny quest as pride swells in my chest at my accomplishment.

Looking over to Zane as the shadows clear around us, I see Liam's dead body lying at Zane's feet. His war scythe is still soaked in blood. Liam's soul has gone to Death. Zane walks over to Sage. He sticks his war scythe into her as pale green light glows from his war scythe. He's reaping her soul, sending her to Death. Seconds pass, and his scythe stops glowing. Zane then repeats the process with Ghost's body.

"I've called a clean-up crew. They will be here shortly. We can go home." Cade announces as the four of us come together. Blair and I are still in our animal forms.

"Home is exactly where I want to go. I'm proud of us. We have made the Five proud today, and they will surely bless us for our success. Time to go home and wash the grime of battle off us." Zane replies, waving his hands, causing shadows to come around us.

Once we are home, Zane and I shower together, but we don't have sex this time. We are both far too exhausted from everything. Emotions are high for both of us. Zane may not have been close to Mags, but her death affects him even if he doesn't show it. I know him. I've learned to see through the stone mask he wears for the world. I'm dealing with killing someone I both liked and hated. Regardless of how things ended between us, she was still a huge part of my life in many ways. It hurts losing her, yet there is a sense of peace I have about her death. It's the same feeling I had when my parents died. Conflicting emotions of love, hate, admiration, and resentment all mixing together with grief is a tough pill to swallow.

After getting cleaned up, Zara feeds us as she had prepared a massive meal for when we got home. Blaine is currently bringing Cade and Blair their food. Everly is awake, trying to roll around in her pack and play. The little girl is already growing too fast. Everly is bound to advance quicker than usual. I suspect she will be walking before one. Everly is the beginning of a new legacy for our coven. A symbol of hope.

Part of me worries about what kind of burdens she will carry. The weight of being something extraordinary and simply wanting to be unextraordinary. I know how that feels to some extent as I was a lycan living among a pack of werewolves. I was feared and rejected for being extraordinary; however, I know Everly will be accepted and admired. That gives me hope for her. Acceptance and support from loved ones are vital. Our family thrives off of love, support, and acceptance. The coven is open-minded, even excited for a new legacy to take root in our coven, even if the coven is a legacy in its own right.

Deep down, I know Zane is honored to be considered Death's ultimate legacy. Zane is proud to start his own legacy

The Coven of the Crow and Shadows: Legacy

and even share a legacy with his bio dad. It's strange to see them developing an actual father son bond. It inspires hope in Zane that he can have a good relationship with his own children. Secretly Zane struggles with the fear that he will be a bad father. He's terrified of failing our children. Zane won't admit his concerns out loud, but he doesn't have to. I know how to read his mind now. Damn, does it come in handy I get why Zane does it all the time. It's a little addicting. However, Zane and I don't use it against one another. We use it to help us understand each other. To communicate when words fail us. It's become a helpful tool for us. It's just another way we have strengthened our bond and relationship.

Every day our love for each other grows stronger. We are learning to grow together and to grow as a family. Many things change when a child enters the family: dynamics change and shift. As new parents, Zane and I have to work together on new things, on having a united front with our children. It's exciting, though. Exciting to see how things will change for the better. Exciting to see how our daughter has only enhanced our family and how the love of our family has grown in strides.

Hopefully, with our missions complete, we will have some downtime to bond with Everly as a family. The downtime will be good for Zane and me. I know Zane won't be able to take too long of a break as he is a vital operator of the coven. I will do my best to help him where I can, but my main focus will be Everly for a bit. I still plan to go on small missions with Zane. Zara and Blaine are more than happy to watch their granddaughter. The two of them spoil her rotten already.

Zane and I will have to find a balance between work and family life while making sure we have time for each other. It will be a bit of a bumpy road, but I have faith that Zane and I will find our balance in no time. Besides, Zare and Blaine are in our corner. They are wonderful after offering guidance in relationships and most life events. Then there is also Blair and Cade, who are great to talk to. We like doing double dates with them. While I was pregnant, it was a weekly thing to help me not have total cabin fever.

Then I have the other women of the coven who I've just started to build relationships with. I have a new life filled with friends and family. Life has turned out well for me. I know it won't always be this blissful. I'm sure there are new challenges around the corner, but I know I don't have to face them alone. It's been a beautiful journey finding a place to call home. I often wondered if I'd ever experience what it's like to have a home, have a family, be accepted, have quality friends, and find love. I'm thankful to have found all of that. To experience it in such a way that many only dare to dream of. I always feared I was cursed. As it turns out, I was blessed. My dreams have been fulfilled. Now, I can look forward to a future filled with hope and new adventures. Right now, all is right in my world, and for the first time ever, my mind, body, soul, and spirit are at peace.

The End

The Shadow family will be back in Book 2: Ghost Opera

EPILOGUE
Zane

Everyone is gathered in the dining hall of the coven to celebrate Blaine as he is officially retiring today, and Cade is now the official leader of the Coven. Ever is a little over two now and a clever little thing. She's also adorable, and everyone fawns over her. She absolutely loves the attention. Watching Ever bob and weave around people as she makes her way over to me. She runs into my arms, and I scoop her up. She looks so much like Ari with the same hair and facial features, but she has my dark gray eyes. Ever's light wavy hair bounces as we make our way over to Ari, who is rubbing her growing belly.

Ari and I got smart and started using some magical protection till we were ready for baby number two. Blair is standing next to Ari, also rubbing her baby bump. Cade and Blair took their time starting their family. They procrastinated a lot. I'm not totally sold that they wanted to have kids. They say they do, but I think they only are having a child to have an heir to take over the coven for Cade.

Shortly after we got back from completing our missions, I talked with Cade. I've always known my brother has reservations about having children. I told him if he didn't want to have a child, he didn't have to. There was no need for him to have heirs as I already had one that could take over the coven. I didn't want Cade and Blair to feel pressure to have heirs if they didn't want kids.

The topic of kids has always seemed to be a sore spot for Cade, and I never understood why unless there is something I don't know about. I worry for my brother and his family. Something has been off with Blair and Cade lately. Ever since Ari and I had Everly, Cade and Blair have been acting odd when the topic of kids comes up, which happens a lot with an adorable toddler running around.

Balancing Ever on my hip, I stop in front of Ari and briefly kiss her on the lips. Ever giggles. She thinks it's funny when we kiss. She finds it funny now, but she definitely won't find it funny in a few years. Ari hands Ever her juice cup, which Ever can't seem to chug the damn juice fast enough. I've learned that juice is toddler life, and without it said toddler will have a mental breakdown.

Cade comes over and puts his arm around Blair's shoulders. They smile at each other, but it's a strained smile. What the hell is going on with them? I'm going to talk to mom and dad to see if they know what's going on. Speaking of my awesome adoptive parents, they are getting ready to do some traveling and enjoy some time to themselves. They won't be gone too long as they want to be back for when Ari and Blair give birth. Ari is due a month before Blair. I'm sure my parents will be in and out of the coven's realm as they balance their retirement between enjoying their free time and enjoying their grandkids.

Death shocked me the other day when he asked me if he could meet Everly. Death and I have gotten closer over the last few years. I've spent time learning from him how to run the underworld. I'm not sure I want to run the underworld, but I couldn't say no to learning how. Besides, it offers bonding time for Death and me. As Everly grows, I realize how strong her powers will be and how powerful she will be. Having Death and I on excellent terms will be useful when it comes to Everly's future and the future of her baby brother.

The Coven of the Crow and Shadows: Legacy

Blaine and Zara are mingling around the room as coven members pay their respects to them. Even though Blaine and Zara will still be around, they won't be involved with much anymore. Anything they are involved in will be either because they are helping us with something important or volunteering to help out. I'm not sure they are totally going to give it all up because they loved running the coven. They were good at it. I used to have the same faith in Cade and Blair, but lately, I'm worried about them. Cade, I know, can run the coven. It's what he's spent most of his life learning. There is a lot of stress that comes with running the coven. I'm sure they will pull through whatever issues they are having.

Ari and I have had our issues over the years, as every couple does. We work hard to keep our relationship healthy. Sex has never been an issue for us. Part of the problem at one point was we were fucking more than talking, and it caused some miscommunication. We worked it out and refound our balance with things. It's complicated and challenging but worth it. Then, of course, there are the disagreements and arguments that come from having children together. Thankfully, we don't disagree too often, but Ari is very worried about our children and the pressures on their shoulders.

It's hard for her to understand that they won't break from the pressure. Cade and I both grew up with extreme pressures on our shoulders. Cade was being groomed to run the coven, and I was groomed to become the perfect asset to the coven, growing my powers and abilities to be everything I was meant to be and more. Ari didn't grow up with anything like that. She grew up in the shadows hiding. I've gotten a further glimpse into Ari's life in her pack. She is scarred from it, which sometimes clouds her judgment when it comes to Everly.

I do my best to see things from her point of view. It's not always easy, but it saves me a lot of trouble if I attempt to view things from Ari's point of view. I know she appreciates it when I do it. Ari is terrified of being a lousy parent because her parents were so horrible to her. They made her feel so unwanted and unloved. I understand that to some degree. Mags certainly left her scars on me as a shit parent. Death at least tries and has always tried with me. He and I are closer than we have ever been. It's not even strange for me to consider myself close to him anymore.

Blaine and Zara were my saving grace, though. They showed me a nurturing environment and did everything they could to be great parents. They weren't perfect because none of us can be perfect. Even the Five have flaws. Zara and Blaine are amazing parents and great models to look up to in parenting and relationships. They are great people, and I'm happy to be a part of their family. I'm thankful that they loved me like their own and never once made me feel like I was just some adoptive kid they got stuck with. Sometimes that is what I would think. I would think they just got stuck with me. Afraid that they would ditch me as Mags did. They worked hard to change that line of thinking.

It will be strange not having them around all the time, but they deserve retirement. They deserve time to relax, enjoy the rest of their lives, and do what they want to do. A season of change is upon the coven, and while it's exciting, it's always concerning when there is a major change in leadership. I'm not doubting Cade and Blair. I'm hoping that whatever they have going on between them doesn't affect their ability to run the coven or negatively affect their family. I'm prepared to step in wherever I need to. Ari is already prepared for me to be busy and to handle the kids on her own for the most part. I will, of course, help her wherever I can, and I know she will help me where she can. She and I are a team in everything.

The Coven of the Crow and Shadows: Legacy

Change brings new beginnings, and new beginnings offer hope. The future is uncertain unless Fate decides to give Ari premonitions. Ari has honed in on her gift from the Five. She can even trigger her own premonitions if she tries hard enough. Her gift tends to be very handy. It's unclear whether Ever or our son will have Ari's gift. Gifts don't tend to get passed down throughout generations, but this isn't a normal situation. Death has done his best to prepare me for training my children as they will need special training. They are going to need magic lesions even earlier than I did. Ever is already showing signs that she is close to doing magic. I have no idea how I will train a toddler in magic, but that's what I have Death to help me with. This was his idea, so he could help see it to fruition.

After the party, we head back to our apartment. Ari tucks Ever into bed. The party went pretty late, and Everly is passed out hard. She burned up a lot of energy today. Ari looks like she is about to pass out as well. Pregnancy takes a toll on her energy levels. I'm tired myself. The next few months will be busy as the transition of leadership always shakes things up a bit. It's not usually a bad thing.

Climbing into bed with Ari, we get comfortable. Ari passes out quickly. I chuckle at her and her ability to pass out anywhere while pregnant. Ari is enjoying this pregnancy a little more as she doesn't have a destiny quest looming over her head as she did with Everly. Our future is bright and happy, but I'm sure something will come along to shake it up. There is always something to shake life up, but at least I don't have to face it alone. I have my beautiful soulmate, family, and coven to face all the good and bad. This is why I know no matter what challenges Everly and her baby brother face. They will never have to do it alone. Besides, both their parents are total badasses; they will be just fine.

Other Books By Birdy Rivers

Children of the Empire: *World on Fire*

Children of the Empire: *Reflected Mirrors*

The Voice of the Sea: *A little Mermaid Retelling*

All book are available on Amazon

Made in the USA
Columbia, SC
01 May 2025